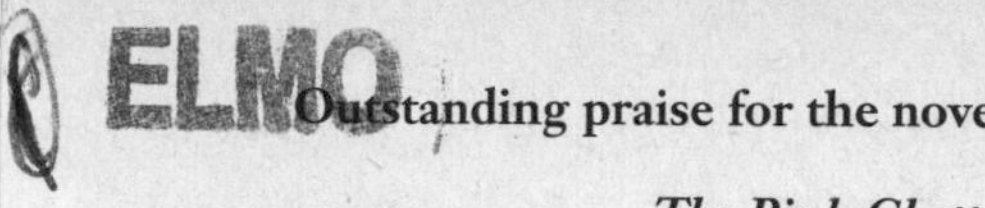

Outstanding praise for the novels

The Pink Ghetto

"Liz Ireland's breezy new novel sends a gust of fresh air through familiar chick lit territory. Ireland's wry prose deftly captures a lovable heroine and a world where overdue rent and padded resumes are as prevalent as roommate crushes and Amex'd takeout pizza. Ultimately, this is a post-millennial Cinderella tale featuring a heroine in a hand-me-down Chanel suit—and rose-colored glasses—instead of glass slippers, entry-level grunts in place of wicked stepsisters, and a Manhattan office building standing in for a castle."

—Wendy Markham, author of *Slightly Engaged*

How I Stole Her Husband

"An entertaining read." —*Booklist*

"A hilarious and compelling story about first love, lost innocence and payback. Liz Ireland has created a cast of multifaceted characters who are deliciously twisted and yet completely sympathetic. From downtrodden diva, Alison Bell, to the serial adulterer, Pepper Smith, you can't help being pulled into their tangled web. Wickedly clever one-liners, outrageous abuses, and a page turner of a story make *How I Stole Her Husband* a must-read for chick-lit fans."

—Jennifer Coburn, author of *Tales From The Crib*

"*How I Stole Her Husband* is a wonderfully written, often hilarious story of a young woman's journey from all-around discontent to hard-won acceptance of life in all its crazy splendor. Alison Bell is the most likeable heroine I've met in some time—charmingly down-to-earth, sometimes painfully self-aware, and just a little bit desperate to make something of her life. How she plans to pluck herself from the depths of poverty to which she imagines she's sunk, how she rediscovers the love of her life, and how she recovers triumphantly from the havoc he wreaks makes for an utterly absorbing read. Liz Ireland takes a clever concept and raises it to an unexpected level of sophistication. Don't miss this book!"

—Holly Chamberlin, author of *Back In The Game*

Three Bedrooms In Chelsea

"The three-girls-in-the-city formula gets an extreme chick-lit makeover in *Three Bedrooms In Chelsea*, an amusing sexy read."

—Lauren Baratz-Logsted, author of *The Thin Pink Line*

"The sexy singles occupying *Three Bedrooms In Chelsea* are heartwarming, funny and unforgettable. Liz Ireland has created an absolute delight!"

—Patti Berg, author of *I'm No Angel*

Charmed, I'm Sure

"Captivating! *Charmed, I'm Sure* is an enchanting blend of hex and sex! A rollicking romp that will make you believe in magic."

—Stephanie Bond, author of *In Deep Voodoo*

When I Think Of You

"Fresh and funny!"—Jennifer Crusie, *New York Times* bestselling author

Books by Liz Ireland

HUSBAND MATERIAL

WHEN I THINK OF YOU

CHARMED, I'M SURE

THREE BEDROOMS IN CHELSEA

HOW I STOLE HER HUSBAND

THE PINK GHETTO

THIS CHRISTMAS
(with Jane Green and Jennifer Coburn)

Published by Kensington Publishing Corporation

The Pink Ghetto

LIZ IRELAND

KENSINGTON BOOKS
www.kensingtonbooks.com

KENSINGTON BOOKS are published by

Kensington Publishing Corp.
850 Third Avenue
New York, NY 10022

All Kensington titles, imprints and distributed lines are available at special quantity discounts for bulk purchases for sales promotion, premiums, fund-raising, educational or institutional use.

Special book excerpts or customized printings can also be created to fit specific needs. For details, write or phone the office of the Kensington Special Sales Manager: Kensington Publishing Corp., 850 Third Avenue, New York, NY, 10022. Attn. Special Sales Department. Phone: 1-800-221-2647.

ISBN 0-7582-0839-1

First Kensington Trade Paperback Printing: April 2006
10 9 8 7 6 5 4 3 2 1

Printed in the United States of America

The Pink Ghetto

For a certain type of man—and I plead guilty to being that type to a T—Renata Abner was like catnip to a lean, hungry Siamese tom.

When we met in college, she was frisky and eager for new experiences as only a recently slimmed-down co-ed can be. Unbeknownst to those around her, her first eighteen years had been as Renata Abner, chubbette; her highest social attainment had been co-captain of the pep choir. Due to a graduation night trauma, she had spent her postgraduate summer on a potent regimen of Jenny Craig meals and Ex-Lax, and was at last a slender shadow of her former self. Now, in her new size-ten incarnation and self-schooled in the Sex and the City *Tao of high heels and cleavage, she was eager for those dating experiences her cohort had all been having since crawling out of the post-pubescent ooze.*

She certainly had me fooled. But after three beers purchased with our just-hatched fake I.D.'s, the newly acquired sophistication fell away like her resistance to the cheese straws in the bowl at her elbow, and the real story came spilling out: the rowdy houseful of siblings that a pudgy middle child could get lost in; the taunts of classmates from preschool onward; the playground depredations that led to her finding solace in imaginative but not physical play; the lack of social life in high school, the only compensations of which were an encyclopedic knowledge of old movies and a very respectable 3.6 GPA.

So what was the big attraction, you ask?

Simple. Some men go for the geisha types (harder to find these days, but still out there). Others inexplicably veer to those domineering, she-who-must-be-obeyed fright dolls. What's my poison? She who has been overlooked.

Chapter 1

After all that's happened, most of the people think it was *that book* that changed everything for me. It's not hard to understand why. I blamed everything on the book at first, too. I was bitter, I'll admit that. In my shoes, anyone would have been.

But recently, thanks to the support of my friends, my family, and the personal growth section at Barnes and Noble, I've adopted a more zenlike attitude toward the whole episode. To put it in a string of clichés: I am bowed but not broken. That which did not kill me has made me stronger. I have washed that man right out of my hair.

Taking the longer view, I can see that it wasn't heartbreak or even *that book* that altered my life. Not really. It was the job. The job changed everything, which is weird, because at the time I was so desperate to earn money that I didn't even pay attention to what I was applying for.

The ad didn't name the company. Lodged as it was in the middle of the employment section of the *New York Times* without a box or even much bold lettering, it seemed anonymous, non-threatening, almost forgettable. A little brown bag of an ad. *Well-known publishing house seeks assistant editor*, it said. Or something to that effect.

Well-known publishing house. Lurking behind those four innocent words was a whole new world, amazing to the uninitiated and fraught with unseen traps that a novice was bound to step in, like those pits camouflaged by leaves in an old Abbott and Costello jungle movie.

I didn't realize it myself for months, until I was sprawled on the ground, shaking the banana leaves out of my hair.

Not that it would have mattered at the time when I spotted the ad. Like I said, I was desperate. If Pol Pot had been hiring, I probably would have fired off my resume. I was sending out that document, so heavily padded that it could have played tackle in the NFL, to any and every business that sounded as though they required a semiliterate being to park at a desk all day. In a blizzard of cover letters blanketing the human resources departments of Manhattan that month, I professed my profound desire to be a proofreader, executive assistant, editorial assistant, or any type of flunky imaginable sought by the worlds of advertising, public relations, or broadcasting. I needed a job, and the sooner the better.

For two and a half unbelievable years I had been living on easy street. Actually, the address was a floor-through in Williamsburg, Brooklyn, land of the trust fund bohemian. I had no trust fund, but I had been incomparably lucky since getting out of college, when, through a professor, I had landed a position as a personal assistant to Sylvie Arnaud.

Sylvie Arnaud was one of those people that the early Twentieth Century popped out now and then—magic people who were simply famous for being around all the right people.

How she had become famous, no one remembered. Perhaps sometime circa 1935 she had written something, or painted something, or slept with someone who had written or painted something. Her name would occasionally pop up in *The New York Review of Books*, during the course of a discussion of a review of books about German Expressionist painters, say. She knew everybody. Ernest Hemingway. Salvador Dali. The Duke and Duchess of Windsor. Harpo Marx. You can play a highbrow *Where's Waldo?* with her in pictures of intellectuals and rich folk gathered in salons in Paris and London between the wars. Chances are she'll be there somewhere, maybe sitting next to Cole Porter and looking impossibly elegant in her slinky bias cut dresses, with a drink in one hand and a stretch limousine cigarette holder in the other.

By the time I knew her, she was a beaky, wizened old creature on toothpick legs, with jaundiced flesh as thin as onion skin parchment. She lived in a dark, musty brownstone on the Upper East Side, in Turtle Bay. When my old college professor who helped get me the job told me about the position, he said that I would probably be helping her assemble her personal papers so she could write her autobiography. But I was not taking down her memoirs; instead, I spent most of my time chasing after her favorite groceries, like these nasty chocolate covered apricot filled cookies that she practically lived on. Believe me, I am not picky when it comes to food. There's nothing I can't deem binge-worthy if I stare at it long enough, but even I would make an exception for those cookies.

And her peculiarities didn't end there. She also liked a specific kind of hot pickled okra that could only be found in Harlem; butter mints from the basement at Macy's; baguettes and croissants from a French bakery in Brooklyn Heights. She preferred cloth hankies to Kleenex and Lava soap to the expensive kind I bought her once on her birthday, and woebetide the person who made the mistake of serving her ice in her drinks.

She was one peculiar old lady.

She didn't talk to me much about Picasso, or Earnest Hemingway, or the Duchess of Windsor. I arrived too late for that. Mostly I heard about her ingrown toenails and her skin problems. I guess when you're ninety-four and you itch, dead painter friends become a second tier concern.

When I first started working for her I would bring up the subject of her memoirs.

"What are these memoirs you are always pestering me about, Rebecca?" She had a trace of her native accent, but it was an off-and-on thing. She could lay it on thick if she wanted, turning *these* to *zeez*.

I tried not to let on that I was disappointed not to be doing important literary work. "I just thought . . . if you needed any help going through your journals . . ."

She would laugh throatily at that idea. "Ah, you see me as some sort of crazy old artifact, *non?*"

"No, no," I would stutter. (A lie. I did.)

"Naturally! You want to know all my little secrets, like whether Cary Grant was good in bed."

"No, I . . ." I gulped. "Wait. *Cary Grant?*"

She would bark with glee at me, tell me to take her laundry down to the basement, and then ignore me for the rest of the afternoon. I began to suspect the diaries didn't exist anyway. Maybe she'd never been any closer to Cary Grant than I had been.

Or maybe she had.

Occasionally an academic would make his way to the brownstone, but he always left disappointed. He might sit in a chair with a plate of those apricot cookies and listen to Sylvie rave for a few minutes about John-Paul Sartre's bad breath; generally it didn't take much longer to realize that Sylvie wasn't going to divulge much useful information. Even though Sylvie had been living in New York since the sixties, her principal visitors while I was there were not glitterati or even academics, but a physical therapist named Chuck and an old lady from the Bronx named Bernadine.

Sylvie was a mystery to me, right down to the question of what I was doing there. I couldn't figure out why she wanted to pay even my nominal salary to have me around. I couldn't even figure out why this old French lady was in New York.

Then again, I didn't waste a lot of time worrying about it. When I began working for her I was twenty-two and it was the first time I'd ever lived in New York City, so I wasn't exactly consumed with curiosity about my nonagenarian employer.

And I had nothing to complain about. On the first day of every month a check arrived from the manager of Sylvie's estate, R.J. Langley, CPA, which made me the prime breadwinner among my roommates in our apartment in Williamsburg. At the time I was too young to appreciate that getting paid a living wage for buying an old lady's baguettes was really nothing short of a miracle.

Then one morning as I was getting ready to hie myself off to Manhattan, I received a call from R.J. Langley, the first time I had ever spoken to the man personally. He asked me—commanded me, actually—to go to his office in midtown first thing.

"Why?" I asked. "Is something wrong?"

"Actually, yes. I have bad news. Miss Arnaud has pneumonia."

"Oh, no! What hospital?"

There was a pause. "I can give you more details in person."

During the subway ride over, I was filled with sadness. Poor Sylvie, stuck in the hospital, eating Jell-O. She hated being away from her apartment, away from all her musty old crap. I made out a mental list of her favorite things I could put into a hospital care package for her.

When I arrived at the accountant's office, however, I was hit by a real shocker. Mr. Langley pushed an envelope across the vast oaken plateau that was his desk. "We would like to thank you for your service to Miss Arnaud."

I gawped at the check, which was for twice the amount I usually received.

"That's for your last weeks of work, plus two weeks severance," Langley said. "I'm afraid we have to let you go."

He kept saying *we*. "But what about Sylvie?"

"If she recovers—"

"*If!*" I bleated.

He winced at my outburst. "Miss Arnaud is at a very advanced age, as you know, and her condition is serious. If she survives, it is her wish and the wish of her beneficiaries that she be moved to an assisted living community. You must understand."

I did not. And who were these beneficiaries? They had certainly not visited her while I had been there.

"I'd like to see Sylvie."

The wrinkles of studied concern that had creased his brow

disappeared. "I don't think that will be necessary, or even advisable considering her present condition."

Growing miffed, I asked, "Will you at least tell me where she is?"

"I will take that up with the beneficiaries."

I stood up, filled with righteous anger. I had a feeling I was talking to the primary beneficiary. Maybe the only one. The weasel. "Fine. Please ask them, Mr. Langley. Please assure *the beneficiaries* that all I want to do is bring Miss Arnaud a box of her favorite cookies."

I sailed out of his office, my indignation at full mast.

Needless to say, I never got a call telling me Sylvie's whereabouts. But to be honest, I didn't knock myself out trying to find her on my own. I didn't work at it at all. When it came down to it, I rationalized, I had just been Sylvie's employee. She wasn't my responsibility. And if her heirs worried that I would somehow winnow my way into her will, then fine. Let *them* comb the island of Manhattan for butter mints and hot pickled okra.

It didn't take long for my severance money to dry up, and no one came forward offering me another cushy job. One of my roommates, an aspiring playwright named Fleishman, was working sporadically at a part-time job with a telemarketing company selling vinyl siding one day and ballet subscriptions the next. My other roommate, Wendy, was studying lighting design at NYU and honing her barista skills at Starbucks. We had known each other since college. We were the three musketeers, but without my paycheck, we were more like three shipwrecked souls on a leaky lifeboat.

Wendy was somewhat worried, but she was too busy to do much to solve our financial conundrum.

Fleishman was not worried, because he never worried, especially about money. He came from serious money—he was a descendent of an established chain of discount shoe store owners. He himself had no interest in shoes (at least not the discount variety), and since his parents did not consider playwriting a good use of their son's life, at the moment he was supposed to be cut off from the family. His mother, however, would occasionally suffer a wave of maternal guilt and come into the city to take Fleishman out to lunch (and take in the stores, no doubt.) On these days, Fleishman would return to our apartment with a wad of cash in his pockets. Or maybe sporting a new leather jacket. Christmas and birthdays—even in his disinherited state—tended to be accompanied by a thin envelope bearing a fat check. Broke was always a temporary thing to Fleishman. He always had hope.

My dad owned a plumbing supply business, which, while lucrative, did not provide for periodic windfalls. I was the fifth of six kids. My parents bankrolled me through college with the tacit understanding that afterwards I was to be completely on my own. My dad, in his usual self-effacing way, called this kind of generosity paying for the privilege of getting rid of me. Given that they still had my little brother in college, and now grandchildren to juggle, I would have died before I asked them for more money.

In February, my roommates and I were one hundred and forty dollars short on the rent, so I sold my notebook computer on eBay. This was a psychological low-water mark. Not that I actually needed my notebook. When I had come to New York, I had thought I would write something. Sylvie's memoirs. Maybe short stories; I had done a few of those in college. It had been two years, though, and I hadn't written anything more taxing than a grocery list.

Unfortunately, my notebook was my only valuable. I couldn't hock anymore even if I'd wanted to. I needed a job. Fast.

Out flew the resumes. But the expected responses never came pouring in. After three weeks, I'd had exactly two interviews, neither of which had borne fruit. The calendar advanced relentlessly toward the next rent due date. It was nail biting time. So when my phone rang and the person on the other end of the line said she was calling from Candlelight Books and that I had an interview, it felt like a lifeline was being thrown at me. I was ecstatic.

I knew what Candlelight Books was, of course. Who didn't?

They were the colossus of romance, the books everyone's aunts read but that they never read themselves. You couldn't walk through a superstore in the heartland or a drugstore anywhere without seeing racks of them, all branded with the flickering candle logo.

I just didn't remember applying there. Not that I was about to tell that to the woman on the telephone. I wasn't about to say anything that might risk my chances for getting my foot in the door. She instructed me to appear at the offices on the following day at one o'clock, and I assured her I would be there.

"What's the job?" Fleishman asked when he saw me dragging my interview suit out of our closet.

A railroad flat is not an ideal setup for communal living. The apartment took up an entire floor of a rowhouse, and there were three rooms, sort of (one had surely been meant to be a hall, or a dining area), but there were no doors between the rooms. It was just one long breezeway. In other words, for having blowout parties or as a roller rink, the place would have been ideal. For trying to section off three bedrooms, it was a challenge. We all had to share the one closet, which during the residency of some previous tenant had lost its sliding door and now was "closed" with a shower curtain with a tropical fish motif.

"It's with Candlelight Books."

Fleishman barked out a laugh. "You are *kidding* me. You're going to work on romance novels? *You?* You've never had a successful romance in your life."

I didn't really need to be reminded of that. Especially since one of my failed romances was with *him*.

"They aren't looking for Masters and Johnson," I said.

"Good."

I eyed him sharply. I admit it—I could still be a little defensive when it came to our relationship. "What's that supposed to mean?"

"Nothing," he said, rolling his eyes. He always complained that I was too sensitive. "I'm amazed you applied there, though."

"I didn't even know I had. The ad didn't give the name of the company."

"They were probably afraid that people wouldn't answer the ad if they knew it was for Candlelight Books."

"Probably." No doubt there were some people who would turn up their noses at working around romance novels. I was not one of those people. *Correction:* Since having to auction my belongings on eBay, I had ceased to be one of those people.

"I think you'd make a great editor."

"I think it's just secretarial. Or something."

He raised his brows. Fleishman had very distinctive, Dracula-like brows, so it always seemed very dramatic when they arched at you. "You don't know?"

"I'm sure it's an editorial assistant job." I was fairly certain I had applied for a few of those. Not that I had any idea what an editorial assistant actually did. "Or assistant something-or-other. I answered so many ads . . ."

I once read in a book about job hunting that you should keep a tidy folder documenting all the places you've applied, and listing all the relevant dates for callbacks and interviews. But if I had been that organized in the first place, I probably wouldn't be the kind of putz who was scrabbling for a job, any job.

Now Wendy, she would have made a folder. Wendy was that way. She kept a chart on our refrigerator to keep track of whose week it was to take out the garbage.

Fleishman was more like me. (Which made it extra fortunate that we had Wendy.) "Well, whatever," he said. "Once you have a bundle saved from your lucrative new career, you can produce *Yule Be Sorry.*"

"Don't hold your breath." I quickly added, "The position's not that lucrative."

But what I really meant was, fat chance I would ever help *Yule Be Sorry* see the light of day.

Yule Be Sorry was Fleishman's latest unfinished theatrical masterpiece, dreamed up after he had spent Christmas with my family in Cleveland. Fleishman's plays, which had made him the Noel Coward of our little college, were airy, funny pieces with just enough message to justify their being written at all. *Yule Be Sorry* continued in this tradition. But even in the one act he had written, the thinly disguised picture of my family was not pretty—the Alberts came off as a collection of airheads and rubes. And the girl protagonist of the play, the one who brings her ex-boyfriend home for the holiday—in other words, me—was especially grating. She had a few good lines, but for the most part she was a scold, a former fat girl who secretly scarfed down spritz cookies when no one was looking.

Okay, maybe that last part was me spot-on, but come on. *Was* I *a scold?* I didn't think so. Yes, I was just more practical than Fleishman, but that was setting the bar so low the midgets of the Lollypop Guild couldn't have limboed under it. Anna Nicole Smith was probably more practical than Fleishman.

This play would have weighed more heavily on my mind if I had thought that Fleishman would ever finish his masterpiece. But he had been completely unproductive since graduation. What really went over big in a small school in Ohio was not exactly what the Great White Way was clamoring for. I could sense Fleishman getting discouraged. He hadn't written much of anything in the past year, and he had lost that glow of the big-fish-in-a-small-pond celebrity he had when we first met. Lately it seemed that he mostly misspent his nights drinking too much cheap wine and watching *Green Acres.*

Nobody tells you this growing up, but the reason you're supposed to develop good work habits is so when the academic world spits you out at the age of twenty-two, your personal ambitions won't be sidelined by the seductive lure of TV Land.

Fleishman squinted in despair at my gray interview suit, which had been a college graduation present from my mom. I had never had to use it until that month. "You think that's the right outfit for this job interview?"

I furrowed my brow. During the last interview, I had splooped coffee on the jacket and I hadn't been able to get it out with a Shout wipe. "Why not?"

"Because that suit is not the right suit for any job interview."

I couldn't argue. The suit was pretty much ugly all day: a slate gray color that would wash out even the most Coppertoned skin, a Mao collared jacket that made my bust look like one vast gray rolling plain, and a skirt with a hem that hit at mid kneecap, which was a flattering length on no one.

"Plus I imagine people at Candlelight Books all run around the offices in pink sequins and feather boas," Fleishman said.

"It's a *business*," I replied. "The woman on the phone sounded very businesslike."

"Right. It's probably just the authors who run around all day in lounging pajamas." He flopped onto the couch. "I hope you get this job! It'll be so entertaining to hear you talk about. You'll get to talk to people like what's her name."

"Who?"

He snapped his fingers. "You know—that one who's on the bestseller lists all the time."

"I have no idea who you're talking about."

Neither did he.

"It's probably just some flunky job. I might just answer phones or something."

"You're always downpeddling," he said. "What if this is actually the beginning of something big?"

He flashed those gray eyes of his in a way that, I admit it, could still make my insides go fluttery. Which was amazing, considering all we'd been through. I mean, we'd been friends, and—briefly—lovers, and endured a breakup, and then become roommates. One New Year's after we'd just moved to New York, we had re-succumbed to each other, but now our romance was officially in full remission. I'd watched him date other women. Worse, I'd watched him floss his teeth in front of the eleven o'clock news. That alone should have squelched any residual fluttering, but no such luck.

I shook my head. "Big, as in . . . ?"

"Think of it. We've both been knocking around this city for almost three years now. It's time one of us got a break, isn't it?"

"In other words, you think I'm going to go to that interview a youngster, but I have to come back a star?"

"Don't be so cynical. This could be a really great career turn for you."

Could it? I tried to stay guarded. Sometimes Fleishman exuded this crazy enthusiasm that could carry me aloft. He could go nuts over an idea, or some wacky plan, or even a new Web site he'd found. It's part of why I found him so appealing. He could pull enthusiasm out of thin air and toss it over me like fairy dust. A little of it was twinkling over me now.

Chapter 2

Candlelight Books was located on two floors of a mammoth New York office building in Midtown. I huddled in a coffee shop in the lobby until it was just time for my appointment, then I hurried up. The only other person on the elevator was a tall, good looking man. *Really* good looking, I decided, doing a double-take. Dark blond hair, brown eyes. A combination of buttoned down and hott, with two Ts. I took all this as a good sign. Despite the butterflies in my stomach, I couldn't be too nervous if I still wanted to take the time to ogle some man-flesh.

He tilted his head at me. I smiled.

He frowned.

I averted my eyes.

"Job interview?" he asked.

I swerved back toward him, amazed. It was like he had powers, or something. "My God, you could be on *Oprah*. How did you know?"

Laughing, he lifted his shoulders. "You looked nervous."

I sank against the wall. Damn! "Nervous isn't exactly what I'm trying to convey."

"But you shouldn't be nervous at all," he said. "I'd hire you."

He was just being nice, but I was grateful. "You don't happen to work at Candlelight Books, do you?"

"Uh, no."

"Well, thanks anyway."

"Just the same, you might want to check your teeth." A fresh Kleenex materialized in his hand, and he offered it to me. "Lipstick."

Startled, I glanced into the stainless steel of the doors and just before they opened, I saw a smudge of red on my left front tooth. "Shit!" I murmured, grabbing the Kleenex and scrubbing frantically. How embarrassing. I felt like a dumbass (with two Ss).

"Break a leg!" he called after me as I stumbled off the elevator.

I was standing in a carpeted lobby whose walls were lined with glass-covered bookcases. The cases gave the appearance of guarding something valuable, though the books inside them were rack-sized paperbacks you would see at any Walgreens in the country. Many of the covers bore pictures of men (usually shirtless) and women (usually in the process of tastefully losing their shirts), undulating against each other in various chaste and not-so-chaste ways. Some of them just had couples staring at each other, or the horizon, with dramatic urgency. A few just had a single man, usually in a cowboy hat, standing rugged and alone and staring ahead with what I supposed was meant to be a sensual glower.

A woman about my age was doing phone duty at a large, double-tiered reception desk. All that was visible of her was her heart-shaped face, long blond hair, and a Peter Pan blouse in baby blue with navy blue piping—a hideous early Donna Reed thing that I hoped for her sake was being worn as an ironic statement.

She smiled briskly at me. "May I help you?"

"I'm Rebecca Abbot. I have an appointment with Kathy Leo."

"Kathy will be out momentarily," the receptionist announced after buzzing her.

Momentarily left me five minutes to stare more closely at the books in the cases. I recognized very few names. I had spent all my college years reading. I had been buried in books, but I knew nothing about romances. It was like I was discovering a counterculture.

"Good, you're on time!" a voice said to me before I knew I had been spotted. Kathy Leo strode toward me with her hand outstretched. "Nice to meet you. Come on back."

I was ushered through a maze of hallways, all buzzing with romance novel–related activity. Little clumps of people gathered together talking looked up with obvious curiosity at me as I walked by. Along one corridor we passed a lone young woman standing at a copying machine, staring mesmerized at the flashing light of the Xerox.

My future, I thought.

But it looked good! Earning money as a copying machine zombie sounded just fine. I'd take it.

Kathy escorted me into an unadorned beige box of an office. Her desk had children's pictures on it, a computer, and a Rolodex, but little else. "I showed your resume to the editorial director, Mercedes Coe, and she thought it looked good. Really good. So I want you to meet with her today. She's got a meeting at one-thirty, but we should be able to just sneak you in."

"Great!" I said, wondering when she was going to ask how fast I could type. (I was prepared to lie.)

"Good—let's go."

And that was that. The next thing I knew, I was being led back through the maze again, until we arrived at what was clearly set up to be an outer office—a woman in her early twenties was sitting in front of a computer next to a door with a plaque that read *Editorial Director*. The absence of a name made me wonder if editorial directors came and went with such regularity it didn't seem worth the effort.

"Is she in?" Kathy asked.

"She's in," the assistant said, giving me a quick visual going over. Her gaze seemed to linger on my Mao suit mono-bosom.

Damn. I should have taken Fleishman's advice and worn

something else. The tricky part was, what would something else have been?

Under her breath, the assistant started singing a bluesy song as I was shown into the office. "Stormy Weather." I flicked a glance at her to see if there was some sort of message in it, but she seemed completely absorbed in whatever was on her computer screen.

Inside the editorial director's office, Kathy parked me in front of a desk that was a mass of stacked papers, pink message slips, paperback books, and yellow legal pads. Kathy made a quick introduction, and Mercedes Coe hopped up from her chair and came around.

"Oh good! You're here."

She was tall, slender, and wore a suit that was amazingly like the one I was wearing, only it was navy blue and looked a lot better on her. Her blond hair was swept up into some kind of coil on the back of her head, and her lips were bright red against her pale skin. Around her neck she had knotted a silk scarf in an elaborate stab at being Catherine Deneuve.

"I have to be at a meeting at one-thirty," Mercedes informed us.

It was one-twenty already.

"I told her you didn't have much time," Kathy said.

"I've got a senior ed meeting," Mercedes told me.

Kathy left us alone, and I expected a rushed five minutes full of questions, after which I would be shown the door.

Mercedes told me to take a seat, and then she lowered herself down in her leather desk chair. "I was very intrigued by your resume. *Very intrigued,*" she said, rifling through the mess on her desktop. "If I can find it . . ." she muttered. "Where did it scamper off to?"

I didn't see it there.

She lifted her shoulders. "Oh well! I suppose it's times like these when one is glad to have a photographic memory."

I chuckled. I appreciate sarcasm.

But her expression wiped the grin off my face. "No, really. I do," she said, with a little roll of her eyes to let me know what a burden this kind of super intelligence could be at times. "That's how I ended up graduating *cum laude* from Stanford. It couldn't have been hard work, I assure you!" She laughed modestly, all the while staring pointedly at the Stanford diploma hanging on a wall to my right. "And you went to school . . . where?"

I gave her the name of my private college in Ohio; it was a good school, a little liberal arts haven, but not that many people knew about it. We had no major sports team.

"Small schools have great benefits," Mercedes observed consolingly. "Your major was . . . ?"

"English literature," I said.

"Right! English lit." She chuckled. "Now I remember—it seemed strange to me that you didn't major in French, because you went on to work with Sylvie Arnaud. You were her ghostwriter-editor?"

I gulped. *Had I written that?* I was prone to resume inflation—it's hard not to be when you're starting out with the flaccid balloon of resumes. "Well, some might say that I was something more like an all-around personal assistant."

"Right! Interesting!" She leaned back, clearly impressed. Clearly having no clue that I had spent the past two years combing Manhattan for jars of okra. "She knew Albert Camus, I'm sure."

I had no idea. I nodded. "She knew everybody."

"I did my senior thesis on Camus."

"Oh!" I was trying to remember who that guy was, exactly. Had he written *The Little Prince?* "How fascinating."

"In French, of course." She rattled off a question at me in rapid fire, extravagantly accented French.

I had studied French in school, but I hadn't given it much of a thought in years. Sylvie had always spoken to me in English. And even in my heyday of Continuing French Conversation during senior year, I never knew the language so well that I didn't panic when someone was talking at me full speed.

In this case, I did what I always did when I didn't exactly understand. I agreed. "*Bien sur!*"

This seemed to satisfy Mercedes. "You know, I saw her mentioned the other day somewhere . . ."

"*The New York Review of Books.*"

"Exactly!" Mercedes seemed gratified that I would assume she read that magazine. Actually, I assumed she didn't. Did anyone? "So . . . um . . ." She was searching her *cum laude* brain for my name, I presumed.

"Rebecca," I reminded her.

"Right! Tell me a little more about yourself, Rebecca."

If there had been a BS meter on Mercedes's desk, for the next five minutes its needle would have been tilting frantically into the red. I was an unrecognized child prodigy, torn between all of my varied interests, but what I had always been attracted to was the written word. I had edited my school literary magazine. (True enough.) We had worked mostly on student work, but also with professionals like Margaret Atwood and Jane Smiley. (Almost true—I had written those esteemed women to ask if they would contribute a story, and each had written back to politely refuse.) My dream was to edit books, but I knew I needed to start small, pay my dues. Working with a woman like Sylvie had taught me all about patience. (I had to mention Sylvie again, since Mercedes seemed so impressed by her.)

But Mercedes didn't have a BS meter on her desk, and she didn't seem to have one in her brain, either. All during my tall tale, she tapped a silver fountain pen on her desk blotter and didn't appear to notice that it was dribbling puddles of ink everywhere. "Well! I am impressed."

The minutes were ticking away. The meeting she had needed to rush out to had surely started by now?

"Very impressed indeed!"

I felt a surge of hope. I started ticking the days off in my head. If I started work the next Monday, maybe I would be getting a paycheck two weeks after that. Which meant that we might fall short on the rent the next month, but after that we would be on easy street.

Which reminded me. Money. "How much does this job pay?" I blurted out.

Mercedes's face fell, and I knew instantly that I had made a mistake. Her expression couldn't have looked any more uncomfortable if I had farted.

She tapped her fingers, shifted in her chair, and finally cleared her throat. "You didn't go over this with Kathy?"

I shook my head. Kathy! *That's* who I should have asked.

"Well, an assistant here starts at . . . generally speaking . . ." She named a figure in the low thirties. My heart pounded. It was unbelievable. I couldn't help saying the number aloud.

Mercedes's eyes narrowed. "Did you have a specific salary requirement?"

"No!" Then, realizing that I probably sounded very uncool, I added, "That is, not really . . ."

"Because, naturally, with your experience . . ."

My lips twisted. *Right.* With my experience I was lucky not to be asking people if they would like to supersize that.

"I'll be pulling for you to do well on the test," she said quickly.

That word, *test*, stopped me cold. I stopped balancing my checkbook in my head. I'd been hoping to bluff about my typing speed. "When do I take that?"

"I'll give it to you to take home now," she said.

Take home? This was obviously not a typing test.

She turned and pillaged the top of a file cabinet stacked with papers, then came back at me with a large manila envelope. "That's a book proposal. Read it, write an acceptance and revision letter and edit the first chapter, and then drop it off at the front desk."

I gulped. *Edit?* They wanted me to be an editor and not just some kind of secretary?

"Oh! And let me get you some books." She grabbed handfuls from her shelves and shoved them across the desk at me.

I stumbled out of the building with my bundle of stuff, feeling conflicted. A job like this would be great, but what were the chances I would get it?

Nil.

I really needed to be more careful about these jobs I was applying for.

Fleishman and Wendy were thrilled with my freebies. Wendy found a baggy family saga in the pile that piqued her interest. "I love stuff like this."

"I thought you didn't read romance novels," I said.

"I don't," she said. "I just like these."

Fleishman went straight for the category romance novels; he seemed more interested in the camp factor of it all. "Look at this! *The Fireman's Baby Surprise!*" He sniggered as he leafed through the front pages. "Is that what women fantasize about now? Having babies with firemen?"

"Don't ask me," I said. "I just fantasize about having a paycheck."

Fleishman stole away with a little hoard of books.

Wendy shot the manila envelope a look of concern. "What's that? Homework?"

"It's an editing test. I have to edit a chapter of a manuscript and bring it back to them."

Wendy tilted her head. "Do you know how to do that?"

"Oh, how hard can it be?" Fleishman piped up from the futon sofa. Then he turned back to his book. "The fireman's name is Chance. Are there actually people in the world named Chance?"

"Coming from a man named Herbert Dowling Fleishman the Third, I don't think you have room to sneer."

He glared at me and sank down on the couch. He always hated it when I reminded him of his name. There was a good reason he went by Fleishman.

"What are you going to do?" Wendy asked me.

"I guess I'm going to treat myself to a crash course in editing."

For the next two days, I was a slave to the *Chicago Manual of Style*. I went through two red pencils marking up that manuscript. And in the meantime, I read several of the books. I read *The Fireman's Baby Surprise*, *Beauty and the Bounty Hunter*, and I skimmed a long book that was a retelling of Cinderella set in Scotland in the 1700s called *Highland Midnight Magic*. I steeped myself in romance.

I don't know what I was expecting. Hilariously purple prose, I guess. And it had been a long time, maybe forever, since I had heard a man's sexual organ referred to as his manroot. But for the most part, the thing that surprised me was that the books were so not focused on sex. At least the little modern ones weren't. (The Scottish book was half sex, half clan war.) The fireman had firehouse politics and an arsonist to deal with, along with his paternity dilemma. The bounty hunter was chasing an heiress wrongly accused of jewel smuggling—so that was a big mess to have to work out. Every step of the way, these poor people had problems, *and* they were falling in love.

By the end of the week I was beginning to see the appeal. If some schmuck has time to find an arsonist, expose his boss for corruption, find good daycare, *and* fall in love with a sassy local news reporter, the authors seemed to be saying, there was hope for us all.

I must have done something right, because the day after I turned in my test Kathy Leo called me to tell me to come in again, this time to talk to someone named Rita Davies.

When I was led back to Rita's office, I was struck at once by the mess. If Mercedes's office was disorganized, Rita's could have qualified as a Superfund site. Manuscripts piled up precariously in teetering Seussian columns. I counted six different in-boxes, and all of them were full. Rita was a blousy, heavy-lidded woman with frizzy red hair. She looked up at me when I walked in and took a sip from one of the three coffee mugs on her desk.

"Do you smoke?" she asked by way of greeting.

I was a little taken aback. Was this a trick question? I took a deep breath and sensed a definite smell of tobacco. "Uh . . . not really. I mean, occasionally I'll bum one at a bar or something . . ."

She cut off my answer with a wave. "Because if you want, we can go outside."

It was drizzling outside. And cold. It wasn't yet March. "No, I'm fine here."

"Okay, great. Just a second." She opened a drawer, tossed

out several old pens, what looked like an ancient bagel wrapped in wax paper, and a box of nicotine patches. She took a moment to slap on a patch, waited a moment for the burn to begin, then turned back to me with an easy smile. "Great job on the test, by the way."

"Thanks. I really liked that story."

"Yeah, she's a good author for us. I'll give you more of her books, if you want."

"Terrific!" I could give them to Fleishman. Ever since my first interview, he'd been on a romance reading jag.

"Mercedes told me all about you. She said you're just what we need around here."

"Oh, well . . ." What she really needed was a Mighty Maid service.

"She said you had worked with Sylvie Whatsawhosit and really were invaluable to her."

I just shrugged modestly.

She squinted at me. "Sure you don't feel like a cigarette?"

I was pretty certain there was a hard and fast rule about not smoking on your job interview. It was probably up there with not showing up shit-faced drunk or wearing flip-flops. I shook my head.

"Nicorette?" she asked, offering me a box.

"No, I'm fine. Really."

"Wish I could say the same!" She sighed and popped a piece of gum into her mouth. "I guess I should tell you how we work around here. This little area here is referred to as the Pulse Pod."

"Pulse?" I asked.

"I'm senior editor of the Pulse line." She pointed to a shelf of books with identical red and white spines that were for the most part obscured by random piles of other books, souvenir ashtrays, and, inexplicably, a pair of beige suede boots. "It's Candlelight's line of medical romances. You know—doctors, nurses, paramedics. Even a phlebotomist or two." I was going to laugh, but she didn't give me a chance. "As far as staff goes,

I'm the senior editor of the pod, and I've got an ed assist. Then there's an assistant editor and an associate. Another person would be such a big help, I can't tell you. I hope you don't mind having a ton of work thrown at you all at once. You wouldn't have much of a learning curve."

"Learning curves? Who needs 'em?" I joked.

"Right. Well, what I could use is a vacation, but I doubt that's coming anytime soon, unless it's in a place with padded walls."

She went on to explain to me that Pulse Pod people worked on all sorts of books aside from medical romances. "We also work on Hearthsongs, Flames, MetroGirl, Historicals, and occasionally Divines."

She might have been speaking to me in a foreign tongue. I was lost. All I could think of when she said *divine* was the cross-dresser who starred in *Lust in the Dust.* I was pretty sure that wasn't what she meant.

She stopped. "Divine is Candlelight's inspirational line. Those books are *really* hot right now. You might say preachers are the new vets. Vet heroes came into vogue a decade ago. And cops are always the rage." She sighed. "We don't do a lot of Divines in this pod, though. Mary Jo is pretty possessive of those. Have you met Mary Jo Mahoney?"

I shook my head.

"You will." She inhaled on her pen. "Lucky bitch—she knows she's sitting on the gold mine over there in the God Pod. It's where the real growth is now."

I left the interview with mixed feelings. I couldn't decide if the job looked like a great thing or a nightmare. When I got home hauling a totebag full of books, Fleishman was all over me. (Well, all over the totebag.)

"More books? Yay!"

I was beginning to worry about him. "Aren't you supposed to be at work?"

"I called in sick." When I leveled a stare at him, he smiled impishly. "I had to see how your interview turned out."

"It went fine."

"I'll say—there's a message from Kathy Leo on the machine."

I gasped and scrambled over to the phone. When I called Kathy, she announced, "I was calling to offer you the position of associate editor for Candlelight Books."

Associate? I gulped. Maybe I'd heard her wrong. "I thought . . ."

She laughed. "I know. You could have knocked me over with a feather when Mercedes came to plead your case. The thing is, we can't up the starting salary for assistants without causing a revolution around here, but she really was impressed with you, so we decided that we should bump you up a job grade."

Fleishman, who was practically shoving me out of hearing range so he could stick his ear next to the receiver, too, gave me a high five.

"I-I don't know what to say," I stammered. "Except . . ." *Except I think I'm in way over my head now.* "Except how soon can I start?"

Chapter 3

Kathy Leo's call put me in a panic.

What was I getting myself into? Sure, I could bluff my way through a half-hour interview or two. Apparently I had bluffed beyond my wildest dreams. But how could I bluff my way through eight hours a day, five days a week, fifty weeks a year?

Answer: I couldn't. I was so screwed.

I didn't even own the clothes to look the part. Aside from my Mao suit, my wardrobe leaned heavily toward the ultra-casual, as befitted an ex-grocery shopper. I was utterly unprepared to enter a world where I needed to look like a grownup. I wasn't even sure I still owned a pair of panty hose. Didn't people still wear those?

On Friday, the day after the call from Kathy Leo, I was still flat on my back on the futon in the living room, awash in worry. Worrying was about all I could do, since God knows I didn't have the funds to remedy my fashion deficiency. And no amount of money would render me suddenly competent for a job I was in no way qualified for.

I had a versatile skirt made out of some kind of tensile material that was supposed to be breathable but really felt like Saran Wrap, and I had the Mao suit. Wendy had an actual dress I could probably borrow to throw my new coworkers off my feebly garmented trail. That was three outfits—maybe five if I accessorized cleverly to disguise the fact that I was wearing the Saran Wrap skirt in three different incarnations. If I did that for two weeks, maybe three, I would probably be able to splurge for something new at Filene's Basement with my first paycheck.

I envisioned myself at the end of those three weeks in my gamey black skirt, already the office pariah. Possibly by then the powers that be would have found me out—that I, *ahem*, stretched the truth in those interviews. That I had no business even applying for such a job. That actually, despite four years of college English, none of which remotely touched on the subject of grammar, my relationship with the technical ins and outs of my native tongue was haphazard at best.

In other words, that I was a fraud.

Just as I was considering holding up the nearest Duane Reade for some Zoloft, the apartment door flew open and Fleishman rushed in. At least I was pretty sure it was Fleishman. His distinctive features were almost indistinguishable behind heaps of colorful shopping bags.

"Where have you been?" I asked. "I thought you had work today."

"I did, but then I got a summons from Natasha." Fleishman was the only person I knew who called his parents by their first names, a practice that in my family would have earned any kid a whack upside the head. But Natasha Fleishman never seemed to mind; she seemed to think it was part of her son's bad-boy appeal. Fleishman's attitude toward his family was always that of a beloved scapegrace. His father might not be speaking to him, his mother might have to sneak into the city to see him, and he might profess contempt for everything they stood for (up to and including budget footwear), but he acted as though he believed they would all eventually come around to see his undeniable value and charm.

I wondered, though. Fleishman took an awful lot for granted. No person, even a father, wanted to be called a miserly old fascist forever. I mean, language like that tended to alienate people.

He grinned and explained his mother's surprise appearance in town. "Natasha came to have lunch and to drop off part of the Fleishman fortune on Fifth Avenue. She called me at work before heading over, so I took the rest of the day off and here I am."

I eyed those bags. One said Sak's, one said Barney's, and a few others boasted names of stores that I didn't recognize.

"She took you to all those places?" I asked.

"No, no, no. Natasha just took me to lunch. I told her that we were collecting clothes for a charity drive, though, and so before coming over she loaded up the Benz with all her cast-offs."

"What charity?" I asked.

"The Rebecca Abbot foundation, dedicated to clothing the intolerably attired."

He laid all the bags at my feet. I could hardly believe it. There had to be thousands of dollars worth of stuff in there!

"Oh my God. It's like having a fairy godmother burst through the door!"

"I hope you don't mind hand-me-downs," he said.

He was joking. How many times had I repeated the factoid that I had not owned a first-hand coat until I was thirteen? When you're the fifth of six kids, you learn to look at the closets of your siblings as your own personal thrift store. But this—this was a big step up in closet class.

I tossed my arms around Fleishman and gave him a noisy kiss on his cheek. "I can't believe you did this for me, Fleish."

"Who else *would* I do it for?" he asked, his grey eyes practically sparkling at me.

When people ask me to describe Fleishman, I usually say he sort of resembles the young Martin Landau from his *North by Northwest* days, only that doesn't really do him justice. He's that tall, thin, and angular, but he's dapper. When you look at him—and he's so distinctive that people always do crane around to look at him on the streets or in restaurants—you would think that he must be an actor, or some other person used to being in the public eye. He might not be handsome in the way

Brad Pitt is handsome, but he carries himself like a man accustomed to thinking of himself as exceptional. Aside from his bearing, he has these steely blue-gray eyes—they can seem intense, or full of humor. They are mesmerizing.

On many an occasion those eyes have been my undoing.

I knew better now than to get tripped up by those eyes now. I knew my limits. Both of our limits. I was well aware of what all the sparking and smoldering could lead to: Wild abandon chased quickly by abject regret.

"Well, c'mon," he said impatiently when I broke eye contact. "Let's see what the old dame brung you."

Say this for her, Natasha Fleishman did not skimp on charity. From those shopping bags, which still had a perfumey smell lingering on them, we pulled out a wealth of stuff. Twinset cashmere sweaters, fabulous lightweight wool outfits in rich tweeds and checks, silk shirts, and so-called casual wear that would only be casual to people who actually wore formal wear on a regular basis. Putting on Natasha Fleishman's casual chic, I would feel like a kid playing dress up.

Yet after a few minutes I was pawing over garments bearing tags with Prada and Dior with a critical eye. The trouble was size. Natasha Fleishman was both taller and smaller than I was. That ruled out pants. I could, however, squeeze into most of the skirts and tops if I was careful to keep my breath sucked in.

Fleishman, who had begun to look like he was losing interest, dug out a vintage dress. "Wow—I think this was my grandmother's." It was a fitted turquoise and deep purple houndstooth shift. "I think you should wear this on your first day."

I took the dress from him and frowned as I looked it over. The tag read Mainbocher, whom I thought was a really big designer at some point. "I'm not sure . . ."

Fleishman looked hurt. "Why not?"

"Because it's not the kind of thing you wear on your first day to a job. Unless your job is as a guest star on *The Doris Day Show*. It's loud."

"You need to be louder," he grumbled, putting the dress aside.

I wasn't so sure. It was both loud and fitted, and things that were so fitted played right into my paranoia about body issues. Growing up, I had been fat. The kind of girl to whom people would say things like, "You have the loveliest brown eyes!" Or, "You look just like Winona Ryder!" Meaning, Winona Ryder, but fat. I had brown hair and brown eyes, and there our similarities ended.

When I lost weight, I actually did look a little more like Winona Ryder, but by then she was more known for shoplifting than good box office, so the resemblance was no longer in my favor.

"Do you think this is too tight?" I asked Fleishman as I stepped out a few minutes later to model a newer black scoop-neck dress with a Prada tag. I couldn't believe this stuff was from someone's discard pile.

Fleishman eyed me critically. "Sit-ups," he said. "A week of sit-ups and you'll look like a million dollars."

"I don't have a week," I reminded him. "Besides, I haven't done a sit-up since P.E. in seventh grade."

"Okay, we just won't eat for the next three days."

I nodded. If it meant fitting into a free wardrobe, that sounded like a reasonable suggestion.

That was the other thing about Fleishman. We'd known each other so long, he knew my history. He knew that growing up I was the little girl other kids had called Shamu in swim class. My weight had been a torment, but in a perverse way it had also seemed like my security blanket. Fat was who I was. The idea of losing weight and showing up at school thin (I always dreamed that it would happen overnight or something), which according to everyone was supposed to be my dream, made me feel even more self-conscious. I would be like the bald guy who suddenly shows up at work with a toupee.

The summer after high school, though, I took the plunge. I dropped forty-five pounds, and not by a method I would recommend to anyone. But by the time I got to college, I was average size. No one there knew I was only masquerading as a normal person.

At first, Fleishman was the only one at college I told about my deep dark secret. He knew all about me, and understood the yo-yo diet mentality and why I would panic when my size ten jeans started to feel tight. I have developed discipline over the years, but it's the cockeyed kind of discipline that says that it's fine to inhale a Krispy Kreme donut (or two!) for breakfast as long as you don't eat again for the rest of the day.

It's the kind of discipline Fleishman understood.

"Okay, modeling time's over," Fleishman said, two outfits later. "I'm taking you out."

I tilted my head. "Out where?"

He reached into his pocket and pulled out a wad of cash. "Natasha made a generous donation to the Fleishman fund, too, so I'm treating us both to haircuts."

Fleishman and I had been so tight knit for so long that we tended to treat financial windfalls as community property. We were so close we sometimes acted like twins with an extra set of parents. The fact that we had actually been an item—and that we had weathered not only a breakup but also a romantic lapse since—only made us that much more inseparable.

Wendy was always telling me that I should be more cautious; if Fleishman considered me his scold, Wendy was mine. Typically, she would wait until Fleishman and I had one of our periodic dust-ups to swoop down on me with advice.

"Someday you might want to put a little distance between yourself and the boy wonder," she would warn. "I like him, too, but I've never been in love with him."

"I'm not in love with him! We're *friends.*"

That was her cue for the piercing stare. "Works out great, too. You get a Svengali, and he gets an entourage."

I think the old college ties were beginning to grow frayed for Wendy. Luckily, she was in the middle of graduate school now and didn't have a lot of time for conversations like these anymore. She was too busy working on lighting designs for *Waiting for Godot.* She was up to her armpits in lighting gels and asbestos cables and didn't have as much time to devote to our ongoing domestic drama.

It was a beautiful winter day and Fleishman and I larked off into the city like two teenagers playing hooky. First we headed to Soho, where we were coiffed, and then we flitted down busy streets, in and out of stores, buying shoes and little trinkets and basically depleting the Fleishman fund to its previous shaky state. I charged a few things I shouldn't have, and accepted a few freebies from Fleishman, including the haircut, without much protest. After all, I was usually the big breadwinner.

When we had worked our way all the way up to Union Square, Fleishman sighed contentedly. I'll say this for him—you'll never meet a man happier to be down to his last dime. Maybe that was because he was always assured that it never really was his last dime. Another dime was always around the corner. Poverty was just a temporary mix-up to him. "I have just enough for dinner and train fare back to Brooklyn."

"I thought we weren't eating until Monday," I reminded him.

"But all this shopping—I'm starved!" he whined.

Fleishman was never big on deprivation.

"Okay," I said, "but after this . . ."

Let's face it. I wasn't big on deprivation, either.

We ambled over to an Indian place we liked.

Once he and I were settled in our booth soaking in the comforting scent of curry, with our respective beverages of wine and tea, we both took what seemed like our first deep breaths since we had started our retail debauch.

Fleishman slipped down in the booth until his torso formed a leisurely C. He sipped his wine. "You know what? Your big success at finding work has given me a shot of ambition myself."

I tilted my head. "You mean you're going to look for a job?"

His eyes widened in alarm. "What? Why would I do that? I have a job."

"A permanent job, I mean." *One that you actually go to.*

He shuddered. "I still feel that I'll make my mark in the world through writing. I haven't given up on *Yule Be Sorry.*"

I groaned. "I wish you would."

We had been over this before, gingerly. "It isn't about you and me," he assured me for the hundredth time.

"No, it's about an idealized you and a caricature of me."

"Not at all. You make Ramona sound like a cartoon. She just has a few traits you share. I'm culling from all over, though. She's a composite."

Don't be fooled; the woman was me.

And really, I had to wonder. Because the woman was doggedly conventional and a bit of a killjoy. One of those tiring people who believed every argument had a flipside—who would come out with expressions like "different strokes for different folks" as if she were delivering original kernels of wisdom. (I *never* said things like that!) The boyfriend, an artistic free spirit, comes to realize that what is holding him back is this girlfriend he's attached to who doesn't believe in him and reins in his phenomenal creativity out of subconscious jealousy.

That's just what I gleaned from the first act.

I didn't want to be unreasonable. I knew that writers had to cull a little of their work from real life. This one just seemed a little *too* culled. But what was I going to do, take his computer away from him? I suppose I could have put my foot down, but the hold-it-right-there-buster impulse was never strong in me. And as much as I hate to admit it, I was scared. I liked having Fleishman for a friend, if nothing more; I didn't want to alienate him.

I consoled myself with the knowledge that it would probably never be finished, or if it were, that it would never see the light of day. The theater world was a lot tougher to crack than we had assumed back in our little college in Ohio. Wendy was going the academic route and following her dreams that way, but Fleishman professed to be burned out on school.

"I'm glad you're feeling inspired," I said. Supportively.

Maybe he would feel inspired to write something else.

He raised his glass of cheap house wine. "To new beginnings," he said.

I clinked my chai tea against his glass. "Here, here."

He leaned back and sighed dreamily, pinning me with that gaze of his. "I don't know what I would have done without you."

I chuckled uncomfortably. "You make it sound as if you're either about to accept an Oscar or to ship out overseas."

"It just seems amazing to me sometimes. We've been friends for so long."

"Six whole years," I said.

"Isn't that a long time?" he asked.

"An entire lifetime . . . if we were six."

He shrugged. "Well, it's longer than most friendships I've had, and the amazing thing is what we've weathered. How many ex-boyfriends have you stayed friends with?"

I had to admit that he was it.

"And you're the only ex-girlfriend I've ever been able to be around, too. Most of the time I duck down store aisles and sidestreets to avoid them."

"I feel honored."

"I guess the difference is we always knew getting together was a mistake," he said.

I swallowed. *We did?*

He explained, "It would be like the old *Dick Van Dyke Show*, if Rob had run off with Sally."

I laughed, then stopped abruptly. Being compared with Rose Marie wasn't exactly my dream.

Besides, what if Rob *had* run off with Sally? Would that have been so awful? Sure, she wasn't Mary Tyler Moore, but she could make up jokes, and she could sing. Think of how much fun Rob had at the office. At the *Alan Brady Show* they were always laughing, but at home, it was just mixups and headaches, the Helpers and Little Richie. (Sally would never have saddled him with Little Richie.)

Fleishman snapped his fingers. "Rebecca!"

I jerked back to attention. "Huh?"

"You were about to start defending Sally, weren't you?"

I choked on my tea. "Okay, I get your drift. We weren't meant to be."

"Right. Most people aren't meant to be. The miracle is that we realized it was all a big mistake before our feelings got hurt."

I nodded. "Exactly."

At the end of the meal he looked at his watch and nearly knocked over his water glass in his hurry to wave down the waiter for the check.

"What's the matter?" I asked.

"I gotta get back," he said.

I frowned. "Back where?"

"To the apartment. I have a date."

So much for companionability. I gritted my teeth. "Really? Who?"

"This woman from the telemarketing job. Dorie. She's got a painting at some gallery, but I think the gallery's more like a coffee shop. It's probably going to be really lame, but I promised to go." He shrugged. "Dorie's not really my type. She's mousy and insecure, but for some reason she's latched onto me a little."

I bolted the rest of my tea, cold by now. Fleishman generally went out a lot on weekends. I went out too, if less frequently. (Confession: A lot less frequently.) Still, every time I heard him say he was going out with someone, I could feel a little knife twisting in me.

I could also hear Wendy's warning voice.

But I ignored it. Like Fleishman said, he and I were lucky that we had realized our mistake before any feelings got hurt.

My first day of work, and wouldn't you know it, it was pouring rain. The cats and dogs kind of rain where there's no way to avoid getting soaked. I had a dorky all-weather coat that I threw over one of Natasha Fleishman's suits. It was Chanel, and pretty snazzy, if I did say so myself. Then I grabbed the biggest umbrella I could find and shivered and sloshed my way into Manhattan. When it rains the subway can be so gross. Even when it's not hot, there's something about so many wet bodies crowded into a confined space that starts making everyone look limp and slightly mildewed. Glancing around my crowded car, the moment did not seem to auger great things for the new beginning that Fleishman had been toasting a few days earlier.

As I was scurrying toward the building, I walked through a cloud of smoke and heard someone call my name. I turned. Rita, AKA my new boss, was huddled under a plaid umbrella, puffing away.

She had to speak loudly over the sound of the rain beating down. "Aren't you early?"

"First day," I confessed, though I had never had a boss complain about someone being on time. "I wanted to make a good impression."

She lit another Benson and Hedges. She looked anxious. "I should show you around . . ."

"I can find my office," I assured her, even though I was a little doubtful about whether I actually could. My memory of that place was that it was a confusing maze of hallways.

She flagged down a passerby. "*Andrea!*" Another figure under an umbrella stopped in mid-scuttle toward the doors. "This is Rebecca Abbot. She's starting today. Think you could give her the tour?"

Andrea and I gave each other once-overs. She had dark curly hair, a Roman nose, and a mouth that turned down at the corners. She was tall and, I have to say, slightly intimidating. "So you're the latest victim." Her voice was loud, with a little bit of a scratch in it. "Okay, let's go in before you float back to wherever you came from."

"I'm right behind you!" Rita called after us.

We shook ourselves out like rain-drenched dogs in the lobby, causing the marble floor to get that much more slippery. In the elevator, Andrea turned to me. "So where else did you interview? Did you get in over at Avon?"

"No . . ."

She looked surprised. "They were looking for someone. But they didn't call me back, either."

"You applied there?"

She laughed as though I had delivered a zinger. "My resume has been to every company in this whole damn town. I'm not going to get myself out of this place depending on telepathy, you know. Did you interview at Warner?"

"Uh, no . . . I did interview at a trade publication. I think it was legal books . . ."

Andrea shook her head disdainfully. "Oh God! You're better off here."

An uneasy feeling nibbled at me. Could it be a good sign when the first coworker I met was scrambling to find a job elsewhere?

"I noticed Random House was looking for a full editor," she said. "You didn't apply there, did you?"

"No."

She nodded. "Probably best not to waste your time. I interviewed with them before I came here."

"What happened?"

"They hired someone else. Jackasses!"

We faced forward for a moment.

"How long have you been here?" I asked.

"Four years." Before I could register whether I thought this was a long time or not, she answered the question for me. "I know, I know. I gotta get out—but the market is so tight right now." She sighed. "My luck, I'll probably spend the rest of my life in an efficiency in Queens."

The doors opened, and Andrea waved me out with a sarcastic flourish. "Welcome to Alcatraz."

First stop on the tour was the receptionist desk, where the woman with the Peter Pan collar still sat at attention with her headset, looking like the proverbial operator standing by in those TV commercials of old. And was that actually a cameo she was wearing today?

"Muriel, this is . . . um . . ." Andrea darted an uncomfortable glance at me.

"Rebecca," I said.

"Yes, Rebecca, I remember you," Muriel said. "Kathy Leo alerted me to your arrival this morning, so I have already put you into our message center." She whirled a little plastic caddy around to the point where my name in a red colored tab was prominently displayed. "This is where you may retrieve messages left in person, or urgent messages that callers do not wish to leave on your answering service. But please keep in mind that the answering service is the most efficient way of retrieving your messages. I do my best to relay communications efficiently, but the human factor is always fallible, and I have noticed that *some* people forget to check for their message slips. So do set up your answering service at your earliest possible convenience. Your extension is fifty-six, which is written on the phone in your office, along with detailed instructions about setting up your personal recorded message. Of course if you have any questions, I will be more than happy to help. Welcome aboard!"

She ended her introductory monologue with a smile that was one hundred percent lips.

I felt like I should applaud. "Thanks."

"You're welcome, Rebecca."

Andrea tugged impatiently on my sleeve. During Muriel's monologue, she had removed her raincoat and shaken herself out a little more, spilling droplets on Muriel's carefully tended simulated wood grain work surface.

"Let's show you to your cave so you can dump your junk and start to dry off," she said, ignoring Muriel's pursed lip parting glare. When we were out of earshot, she said, "She's always like that."

"Like what?"

"Prim," Andrea grumbled. "I don't know how she keeps it up. It makes me wonder if she's not moonlighting as a lap dancer."

We made our way through a labyrinth of hallways that I vaguely remembered from my last visit. As we were turning a corner, Andrea looked around furtively and asked, "When you were at Random House, did you talk to Margaret Wyberry?"

"I didn't interview there," I reminded her.

"Oh, that's right." She let out a puff of breath. "Oh well.

I've heard there isn't a lot of opportunity for advancement there anyway."

"Is there here?" I asked.

She arched her brows. "Why? Are you bored already?"

"Well, no . . . I . . ." I had just been making small talk.

"Here!" She stopped at a small windowless office and flipped on the lights. There was a seascape watercolor gracing one wall and a large empty peg board over the desk. Andrea gestured grandly, like the hostesses on *The Price is Right.* "Home sweet home. I stole your chair and gave you my shitty one. Hope you don't mind."

I looked at the desk chair, which looked like standard issue office rolling thing. "I'm grateful not to be sitting on a plastic crate."

"That's only the ed assists," Andrea joked.

I took off my coat and tossed it on the spare chair in the corner. As I did so, I noticed a bookshelf with piles and piles of manuscripts on it. "What's that?"

"Your inheritance." Andrea went over to inspect it. "Looks like slush, mostly, but there are a few agented proposals in here . . ." She whistled. "This one's cover letter is dated 2003! Damn! That Julie had more nerve than I gave her credit for."

"What happened to Julie?"

"It was very sad. One day she decided to end it all right there at her desk."

I swerved in alarm, whereupon Andrea blasted out a laugh. "*Kidding!* She got knocked up." She sighed. "That's one way off the treadmill."

"Yeah, but then you have a baby to deal with."

Andrea snorted. "Here you have twenty."

I looked at her, puzzled.

"Otherwise known as authors." She gave my suit a once-over and whistled. "Snappy!"

"Thanks—it's a hand-me-down."

"What, are there tycoons in your family?"

"In my roommate's family, actually."

"Nice!" She frowned. "But can you breathe?"

I sucked in. I had never gotten around to those sit-ups.

Or starving.

When we ventured out again, our first stop was Rita's office, which was dark. "She must still be downstairs," Andrea said.

In the cubicle outside Rita's office, there was a commotion, and we turned as one. Before, I hadn't noticed anyone sitting there. "*Lindsay?*" Andrea asked, her tone doubtful.

A figured hunched on her hands and knees on the floor jerked up, banging her head on her desk. "Shit!" she cried. Then she saw me. "Oh—sorry." She jumped to her feet and darted out her hand for me to shake, then thought better of it since it was holding a paper towel that was dripping some sort of fluid all over the carpet.

And that wasn't the only odd thing about her. She was wearing a nubbly tweed jacket over what appeared to be an old taffeta formal. I usually wasn't too judgmental about outfits. I had been around theater people, so I was used to creative dressing. But this girl looked bizarre. Plus, I have this thing about taffeta. I don't like it. (It's a long story.)

"I'm having *the worst* morning." Lindsay gestured to her desk, where an overturned Starbucks cup told the whole tale. "I spilled my latte all over this manuscript. Rita's going to kill me!"

Andrea waved off all her worries. "It's no big deal. Stuff like that happens."

"But it's a Rosemary Cain proposal—and she's rejecting it!"

Andrea went still. "Oh."

I knew the name Rosemary Cain, but not well enough to be able to name any of her books by title. But I got the gist of what was going on. Big author, stupid boo-boo. "It's just a few pages," I said. "Why don't you retype them? The author probably won't even notice."

It seemed a pretty obvious suggestion, but Lindsay latched onto it as if it were a pronouncement coming straight down from heaven. "That's right! I could retype them. She'll never know! Rita won't even have to know."

She thanked me profusely, and I felt a little embarrassed. It hadn't taken a genius to figure out what to do. Lindsay was probably a few seconds away from figuring it out herself.

Or maybe not. She obviously hadn't figured out not to wear prom dresses to work.

"She's a mess," Andrea whispered to me as we walked away. "Something like that happens every day. I call it the crisis cubicle. She and Rita together are a train wreck."

At the next office we passed, a woman about my age with dishwater blond hair was sitting at her desk with an untouched bagel next to her.

"Hi, Cassie," Andrea said. "This is Rebecca. You know, the new inmate."

Cassie's blue eyes fixed on me. "Cool!" Her office was a duplicate of mine, with the exception of romance covers covering her cork board, and a single framed picture on the desk. It was a picture of a younger Cassie in a blue gown and mortarboard. Her hair was longer, but it was also frizzier; she had the Jan Brady effect going big time.

Cassie stared unblinkingly at me. "Mercedes made you sound like Wonder Girl. She couldn't stop singing your praises."

"Really?" I asked, surprised.

"She said you worked for Sylvie Arnaud."

"Oh, right." I nodded.

Andrea tugged on my arm. "Okay, well I guess we should—"

"You must have really wowed Mercedes at your interview," Cassie broke in. "I thought they were just looking for another assistant editor, not an associate."

"I had thought so, too, initially . . ."

Her lips tensed into a toothless smile. "I'm an assistant editor. This is my third year here. I was Rita's editorial assistant one of those years."

"That's . . ." I really couldn't figure out what I was expected to say. ". . . good."

"You think so?" She shrugged. "I guess I just have high standards."

Andrea laughed and told me, "We'll probably all be working for Cassie next year."

Cassie smiled, but I had a feeling she actually felt that we all really should have been working for her already.

The rest of the tour was a blur. We ventured out into other pods, but after twenty minutes of meeting people, my brain started to go numb. Andrea introduced me to coworkers I knew I wouldn't remember if I bumped into them five minutes later.

But I did learn the important things—where the bathrooms were, and the mail and supply room. The mailroom was headed by a guy with a long blond ponytail named James. According to Andrea he had been a bike messenger until he had been hit by a bus. He still had the restless energy that I had noticed in bike messengers, that same way of catching your eye just long enough to let you know that he would be glad to run right over you.

The only other guy I detected in the office was the head of the art department, named Troy Raymond. His office was cavernous and wallpapered with huge prints of cover art—which was to say, men with no shirts. There were two couches in his office ("For meetings," he explained. "I like to be comfy.") and a huge desk, and to the side, a drafting table.

"Troy's our link between the production folk downstairs and editorial," Andrea explained.

"Downstairs?"

He laughed. "The mole people. Art, copyediting, production. The unglamorous folk."

"Right, like *we're* glamorous," Andrea said.

Troy gave my outfit a pointed once-over. "I wonder. That's an awfully nice Chanel there. Who'd you have to sleep with to afford that?"

I began to sputter about it being a hand-me-down, and Troy burst out laughing. "I was just zooming you."

As Andrea and I left Troy's office, she laughed. "Those 'meetings' he was talking about are his interviews with cover models. He's the only one here who has any fun."

I shook my head. "Not many men work at Candlelight, do they?"

"There are more in production, but editorial's almost exclusively women right now. The president of the company is a man, of course. Art Salvatore."

"I didn't meet him."

"And you probably won't until the Christmas party. His office is over there"—she pointed to a long, dark corridor—"but he rarely walks among us."

"Oh, I see. Head honcho."

"More than that." She lowered her voice. "It's said that the Salvatore family used to be in the laundry business, if you know what I mean."

My mouth popped open stupidly, and my voice came out in a squeak. "The mob is running Candlelight Books?" Being from Ohio, I was still fascinated when I bumped into anything vaguely Godfatherlike, even after two years of living in Brooklyn. I never expected organized crime in romance publishing, though.

"It's all just a rumor, I think, but we like to keep it going. It's the only thing lending this place even a little bit of mystique."

Apparently the tour was over, but Andrea seemed reluctant to go back to her desk. "Okay—pop quiz time," she said. "Show me the way to the coffee room."

That was one quiz I could ace. Asking me to put names to faces of ten percent of the people I'd just met would have stumped me, but caffeine was important. I couldn't have made it to the coffee room any faster if I had been laser guided.

"I'm impressed," Andrea said.

"Impressed by what?" A woman dipping her Celestial Seasonings tea bag into a mug of hot water turned to us. I had met her at her desk already. Her name was Madeline, and she looked like she had stepped off the pages of a magazine cover. She towered over Andrea and me. And she wasn't just pretty, she was stunning.

"Rebecca found the kitchen on her first try," Andrea said.

Madeline smiled big, as if I really had achieved great things already. "That's terrific."

When she sashayed out with her cup of herbal tea, Andrea leaned toward me. "She's an associate editor, and very well connected. From the mailroom to the boardroom, she's got this place covered. Both James and Art have the hots for her."

"What about Troy?" I asked.

"He's got the hots for both Art and James."

"Well! Who have we here?" a new voice asked.

"Hey, Mary Jo. This is Rebecca."

Mary Jo smiled but didn't stop what she was doing. She wore chic rectangular wire frame glasses and was anorexically thin. Arms stuck out through the holes in her sleeveless shirt like chicken wings that had been picked clean. She poured coffee into a mug that had a Cathy cartoon on it. Cathy was sitting behind a desk; the caption read, "*I hate Mondays!*" Into that cup Mary Jo emptied two packets of sweetener and about a quarter cup of non dairy creamer. My mouth started to pucker just looking at that concoction.

"Mercedes told me a lot about you," she said.

She never stopped smiling, or stirring her creamer, but with one sharp flick of her eyes, I felt she was telling me something. And that something was that she had my number.

I muttered something about hoping it wasn't all bad.

She dropped her stir stick in the garbage and picked up her mug. "No, it was mostly good."

Mostly?

"Of course, too much praise begins to sound suspicious, doesn't it?" She laughed tightly. "Oh, well, you two go back to your tour. Don't let it last all day, though."

The moment she was out of earshot, Andrea mimicked, "Don't let it last all day!" in a snippy little whisper.

"She didn't seem too friendly . . ." I ventured.

Andrea rolled her eyes. "Ignore her when at all possible. She's a tyrant."

I nodded.

"Don't get on her bad side, though," Andrea advised. "You get on her bad side, and . . ." She stopped and made a slitting motion across her throat.

"For some reason, I feel like I already am on her bad side." Like my house just fell on her sister, basically.

"That's just her way. You know the type—she's a . . ." She frowned. "Well, a bitch. And she's second in command under Mercedes, so she tends to get a little nervous if Mercedes takes too much of a shine to anyone. As if any of us would want her stupid job!"

"Yeah, that's crazy."

"That's Mary Jo. You know that coffee cup with Cathy on it? She's had it ever since she was an editorial assistant. Almost twenty years! The first year she started work, her Secret Santa gave it to her. She's got a real thing about it."

"Maybe there's some deep psychological reason, or . . ."

"Yeah, and that reason is she's a controlling, obsessive loon." She sighed. "Okay, back to work."

As we trudged back to our offices, I felt a knot of dread in my tummy, like I was being dropped off at kindergarten or something. I could handle meeting people. That was a snap.

But work. *That* was the tricky part.

Chapter 4

By lunch, I was finally beginning to relax, if only because it finally dawned on me that chances were good that I wouldn't be fired on my first day.

I had worried that once Andrea dropped me back by my office, I wouldn't know what to do with myself, besides stare at those ominous manuscript piles on the bookshelves. But if there was anything I really knew how to do, it was fritter away time. First I had to check out my computer. Solitaire had not been removed, and I even had pinball! This reminded me of the e-mail question, so I set up my account at *rabbot@candlelight.net*. Then of course I had to e-mail all my family and friends and brag about my new corporate identity.

My sister Ellen replied immediately. She had just finished law school the year before and was working in a law firm back in Cleveland.

> I'm psyched about your new job. Congrats! I don't read romances, natch, but what a hoot to be working there. Maybe you can send me a few beach books next summer. (I guess I do read a few of those . . . just don't tell anyone here at the office!) XOX, E

Once I started looking at it, *rabbot* seemed like a really bizarre handle. Like rabbit misspelled, or a combination of rabbit and robot. I started imagining bad sci-fi movie titles. *Attack of the Killer Rabbots!*

So after much contemplation and doodling on my notepad, I changed my address to the more respectable *rebecca.abbot@candlelight.net*. And then, of course, I had to send out my change of address.

Ellen wrote back in a flash.

> Stop procrastinating and get to work!
> XOX, E
> Oh, and one of my coworkers wants to know if you publish something called Regencies? I think they're like fake Jane Austen books . . . which actually sounds kind of good, now that I think about it. Do you really get freebies?

I made a note to send Ellen books.

All in all, setting up my e-mail killed a good hour and a half. A few games of pinball later, Andrea was knocking on my door. I reduced the screen and swiveled toward her.

"How's it going?"

"Great!" I said.

"Lunch?"

I was up like a shot. "Sure."

Rita was right behind her. "My treat."

"Which means she's expensing it," Andrea translated.

We stopped by Cassie's office on our way out. "Want to go to lunch with us?" Rita asked her.

A plastic serving container of breadsticks and celery sat on the desk next to the manuscript she was reading, along with a half-eaten apple. "I'd love to, but I promised myself I would read this book today." She eyed me staring at her meal. Like any veteran of Weight Watchers (ages twelve and fifteen), I was no stranger to breadsticks. I sometimes wondered if there were any other people besides WW veterans who actually ate those things.

I smiled at her, sensing a kindred spirit.

She did not smile back. "I like to stay up on things."

"Well, carry on," Rita said. "We'll be back in forty-five minutes."

Two hours later, we ambled back to the office, full of Chinese food. I had expected to get the lowdown about what they expected from me in my job. Instead, I got gossip. Gossip about everyone. There were no affairs reported, no embezzling or money scandals, no shocking Candlelight secrets revealed, although you wouldn't have guessed it from the urgent tone in Rita and Andrea's voices.

"Did you know Ann takes her Maltese to doggy daycare every day?"

"It must cost her a fortune."

"What else does she have to spend it on? The woman has no life. It's pathetic."

"Sad. She should try online dating."

"First she should try to do something about that acne scarring."

"Would insurance cover plastic surgery for that?"

"She could pay for it herself if she weren't wasting all her money on her canine."

They asked me a few polite questions about myself, which I evaded to the best of my ability. (If Ann and her doggy daycare were worth a conversational massacre, imagine the hay they could have made out of my living with my ex-boyfriend.) By the time the fortunes cookies rolled around, it felt like I had been working with them for months instead of hours.

When I got back, I continued to pile up accomplishments. I played a few rounds of solitaire and did very well. A few people, some of whom I had met that morning, came by to ask how I was settling in. Actually, I think they had afternoon restlessness and just wanted to get away from their desks for a while.

At one point, I had three other editors and Lindsay the editorial assistant all squeezed into my office, talking about famous person sightings they'd had in New York City. Ann—she of the pampered pooch—had stood in a deli line behind Leonardo DiCaprio, which was pretty damn impressive. The only famous person I'd come in that close contact with was Al Roker, who Fleishman and I had seen coming up the theater aisle the night we had gone to see *Gypsy*.

Lindsay had a good one. "Whoopi Goldberg goes to my dentist."

This revelation brought gasps. "No *way!*" Madeline exclaimed. "*Your* dentist?"

Lindsay puffed up a little, sensing she had scored. "I saw her in the waiting room once, even. She was there for a cleaning, the hygienist told me."

"Where? What dentist?"

"His name is Dr. Stein, and he's on Eighty-fifth Street."

Ann's forehead wrinkled. "Does Whoopi Goldberg have good teeth?"

"Of course she has good teeth! She's a movie star."

"I'm sure they're capped. All actors have caps."

"Be crazy not to. In a movie close-up an incisor can look twenty feet tall."

"Wait," Andrea said. "*Our* insurance pays for Whoopi's dentist?"

Lindsay nodded her head.

"That's it. I'm switching."

"Just like that? Because Whoopi goes somewhere else?"

"Why should I settle for substandard?" Andrea asked defensively. "You can bet with all that money she has, Whoopi's checked out her dental care options."

"Do you know she travels in her own bus?" someone asked. "Like a rock star."

Just as the conversation was about to turn full tilt onto the subject of celebrity transport, someone rapped on my doorjamb. Standing behind Lindsay was a woman of medium height, with dishwater blond hair cut in an unflattering page boy, and wearing an olive green pantsuit of the most aggressively dumpy design imaginable. She surveyed the crowd through an owlish pair of glasses.

Suddenly, it was as if someone had shot off a bird gun at a duck pond. Coworkers flew out my door, leaving me floating all alone in the sights of . . . well, whoever this was. I still didn't know, but a knot of foreboding formed in the pit of my stomach.

"Hi," I said, attempting to keep the uneasiness out of my voice.

She smiled tightly. "I didn't mean to break up your little party."

I blushed self-consciously. "No—it's just my first day. I'm Rebecca, by the way."

"Hi, Rebecca, I'm Janice Wunch."

I really had to keep my lips from twitching. If ever a person looked like a Janice Wunch, it was this woman. Poor thing. You would think she would have changed her name, or at least her glasses.

"I'm the production manager."

I kept the polite smile frozen on my face. I had no idea what this meant.

"I have a little list here—well, actually, it's quite long—of things of yours that are late to production."

"Of mine?" I asked, confused. "But I just got here."

"I'm sure many of these are projects that were originally Julie's, but of course they're your babies now."

"Oh, I see . . ."

She handed a list to me, which filled up an entire page. It was staggering how late I could be on everything on my first day.

"In terms of priority, of course, the edit for *The Baby Doctor and the Bodyguard* needs to get done first. It's nearly a month late. I have told Rita about this repeatedly, and she said she was going to get Lindsay to do a preliminary edit, but then apparently she changed her mind when Lindsay left the manuscript on a crosstown bus and they had to ask the author's agent for a duplicate."

I nodded. As urgent as the situation was with *The Baby Doctor and the Bodyguard*, there were two other late edits on the list, along with other stuff that I was completely clueless about. What was an art info sheet? I owed five of those. Where was cover copy supposed to come from? (*Me?* I wondered with growing hysteria.)

"No big deal," Janice said. "Just get it to me ASAP—or by the end of the week, if you can."

I gulped. The end of the week was sooner than what I had in mind. She had to be kidding. "If there's a problem getting some of this stuff in . . ."

She blinked at me with what appeared to be sincere incomprehension. "Why should there be?"

Maybe because I don't know what the hell I'm doing?

My heart started to pound. This was why you should never stretch the truth in a job interview. Eventually someone was going to expect you to know something.

When Janice Wunch left my office, I closed the door behind her and succumbed to a moment of blind panic. What the hell was I going to do now? I was contemplating simply running away and spending the rest of my life as an editorial fugitive when my phone rang. I leapt for it. I didn't care if it was bad news. At least someone from the outside world was trying to contact me.

It was Fleishman. "How's the little editor doing?"

"She's dying."

He laughed. "You sound stressed."

I told him about the late list. I told him I didn't even know what most of this stuff was. I told him to prepare for my impending departure from the ranks of the employed. "I'll send the clothes back to your mom," I promised.

"Just go ask that assistant person what to do," he said.

"Lindsay? But she'll think I'm an idiot."

"All the better—that'll make her day. Assistants love to think people working over them are incompetent morons. It reinforces their own suspicions that they should actually be running things themselves."

"Yeah, but this girl seems . . . well, incompetent. I would be happy to give her ego a boost, but I don't trust her to give me correct information."

"Hm. Is there anyone else you could ask?"

I thought of Cassie, who looked as if she had never made an incompetent move in her life. "Well, I'll give it some thought."

"That's the spirit!" Fleishman said.

"Anyway, I should be home around six-thirty." I felt a sudden longing to be there now.

"Good, because I've got a huge surprise for you."

"I hope it involves a large pizza box." After this afternoon, I had a feeling I was going to need some serious comfort food.

He laughed. "Oh, it's better than that."

There was a knock on my door and I hung up the phone to answer it. James, the mailroom guy, was standing there, his stance impatient. He was wearing headphones. "Mail," he mumbled.

He handed me a plastic tub full of manila envelopes, business letters, and fat padded mailers, all addressed to Julie Spears. I grabbed it automatically and then staggered back under its weight. "Hey, wait a minute!"

He frowned and asked loudly, over whatever was being pumped into his ears, "What's the matter? You're her now, right?"

He pointed to Julie's name.

As much as I would have loved to refuse delivery at that moment, I had to admit that I was indeed Julie now. Damn.

I began to sort through the top of the pile, separating the letters from the packages. I decided that I would come in early tomorrow to open the packages. I needed to think of some kind of logging system, since I didn't see any evidence of one among Julie's stuff. Gingerly, I opened a few letters.

Happily, most of them seemed manageable. A woman wanted to know if she could send me her book about a nurse midwife who finds herself pregnant after having a fling at her ten-year high school reunion. Sounded good to me. Another writer was dying to have me read her romantic suspense novel involving a female paratrooper who is taken hostage in a war-torn country and falls in love with a Norwegian Red Cross worker. That sounded good, too. But what did I know? I fired off letters to basically everybody telling them to mail me whatever.

A reader wrote to inform me that she had found several typographical errors, including the misspelling of the word gynecological, in a book called *Twins on His Doorstep*. She wanted to know if Candlelight books wanted to hire her to proofread their books. I looked up the word *gynecological*.

Then I looked up *misspell*.

I put the letter aside with a note to query Kathy Leo.

Several people had written requesting guidelines for writing romances. I searched Julie's file cabinet, but found nothing under guidelines. When I went over to Lindsay's cubicle to ask her about guidelines, she wasn't there.

I was pondering how unethical it would be to rifle through someone else's filing cabinet when Rita flew out of her door and almost slammed into me. She looked wild-eyed. "Where's Lindsay?" she asked, practically hyperventilating.

"I don't know. I came here to ask her about guidelines."

"She didn't go to the mailroom, did she?" Her voice cracked on the word mailroom.

"I don't know," I said again.

"I hope I didn't miss her."

I tilted my head. "Is everything all right?"

Rita sighed. "Probably. But one time she sent a manuscript to the wrong author, and since then I've tried to keep my eye on her when she goes to the mailroom so I can follow and double check them."

"You check *every* package?"

She frowned. "Is that nuts?"

"Um. . . ." After all, she was my boss. But no wonder she hadn't taken a vacation in forever.

"You're right. It is." She released a long breath and combed her hand through her frazzly hair. "I mean, she's my assistant, for heaven's sake. I shouldn't have to sneak behind her and double check every little parcel."

"No, you shouldn't."

Rita chuckled a little, then stopped just as suddenly. "Maybe this one last time." Before I could get in a word about guidelines, she darted toward the hallway.

I wandered back to my office, but happened to catch Cassie's eye as I walked by her open door. I hesitated to ask for her help, but maybe this would be a good icebreaker.

"You wouldn't happen to have guidelines for the different lines of books, would you?"

She stretched her back as if she had been hunched over a manuscript nonstop since the last time I had seen her. "I think so—let me check."

She swiveled toward her file cabinet and opened what could have been an advertisement for a perfectly organized file drawer. All the colored tabs were perfectly staggered. No messy stray papers sticking out of file folders.

"When was this picture taken?" I said, pointing to Cassie's graduation photo.

"High school," she said as she flicked through her files. "I was salutatorian."

I made a humming sound of approbation. It seemed expected.

"I should have been valedictorian, but the varsity quarterback had gotten extra credit for doing independent study. All he turned in was a five-page paper on the history of the NFL, but he got as much credit for it as I got for calculus. It was sort of unfair."

I frowned. It was unfair, and now she kept that photo on her desk as a . . . a what? A testament to having been passed over? Cheated?

"Here they are!" she said brightly, pulling out a small stack of stapled-together pages. She flipped through a couple of multicolored sheets. "I knew I had restocked recently."

"Great."

She smiled up at me. "You can get them from Mercedes's assistant."

I froze, momentarily confused. Did this mean Cassie wasn't sharing? I looked pointedly at the pile of papers in her hand. "I just need one."

"Oh, no. You'll need more than that," she said. "People ask for them every day. You should keep a stack handy."

"Okay, so if I just took one of yours and made copies. . . ."

She shook her head. "Mercedes wants them all to be uniformly color coded. A different color for each line of books, see?" She flipped through her stack again, to demonstrate. Or to taunt me. "We had a meeting about this a few months ago. Guidelines should be color coded—she doesn't want the Pulse guidelines to be green, for instance. They should be this pale red color."

"Uh-huh." She kept leafing through those guidelines so that it was all I could do not to snatch one out of her hands and make a run for it. She clearly was not going to cough one up. "Okay . . . guess I'll ask Mercedes."

"Her assistant, Lisa, is who you should ask. She usually has a whole stack of them."

So do you, but a fat lot of good that's done me. I grinned at her. "Well! Thanks for your help."

She tilted her head and aimed a reptilian smile at me. "First day going well?"

"Going great," I said.

"Terrific!"

I got the guidelines from Mercedes's assistant without further ado, but the next time I saw Andrea, I had to ask her, "Have you ever sensed any animosity from Cassie?"

"Oh, that one's a real go-getter," Andrea said. "And a stickler for the rules, too. It's probably eating her up inside that you got hired in a level above her."

I told her about the guideline incident.

Andrea's brows knit into a puzzled frown. "I'm sure Julie had tip sheets here somewhere . . ." She turned to my file cabinet. In five seconds, she was handing me a little stack of guidelines.

I sank down in my chair, feeling like a dope. "*Tip sheets,*" I said. "I didn't think . . ."

Andrea shrugged. "Give yourself a break. It's your first day."

My first day. Right. I needed to get a grip. "Forget what I said about Cassie," I said. "I'm just being paranoid."

Andrea laughed. "Maybe, but don't forget the immortal words of Richard Nixon: 'Just because you're paranoid doesn't mean someone's not out to get you.'"

At six-forty I straggled up the stairs to the building lugging my copy of *The Baby Doctor and the Bodyguard.* Every muscle in my body felt tired, even my mouth from holding it in a tense friendly smile for half the day. I really needed to have a Calgon evening, but unfortunately the apartment was tubless. Maybe I could have a hot shower and relax for a little bit before tackling the editing of the manuscript, which I was determined to make considerable headway on that night.

As I reached the third floor where we lived, the door was flung open. There stood Fleishman, shifting impatiently from foot to foot. "You're finally home! The pizza's cold."

He took my totebag full of manuscript as I dragged myself through the door. "Cold is okay," I said. Even after pigging out at lunch with my coworkers, I was starving now. "Sitting at a desk all day really gives you an appetite."

Fleishman had set the little table in what we laughingly called our entertainment area. It was the ten-foot square of space into which we wedged a round eating table, a futon couch, a thirty-five-inch plasma screen television, a bookcase, and the microwave oven. (The kitchen didn't have room for the microwave.) He had even put out cloth napkins and lit a candle. At the moment I would have been happy to collapse on the couch with a pizza box in my lap and an IV hookup to a box of wine, but it was really thoughtful of him to try to make the apartment nice for the occasion.

Though I wondered what kind of occasion he thought this was. It wasn't as if I had never worked before.

"Have a seat." He guided me over to a chair and pressed me into it. "I have to show you the surprise."

"Oh." I assumed that this was the surprise—pizza by candlelight. That would have been enough.

But Fleishman had never been one of those people for whom *enough* would suffice. He was fond of over-the-top gestures, and as he skipped back to Wendy's closet of a room to retrieve whatever he had hidden there, I wondered what on earth he could have gotten. I mean, he had already arranged a wardrobe for me. At the moment, I felt I lacked for nothing except self-confidence and a modicum of editorial know-how.

He came running back with a large cardboard box, which he put carefully on the floor in front of me. It was just a plain brown box, though it had a big white bow around it. I was just so exhausted I couldn't focus, because it appeared to be moving.

"Open it," he said.

I frowned at it suspiciously. "What is it?"

"*Open it.*" When I hesitated, he yanked the bow off himself.

After that, I didn't have to open the box. It opened itself. Suddenly, I was staring into the face of a tan colored puppy. His little pink tongue was sticking out at me, panting like mad, and his paws were scrabbling pointlessly against the cardboard. He wanted out of that box and onto my lap. Onto *someone's* lap. Like all puppies, the eagerness in his eyes gave you the impression that he wasn't going to be too particular. Anybody would do.

He yelped. I jumped.

"Isn't he cute?" Fleishman said. He picked up the puppy and plopped the squirming mound of fur onto my chest. My neck and face were immediately assaulted by that tongue and the Mighty Dog breath that went with it. "His name's Maxwell."

"Maxwell?"

"For Maxwell Perkins, the editor. I thought your dog should have a publishing name."

"*My* dog?" Maxwell let out another yelp, letting me know that was A-OK with him.

"I thought it would suit him better than naming him some lame author name, like Hemingway. That's so unoriginal. Of course, *Max* isn't exactly original, either. We could call him Perkins, but people might think we named him for Anthony Perkins—"

It was time to interrupt his soliloquy. "*My* dog?"

"Of course. He's a gift."

The dog was having a hard time balancing on my lap, so I put him on the ground. He proceeded to try to crawl up my leg. I had to admit he was awfully cute. His fur was short and bristly in appearance but soft to the touch, and his little face was like something you'd see in a Puppy Chow ad. The tips of his ears folded downward, giving him a look that was goofily rakish.

"He's a purebred Norfolk terrier," Fleishman said. "He's even got papers."

It was hard to believe something so small and silly looking had a pedigree. Also, pedigree was usually accompanied by a healthy price tag. Last I heard, Fleishman was supposed to be broke. "What did you do, rob a pet store?"

Fleishman laughed. "I put him on American Express."

"Since when do you have one of those?"

He looked offended. "I've been a proud member since ten AM this morning."

"You know AmEx makes you pay off in full at the end of the month, don't you?"

"Okay, so at the end of the month I'll find some money."

Shame he couldn't have found some when we were scrambling for the rent.

He laughed. "Rebecca, will you lighten up? I charged the pizza, too—and you don't mind that."

Speaking of pizza, I grabbed a piece and chewed as I stared at Maxwell. At the first whiff of food, he plopped down on his rump and started to wag his stubby little tale. His big brown eyes melted me. They could have melted the polar ice cap, what was left of it. "Hey Maxwell, you want some pizza?"

"No—no pizza. I got some Science Diet puppy formula."

He said it with such paternal sternness, I drew back in surprise. "I can't believe you got a dog. Dogs are a lot of work, you know. They're a responsibility. They have to be fed regularly, and walked, and housetrained . . ."

Not to mention, I started thinking about Ann and her Maltese. *No life. Pathetic.* Would that be me soon?

"Yeah, but puppies are so cute," Fleishman said. "How can you resist?"

Maxwell was chewing on my shoestring. The truth was, I couldn't resist. Outside of a goldfish, I hadn't had a pet since I was a little kid. I had always wanted a dog.

"I felt it was time," Fleishman said. "We're getting older, you know. Besides, won't it be nice to have a warm body to come home to?"

I glanced into Fleishman's eyes and felt the pizza like a lump in my throat. I looked back down at Maxwell, who was still gazing at me adoringly. Or maybe it was just hungrily. It *would* be nice to have a warm body waiting for me, I supposed, even if it was canine. And as long as I kept food in my hand, I would always have his undivided attention. How many relationships could you say that about?

"So what do you say . . ." Fleishman looked at me. "Can we keep him, ma?"

I laughed. "Did you really think I could get rid of *that?*"

As if knowing his cue, Maxwell barked. Which reminded me. "Did you check this out with the landlord?"

"It's okay. I bribed the super when I got home."

"How did you do that?"

"Cash advance."

I would have loved to lecture on the fact that he would regret being so financially reckless someday, but the fact was that he probably wouldn't. Fleishman lived in a parallel universe where the chickens never came home to roost. Or when they did come home to roost, they ended up laying golden eggs.

"So how was your day?" he asked. "I mean, up to now. I know you're blissfully happy now."

"Half okay and half awful." I told him about what had happened with Cassie after I talked to him on the phone. "I think she has it in for me, I really do. If you could have seen the look in her eye when she was sitting there with those tip sheets . . ."

"Some people are just like that."

"Right." And some people were just psychopaths. I was pretty sure I had put my finger on our office psycho, but I didn't have the evidence. "Plus I have all this work to do now."

"Homework?" He looked alarmed at the idea of work being brought into the house, and eyed my tote bag suspiciously.

"Just till I'm caught up."

"When will that be?"

I thought for a moment. "Somewhere in the year 2010."

"Did you bring any more books home?" he asked.

"Just the one I'm editing."

He seemed disappointed.

"I'd better get to work," I said, reluctantly. It would have been so nice to play with the puppy and then just conk out.

Fleishman got up. "I'll take Max around the block."

I looked doubtfully at that unruly lump of fur. "Does he walk on a leash yet?"

"No, but he enjoys gnawing on it. I'll just carry him down and set him on a patch of grass, if I can find any."

He left and I got out the book. I was already so tired, I wondered how I would be able to stay awake long enough to get anything done. I spent ten minutes just getting myself situated—sharpening pencils, brewing a pot of coffee, doodling on a pad of Post-it notes.

When Fleishman and Max came back, I hadn't even started yet.

"I'll just sit here and read," Fleishman said. "I won't bother you at all."

He settled on the couch with a copy of *Forgotten Nights* by Joy Silver, an amnesia book I think he had already read. Max proceeded to chew on the cover. The next time I looked up, the book had dropped to the floor next to the futon, and Fleishman was asleep with the puppy on his chest.

I wished I had a camera.

Then I shook my head. I was entertaining thoughts I shouldn't. Like how sweet it was of Fleishman to bring Max home, even though the thought of taking care of a dog for the next fifteen years made me a little panicky. It was hard not to feel, there in that little room with just the three of us, that it had been a rather couply gesture. Not that we were a couple in the real sense . . . but still. It made me wonder if he still ever thought of me as girlfriend material.

I shouldn't have cared. Fleishman was my friend, and he was more friendly as a friend-friend than a boyfriend. In the past, every time it seemed that something was starting to brew between us, it seemed he would simultaneously start slipping away. That he would avoid my eyes and suddenly develop a fondness for going with his guy buddies to see loud movies with lots of explosions and sexy girls in tank tops carrying machine guns.

But when we were just friends, like now, he was so something else. We were so comfortable together, like an old married couple.

It was so irritating. Why couldn't the person you want just fall in love with you? That would solve everything.

I forced myself to focus on my work rather than the enigma that was my roommate. Gradually I became more involved in the story, and before I knew it, it was after midnight and Wendy was coming through the door.

She glanced at Fleishman on the futon, and then me camped out on the table. Then she did a double-take back to Fleishman. Fleishman and Max.

I winced. Fleishman and I hadn't discussed what Wendy would say about the dog. But now that I considered it, there *might* be trouble . . .

"Do you know what month a woman's supposed to have an amniocentesis?" I asked, hoping to distract her.

Wendy wasn't looking at me. "What's that?"

"It's the test pregnant women take to . . . well, I'm not sure why, exactly. But the woman in this book is going for an amnio in her second month. Isn't that a little early?"

She put her arms akimbo and affected a Bones from *Star Trek* voice. "Damn it, Rebecca, I'm a lighting designer, not an obstetrician."

I laughed.

"But that's *not* what I was asking you about." She pointed to Fleishman's snoozing form. "What is *that?*"

"Oh, that's Maxwell Perkins. Fleishman brought him home today."

Wendy sank into a chair. Lately she had seemed to chafe about stuff going on in the apartment. "Isn't this the sort of thing we're supposed to have roommate conferences about?"

"When have we ever had a roommate conference?"

"You're right. It's not a democracy, it's a dictatorship . . . and from now on it's going to be a dictatorship run by that little ball of fur there." She seemed genuinely worried. "This is no joke. Dogs are a lot of trouble."

"That's what I was telling Fleishman. But he was being so sweet—he bought the puppy for me for my first day of work."

She crossed her arms. "You don't think that's kind of odd?"

"Why?"

"It's sort of . . . cozy. Giving a person a puppy. Don't you think?"

"Well . . . yeah, it seemed kind of *domestic.*"

"Right. Like Fleishman wants to play house." Her brows arched meaningfully.

I lifted my arms, and suddenly realized how stiff my shoulders felt from being hunched over that book. I had to stretch like Cassie had in her office this afternoon. I couldn't believe I had been working for almost four hours, and I still wasn't anywhere close to done. Maybe I wasn't doing this right.

"How did your day go?" I asked.

"Okay, except I got my next project. I'm going to have to design the lights for *Death of a Salesman*. Another dreary one. My professors must think I should specialize in tragedy and angst, but I tell you what. It's made me want to graduate and go light roller-skating tourist musicals and revivals of *Annie*."

I nodded. I knew just how she felt. Back when I was an undergraduate studying English lit, I spent semesters slogging through James Joyce and William Faulkner when I would dream of getting out and reading fun stuff again. Pure fluff.

I stared down at my marked-up copy of *The Baby Doctor and the Bodyguard*. As wish fulfillment went, this seemed a little over the top.

Renata told me that the catalyst for her weight loss, the event that drove her into the arms of Jenny Craig, was losing her virginity on graduation night.

Her older brother, who was just home from college and working at a country club for the summer giving tennis lessons, had let it drop that Jake Caddell, a boy in her class she'd had a crush on since third grade, was going to be working at the same club as a golf caddy. Not that her brother knew about this unrequited love of hers, or even suspected it. Jake wasn't the best looking guy in her class, and he certainly wasn't the smartest. He was one of the cut-ups, though he was one of the rare boys she'd known since third grade who had never used her appearance as the butt of his humor.

That alone would have made him a dreamboat. But because of his comparative kindness to her, she'd also endowed him with all sorts of attributes over the years: gorgeous brown eyes, wit, incredible aim with a spitball . . .

Right before graduation night, the talk of the school was that Jake's girlfriend, Courtney Rogers, had dumped him for Rance Dumars. Jake was free, wide open, and on graduation night, fortified by two Mickey's Big Mouths, Renata made her move. She waited until the band played a slow number, and then—boldly, bravely, tipsily—she asked him to dance.

The element of surprise worked in her favor. Jake blinked a few times, then said, "Sure, why not?"

Two dances, one long drive, and five cans of Old Milwaukee later, the two of them were huffing away in the back of the Caddell family's Chrysler minivan. Which, even in Renata's state of inebriation, was not all that comfortable. About the time her taffeta skirt was pushed up to her chin, she began to have doubts.

When she felt his erection pressing against her—urgently—she raised an alarm.

"What's the matter?" he panted. He sounded a little annoyed, but she could understand. They had reached a critical juncture. She could feel his sweat dripping down her neck.

"This is my first time."

"So?"

She bit her lip . . . not sure she should take a chance. "So . . . won't it hurt?"

"Nah—and anyway, it'll be over in like, five seconds."

"Really?"

In the movies, sex scenes seemed to go on forever.

He pressed against her again, and she felt a surge of heat between her thighs.

"Trust me," he murmured.

She did.

He was such a liar. He thrust into her, and for a moment it felt like a steak knife going into her vagina. She bit her lip so hard she tasted blood.

But he was right about one thing. He chuffed against her for about five seconds, fast, like a fornicating bunny, then he stopped, groaned, and collapsed on top of her.

"Goddamn!" he moaned.

Renata winced. She could feel something dribbling down her leg and toward the beige upholstery beneath them. She hoped it wasn't blood.

Jake sat up, hitched his pants up from his ankles, and began zipping and buttoning. Following his lead, Renata sat up, too, and tried to pull herself together. Her dress was a wrinkled mess, but she didn't care. Despite the pain, and the curious brevity, she felt lit from within.

I am a woman now, *she thought, not entirely humorlessly.*

When they crawled into the front seat, where Jake chugged the remains of a beer before firing up the van again, she decided to toss out a hint concerning her future availability. She knew he was a sought-after guy, but look where a little initiative had gotten her so far.

"This could be a great summer," she said.

"Oh yeah?" He sounded distracted. "How come?"

"Well . . . I'm not really doing much of anything. If you want to get together sometime."

She imagined going and hanging out at the country club every once in a while. Sharing a Coke.

Maybe he would even give her a golf lesson.

"Oh."

"For dinner, or a movie, or . . ."

"You know what?" he said. "The truth is, I'm not even gonna be around much this summer."

She darted a look at him. "But—" She bit her lip.

"No, see . . . I, uh, I'm going to be working on my uncle's farm this summer. In Pennsylvania. I might be around occasionally, visiting . . . I mean, if you happen to run into me or something, that's probably the explanation . . ."

She faced forward. "I see." He thinks I'm too fat to be his girlfriend. *Her face burned.*

But maybe he wasn't lying. Maybe he'd decided to turn down the country club job . . .

Over the summer, her brother mentioned Jake in passing several times. He was a golf caddy at the country club all summer.

Renata vowed that the next time a guy slept with her, he wouldn't want to toss her away like an old tissue afterward. And the next time she saw Jake, she swore she'd knock him off of his feet.

She waited until she had starved down thirty pounds, and then squeezed into a pair of shorts and went to the country club to see her brother. She happened to pass Jake, who walked right by her without recognizing her. He did a double-take, but by that time, she had noticed that he had a sunburn and a piggy nose. And she recalled that he wasn't very bright.

Besides, she'd spent a lot of time in the library in June, and after researching some back issues of Cosmo, *she was fairly sure that sex was supposed to last longer than five seconds.*

Chapter 5

Lesson One: *Beware of the phone.*

I had never really worked in an office, and my social life and my credit history had always been orderly enough that a ringing phone was nearly always a welcome thing. God knows, sitting in my office, staring at that intimidating pile of manuscripts on my bookcase—which had managed to grow—talk seemed preferable to speechless angst.

"Hello?" I said.

"I got the cover!" The voice on the other end—a female voice with a pronounced drawl—sounded sniffly, congested. Either this woman had a doozy of a cold or she had been crying for a long time. "I'm sorry . . . I've just been so upset . . . I had to call you."

"Well, good. I'm glad you did. But, uh—"

There was a clatter on the line, followed by the faraway sound of a nose being blown. A second later, she picked up the phone again. "Have you seen it? I mean, I know you did, but it seems strange since there was no note attached when you sent it . . ."

Lesson Two: *Beware of the phone, and always announce your name first thing.*

"I'm sorry, you might be a little confused. You see . . . uh . . . I'm not Julie."

There was a pause. A sniffle. "You aren't? I asked for Julie's extension and Muriel put me through to you."

"I know, but—"

"Who are you?"

"My name is Rebecca Abbot?"

"Well, Rebecca, my name is Luanne Seligson. I write as Shanna Forrester. I'm from Venita, Oklahoma, and I'm looking for my editor."

I tried the best I could to clear things up for her, explaining that Julie had a baby—yes, wasn't that wonderful . . . odd that she hadn't heard—and that I was taking on her authors. "It's so good to meet you," I said.

This announcement was met with stark silence. "Nobody told me!" she said in a distraught tone. "She left *how* many weeks ago?"

I cleared my throat. "Just a few . . ."

"A few! Did Julie call Dan?"

"Who?" I asked.

At my ignorance, the voice looped up another notch on the hysteria scale. "Dan Weatherby! My agent."

"Oh—well, possibly." I realized from the rattling in Luanne's throat that this was not a time for maybes and possiblies. I needed to project something more affirmative. More upbeat. "Well, I couldn't say *who* Julie called, exactly, but I want to assure you—"

"Dan never breathed a word of this to me!"

"I'm sorry."

"I'll bet he's as shocked as I am!" she declared. "Julie has always been my editor. Always. Going all the way back to *Too Many Babies!*"

I spent the next five minutes assuring Luanne that I was every bit as eager as Julie was to promote her career.

"Well I very much doubt I'll have a career after this child molester book comes out!"

She was hollering. There was no other way to describe it.

"Child molester book?" I asked, alarmed.

"*Pursuing Paula!* On account of the cover!"

I crooked the phone between my left ear and shoulder as I scrambled to find this cover. After frantically pawing through the file cabinet and then my overflowing in-box for a minute, I had the cover of *Pursuing Paula* in my hand. It was from the Hearthsong line. On the front was a man who looked vaguely like Ben Affleck might have if he had been going gray at the temples. He was standing behind a teenage girl and had his hands clamped on her shoulders. The girl was looking off nervously to the side.

My God, she was right. The pose made the man look like a child molester.

"Hm . . ." I tried to approach this diplomatically. "Is there a reason the art department put a little girl on the cover?"

"That's not a girl, it's my heroine! She's a librarian, and she's twenty-seven years old! How the art department fouled this up so completely is beyond me!"

Me either. Failing to see any other option, I started babbling promises to right this grievous wrong . . . or at least see what I could do.

Lesson Three: *Never make promises.*

When I hung up the phone, I marched across the hall to confer with Rita.

"She's in the outer office," Lindsay told me before I could even knock.

I stopped. "Where?"

"Next to the ashtray in front of the building."

Damn. I turned on my heel debating whether I should wait or go outside to track Rita down, but I stopped as I passed Andrea's office. Maybe she could give me some tips on how to handle this. I rapped on the door.

For a moment there was no response but the sound of paper rustling and a steel file cabinet door slamming. "Come in!"

I poked my head in, and Andrea, who was sitting rigidly behind her desk, blew out a breath and reached for her file cabinet. "For God's sake, it's just you." She pulled out a newspaper and shook it open to the want ads. "The classifieds this week are for crap. Did you notice?"

I closed her door and edged toward her desk. Andrea made me nervous. "I just got this job," I reminded her.

"Oh right." She slapped the paper down. "So what can I do you for?"

"I just talked to an author. She was sort of upset about this cover . . ." I pushed the evidence across the desk.

Who knows? Maybe it wasn't as bad as I thought. Maybe Luanne had just been overreacting.

Andrea recoiled. "*Eww!* What is this book about, some coach that seduces girls on the junior high basketball team?"

I shook my head. "There's no girl in the book. The heroine's supposed to be a twenty-seven-year-old librarian."

"Wow!" she exclaimed, with something between revulsion and awe. "That really is a shitty cover."

"So what do I do about it?"

She blinked at me. "*Do?*"

"To fix it."

She laughed. "There's no *fixing* it. The cover's done. See? The title's on it—probably tens of thousands have already been printed. That's all she wrote, Myrtle."

"B-but if I talked to Rita?"

Andrea nearly doubled over. "What's she going to do? Blow magic smoke rings on it?"

My ever shaky confidence began to tremble like a wet hamster. "I thought maybe since she was senior ed . . ."

Losing interest in my dilemma, Andrea shook open her paper again. "No one in editorial has control over the art department."

"But how could Troy have let this go through? It's so obviously bad."

"He probably took one look at the hunky guy with the sideburns and didn't see anything else. I'm mean—look at that man. He's definitely a good looking child molester. He looks sort of like Ben Affleck."

"But—"

"Forget it, Rebecca. Tell the author better luck next time."

I slid down in my chair. "Okay, here's the deal. I told the author I'd do something."

Andrea's eyes went from squinting in concentration on an ad to popping open in shock at my stupidity. "Oh God! What possessed you?"

"She was so upset . . . Julie left and didn't tell her."

She grunted. "That Julie! Her water broke two weeks early and she tore out of here like a shot, lucky cow."

I frowned. "Why didn't she take maternity leave?"

"That's the most disgusting part. She has this husband who works on Wall Street and begged her to be a stay at home mom. So she knew all along that she wasn't coming back . . . and she even told Mercedes. The dope!" She shook her head mournfully. "She really didn't know how to play the system."

"I don't feel like I do, either."

Andrea waved her hand. "Give yourself a month or so in the pink ghetto. You'll know all the angles in no time."

"The pink ghetto? What's that?"

"You're in it, sugar plum. Romance publishing. It's a world unto itself, always clamoring for respect and getting none. The authors get no respect, and neither do the editors. If you don't watch out, it'll suck you in and never spit you out. You'll be stuck in the hood, just like me."

"You're doing okay," I told her. "I bet when the next job does come along, you'll miss this place."

Withering doesn't really describe the look she shot me. "Is your name Rebecca Abbot or Rebecca of Sunnybrook Fucking Farm?"

I stood up and reached for *Pursuing Paula*. "My name's going to be mud if I don't get this cover situation figured out."

In the hallway I nearly had a head-on collision with Rita. We sidestepped just in time and I began to speak, but she gestured with her coffee cup that she didn't have time. "Senior ed meeting," she explained, rushing past. "I'm late."

I skip-stepped after her down the hall, unloading my burden. "What can I do?"

"Just make up something. Tell Luanne that we made the heroine youthful because we're trying to reach a younger demographic."

"Um . . . I don't know if that will calm her down. She's pretty upset. Julie didn't call her to tell her that she was leaving." I skidded to a stop as a horrible thought occurred to me. "Do you know if Julie called *any* of her authors to tell them she was leaving?"

"Of course she did. I think. Luanne probably just fell through the cracks." Rita stopped outside the conference room door and her brows knitted. "Still, you'd better call everybody."

Oh God.

"You needed to do that anyway," she said. "I guess I should have told you that, huh?"

I schlumped back to my office, feeling defeated. How was I going to call that poor woman back and tell her that a book that probably took her months and months of work to write was going to be sent out with that child molester cover? She would be devastated. She would hate me.

She would know I was a fraud.

When I turned the corner into my office, I found Cassie standing in front of my bookcase, looking through my manuscript pile.

"What are you doing?" I asked.

"I'm taking some of your authors."

"*What?*"

"Just four," she said, then added, "so far."

"Rita didn't say anything to me about giving you my authors."

At the mention of Rita, she looked openly contemptuous. "Of course not. Rita's been out all morning. And I have no idea where *you've* been, but my phone's been ringing off the hook."

I craned my head forward. "Why? Because of Luanne?"

She laughed. "No, because it's all over the romance web

rings that Julie bailed and left a novice in charge of her author list. Somebody who doesn't even know what tip sheets are."

"I just thought . . ." *Wait.* My blood ran cold. "How would anyone know that?"

She froze, realizing she had made a slip, and shook her head. "Well, what was I supposed to say to all these worried authors who called me? Tough luck, you'll have to work with this new chick, this total novice, or lump it? Authors aren't idiots, Rebecca. They have careers at stake here."

"They do, or *you* do?"

She smirked as she grabbed a fat manuscript from my shelf. The rotten thief.

"I'm not a novice," I lied. Well, I had a day under my belt now.

"Right. Like working on some woman's memoirs is the equivalent of four years of hard work. Not that I'm complaining, mind you. Life isn't fair. I've always known that."

I squinted at her. "It's certainly not fair of you to take my authors away before I've had a chance even to talk to them."

Fair was not the way of Cassie Saunders, however. And with Rita in a meeting, there was little I could do for the moment but watch as Cassie made off with her loot.

When she was gone, I sank into my chair, burning with frustration. By all rights I probably should have marched right into her office and shoved one of those pilfered manuscripts down her throat. Instead, I sat there in a funk, wondering if I really deserved to be bested by her. And deciding that I probably did. I was the interloper here, after all.

It was only a matter of time before everybody found that out.

The phone rang, and—still not having learned Lesson Number One—I automatically reached for it.

"Am I speaking to the girl genius?"

If the male voice had asked me if my refrigerator was running, I couldn't have been any more certain this was a prank. "This is Rebecca Abbot," I said.

"Right, Rebecca Abbot. Editor extraordinaire, or so I've heard."

An uncomfortable chuckle burbled out of me.

"I know—the suspense is killing you. My name is Dan Weatherby." The name sounded familiar, but I couldn't place it. "Luanne Seligson's agent."

"Oh! Right!" I suddenly had the urge to put my head down on the table and cry. I was so not ready for this conversation. "I guess you heard I spoke to Luanne."

"Yes, I'm very sorry. Julie called me before she left, but then it slipped my mind to call Luanne. My bad."

A hint of sunshine peeked out through the clouds. Except there was still the matter of the child molester. "About that cover . . ."

He laughed. "Don't worry, I think between us we've talked Lu off the ledge."

We had?

We?

That word had such a comradely ring to it. I perked up. Suddenly I noticed what a rumbly, sympathetic sounding voice Dan Weatherby had. "I've been raising heck around here about it."

I know, I know. But I had to tell the man something. "Raising heck" sure as hell sounded better than "whining to my coworkers."

"I told Luanne you would," Dan said.

How did he know? Or rather, how had he arrived at that very shaky and utterly wrong conclusion? He didn't know the first thing about me.

"I explained to Luanne that there wasn't a lot that could probably be done at this point."

"You did?"

I wondered suddenly what Dan Weatherby looked like. He sounded a little like Russell Crowe, when he wasn't speaking in the Aussie accent. I leaned back in my chair and twirled a Paper-mate pen through my fingers. I really liked Russell Crowe, apart from the jackass movie star behavioral problems.

"I also told her that if you are half of what Mercedes built you up to be over the phone fifteen minutes ago, she's in great hands."

Mercedes, a woman who clung ferociously to her misperceptions. God bless her.

I sputtered modestly, "I don't know about that . . ."

He laughed. "I told Luanne that it's always good to have a new editor anyway. That you'll probably work extra hard on her behalf."

I would, I swore I would.

At this point, it didn't even matter whether Dan Weatherby looked like Russell Crowe or just a plain ol' dead crow. He could have had a face like roadkill for all I cared. I was pretty sure I was in love with him. Such was the power of a seductive phone voice.

We exchanged a few more moments of chitchat before he rang off, with me still assuring him that I was going to see what could still be done about *Pursuing Paula*, and him assuring me that it would all work out, because I was such a sharp young whippersnapper of an editor. By the time he rang off, I was thoroughly schmoozed.

I leaned back in my chair, savoring the image of myself that Dan Weatherby had imprinted in my head. I was one of those go-to types. A problem solver. The sharpest knife in the drawer, and glamorous to boot.

The seconds ticked by. The image began to fade.

I was me again.

I looked at the clock at the bottom of my computer screen and gasped. It was almost noon! And all I had done all morning was deal with this one cover controversy.

And I still had all those authors to call.

I looked at the list, crossed off the four Cassie had stolen, and considered nipping out to a Chinese restaurant I'd spotted around the corner. A large order of lemon chicken and some potstickers would really bolster my courage.

It would also make the already tight button on my skirt pop.

My stomach rumbled. The sad little sack lunch I'd brought from home mocked me. Could I really face twenty-one—no, seventeen—authors on nothing but tuna salad and an apple? Authors who had been told already that I was a hapless newbie idiot, and maybe worse?

Lemon chicken, lemon chicken, lemon chicken.

Sighing, I picked up the phone and dialed. Let the awkwardness begin.

By the time five-thirty rolled around, I felt like something that should be carted off and rendered for pet food. As if being on the phone with authors for three straight hours wasn't enough, at four o'clock Janice Wunch appeared at my door with an updated late list. Somehow my portion of it had grown by another half page in the past day. Something—perhaps the impatient tapping of Janice's Naturalizers—told me I wasn't managing my time wisely.

At the end of the day, I filled up an old Candlelight totebag with homework and staggered to the elevator.

"Good night, Rebecca," Muriel said. The phones were silent, but in her headset she appeared poised for the slightest hint of a ring. The model of efficiency.

" 'Night."

"Is it your intention to burn the midnight oil tonight?"

I grunted.

There was an awkward stretch while Muriel stared at me with her amazing blinkless eyes as I fixed my own drooping gaze at the elevator doors. Finally, they slid open and I escaped inside.

When I got on the elevator, there was someone already on I thought I recognized. At first I thought he must be a movie star or something, then I realized he was the suave elevator guy from the day of my first interview. The one who told me not to be nervous, then informed me I had lipstick on my teeth. He must have thought I was a complete bozo.

"Well, hello!" he said, recognizing me.

He was looking as dapper as he had the last time we had met, while I was sure I had that washed out after-five thing going on. My hair, not brushed since eight AM, hung in hanks around my ears, my makeup had long since faded under the fluorescent lighting, and my skirt had very pronounced sit wrinkles. I was not up to Suave Guy's standard. Suave Guy didn't even have a five o'clock shadow.

"So you got the job," he said. "Congratulations."

I felt like weeping on his shoulder. "Thanks. Never has the phrase 'be careful what you wish for' seemed more apt."

"That's just that new job feeling. It'll pass when you get that first paycheck."

Paycheck! I had forgotten all about that concept, even though it was my entire reason for being here. Now the prospect appeared to me like the light at the end of the tunnel. Or a carrot before the donkey. I was going to be paid for all this eventually. The very idea made my spine straighten.

At the ground floor, Suave Guy held the door and waited for me to exit first. (As a suave guy should.) "Good night," he said as I stepped out.

"Good night." I walked ahead of him out of the building and headed for the subway, feeling a little more hopeful than I had when I'd stepped onto the elevator. I needed a Suave Guy with me twenty-four hours a day. A pocket size Suave Guy.

On second thought, full size was awfully nice.

The train took forever to arrive and then managed to get stalled in a tunnel, so when I finally climbed the stairs to the apartment, it was almost seven o'clock. The door flew open and Maxwell came bounding out like a carnival performer just shot from the cannon. He quivered with energy and let out a series of yips. Finally, seeing that not even his boundless enthusiasm would hurry me along, he slapped his rump down at the top of the stairs and watched with an eagerly thumping tail as I climbed the last flight. Looking at those adorable brown eyes and those goofy folded ears, I had to smile and make a few cooing sounds.

Fleishman leaned against the doorjamb. "How'd it go?"

That was a hard question to answer, mainly because I wasn't sure if there were enough synonyms for the word bad to encompass everything I had to explain. I crossed the threshold with the puppy in my arms and deposited him on the floor. Our apartment smelled doggy now. "Where's Wendy?"

"Where else? Stuck in the NYU gulag."

I collapsed onto the futon—right on top of Max. How had he jumped up so fast? He hadn't been wasting his day, obviously. I let him crawl up on my chest and lick the bottom of my chin. I was too tired to be grossed out.

"Are you okay?"

I slit one eye open. Fleishman was bent over me, looking as one might when trying to discern whether that homeless person you just passed was actually dead or alive.

"Fine."

"Good. How about some dinner?"

I shook my head.

"Come on, Rebecca. You have to eat."

"No I don't. Eating will only prolong it."

"Prolong what?"

"My life."

I could hear his foot tapping. My life was full of foot tappers today. "You aren't on some kind of funky diet, are you?"

"I'm on the exhaustion diet," I said.

"The best thing for that is to go for a walk."

I had just enough energy left to lift my head and glare at that maniac.

He was smiling at me impatiently. So was the dog. "Maxwell and I have been cooped up all day long. We need air."

So he had skipped work again and he wanted *me* to walk the dog?

"And I want you to tell me all about your day," he said.

I allowed myself to be persuaded. Especially when the word gelato was raised. I changed into sneakers and a pair of pedal pushers and out the door we went—my roommate, my dog, and me. We were taking little Max to the park together for the first time.

Wendy was right. This business of having joint custody of a dog did feel intimate. But what was wrong with that? I knew it was dangerous to think this way—to let myself get carried away—but Fleishman and I did go way back. So I occasionally had a, shall we say, fondness for him . . . was that so bad?

Whenever I saw Wendy or one of my sisters shaking their heads over my relationship with Fleishman, it made me want to scream. Was this or was this not the twenty-first century? In their minds—especially my family's—there was simply no complexity allowed when it came to relations between the sexes. But surely we had progressed to the point where a man and a woman could be friends.

Mind you, this enlightened attitude of mine did not prevent me from periodically holing up by myself and something Sara Lee and weeping over the fact that Fleish just didn't love me. I wasn't made of stone. The mere thought of *When Harry Met Sally*, a film most women thought of as the best feel-good movie of the past century, was enough to send me into a week-long funk. I knew, knew it in my bones, that there wasn't going to be any big New Year's happy ending scene for us at the end of the last reel.

Nope. Wasn't going to happen.

See? I wasn't completely unrealistic.

It's just that meeting Fleishman had changed everything for me.

Okay, actually it was losing forty-five pounds that changed everything. But Fleishman was the first guy who ever saw me as I wanted to be seen—in other words, not as a big fat loser. Maybe it was the case of the baby duckling latching onto the first creature it sees, but when Fleishman and I paired off during our first year in college, it felt right.

Likewise, when we split up the next year, it felt wrong. But I was willing to deal with that. To play it cool. You don't spend eighteen years of your life feeling like one of society's castoffs without developing a teeny bit of self-protection. Just friends? Okay, I could handle that.

The truth was, if I tried to envision waking up on a weekend morning without him, it felt like a crater was opening up in my chest.

"So what happened at work?" he asked.

I told him he didn't want to know. He insisted he did. I hedged. He cajoled. We stopped for ice cream.

And then it all came spilling out. I told him all about Luanne, the pedophile cover, Cassie's treachery, having to call all the authors who had been told I was an idiot, then Janice Wunch and the late list. It was good to get it off my chest.

All the while, Fleishman sat across the wrought iron café table from me, barely touching his plastic lavender tulip cup of gelato. I really didn't expect anything more from Fleishman than what he was giving me—a sympathetic ear and a few understanding nods.

But when I was done, and was scraping at the last bit of rum coconut raisin in my cup, I was surprised to find myself getting an earful.

"This is just outrageous!" he exclaimed. "You need to march up to that Cassie woman tomorrow morning—first thing, Rebecca—and tell her to give you those authors back!"

"I'm not sure I can do that."

"Of course you can. Tell her where to get off." He squinted. "Who did she take? Anybody good?"

I lifted my shoulders. "I'm not sure. I still don't know who most of these people are. And anyway, I'm obviously swamped. I'm not sure I should go chasing after more work."

His jaw dropped. "It's the principle of the thing, damn it. At the very least, you need to tell your boss what's going on."

"Squeal, you mean?"

"You have to squeal."

"But wouldn't that just make me look weak twice over?"

He whapped his napkin against the table. "Man, we need to put you on angry pills. This is the corporate world, Rebecca. You have to be ready to show your claws."

I know he was trying to help me, but I couldn't help thinking, *what the hell do* you *know about the corporate world?* He'd been a part-time telemarketer for the past six months. Before that, he'd been a summer intern at *Theater World* magazine, and before that he had enjoyed the shortest ushering career ever in the twenty-year history of the Angelika after chucking a Mike and Ike box at a man who was talking during a Juliette Binoche movie.

Fortunately, the box had been empty. Unfortunately, the man he'd chucked it at was Martin Scorsese.

But I did not remind him of any of this. He was trying to help me.

And maybe he was right. I couldn't let things go on this way.

"If you don't do something now, you'll wind up as this Cassie creature's personal punching bag," he warned.

I sighed. "I wish I could just switch places with her."

His brows scrunched. "What do you mean?"

"I think her nose was bent out of joint when I came in a level above her. Being associate rather than assistant doesn't matter to me. So I wish I could just tell her, here, take your damn promotion and leave me alone. All I want is a paycheck."

Fleishman slammed his tulip cup on the table, I think to free up both hands so he could tear his hair out. "Where to begin?" he moaned, looking up at the heavens. He reached across the table for my hand. "First off, you don't cede the advantage to this person, okay? *Ever.* So what if you got where you are through a freakish stroke of good fortune? Them's the breaks. You're the one who usually complains about having bad luck, remember? Well, this time luck worked in your favor. So you have to take advantage. Understand?"

I laughed.

"This Cassie person sounds like a classic DJB."

"What's that?"

"A demented jealous bitch. She needs to be crushed."

"Right. I'm just the person to do that."

"You have to, Rebecca. You owe it to the rest of humanity to stop this woman before she goes any further down the path of demented jealous bitchiness. You didn't ask for it, but this is your mission now."

"What should I do?"

"First off, you have to watch your back. Lock your office door if you have to."

I laughed.

"I'm serious. Do not leave her another opening. And the second thing is, undercut her at every opportunity. Steam right over her pathetic stalled career. You've already got a head start on her. You can do this, Rebecca. Look how far you've come in the publishing world just by mistake! And I know somewhere in that jellyfish personality of yours is a will of cast iron just crying to get out. You're the woman who lost forty-five pounds in four months, remember? You're tougher and smarter than you give yourself credit for."

Damn. He was right. Why shouldn't I succeed?

There was just one problem. Deep down I still felt that I was only kidding myself. While Fleishman was talking at me, I could believe that I would emerge triumphant in this situation. But unassisted, I am a ten-minute optimist.

As we walked Maxwell along the edge of a tiny neighborhood park, my self-confidence sagged back down to its normal level. I told Fleishman, "I'm so far behind, and Cassie's a little go-getter."

"You'll catch up," he assured me.

"How?"

"We start tonight. First we'll knock out all that late-list stuff out, ASAP. Also, we'll make cookies."

"*Cookies?*" What the hell was he talking about?

"You need to start winning friends and influencing people around that place."

"With *cookies?*" I asked. "This is an office."

He nodded. "Doesn't matter. There ain't nobody who doesn't love Natasha Fleishman's chocolate chocolate chip cookies."

That gave me pause. Those cookies *were* good. "But I thought her cook made those."

"I'll call her for the recipe. I know she's got it. She collects recipes, she just doesn't bake anything herself."

"Isn't this going to be a lot of work for a week night?"

"Week night, schmeek night. We'll get it done."

I could feel my lips twisting into a wry curl. "I don't know if you've noticed, but you've been throwing the word *we* around awfully liberally."

"I'm going to help you."

"I've never seen you make a cookie," I said.

"Then you make cookies and I'll help you knock out some of that work."

"*What?*"

"Why not?" he asked. "Are they going to check your handwriting to make sure you did it yourself? Who would even notice?"

He was right about that.

Warning bells were going off in my head, but I couldn't quite figure out what all the ruckus was about. Fleishman and I helped each other out all the time. I'd done so much work on an *Othello* paper for him in junior year that I might have legally been called its author. We shared half our stuff. We even shared money.

What could be wrong in sharing a little work?

Chapter 6

On Wednesday morning, Lindsay stopped by my office carrying a legal pad. I must have looked startled. It was the first time I had seen her looking slightly businesslike. And believe me, it had to be difficult to look businesslike in that tight zebra print top she was wearing.

"Ready?" she asked.

I tried to imagine what she was talking about, but my mind was a blank. "Did I miss a memo?"

"There's an editorial meeting every week," she said. "All hands, plus Janice and Troy. It's boring and interminable. It's also mandatory. Didn't anyone tell you?"

I grabbed a legal pad and followed her down the hall to the conference room. Aside from being in a somnambulant daze, I was feeling pretty cocky. Fleishman and I had pulled an all-nighter. We had knocked out all the stuff I had brought home. We had made four dozen chocolate chocolate chip cookies . . . and I had only availed myself of five. (Everyone agrees: breakfast is the most important meal of the day.)

The conference room was long and narrow, and almost entirely consumed by the rectangular table that ran its length. On one wall was a dry-erase board nearly as long as the table itself. On the other side stood a row of chairs. When I walked into the ed meeting with Lindsay, those chairs were filled with the ed assists, who apparently didn't rank a place at the table. Lindsay took the last of these seats.

"Sorry," she said, "you have to be a plebe to be in this row."

Andrea waved me over to an empty seat next to her at the table. She was madly scribbling numbers all over her legal pad.

"What are you doing?" I asked.

She tapped her pencil. "I'm trying to figure out how much I would have to earn to pay thirty dollars a month more on my MasterCard, which would make me completely debt free in the year 2026. It's really not that much! I think it's doable."

People started passing around Xeroxed handouts. First there was Janice Wunch's dreaded late list (my items had shrunk down to five . . . a miracle no one seemed to notice). Then there was a page bearing the title, *To be discussed.* With the exception of Cassie and me, all the editors had a few titles under their names. I had none. Cassie had thirteen.

Andrea tapped on my sheet of paper. "Oh! You're supposed to turn in the slush and agented manuscript titles you've read during the week that you mean to pursue."

"Now she tells me," I muttered.

Not that I had read anything new. Still, it rankled to be bested by Cassie once again.

"Cassie always overdoes," Andrea grumbled, as if she could read my mind. "It always takes for-fucking-ever to get out of here, thanks to her."

The editors were all congregated for a full five minutes before Mercedes finally bustled in, scarf fluttering behind her. She sat down at the head of the long table, then took out a judge's gavel and banged it on the table, which seemed a little odd, since all of us were already staring at her anyway.

"A rather surprising memo came down from on high about sales figures," she announced, getting things started. "The new hot sellers last quarter were single titles, MetroGirl, and Divines."

Across the table, Mary Jo and her God Pod were smiling smugly. In front of Mary Jo was her ubiquitous Cathy mug. Andrea might have viewed that beverage container as a sign of

Mary Jo's mental health problem, but I for one marveled at its longevity. It was about the same age as my little brother, who was a sophomore at Ohio State.

"Flames also were selling briskly, as usual," Mercedes said. Flame was supposedly the sexiest line of books we published. "So what do we learn from this, people?"

We all looked at one another nervously before Troy blurted out, "We learn that American women can't get enough of hot sex and Jesus."

I laughed, and Troy, who had been munching on some of the cookies I'd brought him, winked at me conspiratorially.

Fleishman's advice had turned out to be not at all bad. When I'd brought Troy the cookies and explained about the cover, and told him how upset the author was, he couldn't have been nicer about it. He'd explained that actually he had yanked a cover once before when it was decided that the drawing of the hero had too much crotch bulge showing. They had swapped the artwork with art from an earlier foreign edition of a different book, but one which had similar looking people. "It cost us, but it saved on angry reader mail and bad sales."

"And you would do that for me?" I gushed.

"Oh, honey! You sound so disgustingly grateful!" he simpered back at me. Then he laughed. "Yes, I would do that for you, and to keep Art Salvatore from firing my ass. Or worse . . ."

My eyes widened in alarm. He made it sound as if he would wind up with cement shoes in the East River over a bad cover. "But that's just a rumor, right?"

"Oh, yeah. Totally." He nudged me playfully in the ribs.

There's one ally now, I thought.

Mercedes was the only person at the table who wasn't chuckling at Troy's little joke. "That's exactly right," she said. "Of course people don't want religion and hot sex in the same book . . ."

"How do we know?" Madeline interrupted. When the only answer she received were blank stares all around, she asked, "It worked for *The Thorn Birds*, didn't it?"

"Richard Chamberlain was so *hot*," Ann said.

Mercedes cleared her throat. "I just don't think that now . . ."

"Oh!" Lindsay piped up. "Did you ever see Richard Chamberlain in *Shogun?*" She made some kind of weird martial arts moved with her ballpoint pen. "My mom has that on DVD."

"I thought he was gay," someone said.

"*No way!*"

All the people who were half asleep during the beginning of the discussion of sales figures were suddenly alive with opinions on the subject of Richard Chamberlain, gay/not gay.

"I don't care about real life," Madeline proclaimed. "He wasn't gay when he yanked that woman down on the beach to have sex with her."

"That was just like that beach scene in *From Here to Eternity,*" Andrea said, "with Burt Lancaster."

"Burt Lancaster was *hot.*"

Mercedes had to gavel us again. "Of course you all know we're talking about two different demographics—people who read for sensuality, and people who read for spirituality."

"What about people who are just reading something because they're at the laundromat, bored stiff?" Andrea said. "They might like a little naughty priest action."

"I think we're getting off topic," Mary Jo said, trying to rescue Mercedes. "What did the report say the worst sellers were?"

Naturally, having already been assured of her bestselling status, she would want to know that.

Mercedes lips tightened into a smile. "The Pulse books continue to flatline." She'd obviously rehearsed that lame line in her head all morning, but she was rewarded with a chorus of dutiful titters nevertheless.

Mercedes did not look at Rita. She so pointedly did not look at Rita that everybody else did. Rita was sucking so hard on her pen, she looked like she was about to inhale ink.

"The lesson here is we can't get complacent," Mercedes said. "We need to keep generating new ideas. I don't care whether they come from you or the authors or the crazy guy who plays spoons in front of Grand Central Station, we need to keep coming up with new twists."

Cassie raised her hand and waved it.

"Yes, Cassie?"

"Just last night I was thinking we should do a series of books about a police precinct, where every book features a different cop's story."

Mercedes snapped her fingers. "See? That's just what I'm talking about. We need more of that."

If Cassie's self-love had been any more evident at that moment, she would have broken some state indecency laws.

I was seized with the urge to come up with an idea. It didn't even have to be an original one, apparently. I mean, a *police precinct?* Come on!

"And from now on," Mercedes continued, "if you come across a fantastic book with a new twist in it, I want it to come directly to me. Take a red pen and write a big *N* on the front."

Everyone around the table exchanged perplexed stares.

"For *new*," Mercedes explained.

Andrea snorted softly and I had to bend my head over my notepad so I wouldn't start laughing.

After the meeting (which really did seem to go on forever), Rita was in an uproar. She directed us to meet her at her outer office, ASAP.

After we had picked up our lattes, Andrea and I huddled next to the coffee shop door next to Rita, who was smoking up a storm.

"Where's Cassie?" she asked.

Andrea licked the foam off her wood stir stick. "She stayed after the meeting to kiss Mercedes's ass."

"That's probably what I should have done," Rita muttered. "That meeting seemed ominous to me. Didn't it to you?"

"Ominous, how?" I asked.

"Didn't it seem to you like Mercedes was telling me that I was going to be fired?" She didn't wait for us to answer. "Well! Naturally I'm going to be fired. It's just a matter of when."

"Why do you say that?"

"Everybody gets the ax eventually."

"Like cows in the feed lot," Andrea mused.

"And I'm the oldest editor here." Rita exhaled. "I'm old enough to be Mercedes's mother, did you know that?"

"Yeah, like maybe if you were giving birth when you were six, Rita," Andrea said. "You're not going to get fired."

Maybe she wasn't, but she was so nervous she was making me feel sure *I* was going to be fired.

I tried to think positively. *Me!* Not exactly your best example of a Pollyanna. But dear God, around these two, *somebody* had to inject a little hopefulness or we were all doomed. "All Mercedes was saying was that we need to punch Pulse up a little . . ."

"Maybe the series is played out," Andrea said, interrupting me. "People just don't want to read about nurses and doctors all the time."

"Why shouldn't they?" Rita asked, getting a little of her spunk back. "They've watched *ER* forever. We just need to think of some way to make medical romances a little more exciting. Right?"

"Right," I said.

Andrea remained unconvinced. "Do you have any ideas for achieving this feat?" she asked me. "Any big *N*s swimming around in that head of yours?"

"Well, no," I admitted.

"Just think about it," Rita said. "Comb your slush for possibilities."

Dismissed, Andrea and I turned to go back up.

"Rebecca, wait," Rita said. "I need to talk to you."

"Wow, is she in trouble already?"

Rita shot Andrea a look. "Why don't you go to lunch?"

"Thanks, I will." Andrea laughed as she headed down the street toward the deli.

Rita frowned at me, then stubbed her cigarette under her heel. "Before the ed meeting I got a call from Darlene Paige's agent. She said Darlene was working with Cassie now. When did this happen?"

"Oh." I shifted uncomfortably. "Yesterday."

Rita crossed her arms. "You just decided to give your authors away?"

"I didn't give them away, exactly," I confessed. "Cassie took them. Well, four of them."

"And you were going to inform me of this fact . . . *when?*"

I tried to think fast, which is difficult when you're working on three hours of sleep and five chocolate chip cookies. "I wanted to raise hell about it, Rita—but what could you do? The authors were already in an uproar. You couldn't force them to work with a new editor now that they've decided they want a change, could you?"

Rita tilted her head. "What caused these authors to get in an uproar, do you think?"

Much as it pained me, I gritted my teeth and stared into the air. It was like some old school camaraderie kicked in, even toward the odious Cassie. All the world hates a squealer. "I'm not sure," I finally said. "Someone said something about a panic on a Web ring."

"Geez," she muttered. "Well, you're right, unfortunately. It wouldn't be a good idea to tell the authors they couldn't change."

I nodded.

She thought for a moment and grumbled, "Well, you've got one thing figured out."

"What?"

"How to lighten your load."

An idea struck me. Even as the words tumbled out of my mouth, I couldn't believe I was actually saying them. "Well since I'm four authors short, if there's anything you want me to do for you . . ."

Her eyes widened. "Actually, I do have a few edits . . ." She drummed her fingers against her jacket sleeves. "You wouldn't mind?"

"Not at all." What were a few more weeks of sleepless nights?

"That would be great," Rita said. "I could almost get caught up."

She was smiling. Which made it worth the trouble.

Besides, it was one less batch of cookies I'd have to bake.

"What did you bring me?" Fleishman asked when I got through the door.

I tossed down two tote bags of manuscripts on the futon and picked up Maxwell, who treated me to a welcome home faceful of slobber.

Wendy, making one of her rare appearances at the apartment at the dinner hour, was sitting at the table with a newspaper and the toaster in her lap. She wrinkled her nose at this canine show of affection. "That's disgusting."

"But it's adorably disgusting." I gave Maxwell a big kiss on the nose.

Fleishman peered into the tote bags with visible disappointment. "No books?"

"What are you talking about? That's nothing but books."

He sank down on the futon. "But I like the ones with the covers on them."

"I'll bring you some tomorrow. But tonight I need to go through those and see if there's anything good."

He perked up. "Oh! I can do that."

I put the dog down, then crossed my arms. "Aren't you tired?"

"God, no. I slept all day. You look beat, though."

"Well, I've been at work all day, while . . ." I couldn't help staring at Wendy, who was sticking a pair of barber scissors down into the mouth of the toaster. It wasn't plugged in, but still, it seemed odd. "What are you doing?"

Never taking her eyes off the task at hand, she said, "There's a sizable chunk of bagel in the bottom of the toaster. If it's left there, it could start a fire."

"How did you find it?"

"What do you mean? It was in the toaster."

"I know, but what made you look?"

Wendy's voice rose in exasperation. "I was *cleaning* it."

Fleishman and I exchanged glances. It was amazing, really, the things Wendy thought to do. It probably had something to do with all those home shows she watched on television. She was addicted to those, which was weird for someone who didn't even have a closet to call her own.

As she surgically removed the old bagel chunk, Fleishman pulled a manuscript out of one of the tote bags and flipped through the pages as if it were one of those animation books from when we were kids. "This looks long."

They all seemed long to me.

"Can I read it?" he asked.

"Why would you do that?"

He lifted his shoulders. "After this past week, I feel I have a stake in your career. Plus, I just like reading these books. It's opened up a whole new world. Romance novel world."

I tilted my head. "Well, just be careful. Don't spill Red Bull all over anything. They have to go back to the authors."

His eyes widened. "What if you want to buy it?"

I could feel my lip twisting in doubt. "That's a long shot."

"Got it!" Wendy cried. Sure enough, at the tip of her scissors was a sizable piece of bagel that now looked like a miniature charcoal briquette. She squinted at it more closely, then looked sidewise at me. "Aren't you the one partial to sesame seeds?"

Caught! "I didn't realize it fell down there." I couldn't even remember the last time I had toasted a bagel.

"This little piece could have sent the whole apartment up in flames," she lectured me.

I sank down in my chair, feeling like an inadvertent arsonist.

Fleishman scooted back on the couch to get comfy with his chosen manuscript. "I'm going to strike gold, I know it. I think I have a real knack for this job."

"But it's not your job," Wendy pointed out.

The look she shot me contained some kind of warning, but honestly, I couldn't see the harm in letting Fleishman read a slush manuscript.

* * *

I fell asleep in the middle of something called *Special Delivery*, about a male obstetrician who falls in love with one of his patients. I saw several problems with this. First, there was a meet-cute where a doctor described as having bright red hair delivers a baby on a bus. I was imagining labor pains and Danny Bonaduce on the crosstown local. Would anyone find that appealing?

I got most hung up on the whole male obstetrician thing. What kind of guy decides he wants to spend his days measuring women's cervixes and giving episiotomies?

Of course, there was the miracle of birth . . .

But there were also those episiotomies.

Was I the only person in the world wigged out by this?

Somewhere around chapter three, I sank down on the futon, closed my eyes, and never managed to come to again until four AM, when I crawled into my own bed. I could hear the sounds of Fleishman snoring softly in his corner of the apartment. I wondered how long it had taken him to give up his quest for gold.

The moment my head hit the pillow I was out again.

The next thing I knew, sun was squinting in through the open window blinds and Fleishman was towering over me with a cup of coffee. "You'd better hurry, or you'll be late."

I sat up and took the mug from him, with thanks. It was a Ziggy mug we had found at a thrift store one Saturday and for some reason had thought hilarious. Now it sort of reminded me of Mary Jo's Cathy mug; it was probably of an even older vintage.

"I struck gold," Fleishman announced.

I laughed. "Could you possibly have found anything more scintillating than *Special Delivery?*"

He wasn't joining me in my mirth. "I found something that will make you."

"Make me what?"

"Make your career," he said. "And frankly, I'm beginning to wonder if you even deserve it. From your reaction, I feel like I'm casting my pearls before swine."

"It's seven AM."

"You've really got to read it, Rebecca. It's *sooo* good! It gave me goosebumps, especially at the end."

I frowned. "You read the whole thing last night?"

"Of course. You were out like a light at nine, but I stayed up well past midnight."

I groaned. I was supposed to get so much done last night, but instead I ended up zonked out. Now I was going to have to drag all those manuscripts back to the office unread.

Cassie had probably been up all night finding the next big thing.

"I really was scared," he said.

"About what?"

He let out an impatient sigh. "Earth to Rebecca—I'm talking about the book. According to the attached cover letter, it was intended for the Pulse line, but aren't those supposed to be short books?"

I nodded.

"Well, this thing clocked in at five hundred pages. But they were five hundred of the best pages you'll ever read."

That was a pretty bold statement. I think Fleishman was just engaging in a little fantastical wishful thinking.

"What was it called?"

"*Heartstopper.*"

"Hm."

"It's got the creepiest villain," he said excitedly, "and the heroine is this scientist who's working with a cop to find out why all these patients are dying in the ER."

"Hm."

"And then she meets this hotshot surgeon, and for a while you think he's the ER menace. But of course he's wicked gorgeous and our lady scientist has the hots for him."

I had to admit, it sounded better than clown-headed obstetricians on public transportation.

I showered and dressed, then headed out the door, weighed down with the same burden from last night. I had been thinking of getting a briefcase like the soft-sided leather one Ann from the office carried around, but now I wondered whether it wouldn't be wiser to purchase a steamer trunk with wheels.

Luck was with me that morning. I managed to get a plum seat on the subway—next to a window even, so I wasn't stuck in a middle seat wedged awkwardly between two thighs. I reached into the tote and pulled out a manuscript. It was *Heartstopper.* Fleishman had written up all his notes and placed them under the rubber band that held the thing together.

Great! Needs cutting, but pacing is terrif. Compelling characters and suspense. 2 thumbs up! (Heroine's name is Eloise . . . shd probably be changed???)

I looked at the author's name. Joanna Castle. It sounded fake. I'll have to admit, I was skeptical of everything about this book, even after Fleishman's sales pitch. Or maybe because of it. This didn't even sound like that much of a romance, and it was way too long for Pulse.

Sighing, I started page one.

The ambulance screamed through the yellow twilight of street-lamps. Inside, on the gurney, a woman was dying.

Within moments, I was hooked. Honestly. The train clattered in its usual stop-start fashion, but I didn't notice any delays. In fact, I didn't even notice when we arrived at Delancey Street, where I was supposed to switch trains. I didn't look up from what I was reading until we had already reached Wall Street, and by then I was screwed. I was doubling back into Brooklyn.

I leapt out of the seat and jumped off the train. The doors nicked my rear as they closed.

Two train changes, thirty minutes, and two chapters later, I had managed to get myself uptown.

I hurried to the office, forgetting to stop for a bagel. I wasn't hungry anyway. I just wanted to know what was in Eloise's test tube . . . and if it would implicate the hottie surgeon she'd just had sex with.

As I wheeled into the office, Muriel flagged me down. "Good morning, Rebecca. You have a message."

"Oh." I found my name on the wheely deal and pulled out a pink message slip. Dan Weatherby had called.

Suddenly, I forgot about the test tube.

"It appears that you have been busy," Muriel said.

I looked up. She was staring at me expectantly. It took me a moment to register that she was making small talk. "Oh, right. I took some books home last night."

"Mercedes said you seem like a real go-getter."

I grunted. I wondered what Dan Weatherby wanted.

"Rebecca?"

I looked back up at Muriel. "I'm sorry?"

"I asked if you would care to go to lunch today? I have a coupon for Bombay Palace, which has a fairly extensive buffet you might care to try if you haven't already."

"Oh . . ." I couldn't think of any reason not to go to lunch, except for the fact that I really wanted to get back to *Heartstopper.* But maybe I would be finished by then. "Okay."

"Wonderful." She handed me another pink slip.

"What's this?"

"I wrote down the time you should meet me here. My break is from noon to one sharp."

I nodded. She really had written it down, including checking off the appropriate boxes of the pre-written menu provided on the slip. *Reminder of appointment,* it said.

Damn, she was efficient.

As I was walking back to my office, it occurred to me that she must have had the slip filled out before I had even gotten off the elevator.

I called Dan Weatherby. "I'm so sorry I haven't gotten back to you about the *Pursuing Paula* cover."

"I'm sorry, too," he said. "If only because I've missed hearing the dulcet tones of your voice."

I laughed, but I had to admit that a little thrill went through me. I had to ask Andrea about this guy. I was curious to know pertinent facts . . . like what he looked like and did he have a wife.

"I called to ask about a book by Joanna Castle."

I nearly fell out of my chair. "Is she your client?" If she was, what had she been doing in the slush pile?

"I just acquired her. She's written a book . . . I believe it's been buried in your office for quite some time."

"*Heartstopper!*" I couldn't help sounding enthusiastic. "I'm reading it right now."

We discussed the book for a little bit, and I tried to reign in my gushing a little. I would have to run it by Rita, after all. What if she didn't like it? I liked to think that she couldn't disagree with both Fleishman and me, but of course she didn't know who the hell Fleishman was.

Anyway, I told Dan Weatherby that I hoped to be getting back to him soon.

"I hope so, too," he purred at me before ringing off.

It took a few moments for my pulse to calm down before I could settle down to reading again.

The morning flew. Before I knew what was what, my phone rang.

"It's after twelve," Muriel announced in my ear.

I looked up at the clock. It was two minutes after twelve. What the hell was she talking about? Then I remembered. The buffet at Bombay Palace! I jumped up, nearly spilling the last chapter of the manuscript on the floor. I scrambled to keep it all together, then ended up losing the receiver.

By the time I picked up again, Muriel sounded impatient. "Naturally if you are busy, I will understand that you cannot take the time to have lunch today."

"No!" I wanted to finish the book, it was true. But my stomach was also rumbling like crazy. I hadn't had anything but coffee all morning. "I'll be right there."

In what I could only guess was deference to Muriel's schedule (and my tardiness) we sped-walked the three blocks to Bombay Palace. Soon I found myself seated in front of a plate of tandoori chicken and across the table from those unblinking eyes. I struggled to come up with something to say. I failed.

I started scarfing down food and was just to the point of wondering how I could make a second trip to the buffet without looking like a complete glutton when I noticed that Muriel wasn't eating at all.

"Aren't you hungry?" I asked.

"Actually, Rebecca, I don't care for Indian food."

I frowned. "I thought . . ." Well, it was hard to know what to think. I mean, she had picked the restaurant.

"I just had this two-for-one coupon and thought it might be a nice opportunity to speak to you."

"Oh." I put my fork down. "Okay."

"To be perfectly honest, Rebecca, the reason I want to speak to you is on behalf of a friend. She's written a book."

I frowned at a little heap of curried eggplant on my plate. "You want me to read it?"

"Could you?" Muriel asked. "Would you? My friend Melissa keeps pressuring me to give her advice because I work at Candlelight, even though I persist in telling her that I am a receptionist, not an editor."

"Do you have the manuscript?"

"It's back at the office."

She didn't have to drag me out to lunch to ask me to read a book. I almost told her that, but then decided it might be impolitic. At any rate, she didn't argue when I insisted on splitting the bill for the two-for-one buffet.

I was impatient to get back to the last chapter. I made a beeline for my office, shut the door, and finished *Heartstopper.* Then I typed up a report for Rita and trotted the project across the hall. When I plopped the five hundred page manuscript in front of her, she frowned. "What's that? *War and Peace?*"

"You'll want to read it," I said. "It could change everything."

She looked doubtful. I couldn't blame her. I hadn't believed Fleishman, either.

"It's sort of a cross between a Pulse and a medical suspense book."

She waved a hand. "Then it probably belongs as a Signature." Signature was Candlelight's single title program of big books. The trouble was, those titles were usually reserved for our best-selling "name" authors.

"If medical suspense books do well, why not market them through Pulse? Then you're sitting on top of a goldmine." I added, shamelessly, "Just like Mary Jo is with Divine."

Rita tapped her pen. "This must be some book."

"Just read a few pages," I suggested, and left her to it.

When I left the building that night, Rita was hovering outside the coffee shop, a cigarette in one gloved hand and *Heartstopper* balanced in the other. She didn't even hear me tell her good night.

I smiled.

Chapter 7

The book Fleishman found lit a fire under Rita. She started calling meetings like mad. Meetings in her outer office, meetings in her real office. Meetings with her staff, and then private meetings with Mercedes. She wanted to make Pulse more thriller oriented, perhaps to take the mandatory medical element out altogether. "I mean, think about it. The name of the line is Pulse. *Pulse.* Sounds suspenseful, doesn't it?"

We nodded.

"Then why the hell have we been kicking medical thrillers over to other lines? Who was the genius that decided these books would all be country doctor sagas and nurses falling in love with millionaires?"

No one was touching that one with latex gloves.

Cassie had been mostly silent through all the meetings about Pulse. But I could tell there was something simmering beneath that calm exterior. Her idea for the police precinct brainstorm had been scuttled. Troy remembered that Gazelle Books, one of our biggest rivals and where he used to work, had already done a continuity series with that exact theme.

"Maybe that's where you got your idea," he told Cassie during a meeting.

I think he was suggesting that she might have absorbed the

idea on a subliminal level, but judging from the Coke-can hue of Cassie's complexion, she felt she had just been accused of being an editorial thief, a plagiarizer, a second-rate conceptualizer.

Sweet.

The downside was, she had it in her head that I had trumped her somehow. It's true, Rita was giving me credit for finding *Heartstopper*, which in turn made her rejigger the Pulse line a little. But it wasn't as if Cassie blurted out her precinct idea and I ran home trying to think of something to top it.

"I don't see what the big deal is," Cassie said as she bustled ahead of Andrea and me as we returned to our offices after the umpteenth Pulse refocus meeting. "This kind of story has been popular for years."

Andrea sniggered. "Oh, right, but your police precinct idea was a bolt from the blue. You know, if you'd thought of adding music to the concept we could have called it *Cop Rock*."

Cassie stopped in her doorway, looking as if she wanted to kill one of us. And that one was not Andrea. Andrea had sneered at her, but Cassie was glaring at *me*.

I followed Andrea into her office and closed her door, if for no other reason than to escape the sharp daggers of Cassie's gaze. My back was prickling from it.

"Shouldn't you take it easy with her?" I asked. "She looks like she's about to go ballistic."

Andrea picked up the new *Bookworld Monthly*—or as we at the office called it, *BM*—and flipped straight to the back. "Oh, let her," she said, scanning the classifieds. "Maybe that would help dislodge the bug that's been up her ass."

"She seems unnecessarily competitive."

Andrea darted a glance at me. "And what about you and your new author finds? Little miss gangbusters! Are you trying to make us all look bad?"

Even though I was getting used to Andrea's style, I still froze when she trained that acid tongue on me. I stammered, "N-no, I just . . ."

She was shaking her head. "You're going to force me to find a new job before I actually have to start working hard."

My jaw dropped. *I* would force her to get a new job? *Force* her?

"I kid." She laughed. "My God, you look like you're about to fall over."

I returned to my office. A second later, just as I was settling down to think about getting to work, Lindsay collapsed into the chair next to my desk. She was shaking, which was actually audible, since she was wearing a shirt with beaded epaulettes.

"I'm fired!"

"*What?*"

"Or I will be."

"What happened?"

"I screwed up. I sent an author Rita wanted to acquire a rejection letter, and then I accidentally stuck Rita's revision letter for the author she wanted to acquire into someone's slush manuscript."

I was beginning to see why Rita was paranoid about the mail.

"What do I do?" she moaned.

"I think you should go into Rita's office and confess. Tell her you'll call the authors and explain the screw-up. Apologize all over the place."

On top of shaking, Lindsay was now squirming. "That'll be so awful! Can you imagine being an author who's waited six months for an answer and then hearing from some twit like me that we have *screwed up?*"

I could, actually. Sometimes I was surprised some angry writer hadn't stormed into the building with an AK-47 long ago.

"There's no other way," I counseled. In her shoes (or in this case, platform boots), I would have been squirming, too. "You have to suck it up. We all make mistakes."

Lindsay slumped in dread silence. Then she flopped back. "Okay. Yes, you're right." Her eyes narrowed on me. "You know what? I like you. Would you like to go on a date?"

The question caught me off guard. "With you?"

"No." She rolled her eyes. "You see, I know this guy, and he's really great . . ."

"Uh-huh," I said doubtfully.

"I mean, there's absolutely nothing wrong with him. He's perfectly fine."

She said it in that voice my mom used when she was trying to convince us to eat cottage cheese that had been sitting around for a while. Mentally I was already flapping my arms and backing away.

"What's his name?" I asked.

"Rowdy."

Now that wasn't a name you heard every day. It was intriguingly Clint Eastwoody. I leaned forward with more interest. "Is he a cowboy?"

"No, God no. He's from New Hampshire." She shrugged. "His real name is Harold Metzger. His father gave him this nickname when he was a kid to—I don't know—make him seem less like a Harold, maybe." Her forehead crinkled. "Which, when you think about it, he could have prevented by not naming him Harold to begin with."

"Did it work?"

She looked up at me. "Did what work?"

"Calling him Rowdy. Did it make him less of a Harold?"

"Not really." Noticing she was losing me, she added quickly, "I mean, he's really *nice*. I've known him for years." She sighed. "It's not like he would be sloppy seconds, or anything like that. We don't even get along anymore really."

"Wait," I said. "This guy is your boyfriend?"

She nodded.

"Your *current* boyfriend?"

"Yeah, but it's not like we're, you know, in love. We just live together."

"Lindsay . . ."

"He's this really good person, I just think he'd be happier with somebody else. I was going to shop him around at the office Christmas party, but that's months away. I'll probably be fired by then."

"Why are you trying to get rid of him if he's so nice?"

"Because we're so boring together it terrifies me. We used to go out clubbing. Last night we watched *March of the Penguins* on DVD and went to bed at ten." She added quickly, "Not that he's dull or anything. Not really. Before he worked in nonprofit sales he was a bass player for a really cool band. He's just dull because I know him already. And he's so normal. He wants to get married and have kids. I keep telling him that I'm, like, twenty-three. I wasn't expecting to do anything drastic till I was thirty, at least. Rowdy would have been the perfect guy to meet when I was thirty."

"Then why don't you move out? Or tell him to?"

She writhed in agony. "Because he's so nice! Like, a puppy. A puppy who does my laundry on weekends."

Okay, now she had my attention. "He does the laundry?"

"And our building doesn't have a laundry room," she said. "It's not like he drops it off someplace, either. He sits in the Laundromat for two hours every Saturday doing it himself."

"Holy cow, Lindsay."

She looked miserable. "I know, I know. You can't just dispose of a guy like that. It would be wasteful, and wrong. That's why I'm trying to recycle him."

"Why did you ask me?"

She bit her lip. "I just thought maybe you were single. You never talk about a boyfriend or anything."

"Oh."

"So . . . what do you think?"

I shook my head. I wasn't going near this. Though I was sort of curious to find out what someone in nonprofit sales did.

"Just one date?" she asked. "Come on. What can it hurt?"

I was pretty sure it was sneaking up on the six-month territory since the last time I'd had a date. Still. Going out with Lindsay's boyfriend was out of the question. That would be too weird.

But was it normal to be living with a guy I liked and feel so frustrated all the time?

Probably not.

But look at Lindsay. She had a steady boyfriend and was trying to pass him off like a baton in a relay race.

She released a long, sad sigh. "I'm never going to get rid of him, am I?"

I couldn't answer that, but when I watched her go, it was not without pity. Maybe it was as trying to have what you assumed was going to be a brief whoop-de-do turn into a permanent relationship as it was to have what you hoped was *the one* become just one of many.

Then I thought of it from Rowdy's point of view. My God, that was brutal. To have your girlfriend shopping you around without your knowledge. I'd have to remember that the next time I thought my life had reached a new pathetic low.

There were several benefits to this corporate employment racket. The first was my salary. At the beginning of the month, I was actually able to pay the rent and I had enough left over to take Fleishman and Wendy out for a celebratory brunch. And to get Max groomed and buy him a snappy new studded collar. And to dribble away a big chunk on CDs and new sheets, and a buy a nice watch to send my mom for her birthday. Even after these modest excesses, attempting to balance my checkbook now was not something that made me want to toss myself off the Williamsburg Bridge.

And then there was prestige—I mean, let's face it, being a Frenchwoman's flunkie doesn't give you a lot of authority. Now I had the trappings of corporate power all around me for the first time. An office. Personalized stationery. The day I got my business cards I must have spent thirty minutes just staring at them . . . and wondering if there were enough to send one to all my old friends. And a few who weren't friends. I imagined Brooke Meininger—the girl I'd overheard in a bathroom my sophomore year of high school comparing me with Rosie O'Donnell—opening an envelope and having this fall out:

CANDLELIGHT BOOKS
231 THIRD AVENUE, NEW YORK, NY 10055
REBECCA ABBOT
ASSOCIATE EDITOR
212*555*0273
CANDLELIGHTPUBLISHING.ORG
"Books Are Our Passion"

The lettering was crimson over eggshell white. Raised lettering. Classy. I didn't send one to Brooke Meininger—I restrained myself—but I did sprayhose my relatives with them.

My parents were so impressed with me. Among others, they had a son who was a pediatrician and a daughter who was a lawyer, but they still acted as if I had achieved something extraordinary. I think they had expected me to wind up living in a refrigerator box.

My mom kept calling to tell me all the people she knew who read Candlelight books.

"I never read romances myself, of course," she said. "Except for the occasional one I'll pick up at the library. I like the short ones. They're easy to read when I need a break after the grandkids leave."

"Okay, I'll send you some short ones," I told her.

"No, don't do that!" Her voice was anxious. "I'll buy them at Target now that your livelihood depends on them."

I laughed. "Don't worry, Mom. Candlelight already makes piles of money from all the other people who don't read romances but keep buying our books."

Dad couldn't have cared less about the books. He was all brass tacks. "What kind of benefits package did you get?"

"Um . . . pretty good, I guess," I said.

"You *guess?* Didn't you talk about this before you took the job?"

"Well, it didn't seem like something I could negotiate, Dad. I mean, I know I've got medical and dental."

"You should go get yourself a checkup," Dad said.

"A what?"

"A physical. Good God, don't you know you have to take care of your health?" This from a man who loved chicken fried everything. "What about vacation?"

"I think it's two weeks . . . or something like that."

I could hear my dad putting his hand over the receiver and calling back to my mom, "*Listen to this! She* thinks!"

"Dad . . ."

"The best part," he said, "is maybe now you can get yourself an apartment."

"I do have an apartment."

"Well . . ." He sighed. Immediately, I knew what was coming. "At least get a place by yourself. Or have *one* roommate." A female roommate, he meant. He had never been a Fleishman fan. "That fellow always hanging around you . . . what's his name? That fellow who acts like your boyfriend only he isn't?"

"You know his name. He was at your house last Christmas."

"Right. Maybe now you can tell him he needs to scoot. Though I don't know why you didn't do that years ago. You're an attractive girl now, you know."

Now, he said. As opposed to all those years when he'd *told* me I was attractive in spite of being a blimp.

I tried not to let his words stir me up. I knew he didn't mean it that way, really; over the years I had programmed my brain to root out the hidden insults in the most innocuous of comments. Like right now, and all his talk about wasting my time with Fleish. I couldn't help thinking that my dad worried I wasn't going to strike husband material before I ballooned back to obesity.

"Fleishman's my friend, Dad."

"You know, I was reading something in a magazine about men like him. I was at the doctor's office. See, *I* take advantage of my healthcare options."

I squinted at the wall. "Wait. You were reading about Fleishman?"

"Oh, sure. They've come up with a whole new category for his type. He's what they call a *metrosexual.*"

I covered the receiver so he wouldn't here me whoop. I loved to envision my square dad at the doctor's, catching up on his pop sociology. "I think you're right."

"Do you think that's a good thing?" he asked me in a worried tone.

"Well, they've done studies, Dad. It's innate. Some men are just born to exfoliate."

"If you're going to be a smart aleck, I'm going to hand this phone back to your mother so she can tell you more about what all the world and its wife have read for the past thirty years."

I laughed. I knew he wasn't going to do that, because he was one of those people who would talk for ten minutes and then start exclaiming that the call was costing somebody a fortune. (Which I believe was code for *half-time's over.*) He made me promise to work hard and go to the doctor, and I promised not to get fired before I had.

"Fired!" he exclaimed. "Why would they do that? They're lucky to have you, Becca-bunny."

I hung up the phone quickly, so I wouldn't start snuffling. That was my Dad in a nutshell. He could put you through the ringer, and then slap you on the back and try to tell you you were the greatest thing to come down the pike since twist-off bottlecaps.

But after a few weeks I was beginning to think he might be right. Not that Candlelight was lucky to have me, but that I might not need to be quite so paranoid. I began to relax a little. To socialize. I was calm enough now that I didn't always panic when I heard my phone ring, or feel my stomach churn with dread when I stepped on the elevator every morning.

In fact, I almost looked forward to getting on the elevator in the morning. There was always a chance that I would be able to share a solitary ride with Suave Guy.

That's how desperate my romantic life had become.

One morning I got on and found myself sharing the car with Andrea. She looked slightly depressed.

"What's wrong?" I assumed it was another job interview disappointment.

She shrugged. "Just the usual letdown of getting on the elevator and not seeing Mr. Incredible."

Mr. Incredible? "You mean Suave Guy?"

"Who?"

"The man on the elevator. Blond hair. Dreamy brown eyes."

She brightened. "Do you see him, too?"

It was like discovering another person in the world saw giant white rabbits.

I nodded. "I've talked to him several times."

"I've been talking to him for years!"

I tried not to feel jealous. "I wonder where he works."

She smiled knowingly. "I used to imagine he was something exciting—a spy, maybe. But I finally decided it's best not to think about it. He's just floating somewhere above us all. He's heaven-sent."

We compared notes, trying to determine which of us the elevator Adonis seemed to favor. Andrea argued that she was secretly his true love, but I was sure she was wrong. We were arguing when we got off the elevator.

"So what if he held the door for you?" Andrea said. "One time he touched *my* elbow."

"He gave *me* a Kleenex once."

She gasped. "When?"

Before I was compelled to confess that the Kleenex had been given to me to mop up an unsightly lipstick smudge, Muriel called out to me. "Rebecca, may I speak to you for a moment?"

I skidded to a stop. "Whassup?"

Slang—even decade old slang—made Muriel uncomfortable. "I wanted to inquire whether you had the opportunity to read my friend's manuscript."

Already? What did she think I was, a speed reader? It had only been a few weeks since the Indian buffet. Or maybe . . .

Well, okay. A month and a half.

"Not yet. It's on the top of my pile, though."

I had learned this response from listening to the other editors. *It's on the top of my pile!* was somehow supposed to be soothing to authors who had been on pins and needles for months and months. Maybe they were supposed to imagine their words rising like cream to the top of the slush.

"Terrific," Muriel said. "I'll let Melissa know."

That was the woman's name. Melissa MacIntosh. I remembered it from that moment a month and a half ago when I had glanced at the cover page and then tossed it onto one of the piles, where it remained to this very day. Feeling that now-familiar twinge of editor guilt, I made a vow to go straight to my office and read this manuscript. And I did. At least, I went straight back to my office and retrieved the book from the shelf.

As I looked at the front page, my heart sank.

The Rancher and the Lady
A novel
By Melissa MacIntosh

I knew you couldn't tell a book by its cover, but wasn't that what everyone did? Wasn't that why Candlelight spent hundreds of thousands on the art department staff and focus groups? Likewise, you weren't supposed to be able to tell a book just by looking at its title.

Then again, you sort of could. And a book titled *The Rancher and the Lady* was starting off at a disadvantage. For one thing, there had been about two hundred or so ranchers and ladies in Candlelight book titles. I hadn't even been here two months yet and even I knew that.

The thing to do was turn the page and plunge right in. Maybe it would surprise me. Maybe the rancher would be different from all other ranchers. And the heroine would not be the overly prim stereotype whom I saw over and over, the kind of woman who didn't know which end of a cow was up. It could happen.

Rita knocked on my door, looking frazzled. "My niece is getting married the weekend of the fifteenth." She collapsed in my chair. "That's Romance on the River weekend."

I was confused. "What's Romance on the River?"

"A RAG conference."

The Romance Author's Guild was a nationwide writer's organization whose local chapters held meetings all year long. Editors traveled to them frequently. Then, in the summer, RAG held its national conference, which apparently was a huge deal. Entire hotels were overrun with romance authors for a full week of seminars, speeches, and a fancy awards banquet where they gave out their industry awards, known familiarly as the Raggies. That year the conference was going to be in Dallas.

"I've decided to send you in my place," she said.

I assumed I wasn't being asked to sub at the wedding (although, given that this was Rita, maybe I shouldn't have). A conference! My first. It was sort of exciting.

What river were they talking about, I wondered. It couldn't be the Seine. I wouldn't be that lucky.

"Where is it?"

"Portland, Oregon."

Oregon. For just a moment, I felt a surge of interest. I'd never been west of Chicago. Oregon was far away. Far, far. Like, a five-hour plane ride.

I hated planes. No, not just hated. Was terrified by.

My palms started to sweat.

"You'll love the conference. All you have to do is make a short speech . . ."

I stopped her right there. "*Speech?*" I squeaked. "I haven't given a speech since high school—a world history presentation on Latvia that had put the entire class to sleep. Including my teacher."

"Yeah, but you were probably nervous back then. What did you really know about Latvia?"

What do I really know about romance novels?

I left that question unspoken.

"You'll do fine. They'll love you."

I had serious doubts about that. "What is this speech supposed to be about?"

She thought for a moment. "Plot."

That was it? "Just . . . plot?"

"Well! There's a lot to say about plot."

There probably was, but I wasn't sure I was the one to say it. I wasn't the one to say anything in front of groups of people. The very idea made me break into flop sweats.

"I wouldn't lose sleep over it," Rita said. "When I give a speech, I always like to tell them some of my pet peeves. Authors like that."

I leaned forward. "Like what?"

"Well, like how authors will start a chapter with *Two years went by*, or *Nine months later*, or something like that."

"What does that have to do with plot?"

"Nothing, really. I just like to work it in." She shook her head. "*Nine months later.* I can't stand that."

I chewed this over a little bit. "But what if nine months *have* gone by?"

She shrugged. "I just don't like it. It shows a lack of finesse. I can't stand twenty-page prologues, either. Oh, and you might tell them to go easy on the adverbs. That's always good advice."

"Yeah, but . . ." What did any of that have to do with plot?

She chuckled. "Well, I'm sure I can count on you. You'll do great. Make sure you keep receipts, though. Kathy Leo is a stickler for having receipts stapled to the expense report."

When she left, I sat in my office, paralyzed. I hated public speaking.

And then there was that plane ride.

Maybe it was better to concentrate on the speech. I immediately started drafting ideas . . . then tossing them one by one in the wastepaper basket. Every time I got beyond "Hi, my name is . . ." I started imagining a hundred romance writers staring up at me expectantly and a fine film of sweat broke out across my brow.

What would a roomful of romance authors look like? For that matter, what would one romance writer look like? I hadn't actually clapped eyes on one yet.

There was a sharp rap at my door. Cassie was standing there. She looked like she had just been fuming in her office until she had to explode out of her chair. "Did I hear Rita tell you that you were going to Portland? To Romance on the River?"

I nodded. Man, these walls were thin. I needed to be careful.

"Why is she sending *you?*"

"Uh . . . I'm not sure. You'd have to ask Rita that."

She shifted from one foot to the other. "Darlene Paige is *my* author and she lives in Portland."

Darlene Paige was one of the authors Cassie had snatched away from me when I first arrived.

"And Cynthia Schmidt is my author, too! She's from Medford, Oregon, and she's already told me she'll be there. Why isn't Rita sending me?"

Moments before I would have done anything for someone to offer to take my place on this business excursion. But now . . .

"I'm sure Rita has her reasons, Cassie." I was loving this! "In fact, she seemed to think it was important that I go. Maybe she didn't think you were ready."

Cassie's eyes flashed. "Don't condescend to me. I'll have you know that last year I was sent to the Gardenias and Graceland conference in *Memphis!* That's a much more prestigious conference than something in Portland, Oregon!"

I curved my lips up in a smile. "Like I said, Cassie, you'll just have to take the whole matter up with Rita."

"Don't think I won't!" She let out an angry huff, turned on her heel, and stomped away. Five seconds later, Andrea was at my door. "Me-*ow!*" she cried, with tacit approval.

I scrunched down in my chair and put my forefinger to my lips to shush her. "She's really angry."

"I know. She just stomped into Rita's office!"

"What is her problem?" I wondered aloud.

She shook her head. "You know, she was a halfway normal person when she got here, but ever since you got here she really seems to be going 'round the bend."

"I have that effect on a lot of people."

"Well! Rita's had it up to here with Cassie's backbiting these days, so you don't have to worry about not getting to go. She'll *never* back down from sending you now."

I tried on a triumphant smile for size. The lump that had taken hold in the pit of my stomach let me know this was a Pyrrhic victory.

Five minutes later the sound of Cassie's slamming office door rattled the building's foundation. It looked like I was West Coast bound.

The moment Fleishman got wind of my upcoming conference trip, he was beside himself. "I want to go!"

"Where?"

"To Oregon."

"Fleish, you can't go on my business trip."

He looked bewildered. "Why not?"

I craned my head toward him. "Because it's *my* job."

"But I've helped!"

I couldn't deny that. Fleishman had become a little manic about reading romance novels—especially after learning how much Rita and everyone had liked *Heartstopper*. The week before I had even found him perusing the latest edition of *Romance Journal*, a glossy monthly that I had never known existed before I started working at Candlelight. The *Journal* was full of romance author interviews, profiles of the latest hottie cover models, and dispatches from the publisher, a woman from Bethlehem, Pennsylvania, named Peggy Murfin, who in the June 1989 issue of *Romance Journal* had mystifyingly transformed into Marguerite, Contessa of Longchamps. She wrote a column detailing her travels and her brushes with celebrity, and plugging her perfume line, *Contessa*, which she apparently gave away as professional courtesy gifts. I had found three bottles of the stuff, plus a tube of the body lotion, stashed around my office.

The bulk of the magazine, though, was devoted to brief book reviews in which practically every book published under the umbrella of women's fiction was given a rating of one to five kissy lips. According to authors, those lips could make or break a career. I'd had one woman call me in hysterics over getting a one kissy review—in romance review terms, the kiss-off. I had a hard time convincing her not to file suit.

How had Fleishman even found out about the *Journal?*

"Look, you're scaring me. I'm grateful for all your interest, but it's my job."

"But I *need* to go."

Was he nuts? "Why would you need to go to a romance conference in Oregon?"

He folded his arms. "I just do."

There was more to this than what he was telling me. "Fleish . . ."

He lifted his chin. "Well, if you must know, I haven't been idling away my days while you've been at work. I've been at work, too. Writing a play."

So? He was always writing a play.

And then it hit me. This was a new play. About Candlelight Books.

About my job.

"A play!" I stood back, aghast. This was worse than I could have imagined. Fleishman was going to write some horrible play making fun of romance writers; by some fluke it would be produced, become a Broadway hit, and I would be fired. *That's why he wants to go to the conference.* To find material to write a play that would wind up deep-sixing my career.

"No way," I said. "You can't do that."

"Why not? It'll be funny."

Funny. Oh God.

"No, that's not right," he said, bobbing his head to one side in thought. "It will be more than just funny. I want to tell all sides of the story, not just the lampoony cartoon side that people think of when they imagine romance writers. I mean, these writers are pros, Rebecca."

"Yes, I know." I bit my lip.

"Well, did you know that romances are forty-eight percent of paperback book sales? Did you know those sales amount to over one billion dollars each year?"

"Where did you hear this?" I asked.

"Off the RAG Web site."

How did he even know about RAG?

He shook his head in apparent wonder. "The most interesting thing is, most of these authors didn't even set out to be authors. They didn't attend graduate writing programs in Iowa. They started out as nurses, or lawyers, or teachers, and then just started writing because they had this burning urge to tell a story. I mean, that's astounding. You don't hear about people becoming concert violinists after being nurses, do you?"

"I don't think—"

"Yet these women manage to write their way into new careers, and hit the *New York Times* Bestseller List! If you hear their stories, a lot of them have had to spend years writing before being published, working before everyone else in the family is awake, or after putting the kids to sleep. They had to steal time to teach themselves to write. Some of the most famous writers spent years getting manuscripts rejected, but they kept going. It's amazing!"

"Right, but—"

"The thing is, everybody dismisses these books. Like there's some kind of formula. But the formula's no different from a mystery, or a sci-fi book. The formula is the author's own creativity. Plus time. Plus determination."

I gave up trying to interrupt him. He seemed possessed.

"Can't you see?" he asked. "I really need to go."

"You don't *need* to do anything but chill out," I argued. "I'm sure you could write a fine play, Fleishman, but going to Oregon is out of the question. I don't know a lot about business, but taking your roommate along to a writer's conference doesn't sound professional to me."

He sighed. "Well could you take some notes? I know—I'll give you a tape recorder. You can tape record people's conversations for me."

"No! I'm not going to spy on these people. They're paying my way, you know."

"My God, you're a killjoy."

"And you're a pain in the ass." It had been a while since we'd had a fight like this. Once he got an idea in his head, he could buzz on incessantly about it, like a whiny mosquito.

"I thought you were still working on *Yule Be Sorry,*" I said, trying to change the subject.

"You didn't want me to write that play, either."

No, I didn't. But now it sounded pretty good. If Fleishman humiliated my family on stage, they could disown me, but they couldn't fire me.

Chapter 8

"Hello, Miss Plot Expert!"

When I heard Dan's voice on the phone, I swiveled in my chair and kicked my office door closed. Down the hall, Mercedes's assistant, Lisa, was singing "Stormy Weather" again. She had a great voice but a limited repertoire. This was the tenth time I'd heard it today.

Plus, I wanted privacy. "What are you talking about?" I asked Dan.

"Check your e-mail. They just sent out the weekend schedule for Romance on the River."

My spine was suddenly ramrod straight. "Are *you* going to the Portland conference, too?"

"You betcha."

If there had been any confetti handy, I would have thrown it. I had a schoolgirl crush on Dan Weatherby. That bedroom voice and that super schmooziness of his were hard to resist. In the most offhand way possible, I had asked Andrea about his looks and his marital status, and she had burst out laughing.

"If you didn't skip lunch so often, you would know from lunchroom scuttlebutt that you aren't the first person in this office to ask that question."

"And the answer is . . . ?"

"Yes, he's good looking—like a soap opera actor. Early thirties. Divorced."

"So he's . . ."

"Up for grabs, apparently." Then she leveled a forbidding look on me. "Unlike Mr. Incredible the elevator man, who of course is mine. But as far as Dan is concerned, you go, girl. I haven't heard of him squiring anyone around for months."

"*Months?*"

"Yeah, he's a little bit of a lothario. Rumor has it that he broke poor Clea Shafransky's heart. Clea was an associate in the Hearthsong pod. She got sort of cozy with him. Then, right after a conference in Minneapolis where Dan was spotted flirting with an editor from Venus books, she left publishing altogether, moved back home to Buffalo, and opened a knitting store."

"So it wasn't clear that it was actually Dan's fault."

"The evidence was inconclusive," Andrea admitted, "but damning."

It was hard to keep poor Clea Shafransky out of my head when I was talking to Dan now. It was equally difficult to banish the phrase "up for grabs."

"Imagine my surprise." He chuckled. "I thought Rita was going."

"Her niece is getting married."

"Oh, so she's not losing a conference, she's gaining a nephew."

I laughed. Too hard—I'll admit it. A throaty chortle just burbled out of me, caused not so much by Dan's dumb joke as by the confidentially husky tone he spoke in.

"Look, I was going to have drinks with Rita at the conference . . . are you filling in on her social engagements, too?"

Zing went the strings of my heart. "I'm always willing to take someone's place at the bar."

"Actually, I was thinking that since we've never had a face-to-face, we should make it a little more festive. There's an old seafood restaurant in downtown Portland . . . and if you weren't doing anything on Saturday night . . ."

I tapped my pen on my desk and counted to five, pretending to check my calendar. Which, had I looked, would have been as wide open and windy as the Great Plains. "Hm . . . that looks very doable."

"Great—then it's a date?"

"It's a date," I said.

My first in six months. Of course it wasn't really a date. Just a professional business meeting. At night. In a strange city. Just the two of us.

What was I going to wear? Suddenly, all my speech worries and death-in-a-fiery-crash flashes seemed insignificant next to wardrobe woes.

It's not a date, I repeated to myself, while at the same time thinking that my shoe situation was going to be the real crux of my problem. I could keep on wearing Fleishman's mom's clothes (it would help if I stopped eating dinner and maybe breakfast, too), but my scuffed old shoes would show me up as a failed fashion aspirant.

My hair could use some touching up, too.

I started making a list of all the things I wanted. (Shoes, haircut, new bra, soft-sided briefcase like Ann's.) Then, on the other side of the legal pad, I started a list of all the money I didn't have, despite my higher salary: rent, credit card bill to pay off, and next month was my turn to pay the cable bill. I'd paid it this month, too, because Fleishman was broke.

I dumped the idea of wowing the romance writers of Portland with a new soft-sided briefcase. Or fashion footwear. Frankly, I was already in the red when I started trying to figure a way to shoehorn a new bra into my budget.

Damn. A few days ago I'd felt rich. Where did all my money go?

I tried to make myself forget shopping. This was just a business trip; I didn't need anything new. And after what Andrea had said about Dan, it was clear that he was just a romance industry Romeo. I shouldn't take a little thing like dinner with him seriously.

But a little voice kept niggling me. *So don't take him seriously. Have yourself a cheap tawdry fling.*

Maybe that would flush Fleishman out of my system.

Andrea flew into my office, shut the door, and collapsed into my chair. Her arms were folded across her chest, which was heaving indignantly.

"What's wrong?"

"I just had my review!"

"Didn't it go well?"

"Oh, terrific—they gave me a one point five percent raise! It's the lowest raise they give! And to me, of all people. I've been slaving away at this place most of my working life. *Damn it!*"

"Rita did this?"

"Yes! Oh, she tried to fob it off as something Mercedes and Mary Jo had dictated—she did look a little embarrassed to be treating me so shabbily—but come on. She's a senior editor! She should be going to bat for me."

"Did Mercedes give any reasons?"

Andrea snorted. "She said I have *personality issues!* She told Rita I should take an anger management class."

"Hm."

"What?" Her eyes flashed at me. "Do you think I have anger issues?"

"No!" I answered quickly, before she could bite my head off.

It looked like she might anyway. All at once she leaned over, opened the door, and screeched, "Will you please give 'Stormy Weather' a rest, Lisa? *Jesus!*" Then she slammed the door again and turned back to me.

I tried to look calm even as I shrank back in my chair.

"They always talk about how there's no employee loyalty anymore," she continued without missing a beat, "but let me tell you. It's these management types that drive us out. I *have* to find another job now," Andrea fumed. "They're forcing me out. This is just outrageous."

"I'm sorry."

She frowned at my notepad. "What are you doing?"

"My budget."

"Do all those little minus signs mean no money?"

"Unfortunately."

She clucked. "Oh well. Hang on for another ten months, and maybe you'll get a whopping one and a half percent raise, too!"

"What should I wear to a RAG conference?"

She shrugged. "Wear your office clothes. That's what they want—to see a professional in their midst."

I hesitated. "Well, yeah . . . but then there's the matter of going out to dinner and things, right?"

"Dinner? With authors? Don't worry about it! They won't expect you to be dressed to the nines."

"Well, actually . . ." I confessed to my rendezvous with Dan.

Andrea straightened in her chair. "Dinner? It's usually just drinks. Maybe he really likes you!"

"He's never met me."

"So? You haven't seen him, either." She looked pointedly at my black pumps, which I think might have been the ones I wore to my college graduation. "You need some new shoes."

I groaned. "Impossible."

She narrowed her eyes on my messy columns of numbers. "What's that?"

"That's what I owe Discover."

"And what's your credit limit?"

"Five thousand three hundred dollars."

Her eyes widened; she really looked stunned. "Well then, what's the problem?"

"I've been trying to pay it off, not run up more debt."

"So you have to make the minimum payments for a while. Wouldn't it be worth it? For Dan the man?"

"It's just a business meeting," I repeated, fooling neither of us.

"Bloomingdale's is having a summer preview sale this week."

My head snapped up.

"You want to go during lunch?" she asked.

"I shouldn't," I said.

But I did.

For a week I kept my loot at the office. The corner next to my file cabinet became a cache of MasterCard enabled plunder. It wasn't that I was hiding anything . . . I just told myself I was too lazy to lug it on the subway. Besides, there was always the chance I would suffer buyer's remorse and want to return something, so why haul it all the way to Brooklyn if I was going to have to bring it back to Manhattan?

But of course I never did return anything. And finally, just before the conference, I realized I would have to carry it home. All of it.

I left the office that day looking like an upscale bag lady.

All the way home, I prayed Fleishman would be out. Even that he would have a date.

But when I walked in, he was eating a bowl of noodles and watching reruns of *Felicity* on WE. The minute he saw me, he snapped the television off by remote.

"Don't let me interrupt," I said. I meant it. All I wanted to do was sneak back to my bedroom and shove all my new stuff under my bed.

"It's okay," he replied. "I know the ending. She starts out an idiot, and she remains an idiot."

He was standing now, circling me to inspect the names on the bags. I have to confess, my little spree went a teensy bit beyond Bloomingdale's. I had taken in quite a few Upper East Side emporiums on my lunch hours after Andrea convinced me that I was letting a generous credit limit go to waste.

"I just ran into a few sales . . ."

He lifted a bag from an expensive luggage store and peeked inside. Letting out a long whistle, he pulled out my new soft sided leather briefcase. "What's this for?"

"I'm going on a business trip, remember?" I turned and

hurried toward my room to sock away my stuff, dropping a shoe box in my wake.

"Manolo Blahnik? For a business trip?"

"I hadn't bought shoes in a while," I said, as if this explained anything.

He was right on my heels, eyeballing the familiar logo on one of the smaller bags. "An upcoming business trip also required you to go to Victoria's Secret?"

I glared at him. "I'm going to be giving a speech. I want to have all-over confidence."

"And where did you get the money for all this?"

"I charged it." Looking at all the bags on my bed now, I was a little astounded with myself. What had seemed like booty from a modest spree when it was shoved into a corner of my office now looked like shameful excess when strewn across my bed. *Good heavens, what had I done?*

He shook his head. "My God, I always expected you to cut loose someday. But I never expected this."

"I have a good job. It's not like I won't be able to cover it . . ." Unbidden, an image appeared in my mind of wild-eyed Andrea scrawling out her debts and her minimum payments across a pad of paper. What on earth had made me listen to *her?*

"Your salary pays for sprees at Bendels?"

The Bendels bag was tiny. "I didn't go on a spree there. I just bought a . . ." Come to think of it, I couldn't even remember *what* I had bought there. I peeked into the sack. "Oh! A scarf. Just a scarf."

He pulled it out. At the time I bought it, with Andrea egging me on, it had seemed like a steal at $69.95. It was longer than I remembered . . . and it had sparkly things on it that hadn't really seemed so prominent in the store, but here in the apartment it looked garish. Like I was flying out west to become a Vegas showgirl.

It dragged on the ground, and Maxwell confused it for a new doggie bed. He promptly plopped his little rear down on it.

Fleishman took in a big breath and then, to show his forbearance, did not huff it out in one impatient sigh. "You know, it's understandable that when you've never had a salaried job before, you might go overboard with the spending at first." Suddenly he was Ward Cleaver. "But you know, Rebecca, just because there's money coming in doesn't mean you can throw economy out the window."

I couldn't believe it. This was *Fleishman* talking. The man who went out one afternoon to grab a slice of pizza and came back an hour later with a plasma screen television.

My face must have been turning purple, because he added, "It's nothing to be embarrassed about. You just have to watch it."

That was my limit. "I'm not embarrassed, I'm mad. Where do you get off telling *me* to economize? You've probably never made out a budget in your life."

He looked offended. "Of course I have. I budget all the time. I just do it stealthily. I don't walk around announcing to the world that I'm poor."

"Neither do I," I said.

He raised his brows. Okay, maybe I did.

"Besides," I sputtered, "you're *not* poor!"

He leveled a probing gaze on me. "This is not about me, is it?"

"What?"

"This argument. You feel guilty, and so you're taking it out on me."

For a moment, he stopped me cold. He was right, in his usual twisted way. I yanked the scarf out from under Maxwell and started folding it. Then I tossed it in my drawer. "I just don't like being lectured."

"Is there maybe something you're leaving out of this discussion?" he asked.

I slammed the door shut. "What do you mean?"

"Like, maybe there's some really studly guy from Candlelight going to the conference with you?"

That was a laugh. "There is no great looking guy at Candlelight. No straight ones, anyway. Except the mailroom guy, and I don't think he travels."

But really, it was eerie how close Fleishman had come to the truth. It worried me. Was I that easy to read, or did he know me too well?

"Some other guy, then." He gestured grandly to all the stuff still spread across the bed. "This can't all be for the benefit of the romance writers of Portland, Oregon. I can believe you would pace around nights working on your speech for them, but I don't think you would be restocking your panty supply for their benefit."

I should have ditched the Victoria's Secret bag, obviously. Damn.

I decided to confess. Why shouldn't I? "All right. There is going to be a good looking guy there, but I've never even met this person. I've only talked to him on the phone. His name's Dan Weatherby. He's sort of flirty, but I think he flirts with everybody."

"He's a romance writer?"

"He's an agent."

Fleishman sank down onto the bed and drummed his fingers on his thigh.

"It's not that I'm hoping to *seduce* some guy at this conference," I said in my defense. "It's just that I suddenly realized I need to think a little bit about presentation. I went from college to running around doing errands for an old lady for two years. And now I'm supposed to go in front of a hotel full of people and pass myself off as a professional."

He gnawed his lip for a moment. "You're right. Maybe we haven't given this enough thought."

"We . . . *what?*"

"You . . . the conference . . ." He tilted a glance up at me. "What are you going to wear on the plane?"

"I don't know. Something comfortable."

He imitated a game show buzzer. "Wrong. You're going to go from the airport to the conference. It's not as if you'll be changing outfits in the airport bathroom when you get there. You have to look good on the plane, too."

He was right again. It was so irritating.

"And what if this Dan Weatherby person is on the same flight?" he asked. "Did you ever think about that?"

"No." So he didn't mind about Dan Weatherby? A few minutes ago, when he'd been pressing me to explain the shopping spree, he'd seemed jealous.

"Portland, Oregon, is not exactly the travel destination of choice for millions," he said. "And if you're talking direct flights, which I assume anyone in their right mind with an expense account would opt for, your choices really shrink."

How does he know so much about airline flights to the West Coast? I wondered briefly. But he might have been talking out his butt, for all I knew. Fleishman could playact all sorts of expertise he didn't have.

I was just glad he was back to behaving like a reasonable creature. In fact, he was being helpful. There was no more whining about wanting to go on my trip. I had just intended to wait till tonight and toss as much as I possibly could into a suitcase and hope I was prepared. Fleishman insisted I go through the process more methodically, planning everything I needed down to the last earring.

I know, I know. I was twenty-five years old and my roommate was teaching me how to pack. On the other hand, I needed to learn.

He was worried about the dress I had bought to have dinner with Dan Weatherby. "This is low cut. Are you sure this is going to project the proper business image?"

"I needed something nice for evenings."

"There's always Natasha's Mainbocher." He was still a little incensed that I hadn't taken a shine to that purple and teal dress.

"It's a thing of beauty, I know, but I wanted something new. I can't go through life looking like a Jackie O wannabe."

"Okay—but you know it gets cold out there. You'll need a jacket to go with this—it gets down into the forties at night."

How did he come up with this stuff?

"Okay, Mom. I'll bring my sweater."

"Have you practiced your speech?"

"I'm still working on it."

He shook his head. "You'd better get that done. That way you can memorize it on the plane."

"*Memorize* it?" I squeaked.

"Of course." He blinked. "You just can't get up there and *read* a speech. This isn't going to be a radio address, you know. You have to outline what you want to say on notecards and work from those."

"Right." My God. I hadn't thought of doing the whole thing by memory. I had sort of expected to have the speech in front of me. Damn.

With this new worry to add to the already mounting pile, I sat down with a legal pad and started jotting down notes on plot. Fleish, seemingly satisfied with all his accomplishments, went back to watching television. "When are you going out with this guy?" he asked.

"Saturday night."

"That's good. Your speech will be over."

"Right." I was living for that moment, actually.

"Where's he taking you?"

"Some place downtown. Seafood."

"Jake's."

I lifted my head. "How do you know?"

"It's the most famous seafood restaurant in Portland. It's been there forever."

He made it sound like Dan was taking me to a clam shack. Now I knew he was bullshitting. I went back to my speech.

Fleishman went back to the television.

Everything seemed just fine.

For a while I can usually fool myself into thinking that I'll be okay. Airline travel? No big deal.

Hundreds of thousands of people step onto planes every

day, strap themselves in, and get flown to their destinations without a single mishap. Their planes are not hijacked. Or blown up in midair. Their planes do not experience electrical fires at fifty thousand feet, causing them to spiral and then plunge to the ground with their cargo of shrieking passengers. On descent, they do not hit that fatal patch of windsheer that turns an almost successfully completed trip into a nightmare of stomach roiling panic and then terror in a screeching jolt of metal hitting runway, metal being torn asunder, and screams of hundreds of people in their last horrible moments of life.

Hardly ever happens. Hurricanes in Halifax.

I'm not scared, not scared, not scared.

The morning of my flight, I was all confidence. I ate a big breakfast with Fleishman, who insisted I needed pancakes. ("Airlines never feed you anymore. You'll endure five hours of starvation.") I scarfed down way too much, then I took the shuttle out to Newark and just had enough time to buy a new pen and some note cards at 200 percent markup at an airport newsstand.

I could smile at the well-groomed airline lady who took my boarding pass and sent it spitting through the electronic scanner. With an almost insouciant nonchalance, I strode through the twisty carpeted tube that leads to the plane. I was a trooper. My new soft-sided calfskin briefcase, practically empty, was slung jauntily over one shoulder.

And then I stepped on the plane and my knees wobbled. The flight attendant greeted me. I experienced a brief flash of her being sucked out of the plane. Then I shook my head. *That never happens.*

The queue of passengers was shuffling along past first class, where men in suits were already staring at their Powerbooks and drinking Bloody Marys. I've never flown in first class. I probably never will. But that's okay, because I've heard it's really the most dangerous part of the plane to be in the event of a crash. I shook my head. Those poor oblivious men with their laptops and booze. *Enjoy it while you can, chumps.*

The line slowed as I neared my strategically chosen seat

(rear centerish, on the aisle). The plane was starting to feel stuffy. There was no more overhead room left in this area, and people were getting aggravated. They were sputtering. Someone asked for a pillow, and a flight attendant called from the back that there were no pillows anymore. *Your comfort is no longer factored into our business model*, she might have said.

Or, *This is a flying cattle car. Get over it.*

I was finally able to flop down in my seat. God, it felt uncomfortable. I shouldn't have eaten so much. Or worn such a tight skirt. Fleishman's short stack was straining against my waistband.

Luck was with me in one respect—the other person on my row, the person next to the window, was already seated, so there would be no awkward hopping up and letting her squeeze by me. I decided that the best way to avoid brooding over whether this flight was going to mark the end of my tragically short life was to get right to work. I pulled the conference schedule and the legal pad with my speech on it out of my briefcase.

"That's where I'm going," my seatmate announced.

I glanced up. Did she mean Portland? We were all going to Portland. (Fleishman was right. This was the only direct flight there was.)

She tapped on the schedule. "That's me. Alison Rooney, from Gazelle."

I took a closer look. Alison Rooney was in her forties, with dark brown hair (dyed—her roots showed), and deep lines around her mouth. It looked as if she had been pursing her lips for twenty years.

"I'm Rebecca Abbot. I'm with Candlelight."

Her dark brows pinched together. "I've never heard of you."

"I just started two months ago. I work with Rita."

She rolled her eyes. "Oh, that poor thing!" A laugh barked out of her. "Of course I love Rita—everybody does—but she was an editor when *I* was there."

"You worked at Candlelight?"

"*Everybody* has done time at that place. Or maybe it just seems that way."

Just then, there was a rumble and a roar as the plane's engines fired up. Little screens came down and the airline safety video was played. I tried to pay attention—had anyone in the history of aviation ever successfully used a seat cushion as a flotation device?—but Alison Rooney was chatting away next to me.

"Do you know Maris?"

"Who?" I worried about those oxygen masks. How often were those checked? What if mine didn't come down?

"Jesus Christ, if you work on Pulse books, you must know Maris Godfrey."

I scanned my brain. I was bad with putting names to faces, but I was pretty sure I had never seen the name Maris on an employee list. Alison insisted I should have.

"Oh no! Scratch that. She's some muckety-muck at NAL now." Alison shrugged. "It's this neverending game of editorial musical chairs. You lose track of people. Where did you work before?"

"This is my first job in publishing."

"Well it won't be your last!"

Not unless the plane goes down and I can't make it to the emergency door. Too late, I realized I should have chosen an exit row.

The plane was taxiing, and the flight attendants were doing their last sprint to make sure all of our seats were upright.

"What did you do before?" Alison asked.

"Nothing—that is, I was sort of a private assistant." That didn't sound very good. "To an author."

"Oh, interesting!"

"Actually . . ." The plane stopped and the engines revved again. My heart tripped, and then my breath started coming in gasps. Sweat beaded on my upper lip.

Alison Rooney's face loomed closer. "Are you okay?"

I nodded quickly and offered her a limp smile. "Takeoffs are the worst." There was always the chance that you could hit an air pocket, too, caused by the wakes of other planes taking off. That could be fatal.

"You don't look too good."

"It's fine . . . I'll be fine . . ."

"Are you faint?"

"Just a little nauseous."

"Oh God." That voice, so clipped and self-assured just moments before, developed a quaver. Alison rifled through the magazines and safety cards in the pocket of the seatback in front of her. "Dammit, have they gotten rid of barf bags, too?"

"Barf . . . ?"

I lifted hand to my mouth. The plane lifted in a deafening roar. Feeling a new urgency, I, too, began thumbing past magazines and in-flight catalogs, but came up empty. *How could this be?*

As if things weren't bad enough, the plane chose that moment to dip, and then to roll. Maybe it was just turning slightly. Adjusting course. Happened all the time. But that didn't matter to my stomach. A wave of clammy heat hit me, and I felt Fleishman's big breakfast climbing back up my esophagus.

"Oh no," I moaned.

Alison Rooney saw the problem immediately, and the solution. "Here!"

She grabbed my soft-sided briefcase out of my lap, undid the top flap, upended the papers and pens out of it, then held it open for me.

See? I knew that briefcase would come in handy.

Chapter 9

Here's a word of advice: If you're a bad public speaker, and you haven't given a speech since high school anyway, *do not* listen to those who tell you it is amateurish to bring a copy of your speech with you to the lectern. Do not simply prepare a sheet of paper with talking points. Do not rely solely on note cards. That is a recipe for disaster.

I did not realize this, of course, until I was right smack in the middle of my own disaster. I stared at the talking points I had scrawled on the notepad, trying to make sense of them. For instance:

A. PLOT ENGINE!!
i. Toyota
ii. Ford Pinto

At one point, maybe back when I was in my hotel room sucking down minibar vodka, those notes had made some kind of sense to me. I think I was trying to say something about how a plot was supposed to be the motor that moved the story along. And that a good plot was like driving a Toyota—taking you dependably to the end of the story. And then there were those Ford Pinto plots that would blow up on you. Ha. Ha.

Now, in my slightly hungover state, listening to my trembly

voice vapor on through this nonsense, staring into the eyes of about thirty women, I had my doubts. This wasn't the Latvia speech; my audience wasn't asleep. They were sizing me up. They were frowning. Their brows were furrowed.

These women were writers. What was I doing up here telling them how to *write?* I had never written a novel. Never attempted it.

I had never owned a car, either.

A wave of overwhelming certainty hit me, though: I needed to get off that podium.

"And if any of this seems confusing—or if all of it does—I would be happy to take questions now," I concluded in a rush.

There.

My audience seemed surprised, and no wonder. A few people looked up at the clock. My speech, which was supposed to be twenty minutes, was about fourteen minutes too short.

"Any questions?" I asked.

Thirty pairs of eyes blinked at me. No one had a question. These guys were cold.

I couldn't just stand there and say nothing. "Of course, there are some things . . . for instance, you should never start a chapter with the words *Nine months went by . . .*"

In the tremulous pause that followed my voice petering out, I could hear the hand on the clock behind me clicking away the seconds. Sweat trickled down my back.

"And don't use adverbs," I blurted out.

"Wait!" someone from the back belted out in exasperation. "You're telling us not to use *adverbs?* We're supposed to ignore entire parts of speech?"

Grumbling began.

"Yeah—and what if nine months *do* go by?" another writer said.

Just when I thought I would have to slink off the stage in failure—or maybe run for my life—a hand shot up. "What if your plot is a Lexus and it still breaks down?" a woman asked me.

Laughter rippled through the group, defusing a little of the tension. Unfortunately they were now waiting for an answer.

I didn't have one.

Shit. I swallowed. "I guess you would . . ." I looked down at my overpriced notecards. I'd already used up all my talking points. My stomach turned. I was the cartoon coyote who had just run off the cliff—suspended in the blue, waiting for gravity to yank me down.

And my mind was a complete blank.

"Well . . . I would say . . ."

"*Find a good mechanic, Mary!*" some wiseacre called out.

There was more laughter. But in that moment, I wondered if that smart aleck in the audience had just tossed me a lifeline. "Actually . . ." I began, speaking slowly so I would eat up more time, ". . . that's true. When you're sure what you've got is solid but it still doesn't seem to be working, the best thing to do is consult someone who knows what they're talking about. Someone you can trust. Your critique group, for instance. Or your best writer buddy."

Heads nodded. It was the first time in ten minutes that something I said made sense.

In the blink of an eye, a realization hit me. These writers didn't need technical advice from the likes of me. There were editors who could probably hold them in thrall on the subject of plot for hours; I wasn't one of them. I was just a messenger from New York. All I had to offer was encouragement.

I drew a breath. "You know, I could stand up here all day and talk about writing, but you know better than I do that every story is individual. There's *no formula*—we've all heard that, right? *What's the formula for writing a romance novel?* People ask that all the time."

Heads bobbed indignantly.

"And there is a formula, but it's not what people think. The only formula is your own creativity."

Someone whooped.

"Plus dedication."

God, I was channeling Fleishman. But it was working. People were nodding now, and I'd heard a spontaneous clap from the back.

"Plus time," I said. "You know—that time that some of you steal to write early in the morning, before the kids go to school. Or late at night, after the kids are asleep."

By the end of the question and answer session, after I had delivered practically all of Fleishman's talking points, I practically had them on their feet. I felt like a preacher at a revival meeting. When I stepped down from the podium, people were applauding me in earnest and smiling at me. A few women came over to talk to me.

An elderly lady with short iron-gray hair reached out to shake my hand. "Aren't you the girl who vomited on the plane yesterday?"

I had to admit I was. "I get airsick."

"Bless your heart!" a woman standing next to her said. "And that's a long flight, too."

It's even longer when you've splattered your breakfast all over your seatmate, I could have told them.

"Then you came here and gave such a wonderful speech!"

Wonderful speech? I wanted to weep in gratitude. The little coterie gathered around me smiled and nodded, sweeping me up on a wave of love.

I left that conference room—the same one I walked into forty minutes earlier with all the enthusiasm of a convict walking the last mile—feeling about ten feet tall. My new shoes, ghastly uncomfortable things, carried me along as if I were walking on clouds. I was elated. I was not a complete failure, after all.

Barbara Simmons, the organizer of the conference, who, I had sensed on my arrival, had been disappointed that I had been sent as a substitute for Rita, flagged me down across the hotel lobby. "Jennifer, I heard you were *just great*."

I smiled awkwardly. "Actually . . ."

"Your speech is getting raves."

A man joined us. He was about six feet, which made him

loom conspicuously above most of the other people around him. He had sandy blond hair and wore a snappy gray suit with a blue tie over a blue shirt. (The blue brought out the blue in his eyes, which were hard to look away from.) When he smiled, his teeth were pearly white and perfect.

"Who's this?" he asked.

His voice went through me like a bolt.

"This is Jennifer Abbot."

Those blue eyes widened. "*Rebecca?*"

Oh my God. Of course I knew that voice. Dan Weatherby. He really *did* look like a soap star.

My knees went weak. *Sweet Jesus, I'm having dinner with* that*?*

Never in my life had I been so glad to have all new underwear.

The rest of the day felt like I was at summer camp. I had one activity after another to attend to—appointments and luncheons and a group session with editors from other houses where we all sat in a line and answered fairly softball questions from authors. Other than a pointed joke from Alison Rooney about wanting to keep a safe distance from me on the dais, I felt swept along through the day by the current of camaraderie.

Andrea had gotten me quite nervous. She could be a little combative towards authors as a species—she was that way toward everyone, actually—but she had me convinced that I would really have to watch myself. "You can't even use public bathrooms at those conferences without having an author slide a manuscript at you under the stall door. They're *animals*."

But honestly. I went to the bathroom five times (nerves) completely without incident. The only conversation that took place in a restroom was when an author offered me a spritz of her perfume. It was *Contessa!* That stuff got around.

I was beginning to like the smell of it, too.

Still, all through the day, butterflies fluttered around my stomach. This, of course, had nothing to do with authors or chicken breast luncheons and everything to do with the fact I was going out with Dan Weatherby that evening. I kept ticking off the minutes, like a countdown.

Seven hours.

Five and a half hours.

Now that I knew what he looked like, I kept seeing him everywhere. He was hard to miss. He loomed over everyone. Plus he had that halo of blond hair. (Dyed or naturally sun bleached? Hard to tell.) And that smile with teeth so white they occasionally seemed to glint off the fluorescent lighting in the hotel. He was sitting at the next table from me during the luncheon, and I could occasionally hear that husky, sexy laugh of his, which would cause a frisson of anticipation in me that was wholly inappropriate for business.

Four hours and forty-five minutes.

The only downside to the afternoon was sitting next to Cynthia Schmidt, Cassie's favorite author, at this luncheon. I had a whole table of Candlelight authors around me, but Cynthia dominated my attention. "I drove in from Medford last night," she informed me. "I have the room right next to yours, I noticed."

That disarmed me a little. I wasn't aware that my room was being watched. "How did you notice?"

"I volunteered with the hospitality committee to put the goody bag in your room."

All visiting editors and agents got a little totebag stuffed with books from Oregon writers and author promotional material like bookmarks, pens, and notepads advertising their Web sites, and my personal favorite, a chocolate bar with an author's recent book cover as the label. I was saving the goody bag to bring back to Fleishman as a souvenir. He would be over the moon.

"You all have done so much," I said, hoping to draw some others in. "I've never been in the position of feeling like a VIP before."

"That's right." Cynthia craned a tight smile up at me. "Cassie told me it was your first conference."

"It is," I admitted, trying to pretend I wasn't feeling the frosty vibes.

"Well, I thought it was very gracious of her to let you come in Rita's place."

My jaw nearly went off its hinges. *Let me come?* What kind of delusional crap was Cassie feeding her authors now? I was tempted to announce that Cassie had never been scheduled to fill in for Rita, and that Cassie's graciousness was all in her own fevered little salutatorian brain.

"But that's Cassie all over, isn't it?" Cynthia remarked.

I could tell that my answer was going to be relayed back to New York sometime very soon. I swallowed, smiled, and though it nearly killed me, gushed, "Yes! Cassie's one of a kind!"

I decided I should double check my goody bag for explosives.

Even though I met Darlene Paige, the other Cassie author from Oregon, at the luncheon, she had scheduled an editor-author appointment with me. These appointments were usually for unpublished authors to talk about a story to an editor; given fifteen minutes to pitch their life's work to an actual warm body from New York, most authors were so nervous they were no more adept at explaining their stories than I had been lecturing on plot. With just a few months on the job, I really didn't feel like I had earned the right to make anyone nervous.

To put them at their ease, I told one and all that I would love to see what they had, even the woman who came in to pitch a story called *The Reluctant Vampire*, the main conflict of which was that the title character, an emergency surgery anesthesiologist, had to spend his nights looking at the exposed necks of unconscious people and hiding his true nature from his colleagues, including a sexy female heart surgeon.

Because she was an established author, Darlene Paige didn't come with a pitch. She seemed nervous, though. She was all apologies for having dumped me. Which really wasn't all that comforting when it came down to it. I tried to be understanding, even though I had been given the hot potato treatment.

"Of course," she said, "I have no complaints. Cassie's been so nice . . ."

"Yeah, she's one of a kind."

Darlene's smile quavered. "She *is* a doll, but . . ."

I leaned forward. "But what?"

"Well . . . when I was working with Julie, she always seemed more enthusiastic, if you know what I mean."

I didn't. I didn't let on, though. "I never met Julie."

"Oh! That's right." Darlene's cheeks went pink at the reminder that I was the person who had replaced Julie, who she had deemed not good enough. "Well! The thing is, Julie always said that Candlelight saw me as someone to build up. You know, to be given a continuing series, maybe with some special covers . . . maybe with my name in puffy lettering."

"Puffy?" I hadn't heard of this before.

"You know," she said, "the raised kind."

"Oh!"

"With foil," she added quickly.

I nodded. If this woman thought she was going to get foil lettering on a category series book, she was living in la-la-land. Foil was expensive, and therefore meted out like dwindling rations on a lifeboat. I knew this because Rita and I worked on Troy to put red foil lettering on *Heartstopper.* He had agreed, but only after weeks of cajoling, and because *Heartstopper* was going to be the launch book for the revamped Pulse.

"Right now I've got this amnesia trilogy for the Flame line called *Forgotten Grooms,*" Darlene went on, "and it just doesn't seem like anything special is being done for it."

"That's a shame." Sounded like Miss Cassie wasn't doing right by her authors. Evil thoughts did a little fire dance in my head.

I am not a vindictive person by nature. I am not the type to escalate tensions.

But this was too tempting.

"Actually, I always find it refreshing to have authors be proactive in these matters," I said.

Darlene's head tilted slightly. "Proactive? But what could I do?"

I looked at my watch. "It's cocktail hour. Could I treat you to a drink, and we could discuss it?"

It wouldn't hurt to give her a few ideas. Just a few.

After my pow-wow with Darlene, I was able to escape to my room. I was actually considering taking a nap, but the minute I was alone I found myself with a bad case of the jitters. Which was ridiculous.

Just a business dinner, I reminded myself.

That sexy smile, my irrational brain countered. *That husky laugh.*

I soaked in the tub until the skin was ready to fall off my bones. There was something wonderfully decadent about having a hotel room all to myself. A startling fact occurred to me: This was one of the few times in my life when I had been alone. Really alone. Growing up, I had never been by myself. In college I had always had roommates, a trend that continued when Fleishman and Wendy and I picked up to move to New York together.

And now here I was. Solo. I had all the privacy I'd ever dreamed of. To celebrate, I stewed in suds for another ten minutes. I also sang to myself—"Oh What a Beautiful Mornin'." The bathroom had great acoustics. I had never been able to sing in the bathtub before without someone banging on the door or shouting "Spare us!" Granted, this had as much to do with my puny voice and tone deafness as it did with privacy concerns, but now I felt as alone and as free as if I were marooned on a desert island. As an encore, I performed "Somewhere Over the Rainbow" for the water spout. And I must say, if Judy Garland had done it my way, she could have gone back to being plain old Frances Gumm and saved herself a lot of grief.

I left my hotel room feeling pretty good, actually. My new dress fit me perfectly—I really did have all-over confidence. And because it's not like me to have even partial, localized confidence, I was savoring the moment.

I had just closed my door and was heading for the elevator

when the door of the room next to mine opened and out popped Cynthia. I flashed a big smile at her. Her lips tilted up more tentatively. *All right*, I thought, feeling cocky. *Be that way*. We stepped onto the elevator and punched the L button. It was a chilly ride down.

The lobby was full of people, and most of them looked like romance writers. I wasn't expecting that. Technically, the conference was over, but most of the industry people from New York were in the hotel until Sunday morning, when they would fly out.

Barbara, the conference organizer, passed me looking as rattled as I felt.

"What's all this?" I asked her.

"The president of the Greater Portland chapter made her first sale, so her agent and all the girls are giving her a big dinner at Jake's." She flurried away.

Jake's. That sounded familiar.

A hand touched my elbow. Startled, I turned and found myself gazing up into those blue, blue eyes. And, immodest as it sounds, Dan was giving me an up and down look that let me know that all the money I'd spent on my outfit had not been in vain.

"Amazing!" he said.

I broke into a smile, then felt uncertainty start to creep in. Did he mean that I was dazzling him, or simply that it was amazing that I had managed to clean up so well?

Of course, he was no slouch himself. He had changed suits—this one was more of a charcoal gray—and he smelled expensively after-shavy.

"Come on," he said, laughing, "let's get away from this crush."

"I forgot to ask," I mentioned as we were swinging out the lobby doors, "where are we going?"

"Jake's. It's just a few minutes' walk from here."

I stopped.

He frowned. "What's the matter?"

"I think the crush will be following us."

Concerning travel time, Dan was true to his word. We walked to the restaurant—just five blocks—before my impractical new shoes could do irreversible damage to my feet.

The restaurant was not too full when we were seated at our booth. Fleishman had led me to think this would be some kind of greasy seafood dive, but the restaurant was huge, consisting of several rooms of rich dark woodwork and paneling. It felt like something from the days of the robber barons.

Next to us there was a long table set up, around which waiters were hurriedly putting on the finishing touches. I nodded to it.

"Looks like we're about to be invaded."

He laughed. "This place doesn't know what's about to hit them."

About fifteen minutes later, the onslaught began. The restaurant was turned into the hotel lobby all over again, but by that time the rest of the tables were filling up, too. Dan and I were settled and comfortable enough that looking over and making small talk with the writers seemed like a harmless diversion.

When we were through exchanging small-worlds and what-a-coincidences with our neighbors, Dan and I swung right back into our conversation where we had left off, which was right in the middle of Dan's life story. He had attended Cornell, graduated with a degree in international relations, but then got a job at a major New York publishing house through an uncle who worked there. He fell in love with the business. And because he possessed both a love of books and a natural head for contracts and figures, he veered quickly toward becoming an agent.

"It's been a rewarding career."

Judging by the Italian cut of that suit, *very* rewarding. Apparently if you got fifteen percent of enough, it eventually amounted to something.

Or maybe he was just rich to begin with. He seemed the type. And if he had an uncle who was a publishing mucketymuck, that was not unlikely.

When our dinners arrived, he asked me to tell him about

myself, and I quickly sketched out what I could, leaving out details like I was a former fatso with no real qualifications to be doing what I was doing. I did tell him that my dad owned a plumbing supply business.

His eyes widened. "Really?"

"Is that so surprising?"

I admit it. I have a bit of a chip on my shoulder when it comes to my dad. People always assume that if your father has anything to do with plumbing you must have grown up thinking of nothing but sinks and toilets.

Dan shook his head. "No, but I'd say it was an amazing coincidence. My father runs Weatherby's AAAA Plumbing Service in Buffalo!"

"Really?" was all I could think to say. I was shocked. Dan just didn't seem the type to have grown up . . .

Well, you know.

I hadn't been joking, but Dan laughed as if I had. "I know, I know. It's as if certain professions have this stamp on them. People used to be even more surprised when I would tell them my dad was a plumber who loved light opera. I guess the idea of drain clogs and Gilbert and Sullivan doesn't sit well with most people."

"Exactly." My dad, of course, was not a fan of opera, light or otherwise. But like Dan said, he wasn't completely unsophisticated. "Dad put every one of us through college. He said his biggest regret was not going."

Dan nodded. "I was lucky enough to get a scholarship myself, but my own father had that same kind of dedication."

The next five minutes became an ode to our working class backgrounds, with Dan both embracing his parents' blue-collar status *and* assuring me they were atypical. I couldn't blame him too much. I had done a lot of that schitzo stuff, too.

Besides, even when he was being full of himself, the man had a mesmerizing way about him. He brimmed with confidence; I am so riddled with self doubts that seeing someone who seems to have none fills me with awe. It wasn't hard to see how this guy could break hearts and send distraught career women fleeing back to Buffalo.

I was listening to him recount the incredible job he had done with an auction of one of his author's books when someone stopped at our table. Seeing a pair of black slacks and assuming it was the waiter, I barely spared the person a glance.

"*Rebecca? Is that* you?"

That voice was so out of context here, and so startling, that I almost didn't recognize it at first. I turned slowly. Then I froze.

It was Fleishman.

Fleishman?

What the hell is he doing here?

"My God! How strange!" That lunatic was acting surprised to see *me*. He flicked a glance at Dan, then back to me.

I looked over at Dan, who was wearing a puzzled smile. And rightfully so. "Uh, Dan? This is my friend Fleishman. Fleishman, Dan Weatherby."

Fleishman darted out his hand for Dan to shake. "I don't think I've heard Rebecca mention you . . ."

Have I mentioned yet that I wanted to strangle him? I did, but I was also still in such a state of shock that I was frantically trying to imagine scenarios that would explain his being here. Maybe he had an aunt in Portland who died in the past eight hours.

Maybe he followed me because he is crazed.

To my irritation, he plopped himself down on the bench seat next to me, then scooted over until I was wedged against the paneled wall.

A terrible thought occurred to me.

"What about Max?" I asked.

"Don't worry," Fleishman assured me blithely. "He's with Wendy."

"Wendy!" I exclaimed. "She *hates* him."

"So? She's not going to starve him."

I wasn't so sure. A few days before, Max had peed on her

bathrobe—which Wendy had not realized until she had stepped out of the shower and actually put the bathrobe on. My whisking Max out for a walk had just barely prevented a puppycide.

Dan was looking from Fleishman to me and back again. He seemed worried. "I hope Max isn't a child?"

"My dog," I said.

"Our dog," Fleishman replied at the same time.

Dan's face slackened a little. "Then you two know each other well? I mean . . . you're not just old acquaintances?"

Fleishman laughed so hard he nearly choked and had to down half my glass of Chardonnay. "Didn't you tell him?" he asked me.

"Oddly enough, the subject of you hadn't come up," I said.

"Oh! Then he has no idea." He turned to Dan. "We live together."

"We're roommates," I clarified, tossing him a warning glance. "We have another roommate named Wendy." I flicked my gaze around the restaurant. "Maybe she'll show up, too."

Fleishman laughed. "Oh, no. She has rehearsals."

My irritation was beginning to bubble over. "What are you doing here?"

"Attending the conference."

"*What?*"

His eyes flashed in triumph. "I was here all afternoon. I wanted to make it for the morning, too, but my flight got delayed."

"How come I didn't see you?"

"I don't know. Where've you been? I went to a workshop this afternoon on building sexual tension. Very informative!"

I waved for the waiter so I could order more wine. I needed it. "How could you?" I asked. "You don't even belong to RAG!"

"I do now." He smiled at me. "West Brooklyn Chapter. I had to pay a visiting member's fee to get in here, but it was worth it."

When the waiter arrived, Fleishman went ahead and ordered dinner for himself. "You two just go ahead with dessert—or wherever you happen to have left off," he offered generously.

Dan seemed like a man who never got flustered and was experiencing the sensation now for the first time. In fact, he looked flummoxed, and the way his eyes narrowed on Fleishman I was sure he assumed Fleishman was my boyfriend. Which seemed, weirdly enough, to be the vibe that Fleishman wanted to put across.

Had he really come all this way because he wanted to attend a conference, or was he jealous?

The long table full of authors had received their food and was quieter than before. The scene at our booth had not gone unnoticed. A few people were shooting curious looks our way, and Barbara actually bent toward us. "Did you run into an old friend, Rebecca?"

Fleishman swiveled. "Rebecca and I live together, actually."

"Roommates," I bit out.

"Oh!" Barbara said. Clearly, my clarification did not mean a lot to her. Her eyes narrowed. "Aren't you the young man who was sitting next to me during Alison Rooney's speech?"

He had missed my speech but gone to Alison Rooney's?

"Wasn't she awesome?" he exclaimed to Barbara.

I sighed. "Barbara Simmons, this is Herb—"

"Fleishman," he finished for me. Then his jaw dropped. "Wait a second! Are you Barbara Simmons who wrote *The Marquis Misbehaves?*"

She drew back. "Yes, I am."

"I *loved* that book!" He looked around the table, practically licking his lips. "Are you *all* romance writers?"

"We're the Greater Portland Chapter."

The whole banquet table of women grinned at him invitingly.

And within ten minutes, Fleishman knew them all. When his lobster was ready, it was brought to the long table, where he had insinuated himself between Barbara and Darlene Paige. Even Darlene, who had seemed so nervous and unassuming with me that afternoon, appeared animated and at ease. She smiled, she laughed, she made comments that caused everyone in earshot to break out in whoops. Something about Fleishman seemed to bring her out of her shell.

Dan and I had picked at our cheesecakes and now were watching in muted awe as Fleishman worked the crowd.

"Your friend has quite a way with people," he said. "What kind of books does he write?"

"He's a playwright, actually," I said, taking a sip of coffee. I was still seething. "An unproduced playwright."

"Comedies?"

"Sort of."

He looked as if he were considering something, then he shook his head. "I've never represented a playwright."

"Probably wise. There's not a fortune to be made in fifteen percent of zero."

He laughed. "You're not very supportive."

"Oh, I've supported him plenty."

His head tilted and he regarded me thoughtfully. "Are you sure you two aren't . . . involved?"

"Very sure." *After this night, we might not even be roommates anymore*, I wanted to say.

"That's funny. I thought I sensed something."

I flushed. "Well, *once*." I am a very bad liar. "Twice, actually. But now we're just roommates. We have another roommate who lives in the apartment with us. It's a big apartment. Her name is Wendy." I stopped. I'd made it sound as if the apartment were named Wendy.

"I think you mentioned her already."

Had I? I was trying too hard to make sure he didn't get the wrong impression, thus ensuring that he got the wrong impression.

But how could he possibly have gotten the right impression when my ex-boyfriend shows up on the first date I'd had in six months?

Not that Dan knew I hadn't had a date in six months.

Not that this was a *real* date.

Right now it seemed like no kind of date at all. It was just a disaster.

When we were done, Dan very politely offered, "Should we wait for your friend to finish?"

I looked over to where Fleishman was yucking it up with his new romance writer friends. He was having the time of his life, and Darlene Paige looked like she had just discovered the love of hers.

"No, he might be a while."

As we walked back to the hotel, I thought about explaining that Fleishman was not a love-obsessed ex-boyfriend, just a romance-novel-obsessed ex-boyfriend. But would Dan have bought that?

I wasn't sure I did, either. Besides, a phrase Dan had said in passing had lodged in my confused brain. *I thought I detected something between you . . .*

Part of me wanted to ask him if he had really meant that, or at least to get the details of what had made him say it, but that probably would be a real relationship ender.

Not that Dan and I had a relationship.

When we got to the hotel lobby and I worked up the courage to ask him if he wanted to go hang out in the bar a while, he shook his head. "No, thanks. I have an early flight out tomorrow."

I nodded. My cheeks burned. I should have kept my mouth shut.

I turned, as if I were going to the desk to check my messages. "Good night then," I said.

" 'Night."

All those advice books that tell you to seize the intitiative? Burn them.

"I like that skirt."

Renata stood in the midst of my cluttered dorm room, eyeing me as if I were playing some trick on her. "You do?"

"Yes."

Her head tilted every so slightly. When she spoke, her throaty voice was as suspicious as if I had told her that parading through the cafeteria in her bra and panties would make her the most popular girl on campus. "What do you like about it?"

She was the first girl ever to ask me to serve as a fashion critic. In a matter of weeks I had gone from undergrad English major to What Not to Wear *host, the coed version. In the beginning, it was fun. "It's flirty. It shows off your legs."*

For a moment it appeared as if she might collapse on my roommate's beanbag chair. The slightest compliment turned her beet red.

And you know what? I liked that. I liked that she asked for my opinion, then went all fluttery when I approved. I felt myself slipping into the role of her social mentor, a Svengali who could help her navigate the treacherous waters of the aquarium tank that was the social life of our little college. Who doesn't want to be needed?

Just so you don't fall for her, *I told myself. That probably wouldn't work out too well. We were so compatible as we were, as friends.*

Remember nineteen? When you're nineteen, you're convinced of all sorts of things: That you can smoke like Puff the Magic Dragon and not get cancer. That an hour and a half of sleep will leave you daisy fresh for your biology exam. That there will simply never be a better band than Weezer.

Or that you can squire around a pretty girl with great legs and willing eyes and somehow manage not to fall in love.

Chapter 10

When I finally heard the pounding at one-thirty in the morning, I decided that I was not the only person who was going to get a rude awakening on this night.

I marched to the door, already bristling for a fight. "What are you doing here?" I asked as I swung the door open. I didn't have to wait to see who it was. I knew.

"I had drinks with some of the women I met at the restaurant," he said. "We talked shop." As if that were an answer to the question I had asked.

"What are you doing in my room?"

He looked flummoxed. "I'm not in your room. You haven't let me in."

I planted my feet. "No, and I'm not going to, either."

After this statement sank in, his mouth opened and shut repeatedly, like a gasping fish. "The hotel is booked, Rebecca. What do you expect me to do?"

"Find another hotel."

His voice looped up in outrage. "At one-thirty in the morning?"

"Oh?! Is it *one-thirty in the morning?*" I asked. "I didn't realize. Maybe because I was in a sound sleep!"

"Well for heaven's sake," he grumbled. "Just let me come in

and you can conk out again. How am I supposed to find a hotel room this late at night?"

"Maybe you should have thought of that before you flew across the country to crash my business trip."

"Is that what you're so upset about?" He crossed his arms. "I thought you'd be glad to see a familiar face. I just came as moral support."

"I didn't need moral support during my dinner with Dan."

"You said it wasn't a real date!" The elevator doors opened and a woman I recognized as an agent I had seen on a panel padded quickly by us.

" 'Night, Bev!" Fleishman called out with a wave.

She beamed at him, then saw me glowering in my pajamas and hurried past me.

Fleishman turned back to me. "You said it was just business."

"And you believed me?" I screeched.

The sound of a chain lock being unbolted sounded from next door. Cynthia, dressed in a chenille bathrobe and matching slippers, came out into the hallway with her ice bucket. Because, obviously, you never know when you're going to wake up in the middle of the night with a burning need to make highballs. My guess was that she had been listening to every word of our argument and decided she needed visual detail. My other guess was that those author Web rings would not be idle tomorrow.

"Hey, Cyn," Fleishman called.

"Is everything all right?" she asked.

"Oh, sure."

When she had turned her back and started walking, very slowly, to the ice room, I reluctantly yanked Fleishman across the threshold. I didn't want to help him out, God knows, but I was here on business and it wasn't professional to have spats in hotel corridors. I had forgotten Cassie's earpiece was right next door.

Fleishman strolled in and went to the phone. "I'll have the front desk send my bag up."

I rolled my eyes. "There's no room in here for you, Fleish."

He nodded toward the bed. "That's a queen size, isn't it?"

"It is. And I'm the queen. The evil queen. You're the peasant who is going to be sleeping on the couch."

He looked over, aghast. "But that's a love seat!"

"Exactly. Sleep tight." Tight was the operative word. In fact, he would have to fold himself in two.

He opened his mouth to protest.

"Take it or leave it," I warned.

His mouth shut. "I've slept on worse, I guess."

At this point I couldn't have cared less whether or not he got his beauty rest. Fleishman's comfort was really not uppermost in my mind. I would say it was pretty much bottommost. If there had been a bed of nails handy, I would have offered him that.

"What did you hope to achieve by coming here?" I asked.

"Your voice is taking on that scolding tone again," he said, as if I might want to take corrective measures.

The man had crust to spare. "I've got that tone because you are jumping up and down on my nerves!"

He lifted his shoulders in a gesture of angelic innocence. "I told you, I wanted to come to the conference. I wanted to meet the authors." He shook his head. "I can't believe I actually talked to the person who wrote *The Marquis Misbehaves.*"

I shook my head. Had he gone completely around the bend? "That's the loopiest thing I've ever heard. You've just started reading this stuff—"

"*Stuff?* Shame on you!"

"And now you're the voice of romance! Not to mention, you're so eager to hobnob with these writers that you were willing to make me look like an idiot."

"How?"

"By surprising me that way."

"What could I do? If I'd told you my plans, you would have told me not to," he said. "Besides, no one cared that I flew out except for you and maybe that baloney sandwich you were having dinner with."

"I saw all their faces when you showed up. They thought it was peculiar." I stopped. "And where do you get off calling Dan a baloney sandwich?"

"He's a phony."

"He's very nice."

"Right. The silver spoon frat boy type."

"I'll have you know that his father is a plumber. He went to Cornell on a scholarship."

"I don't care if his father was a saint. The man has no soul. Can't you tell that just by looking into those vacant eyes?"

I looked into Fleishman's eyes now. They weren't vacant, but I began to wonder if *he* was the one with no soul. It felt as if he were sucking all the air out of the room, out of my life.

"Honestly, Rebecca," he went on, "if you don't think you rate better than that Brooks Brothers-clad chunk of Styrofoam, your self esteem is beyond rescue."

"My self esteem was doing great before you showed up."

"Right. What was this about your vomiting all over some poor editor?"

I shuddered. "I just splattered her a little."

"Oh my God!"

"It wasn't that bad . . ."

Who was I kidding? It was horrible. Every time I remembered that plane ride, I writhed in fresh mortification.

"See?" he asked, waggling a finger. "You should have let me come with you."

"Why? So I could have thrown up on you?"

Come to think of it, the idea had appeal.

He tossed up his hands. "I don't see why you're so bent out of shape. It's like you're not even glad to see me."

"Because I'm beginning to feel like you've suckered onto my life and now you're just draining it dry. You're a succubus."

He lifted his hands, stopping me before I could go further. "First thing: a succubus is a female. I believe the word you are looking for is *incubus*. As an editor, I think you need to start being a little more precise with your language."

I fell back on the bed with a guttural roar of frustration.

"Second," he said, looming over me, "I'm a little offended by what you're saying. I am not leeching off you. When was the last time I borrowed money?"

I had been speaking in emotional terms rather than financial, but now that he mentioned it . . . "What about the cable bill?"

He blinked. "What about it?"

"You said you didn't have the money to pay it this month, so I did. And then the next day you showed up with a new mini iPod."

"So?"

So? *So?* Did he just not get it? "So how did you afford this trip?"

"The same way you afforded those silky pajamas. Plastic."

I shook my head.

"What?" he asked. "Are you the only person in the world now who should be able to go into debt?"

"I don't care if you're in debt," I said.

"Then what are you so pissy about?" he asked. "The cable bill? My stupid iPod?"

"I'm not pissy!" I exclaimed, sounding . . . pissy.

"All right!" he huffed. "When we get home I'll write you a check."

I lifted my head. "If you can write a check, why didn't you write it two weeks ago?"

"I didn't have the money two weeks ago, just at the moment you asked for it. Okay, maybe I should have put off buying the iPod till I paid you back. Or maybe I should have bought *you* an iPod, would that have made you happy?"

"Forget it." This was so off track, anyway. I was so exasperated with him I was lashing out over details. "I don't really care about cable bills, or iPods, or any of the rest of it."

"It's not like I've been stingy," he pointed out.

"No—you're generous. Too generous. Maybe because you don't make money. You just catch it when it falls toward you."

"I work!"

"Fleish, you don't. Not with any regularity. You don't work, and you don't finish anything. I'll bet you never even finish this thing you're working on now."

"Wanna bet?" he asked.

"No."

I glared at him. He glowered back.

This was so ridiculous. We were *roommates*, yet this felt like something so much more. Like a marital spat. Like a spat in a marriage headed for divorce court, actually. If Fleishman had sashayed into the room announcing that he had to come to Portland because he felt so jealous of Dan, that would have been a different matter. I probably would have melted on the spot. His trip would have seemed gallant, almost.

Instead, he seemed to have some twisted desire to see romance writers in person, and he didn't care whether I wanted him there or not.

"I'll show you," he said. "You'll see. You'll be surprised."

"I will if you actually do anything."

But what was I saying? If he actually finished this horrible play, I would probably come out of it as a laughingstock.

But as always when I became panicked about this issue, I did the numbers. Half the temp workers in New York City were writing plays. If you guesstimated a modest 40,000 temp workers, that was 20,000 plays. Each year on off and off-off Broadway and Broadway, there were about a hundred plays given productions. Therefore, the chances were only about one in five hundred that his play would even see a footlight.

Those were good odds in my favor.

"You'll see," he repeated.

I awoke the next morning to a sharp rap at the door. I flopped over in bed, groaning, and prayed whoever this was would simply go away. Then I heard the chain lock unlatch and male voices in the hallway. I squeezed my eyes open in time to see a cart being wheeled into the room by Fleishman.

"Room service," he announced, unnecessarily.

I shot up to sitting. "When did you order that?"

Fleishman seemed to have cast off the animosity of hours before like a snake that had shed an old skin. He was showered, shaved, and his old self. "Last night, after you went to bed. I wanted to surprise you. Also, I figured that since you're probably on an expense account, why not live it up?"

I darted a look at him, but I started to feel more charitably towards him when I smelled the coffee. In all my life, I had never ordered room service. It seemed decadent . . . and wonderful.

A few minutes later I had a steaming cup of coffee in my hand and was dribbling croissant crumbs on the bed. I felt wary after last night, but I wasn't going to be the one to restart the argument.

"I want to apologize," Fleishman announced.

For a moment I had to do an aural double take. *I want to apologize* was not a phrase that came easily to Fleishman. In fact, I'm not sure I had ever heard it tripping off his tongue before. And yet there it was.

"I don't know what I was thinking. I guess I got carried away." Then he looked over his coffee cup at me with those disarmingly expressive eyes. "I guess I was jealous."

I gulped. *God, is this going to be our big love scene?* And there I was with croissant crumbs down my front. I dropped the pastry onto the white plate and set it next to the phone. "Jealous?"

"Thinking of you here . . ." He shook his head. "I guess I went a little berserk."

I could feel myself starting to thaw. "Fleish . . ."

"I know it sounds weird, but I'm *so* envious of your job."

The gooey smile that I could feel on my lips collapsed. *My job.* He wasn't jealous of Dan, but my job?

"Because you went out and found this new career, while I'm still floundering." I instinctively opened my mouth to try to say something, but he shook his head. "No, it's true. Floundering."

I bit my lip. This was not the confession I had been expecting. Or hoping for. It called for a moment of readjustment.

"And you're right," he said. "I have no stick-to-itiveness."

At least he's being honest, I thought. "Maybe you just haven't hit on the right idea yet. I mean, let's face it, I'm not sure how much universal appeal *Yule Be Sorry* would have."

He drew back, as if I had just chucked a spear at him. "What's the matter with it?"

I tried to put it diplomatically. "It just seems a little . . . personal."

"Well of course it is. All good art starts with the personal."

"Yeah, but . . ." Too late, I realized I had stepped into a quagmire. "But maybe the fact that it has taken you so long to finish is evidence that it's not the right project for you to work on at this time."

"Man!" he exclaimed in amazement. "You really have that lame editor-speak down pat, don't you?"

It was true. I had become fluent in gobbledegook.

"The girls and I were talking about it last night."

"About me?"

"No, about editors in general and the language they use. We were trying to crack the code of the weird phraseology you guys employ in your rejection letters."

He had gotten chummy with these women awfully fast.

"Still, there's truth in what you're saying. And I want you to know that I'm very sorry if I ruined your trip. I'll never do it again."

"I'll probably never be sent on a trip again."

"Then you can be assured that I will never do it again."

I laughed. I had never seen Fleishman this way. Contrition wasn't his forte, and he seemed inept at it. But he was trying.

That was a start.

"You didn't ruin anything," I had to admit. "Not really."

"But your date with that guy . . ."

"Dan." I sighed. "It wasn't a date."

That had just been wishful thinking on my part.

His pointy brows pinched into a puzzled frown. "What happened to him? Why weren't you guys at the bar last night?"

"He went straight to his room after we got back. He has an

early flight to catch." I frowned in thought. "I hope this whole incident doesn't make working with him difficult."

"So what?" Fleishman asked. "The writers I was talking to last night didn't seem to think much of him."

"He represents quite a few authors with us," I said.

"Really? Who?"

"Shanna Forrester, Joy Silver—"

I needed to go no further. "He's Joy Silver's agent?" Fleishman said. "Really? I love her."

"He has a lot of good clients."

"And you said he's gone now?"

"I think so." He was probably somewhere on the other side of the Rockies already.

We finished breakfast in relative peace. Fleishman seemed subdued, thoughtful. Then, just when I thought it was time to start considering getting back to the airport, he asked, "Hey—you want to go out and look around?"

"At what?"

"According to my guide book, there's a massive bookstore somewhere around here."

My flight was just after noon. "It's almost nine o'clock now."

"Are you worried about our flight? We've got scads of time."

Our flight?

"I'm on the same plane as you," he said.

"Are you sure you want to risk missing the flight?"

He waved away my worrywartiness. "I've never missed a plane."

I showered and dressed in record time, and we headed out to Powell's City of Books. It was a big place, requiring a map to navigate. Of course we ended up losing more time there than we had intended. As a result, we were late getting to the airport, where the security line snaked around for what looked like miles.

One good thing about arriving late, though—it allowed me to forget about the horrors ahead. And Fleishman, very considerately, bought some motion sickness tablets for me at the airport newsstand/pharmacy. This might have had something to do with the fact that we had switched seats upon check-in so we could sit together.

And we did make it, Fleishman pointed out after we had sprinted to our gate. "In fact, it's a good thing we arrived when we did. Otherwise we would have just been sitting around."

That was Fleishman logic for you.

We were all being shuffled like cattle past first class when I noticed a very familiar person ensconced in one of the oversized leatherette chairs, holding a Bloody Mary. *Dan!*

As if sensing my unbelieving stare, he looked up. I detected a brief flash of embarrassment, but he recovered quickly. That dazzling grin was back in place in no time. "Well, fancy meeting you here."

This is his idea of an early flight? Twelve-thirty PM?

I wanted to give him a solid thump on the head. What had been the point of lying to me last night? Was he worried I was going to hold him hostage in the hotel bar?

"Maybe we can get together back in NYC," he suggested.

"Sounds great."

"Let's do lunch," he said in a pseudo-mocking voice.

I chuckled, then moved along.

When we were safely in plebian class, Fleishman looked back at me, eyebrows arched. "But you say he's a good agent, huh?"

"Yeah." I blew out a breath and reached for the in-flight magazine. "One part good agent, three parts baloney sandwich."

Fleishman and I parted ways at the airport, so I ended up going home alone. When I opened the door, Wendy was scrubbing the woodwork with a toothbrush and HGTV was blaring the most recent episode of *House Hunters.*

"Hey!" I said.

She looked up. She didn't seem overjoyed to see me.

Still, it was great to be home. I collapsed in a chair by the table and looked around the apartment, which I had actually missed. I had especially missed . . .

I looked around, feeling a moment of panic. Max was nowhere in evidence.

"What did you do with Max?" It was embarrassing to admit how reliant I was on canine affection these days.

"He's in jail."

She nodded to the corner, where Maxwell was in a plastic dog carrier with a wire barred door. It did look like a jail. He was amazingly quiet, though his brown eyes looked up at me beseechingly and I could tell by his swaying movement that somewhere in that plastic box, his tail was thumping.

"What was his crime?"

"He chewed my boots."

I trembled in fear for Maxwell. No wonder he was quiet . . . it was a miracle he was still alive.

"I'm sorry," I said.

She kept scrubbing. "Where's Fleishman?"

"He decided he wanted to go to Connecticut to wheedle money out of his dad to pay for the trip."

She leveled an exasperated stare at me. "About that trip . . . ?"

"Honestly, Wendy, I had no idea Fleish was going to go to Portland and leave you here alone. None."

She harrumphed. "What is going on with you two?"

"Nothing."

"You always say that."

"I know, and it's always true. Well, almost always."

"So he just followed you on a business trip to . . . ?"

It was embarrassing to say, but I had to admit it. "To meet romance writers."

She sent me an inscrutable look. "Okay, just answer me this. Am I in the way here? I mean apart from serving as an impromptu dogsitter, of course."

"In the way?" I asked, shocked. "What are you talking about? You're my best friend."

"Right. The person you never listen to. The person who gets treated like a fifth wheel."

Oh my God. I had no idea she felt that way. Though I suppose I should have had an inkling. "I'm sorry, Wendy. I never wanted you to feel shut out from anything. It's just that you're always so busy now, with school and your job, and . . ."

From the amount of gunk she was taking off with that toothbrush, I would guess that the baseboards hadn't been cleaned since they were painted, and from the yellow-white hue of the paint, that had been a few decades.

Still, it never would have occurred to me to scrub them.

"And you do realize you're approaching Joan Crawford territory, don't you?" I asked her.

She let out a long breath. "I'll bet Joan Crawford never had to put up with filth and dog pee and weirdness from her roommates . . ."

"You think I'm weird?" I asked.

"Not you . . ." She reconsidered. "Or, yes, you. You and Fleishman are a weird combo."

"I told you, nothing is going on."

"Yes, that's what I'm gathering. And you know what's going to happen?"

I shook my head.

"Nothing."

"That's fine by me," I declared. "We're just friends."

She dropped her toothbrush into the soapy water, where it landed with a splash. "Bullshit. Don't tell me that you don't have expectations."

"I don't," I said.

"You do, and you're going to be disappointed. Over and over and over."

"How do you know that? Can you read into his heart?"

"His *heart?* Are we still teenagers? I can read into his actions. And what I read there is someone who doesn't give a damn about either of us. You don't see it. You're still seeing the glow from college, when he was the cool guy on campus who had taken a shine to you. Back then we all hung out and talked about our hopes and ambitions. But now I'm following my dreams and working my tail off, and you're working your tail off, and Fleishman's still hanging out talking about his ambitions. He's Peter Pan with a writing bug."

"Writing's not easy."

"You think it's easy to become a lighting designer? Or an editor?" She shook her head. "It's not that I don't like the guy, although I'll admit he's wearing thin. I just don't want to be his serving girl anymore."

"Then get off your knees and stop scrubbing," I said. "Don't do more work than you think you should."

"But if I didn't do it, nobody else would, either. I don't want to live that way."

"In other words, you can't win. That's twisted."

She leaned back against the wall. "I think I'm going crazy, Rebecca."

She really did look stressed out. Working and going to school was no picnic, and she'd been doing it for years now. I felt bad that I had added to her stress this weekend. And I shouldn't have compared her to Joan Crawford. "Don't give up, Wen. One more year and you'll be done."

"One more year, and then maybe I'll be an unemployed lighting designer and full time coffee server." She blew out a breath. "You know how some women just want to get married but they suck at relationships?"

I nodded.

"I just want a nice apartment but I suck at making money."

"You'll get there someday." I looked nervously at the television and reached for the remote. "In the meantime, maybe you should stop watching this channel."

"I know. It's like heroin for the home-obsessed."

"It seems like we're all battling weird addictions," I said.

Her lips twisted into a frown and she darted a glance in the general direction of Fleishman's room. "Except some. For some it's indulge, indulge, indulge." She shot me a look that had a twinge more sympathy. "Just watch out, Rebecca. It's a throwaway society we live in. People can get tossed out, too."

Poor Wendy. She'd been doing way too many of those depressing plays.

* * *

On my way in to work on Monday, I met Rita standing in her outer office. She exhaled a cloud of smoke for me to walk through—her version of a welcome mat. "How'd it go?"

"Not too bad," I said.

Now that I was home, just surviving the weekend at all seemed like an achievement. I had never been so glad to be walking into this office building. I got on the elevator—secretly hoping, as always, for a Suave Guy encounter—with a spring in my step. My heels turned to cement, though, when the doors slid open and I saw Muriel's expectant face.

"I told my friend that you were on a conference trip this weekend and probably wouldn't have gotten much reading done," she said, though you could tell she hoped I would contradict her. "Isn't that right?"

"I'll get to it this week," I promised.

I'd forgotten the rule: *Never make promises.*

I did go back to my office intending to get *The Rancher and the Lady* off the shelf, but in the end I spent most of the morning doing my expense report. I deducted Fleishman's half of the room service, not to mention the drinks the scoundrel had treated his new author friends to and then charged to my room.

Around ten o'clock, I got a phone call. It was Lisa, Mercedes's admin assist. "Mercedes would like to speak to you for a few minutes."

My heartbeat stopped momentarily. "When?"

There was a pause, and the pause meant *duh.* "Like, maybe, now?"

"Oh! Okay, I'll be right there."

After I'd crossed the door on slightly wobbly knees, Lisa waved me on through and I knocked on Mercedes's door.

"*Entrez-vous!*"

I poked my head in.

She looked up at me and smiled. "*Just* who I wanted to see," she said, as if my coming into her office were an unexplainable bit of serendipity. As if I hadn't been summoned.

Maybe this was just her way of lightening the mood. I had the awful feeling that I was about to be scolded for bad conference performance.

Mercedes plopped into her chair, let out a long sigh, and muttered, "*Mon dieu!* Where to begin?"

I wondered if bringing your ex-boyfriend to a romance conference, even unintentionally, was a firing offense.

But Mercedes didn't mention that. Instead, she asked, "Have you heard about our counseling benefit?"

I shifted in my chair, wondering where this was leading. "I think I might have read a pamphlet at some time or another . . ."

"Well, the long and short of it is, there are options. Every calendar year you have three free visits to a counselor, *or* you can enroll in a smoking cessation program, *or* one of the other approved programs on the list. I believe there's a Web site that lists them all. One of them is for alcohol abuse counseling."

I nodded.

She kept her eyes fixed on me.

There was something she was trying to communicate to me by imparting this information; I frowned in concentration to try to figure it out. Did she want me to stage a smoking cessation intervention for Rita? Beyond that, my mind was a blank.

"*Comprenez-vous?*" she asked.

"Um . . . not really," I admitted.

She put her hands before her on her desk, threading her fingers. "We've gotten a few reports about your wild weekend in Portland."

Uh-oh. Here it came. I sank down in my chair.

"*Not* from Barb Simmons, whom you probably met."

I nodded. I met her, Fleishman met her . . .

"Barb *loved* your—"

"Friend," I piped up quickly.

Mercedes cleared her throat. "I was going to say, Barb loved your speech."

"Oh." I shouldn't have interrupted her. I felt compelled to

say, "But that man really is just my roommate. *And* he's a RAG member."

"I've heard this man was your roommate in Portland, too."

"I swear, it wasn't planned. At least by me. It just sort of—"

She waved away my protests. "You don't need to explain to me. I think taking an *amor* with you on your business trip is admirably French. Of course, it probably raised *a few* eyebrows."

Oh dear.

"One of the authors of an editor here said you had a lover's quarrel out in the hallway. She said she barely got a wink of sleep all night."

Cynthia. Damn it. And she probably told Cassie, who probably went sprinting to tell Mercedes at 8:01 AM this morning.

I shook my head. "It will never happen again."

"Good. As I said, however, this was not what concerned me."

There was something else?

"Frankly, Rebecca, it's your drinking problem."

I blinked at her. I had a drinking problem? I know I had a few glasses of wine at the restaurant with Dan, but lots of people had been drinking. And I had deducted the minibar charges from my expense report.

She prompted gently, "The airplane?"

That unpleasant memory flooded back, and I practically hit myself on the head. "I was airsick."

Her brows arched skeptically.

"No, really," I said. "I'm terrified of planes, and then my—well, he's just my roommate, like I said—he said I should eat some pancakes and—"

"I see," she said, cutting me off. "Say no more."

I wasn't sure she did see. In fact, I had a sneaking suspicion she actually believed that I was lying through my teeth and that I kept a fully stocked bar in my metal file cabinet. (Or perhaps that would be admirably French, too.) She probably thought I ended up all my business meetings with a lampshade on my head. I'm sure I *looked* guilty as hell.

"It was all just a big mistake," I said. "I'm sorry if I caused any damage to Candlelight."

Contrition seemed to be exactly what she was looking for. "I'm sure you did *fine*."

Fine, except that I came off like a sex-crazed, vomiting wino.

"And it sounds like your speech went over well. So I'm going to see if Rita will send you to Wichita Falls."

I craned my head. "Where?"

"Wichita Falls, Texas. They have a great little conference there every August."

I was dismissed, and I stomped back to my office. The moment I had left Mercedes, embarrassment had been displaced by rage at Cassie. Telling Mercedes I was an alcoholic?

This was war.

Andrea hurried into my office. "What *happened?* This place is buzzing!"

"About what?" I asked.

"About you." She shut my door quietly. "My God, that conference sounds like it was just one nonstop blowout."

"Uh . . . not exactly."

She plunked herself down in my chair and leaned forward. "So who is this incredibly cute guy you're living with, and why didn't you tell me about him?"

"There's nothing to tell."

"And you let me go on about the elevator guy and Dan Weatherby! Jesus. It sounds like your squeeze is much better."

"He's not my squeeze. He's my roommate."

She blinked. "Then what was he doing in your hotel room?"

"He was . . . well, he was in Portland and he needed a place to stay."

I'm not sure she believed me. "What happened at the dinner with Dan Weatherby?"

I shook my head.

"Oh." She looked completely bummed on my behalf, which was comforting. "Jesus, it sounds like my weekend was better than yours, and all I did was clean my bathroom."

"Where is Wichita Falls?" I asked.

"Texas."

"The pleasantly cool, picturesque part?"

She shook her head slowly. "The hot, dry, flat part."

I let out a long sigh. Texas in August. Mercedes might not have fired me, but I had a feeling my stock was falling.

Chapter 11

I was so involved in debating between a low-fat apple cranberry bran muffin and a full-butter blueberry muffin with chunky sugar crystal sprinkles that I almost didn't notice Troy in front of me in the coffee shop line, even though he was practically sagging across the counter for support. I put my hand on his elbow.

He jumped, nearly upsetting the herbal teabag display. "Rebecca. Hi. What are you here for?"

"Just a muffin," I said. "I've decided that not buying expensive coffee is the least I can do to economize. So I buy the muffin and just breathe the fumes."

He clucked in sympathy. "Oh, that's so *Grapes of Wrath*. Like you just climbed off the Joad's rickety truck."

I laughed, but he didn't join me. He seemed down, and I'm sure it wasn't because of my lack of funds. "You *really* look like you could use some caffeine," I said.

He held up a paper to-go cup. "This is round two for me. Triple-shot espresso."

"Is something wrong?"

"I just spent twenty minutes locked in an office with Hurricane Cassie."

"Oh!"

"My God—she's like the Wicked Witch of the west wing of Candlelight Books!"

"If only we could throw water on her and melt her."

"She's got some whackjob author who has decided that we should promote her trilogy about amnesiac grooms as though it's Danielle Steel. It's crazy. But now Cassie is acting as if this woman should actually be given foil lettering on her covers."

Darlene! I had forgotten about her and our conversation in Portland. I trained my eyes on the muffins. I felt like a turncoat. I had only wanted to cause problems for Cassie, not for Troy.

"There has to be something we can do about her," Troy said, drumming his fingers on the glass. "Do you think if we shoved a little money under Art Salvatore's door he would hire one of his goons . . . er, friends . . . to take care of Cassie for us?"

"That's just a rumor, remember?" I smiled. "Besides, where would we get the money?"

"From sending around a collection plate!" he said. "For this job, we'd have money for the hit and enough left over to send me and the Calvin Klein underwear model to Cancun."

"Underwear model?"

He shrugged. "As long as we're dreaming . . ."

I liked Troy too much not to confess to my sin in this matter. "The truth is, you might want to take a contract out on me." As our orders were taken, I explained to him what had happened at the conference. I told him that I had directed Darlene to lean on Cassie for what she wanted. The squeaky wheel gets the grease, and all that. Then, of course, I had insinuated that if she didn't like working with one editor, it was not unheard of for authors to request a switch. Even if it meant switching twice in one year . . .

Troy drew back. "Oh my God! It has claws."

"I only did it because Cassie's been getting on my nerves. I never thought Cassie would start hassling you."

"Stop. It's not your fault the woman is mentally unbalanced. I think she expected she was going to be super-editor when she came here. The Tina Brown of Candlelight Books. When you were brought in at a higher job grade, she snapped."

I shot him a sidewise glance. "So I take it you told her . . . ?"

"N-O."

"And she's still angry?"

"Angry?" He rolled his eyes. "She looked like she was going to explode. We're talking Krakatoa."

I made my way upstairs and to the coffee room, girding myself for friction. I got it sooner than I had expected. No sooner had I found my mug in the lineup on the counter than Cassie pounced on me. It was as if she had been lying in wait behind the mini fridge. Terrifying. I was glad Troy had given me a little warning.

She stood quivering and rigid by the coffee pot, her cheeks stained with red. "What did you say to Darlene Paige at that conference?"

I did my best to keep a straight face. "What did I say to her about what?"

"You know what!"

My, she was huffy. I took a leisurely sip of coffee. "I'm afraid you'll have to refresh my memory."

"About *Forgotten Grooms!* Darlene has it in her head that I'm just not doing enough to promote her series."

I was trying so hard not to laugh that I thought I was going to choke. Or else spew coffee all over Cassie.

"Don't smirk at me. You know what you did."

"Honestly, Cassie, I just spoke to Darlene once at that conference. I don't even remember it all that well."

"You took her out for drinks." She propped a hand on her hip. "Could you possibly have said something to her about getting foil on her next book cover?"

I pursed my lips as if trying to concentrate. "Did I?"

"You know you can't get foil on a category romance cover!"

"Okay, so tell Darlene that."

"I did, believe me." She harrumphed. "Undoing the damage that you did."

I smiled. "But of course you'll probably have to talk her off another ledge when she finds out that an author who has a book out the same month as hers does have foil lettering."

Cassie gasped. "Who?"

"Joanna Castle."

For a moment I thought she just might go into orbit. "*What!?*"

I nodded. "*Heartstopper* has red foil."

"No way."

"I sent it to the author yesterday."

To see the complete shock on Cassie's face at that moment was so delicious. I understood now why football players did victory dances in the end zone after scoring touchdowns.

"Did Troy okay this?"

I nodded.

For a moment such a look of hatred pierced through me that I was afraid she really might kill me. One day I would just be found dead in my office. And Janice Wunch would probably put a late list over my corpse.

"I don't know how you managed that, Rebecca."

I shrugged. "Maybe I went reeling into Troy's office in a drunken stupor one day and forced him at gunpoint to okay foil lettering. Maybe you should run and tell Mercedes that."

Her jaw opened and shut a few times before any words actually came out. "You can bet I will talk to Mercedes about this!" She was so in my face that I could smell Crest Wintergreen. She lifted her hand and poked her index finger at my chest. "You think you're such hot shit, but just wait!"

I flinched and took a step backward to get out of the way of that poking finger. Unfortunately, as I reached back, I bumped against one of the mugs on the counter. It went flying to the floor and shattered.

We both looked down. In unison, we gasped. Blood drained out of my face.

"*Look* what you did!" Cassie exclaimed.

I had broken Mary Jo's mug. Little bits of it were strewn all over the linoleum, but it was unmistakably the Cathy mug. One of the larger shards had Cathy's exasperated little face on it.

"What *I* did?" I shot back as I dropped to my feet to start picking up the evidence. The first thing I did was cut my hand. I sucked on my finger even as I tried to keep gathering up the bits. The shards of doom. What the hell was I going to do? Mary Jo would murder me.

"If you hadn't been in the throes of some lunatic fit . . ." I told Cassie.

Cassie didn't respond. Which led me to believe that something was wrong. Very, very wrong.

I angled my head slightly, and saw a pair of skinny legs in navy blue hose and matching pumps planted next to me. Slowly, I gathered enough courage to look up into Mary Jo's face. She was staring at the floor. Her face was chalky white.

"My mug . . ."

"Rebecca knocked it over," Cassie said in a tone of voice I hadn't heard since I was eight.

Mary Jo turned to me. Her expression was the same one you saw in TV courtroom dramas when outraged parents look into the eyes of child murderers.

"I'm sorry, Mary Jo—it must have been on the edge of the counter, and it . . . well, it fell and broke." No, it was worse than that. "I knocked it over." I was a mug murderer.

Her knees seemed to collapse beneath her and she knelt down. Her eyes flashed at me. "Do you know that I had this mug for twenty years?"

I swallowed, guessing that she wasn't going to accept this with good grace. No "accidents happen" type reassurances would be forthcoming.

"I'm so sorry."

She didn't say anything. Just picked up the pieces and put them in a paper towel that Cassie handed her. Her mug shroud.

"Maybe I could find you a match. On eBay, maybe," I suggested. "You can find everything on eBay."

"It wouldn't be the same."

"Yeah, but—"

"Would you please just *leave me alone?*" she barked.

I hopped to my feet. Fast. Cassie was grinning at me. "You'd better just go, Rebecca. *I'll* stay with Mary Jo."

I slunk out of the coffee room, then realized I had forgotten my coffee. No way was I going back in there. I headed straight for the elevators. Forget economizing. I needed one of those triple-shot espressos.

Unfortunately, this left me standing in front of Muriel in the deserted reception area. "Oh, hello, Rebecca. I have been meaning to speak to you."

I bit back a sigh. I liked Muriel. I shared everyone's intense curiosity about what kind of life she led. (Andrea always theorized that Muriel was probably secretly into leather and whips and submissive men; I preferred to imagine her living a sort of Jane Austen throwback existence in the Bronx.) But she had a one-track mind now where her friend's book was concerned. Every time I saw her I cringed. I kept wishing she had chosen some other editor to give *The Rancher and the Lady* to.

Or that her friend had written a better book.

"I hate to keep bothering you about this . . ."

I did the only thing I could do. I apologized for the hundredth time even as I stabbed the elevator button in hope of rescue. "I'm so sorry, Muriel. I really did mean to read it last night. I even took it home with me!"

That, at least, was true. Unfortunately, the book was no more appealing to me sitting on my bedside table than it had seemed on my bookshelf at work.

"Well have you read any of it?"

"Of course—in fact, I'm almost finished." That was a lie, but only technically. I had decided that if I didn't finish it soon, I would have to send the manuscript back and just comment on the parts I had read so far (thirteen pages). So really, I was nearly through.

Muriel tilted a guarded look at me. "And what do you think?"

"Well . . . so far, at least . . . I think it shows some promise." *As a sleep-inducing narcotic.*

She smiled. "Oh, that's good to hear! It would be so awkward to have to tell my friend her book was a no-hoper."

It sure would be, I thought, wondering how I was going to

manage to do just that. "Naturally, I can't make any definitive comments before I've finished . . ."

Muriel nodded. "Of course!"

The elevator doors opened and I fled inside.

About an hour later, Andrea came breezing into my office. She was all duded up in her best dark blue suit—her serious interview outfit.

She shut the door quietly, and when she spoke, it was in that whispery shriek reserved for really juicy gossip. "Rebecca! Have you heard? The word from on high—from Art Salvatore himself—is we need to cut expenses, and so guess what?"

"We're all fired."

"Even better! Mercedes decided that only associate editors and up will be going to the national convention in Dallas!" She watched for my reaction. I didn't quite get it. I wasn't relishing going to this convention; my last conference hadn't worked out so well, and Dallas in July didn't sound like my cup of tea, either. She lowered her voice and pointed meaningfully at my east wall. "Cassie was just told she couldn't go."

I drew back. The conference was only a few weeks away. The plans had all been made. Cassie had to be crushed.

And furious.

"How can Mercedes do that?" I asked.

"Well, actually, that's the bad news. You and I are going to have to take over Cassie's editor appointments and her spot on a panel."

Andrea didn't seem upset about this at all, though. And it just wasn't like Andrea to be so gleeful when it meant taking on more work. I regarded her suspiciously. "Why are you so happy?"

She flopped down in my spare chair. "Because, if you really must know, I'm pretty sure I won't be going to this convention, either."

My jaw dropped. "You got a job?"

She put her finger up to her mouth. "Shh. Or maybe I'll be going to Dallas as a representative of . . . Gazelle Books!"

I frowned. Gazelle was another publisher specializing in romance. "I thought you wanted out of the pink ghetto."

"Well, yeah, but Gazelle's offering me five thousand more than I'm making here."

"That's great."

"God, I hope it happens!" She leaned back. "I really sparkled in that interview. I could tell the person really liked me. Joan Conyers—you know her?"

I shook my head.

"She worked here ages and ages ago. I've interviewed with her before, but we didn't hit it off so well last time. This time she laughed at my jokes."

"You made jokes?"

"Oh, yeah. You've got to stay loose in these interview situations. At least, that's what always works for me."

I was about to point out that it would be hard to tell what worked for her, since she never got any of these jobs she interviewed for. But I didn't want to come across as hostile. And as much as I would miss her, I really wanted her to get this job. Or any job that she wanted. She seemed to have so many hopes pinned on getting away from Candlelight.

"I tell you, it's so close I can taste it. And after that first paycheck, it's good-bye crappy Queens studio. So long seven train! I'm going to get a really great one bedroom somewhere in Manhattan."

"When will you find out?" I asked.

"Joan said that I seemed like I would be a good fit, but they still had some interviews lined up." She shrugged. "They have to go through the motions, you know."

"I'll keep my fingers crossed, even though it's against my best interests."

"Your interests? How?"

When I first started working there, I had found Andrea scary. Now she was hands-down my favorite person there. "If you leave, who will I talk to?"

Her puzzled frown turned to a look of disgust. "Please! Don't go getting all sentimental."

I laughed at her discomfort. She looked like my little brother used to when I would give him hugs. "If I cried, would you stay?"

"Hon, I wouldn't stay if you said you were going to throw yourself out the window."

"Maybe it's just as well that my office has no windows," I observed.

But I *was* going to miss her.

When I got home that night, there was a puddle of dog pee by the door. Naturally, the first thing I did was step in it and nearly skid across the apartment. Maxwell was skating around me happily. He apparently had relieved himself long enough ago that he had forgotten he was supposed to feel guilty.

"Damn it!"

"What's wrong?" Fleishman called.

I jumped.

He was leaning in the archway. "Sorry, I didn't mean to startle you."

I tossed my tote bag full of work down on the futon. I just assumed since Max had peed in the house that there was nobody home.

Fleishman threw a startled look at the doorway, then turned back to me, annoyed. "You've tracked it all over." He grabbed a roll of paper towels from the kitchen and ran around trying to clean up.

I sat down and watched. "I thought we had made an agreement to double our efforts to housetrain him."

Wendy had bought a book on cage training.

"I know . . . but I had so much going on today . . ."

"Where were you?"

"Here."

I scanned the room. The apartment looked exactly the same as it had when I had left that morning, so it was a cinch he hadn't been cleaning.

"Would you mind if I borrowed your WordPerfect?"

"I sold my computer, remember?"

"But you still have the disks," he reminded me. "I want to load them onto my new machine."

"What new machine?"

"Oh! I forgot to tell you—Natasha was so impressed by how hard I'd been working that she ordered me a new laptop."

He *had* been working hard. At what, I had no idea. "That was awfully generous of her."

He shrugged. "Actually, it's part of our payback plan."

I hadn't heard of this.

"I told her that I wanted six months to concentrate on becoming a writer, and she agreed she owed it to me since she and my dad hadn't put me through college."

I harkened back. I had gone to college with Fleishman. He had not been on workstudy. He had not received grants, or taken out loans. He had never scrabbled to come up with tuition at all, as far as I knew.

"They paid for it out of my trust fund," he explained. "But that was my *grandparents'* money."

I nodded. It was so like Fleishman that he could explain all of this without a hint of irony. "I see. They do owe you. And maybe I should hit up my parents for a European vacation, since they saved so much by sending me to public schools all those years."

He sent me a long-suffering look. "That's sort of apples and oranges, Rebecca. Anyway, Natasha agreed that since a good presentation could make all the difference in my line of work, I need to have a reliable computer and a new printer."

He escorted me to his bedroom nook and introduced me to his new computer. "It's just a Dell, but I like it."

My computer had been a Dell, only his was the streamlined, light-as-a-feather model. I felt a spike of envy. Not that I had any use for a computer now. I knew I wasn't going to write anything. I just wished I had a benefactress.

"They delivered it this morning. I set it up and registered it and all that jazz. And I was looking for your WordPerfect disks in your room—hope you don't mind—when I found that manuscript."

"What manuscript?" I asked.

"*The Rancher and the Lady!* Or, as I like to think of it, *The Writer and the Bowel Movement.*"

I flinched. "It's not that bad. There's *something* there." Just not something very interesting.

He hooted. "It's terrible! What are you doing bringing drivel like that home?"

"It was written by a friend of an employee."

He rolled his eyes. "I knew there had to be some strings being pulled somewhere. You wouldn't have made it past the first paragraph, otherwise."

"What do you think is wrong with it?"

"What isn't? First off, whoever the author is writes like she was teleported from the eighteenth century. Either that or she learned English by reading Victorian literature. Or else she's just a kook."

If Muriel's friend was anything like she was herself this was entirely possible.

"To me it doesn't seem very original," I said. "I was going to read it tonight and write a rejection tomorrow."

"Save yourself the headache. Write the rejection tonight and get a good night's sleep, your head clear of all thoughts of *The Rancher and the Lady.*"

That was an enticing idea.

"But first, come have dinner with me," he said.

I sighed. "I shouldn't. There's pasta in the kitchen."

"There's always pasta in the kitchen," he said. "Wouldn't you rather go to Senor Enchilada's?"

He had said the magic words. Senor Enchilada's was a place on Flatbush Avenue we'd found once in our wanderings. It was just a really good taqueria, actually, but we liked the name and the fact that it was decorated with fading piñatas and marionettes hanging from the ceiling. Going to Senor Enchilada's was an occasion.

"Maybe we should wait for Wendy." I didn't want her to feel any more left out than she already did.

"Nah—she might not be home for hours," Fleishman said. "Besides, I sort of wanted to be just with you."

If you think those words didn't strike straight through my heart, maybe it's because you didn't see the slight yet oh-so-sexy waggle of his brows. Or maybe you just haven't been paying attention.

I grabbed my purse, and we were out of there.

The stress of the day fell away from me the moment I was settled in front of a chalupa plate. I always order them, telling myself that I will eat the stuff off the top and leave the chalupa shells—really just a giant round tortilla chip. It rarely works out that way, but as my weight counselor used to say, sometimes you have to applaud the impulse even if you don't follow through.

"Have you spoken to Dan Weatherby lately?" Fleishman asked as he began to tuck into some enchiladas. They looked better than what I got. His plate was a sea of melted cheese.

"No," I said. "I guess I'll see him at the big conference in Dallas."

His eyes widened. "Really? That's soon, isn't it?"

"I don't mean I'll see him, see him. I'll probably just see him."

Somehow, this made sense to Fleishman. "Maybe you should do more than see him."

Why would Fleishman possibly be asking me about Dan at this late date? I had just now stopped kicking myself over how I had handled all that. I should have played it more cool, I'd decided. Like Fleishman's showing up was just no big deal. I looked uptight and paranoid . . . which is, of course, a pretty accurate description of my personality type.

"I guess I really mucked things up there," Fleishman said.

I was amazed. He had already apologized. It wasn't like him to dwell on wrongs he had committed. "It's okay," I said. "Obviously, it was not meant to be."

"How do you know?"

"If he liked me, he would have called. It's not like he couldn't have come up with an excuse."

"He wouldn't have called if he thought I was in the picture."

Are you in the picture? I wanted to ask. Fleishman wasn't

seeing anyone, and we had reached a comfortable détente. Part of this had just been because he had been working so hard. We hadn't really had the opportunity to squabble. But there was also this thought in the back of my mind . . .

I'd had thought that before. Foolish.

"I don't think Dan was ever interested in me. His natural schmooziness just bamboozled me into thinking he was."

"I think you're wrong."

"Why?"

"When I saw you two together, he seemed interested."

"After you saw us together, you called him a baloney sandwich."

"Because I was jealous," he admitted.

My heart stopped. Jealous? Fleishman? Of Dan?

"But that was selfish of me," he went on, "I can see that now. I probably broke up something that could have worked out."

"No," I said, forcefully. "I mean, I seriously doubt that."

He shook his head. "There you go again—undermining yourself. The smallest obstacle makes you retreat. The thing you should be asking yourself is, *who do I want?*"

You, dumbass, I could have said. I tilted my head. After all these years, couldn't he tell?

"Have you ever considered calling him, asking him out for a drink?"

So now he wanted to throw me into the arms of Dan Weatherby? I was confused.

Or maybe he was just testing me, to see if I was still carrying a torch.

"It seems awfully altruistic of you to want to matchmake Dan and me."

He shrugged. "I owe you."

"No you don't."

He leaned forward, practically pushing his plate aside. "But I do! Oh, I know we fought—you were right about a lot of things, Rebecca. You really gave me that swift kick in the pants I needed. I feel like I'm really back on track again."

I couldn't remember a time when he had ever been on track to begin with, but he seemed so optimistic I didn't want to point that fact out to him.

"You do seem to be getting a lot done." Of course, it helped when you had a mother bankrolling you.

"It's all because of you."

I shook my head. "You're obviously forgetting your mom."

"Oh sure, Natasha gave me some financial support. But you really got me going."

"I'd love to read what you've done," I said.

He shook his head. "I don't want to jinx it."

"Thanks!"

"What I meant was, I respect your opinion too much to give it to you before it's the best I can make it."

It seemed odd. In college he couldn't wait to show me whatever he was writing for class. And I had already read five drafts of the first act of *Yule Be Sorry*.

But how could I argue when he was showering on compliments this way?

"I think you're going to be surprised," he said.

Chapter 12

Someone called my name, but I didn't hear them at first. I was in that Xerox machine daze, waiting for retina burn to set in as I made a copy of Joanna Castle's edited manuscript. Publishing seemed to be the last bastion of the pencil and paper world. Edits were done in pencil; copyedits in red pencil. A single original manuscript was shuttled between author and publisher and production, piling on corrections as it went. And every stage had to be copied. Mass tree slaughter.

"*Mademoiselle* Abbot!"

That got my attention. If someone was speaking French to me, it had to be Mercedes. And if Mercedes wanted to see me it was probably bad news. More Cassie backstabbing, perhaps. Or who knows what else. I'd felt vulnerable ever since I'd killed Mary Jo's coffee mug.

"Come see me, *s'il vous plaît*," Mercedes said. It wasn't even a question.

"Sure—just finishing up here."

I was filled with dread as I trudged back to her office. Mercedes gestured to the squirm chair and I dutifully sank down into it.

She placed her hands on the desk in front of her and threaded her fingers together. "I got a call from *Bookworld Monthly*. A reporter there is doing an article called 'Making Waves,' which is going to be about up-and-comers at different publishing houses. I told her she should give you a buzz."

"What about?"

Mercedes gave me a good strong eye blink, and who could blame her? "About being an up-and-comer."

"Oh!"

She chuckled. "Of course modesty is a good thing . . ."

I hadn't intended to be modest. I was just slow on the up-take.

". . . but in this instance," she continued, "your job is not to be too modest. In this interview, we need you to highlight all the fabulous things we're doing at Candlelight. Toot your horn about your own achievements, by all means, but we need you to crow a little about all of our products—Signature, MetroGirl, the revamped Pulse."

I nodded. I was still trying to think what on earth I could toot my own horn about.

"You've got to be our cheerleader," Mercedes said.

"But with no skimpy outfit," I joked.

Mercedes's smile froze, and I saw a cloud of doubt cross her face. *I chose the wrong one*, that look seemed to say. *I should have picked Cassie.*

That thought sobered me. Maybe I did feel insecure and unworthy, but damned if I wanted to let Cassie grab any glory. In fact, just the prospect of my being a subject of the "Making Waves" interview filtering down to Cassie made me giddy with glee.

Mercedes got down to particulars. The woman from *BM*, Alex Keene, would be getting in contact with me, but I probably wouldn't be meeting with her until after the Dallas convention.

"And of course, I don't have to remind you that you must keep your ears open in Dallas." Mercedes always wanted us to keep our ears open. "New trends, that's what we're looking for. No one but Cassie is giving me manuscripts marked *N*. We need to stay hot on the trail of the next big thing!"

When I left Mercedes's office, Lindsay came running up to

me. "What happened?" Her whisper was loud enough to carry all the way to Jersey. "I saw her ambush you in the hallway."

"She just wanted to talk to me about some magazine article."

She sagged an arm around my shoulder in relief. "That's good. For a minute I thought . . ."

I tilted my head. "That I was going to be fired?"

"We've all been worried, ever since Mary Jo's mug . . ."

It was sort of comforting to know that someone had been that anxious on my behalf.

"Not that you need to worry," she hastened to assure me. "Rita likes you. And hell, they still haven't fired me, so their standards must be pretty low."

"Don't sell yourself short," I said.

She practically bobbed on her heels. "Oh, I don't. I'm a world champion fuck-up."

Say one thing for Lindsay. She hadn't let incompetence damage her ego.

As I was talking to Lindsay, I caught sight of Muriel walking out of my office. I frowned. It was rare to see Muriel away from the reception desk, much less venturing back here. Obviously, she wanted to check up on her friend's book. *That book!* It was now the albatross around my neck. I still hadn't written the rejection letter, though I had a few notes.

Actually, they were transcriptions of Fleishman's notes.

When Muriel was gone, I went to my office, determined to finally have that troublesome book out of my life for good. And I meant for good. When I started typing the rejection letter, I tried to use terminology that would let the person know in no uncertain terms that I didn't want to see *The Rancher and the Lady* in a new and improved incarnation at any point in the future. I didn't even tack on a "I would be happy to see any future projects . . ." blah, blah, blah that I usually wrote as my final paragraph. The truth was, now that I was finally ridding myself of this thing, I hoped never to see this author's name again.

And this was after only reading twenty pages. I tried to rationalize my strong feelings on such limited evidence by the fact that Fleishman had read the whole book and hated it. It had been given a thorough reading . . . just not by me. As a love interest, Fleishman had his shortcomings, but the man knew his romance novels.

I printed the letter, signed it, stuffed it all in an envelope, and carried the package to the mailroom. Dropping it into the outgoing mail folder, I felt as if a hundred-pound weight had fallen from my shoulders. I felt like toe dancing.

On my way out of the office that afternoon, I told Muriel that I had returned the manuscript to her friend.

Her mouth was twisted into a frown, but she nodded. "I had secretly predicted that would be the end result," she confessed. "Thank you for the time you took with it, Rebecca. At least I can assure her that it was given every consideration."

Did I feel guilty? Well, no. I *had* spent a lot of time with the book. It had been my houseguest, even.

As I clung to a subway pole on the way home that night, I suddenly had a psychological surge. I don't know why. Maybe it was finally getting that manuscript of Muriel's friend off my desk, or the fact that Mercedes had called me an up-and-comer. I felt almost self-confident.

The sensation was disconcerting.

At home I found Fleishman in an expansive mood, too. In fact, if I was in a good mood, then he was off the charts happy. "I'm done!" he exclaimed before I had even shut the door.

I was amazed. "When can I read it?"

Whatever it was . . . I still wasn't sure about that. He hadn't even told me the name of this new play of his.

"I want to go over it one more time," he said. "Maybe when you get back from Dallas."

"Okay, but you should let me take you out for a celebration. I believe I owe you something."

I had told him he would never complete anything, and now he had proved me wrong.

But he was hearing none of it. "Are you kidding? I owe *you*—big time. You're my muse."

I have to admit, those words did something to me. First of all, they made me imagine myself perched atop Fleishman's desk like that famous picture of Lauren Bacall on Harry Truman's piano. Only I pictured myself in a diaphanous gown, one that both covered all my flaws and made me look inspiring. I saw a spark of admiration in Fleishman's eyes that I hadn't noticed in . . . well, too long. I'd been hungry for that.

Or was I imagining it?

He reached out for my hand, playfully threading his fingers through mine, and oozing charm at me via those gray eyes of his. Like I was his favorite person in the world.

His muse.

Anyway, it was as if by some miracle all the friction between us had seeped away and left us as we had been—as more than friends. I felt that old spark of hope flickering inside me again.

"C'mon," he said, tugging on my hand. "White Dragon."

White Dragon had our favorite Chinese food outside of Chinatown. Usually I had to hold myself back from making a pig of myself, but tonight it felt like my appetite was gone. Another miracle. I picked at a potsticker while Fleishman gulped them down like vitamins.

"I can't tell you how great I feel," he said.

"You seem . . . exuberant."

"This time I've done it. I've really done it. I feel like I've created something worthwhile, and lasting."

"That's great."

He jabbed another dumpling with his chopsticks. "And the greatest thing is, it's not just some juvenile masturbatory thing like the stuff I did in college."

"I loved those plays," I said.

He shrugged. "They were great, too, of course—but not for a wide audience. I mean, I don't want to start saying that what I'm doing now is *commercial*—"

"Nothing wrong with that."

He blinked. "Jeez, you're right. Listen to me! And the truth is, I *wanted* to write something commercially viable. What's the matter with that? I mean, you think if any writer could change places with Stephen King, or Nora Roberts, or Tom Clancy, they wouldn't?"

"You're going to be the Nora Roberts of the New York stage?"

He laughed mysteriously. "Just wait till you read it."

I felt a prick of doubt just then, but I ignored it. I was having too good a time.

The Szechwan pork arrived, and for the next hour we drank Tsingtao and talked about how my job had changed his whole outlook. Fleishman and I hadn't talked like this in such a long time, just riffing on our lives. Of course, right now we were just talking about *his* life, but I was sure we would get around to me eventually.

Three beers later, eventually had still not arrived.

Maybe when he said I was his muse, he really meant that I was his microphone.

He was still in an ebullient mood as we stumbled back to the apartment, but by this time I was feeling a little disgruntled. And frustrated. Just like old times.

Why was I such a dope?

"I think I have to go to bed now," Fleishman said, yawning. "I don't know how I got so tired."

Maybe from running your mouth for two straight hours, I thought.

"Max still needs a walk," I said.

"Having a dog is such a pain in the ass, isn't it?" he said.

I grabbed the leash.

"Thanks for doing that," he said, volunteering me. "I don't know what I'd do without you, Renata."

I froze.

"Something wrong?" he asked.

"You called me *Renata*."

He laughed. "No way."

"Yes, you did."

"Okay, maybe I did. *Rebecca*. There. I couldn't live without you, *Rebecca*."

"Thanks!" I hooked the collar around Maxwell's neck. "That makes me feel super special."

"God, you are so bipolar tonight. First you seemed so happy and now you are acting like I insulted you."

"We've been best friends for six years and you just called me by the wrong name!"

He looked like he was beginning to get miffed. "So I have early Alzheimer's or something. Jeebus, get over it. It wasn't as if I called you the wrong name while we were having sex."

I snarled, "No, *that* wouldn't be likely to happen, would it?"

He blinked at me. "Well, no."

I let out a roar of frustration and steamed out of the apartment.

On the street, I just let Maxwell drag me around the block. It was hard to be annoyed with a creature who took such exuberant pleasure in parceling out pee to every tree, hydrant, and other protuberance along his route. But I just couldn't shake off my irritation with Fleishman—which of course was partially irritation with myself. One reference to being a muse, and I'd started thinking wild thoughts. I'd started having hopes again.

Idiot.

Renata, he'd called me.

I had to get over him, once and for all. I had to stop thinking that I would suddenly become the dream girl of this guy, who, let's face it, had passed me over twice already. Maybe I should even move out.

That thought left me paralyzed until Max tugged me onward to a newspaper box.

I'd think about all this later, I decided. After Dallas.

During the following week, when I was getting ready to go to the big convention, Fleishman became a hermit. He disappeared. He was revising his masterpiece, he said, and he couldn't have any disturbances. During the day he went to the branch library; at night he took his iPod and his computer and haunted the coffee shops.

On my last day of work before Dallas, I loaded up everything I needed—the conference schedule, a fistful of business cards, tip sheets to give out at the author appointments. Even though it was July and Dallas was reporting a record heatwave, I couldn't wait to go. Maybe this little break would be good for me. I was so focused on getting away from Fleishman that I didn't even worry about the flight, or the panel I was going to be on, or the million other things that could go wrong.

As I was leaving the office that evening, Cassie called out to me. Startled by this unusual summons, I peeked into her office. "Have a good time in Dallas, Rebecca."

For a moment, I was stupefied. Impressed, even. Tossing out even that little crumb of graciousness had probably cost her a day of agonizing.

Then she added, with extravagant sarcasm dripping in her voice, "I just know you'll be *making waves.*"

So she had heard about the article. A little voice inside my head did a gleeful cheer.

"I'll try," I said, flashing a big grin. "And you keep the home fires burning, Cassie."

She sent me a cool, secretive smile that made it appear that she might just do that. In fact, she looked like she would enjoy burning down the entire building. "I will, though of course I'd love to be in Dallas. *Really* love it."

I puzzled over this on my way to the elevator. It wasn't like Cassie to openly express envy. Openly anything wasn't her style.

But I let it go. I had other worries. I had to leave early the next morning. A car was picking me up at five-thirty to take me to the airport. Five-thirty AM. I hadn't been up and about at five-thirty AM since my sophomore year of college; of course there was a big diff between staying up till that hour and *getting up* at that hour. Hauling oneself out of bed any time before seven is a daunting task.

So it was doubly surprising when Fleishman met me on the

street that morning, dressed and daisy fresh. I had assumed he was still in bed.

I don't think I had seen Fleishman this early in the morning before.

"I sneaked out while you were in the shower." He pulled his hand out from behind his back and presented me with a deli bouquet of flowers. "Have fun on your trip."

I stood next to the car, in which the driver was drumming his fingers impatiently against the steering wheel. I didn't know what to say. It was early enough in the morning that I was confused as to his motives.

"I didn't want you to go to Dallas angry at me," he said.

"I'm not angry." It had been days since he'd called me Renata; I hadn't forgotten about it, exactly, but out of self-preservation I had pushed it to the back of my mind.

"Then thinking badly of me," he amended. "I didn't want you thinking that I was . . . well, you know."

I didn't know, but I gave him a hug. He squeezed me back and said, practically whispering in my ear, "I hope you see Dan Weatherby. I hope you two hit it off."

Dan Weatherby?

I pulled back and fixed my gaze on him. "Hit it off . . . how?"

He lifted those broad thin shoulders in a shrug. "Like you were before I came along and messed things up."

In other words, he wanted me to go to Dallas and sleep with Dan? Was he nuts?

With as much fury as I could muster at that ungodly hour, I huffed, "So you woke up at five fifteen in the morning to tell me to find someone else?"

Great. I think everyone had told me that, and now Fleishman was chiming in. Once I finally got it through my own thick skull to give up on Fleishman, it would be unanimous.

"You said five-thirty," the driver grumbled at me over the roof of the car. "It's five-forty now."

"Okay," I told him. I opened the door.

Fleishman put his hand on my shoulder. "Enjoy yourself, that's all I'm saying."

At that moment, I would have enjoyed giving him a sharp thwack over the head with those flowers. As it was, I thought I showed great restraint by waiting till I reached LaGuardia to stuff his farewell bouquet in a garbage can.

When it came to sex, Renata had a strict lights-out policy. She wanted darkness. But her definition of dark was a little different than everyone else's. Not for her the single flickering aromatherapy candle on the dresser. Even romantic moonlight filtering through the blinds was verboten; Renata had installed window coverings so aggressively opaque they would have served with honor during the London blitz.

When she beckoned me to join her on her Flying Cloud futon bed and turned out the lights, there was nothing but a blanket of inky blackness. We groped at each other not just out of frantic desire, but also because we couldn't see a thing.

I assume her mania for darkness stemmed from her horror of my being able to detect a single bulge or stretch mark on her skin. Who did she think I had been sleeping with before, Natalie Portman? She, like most nineteen-year-olds weaned on *Cosmo* and *Glamour*, seemed to assume all women were supposed to have perfect airbrushed bodies, and that if they unwittingly revealed a flaw, their prospective lovers would run fleeing into the night.

Her tactic did have one thing going for it: I couldn't have fled. I doubt I could have found the door.

It was a little ridiculous—like those old Warner Brothers cartoons where the characters could only see the whites of each other's eyes. The ones where Elmer Fudd thinks he's with a dazzling long-lashed lady when actually it's Bugs Bunny. Come the light of day, I was certain I would not be waking up next to a wascally wabbit, but with Renata by my side—funny, sexy, lovably insecure Renata.

She, unfortunately, seemed equally sure that I would find myself in bed with a gargoyle. An ankle-length yellow terrycloth robe was at the ready to prevent my disillusionment. To say she had self-esteem issues was like saying Donald Trump had a slightly inflated ego. Casual terminology just didn't begin to cover this level of psychosis.

Chapter 13

In Dallas I was full of nerves. Thanks to some Dramamine and anger about Fleishman, I managed to make it through my flight without throwing up on anyone this time. But once I was at the conference, the jitters set in. I am not at my best in crowds, with a minute-by-minute itinerary in my hand and a hoard of women teeming around me speaking in those high boisterous voices. The conference hotel, the largest in Dallas, was a madhouse. Every square inch—every guest room, meeting area, dining room, and bar—spilled over with women bearing RAG name tags on their shirts. More confusing yet, I would sometimes think I saw someone I knew, then realize that I only recognized them from the backs of book jackets.

When I did happen to have a moment free, as when I retreated to my room to change clothes because I spilled a Diet Coke down my front, I would stew about Fleishman. And those flowers. And that awful name, *Renata.* And all the years I had spent as his hanger-on, his groupie, his default girl. It was absurd, mortifying, depressing.

So it was probably best that I was kept busy.

This was Madeline's first time at the big conference, too, and when I ran into her at the registration line, she seemed as dazzled as she could be in a hotel in which practically the only men were the busboys. "Susan Elizabeth Phillips was in the restroom line!" she whispered to me excitedly.

It was as if overnight she had turned into a true romance groupie. But I could understand. It was hard not to catch the fever. Not if you'd spent the past months perusing the *Romance Journal.* There were giants among us.

By the end of the first day, I hadn't run into Dan Weatherby at the conference yet. Then again, I hadn't seen a lot of the people from Candlelight, either. Andrea and I hadn't actually spoken to each other since sharing a cab from the airport, and Rita I had only caught a few sightings of, holding court with the last remnants of the Smoking Author's Guild. I was on a panel about romantic suspense, which I managed to get through, and I spent the rest of the time rushing from appointment to appointment with my authors. I'd tried to squeeze most of them in early on, before conference fatigue set in, and also because I was filling in for Cassie's panel the next day.

Everything had gone smoothly until the author appointments. Then—sometime just before noon on day two—something went wrong. Really, really wrong. Eerily wrong. I always think people are reacting to me oddly, so perhaps it was natural that I wouldn't take in the fact that people I met seemed friendly at first and then turned stony, if not downright hostile. It took me a while to pick up on the dropped jaws, the glares, the mutters.

But at some point, the fact that something was amiss was undeniable. I think it was during the author appointments that I realized that people were treating me not so much like an editor as a carrier of the Ebola virus. At first the appointments would start just as they always did, with an author telling me about her latest masterpiece of hospital romance or clan war romance, and I would nod and smile and ask her to send it to me. I would then hand her my business card, and she would either thank me profusely and make her exit, or her face would redden and she would curtly take her leave. The longer the appointments dragged on, the more often the latter occurred.

At first I thought it was just the stress of the big conference getting to everyone, but after a few hours I realized that people were becoming decidedly more hostile. They weren't even waiting for the end of the appointment to glare at me.

When I left the little room where I was doing my author appointments, glad to escape the glares from people I barely knew, a woman on the conference committee nearly crashed into me. She smiled, then glanced at my RAG tag and let out an angry harrumph.

"Hope you're enjoying yourself, Rebecca Abbot!" she sniped.

I wasn't just imagining it.

For a minute I wondered if someone had pinned a sign on me. I was skulking off to the elevator when Mary Jo bore down on me so fast that there was no chance of escape. Her face was fiery red.

"*Here* you are!" she exclaimed, as if I had been hiding. "Just what is it you think you're doing?"

Having Mary Jo huff at me was nothing new. Right after the fateful incident in the coffee room, the God Pod had presented her with a Dilbert mug, but she had put it on her shelf. "For safekeeping," she had announced, pointedly, when I was in earshot. At all subsequent editorial meetings, she had brought her coffee in a Styrofoam cup.

Still, at a conference you would expect *a little* friendliness from your coworkers. Especially when the rest of the attendees seemed to be giving you the frost.

"I was going to my room to freshen up before my panel," I said.

She folded her arms and sent me a positively withering look. "You're not on the panel."

I did a double take. I was sure I was on the panel, which was called "From Boardroom to Bedroom: White Collar Alpha Heroes." It was originally Cassie's gig, but when Cassie was sidelined, I had been chosen as a fill-in. Andrea was taking Cassie's author appointments.

"In the schedule, it said that I was going to be on the panel," I insisted.

Mary Jo bellowed, "Well you're not! After the stunt you

pulled, Mercedes decided she needed to fill in for you herself. Mercedes Coe, the editorial director of Candlelight, on an alpha hero panel!"

There was so much indignation in her voice, it was as if she were talking about Meryl Streep being forced to go back to community theater. All because of me.

"Why?"

"I think you know," she said.

"But I don't know."

"Oh, I think you do know."

It was tempting to reply, "But I don't," and make a real Abbott and Costello routine of it, but Mary Jo cut me off. In fact, the words nearly exploded out of her, as if she were so exasperated with my obstinacy, my obtuseness, and my feckless destructiveness that she just couldn't hold back the tide of anger anymore. "Your business cards, Rebecca!"

I frowned. I had no idea what she was talking about. "What about them?"

She held out her hand. "Give me one."

I hesitated. I'd already handed out a fistful.

She snapped her fingers. "I know you have them with you."

"Well, yeah, but I only brought about fifty, and I've given out over half of them."

There was another day of conference left. I couldn't afford to start handing them out to coworkers.

Mary Jo nearly snapped my head off. "We *know* you've been giving them out like candy, Rebecca! The directors of the conference are about ready to expel us all from the hotel because of the damn things. Mercedes and I have been doing damage control for the past hour."

Confused, I yanked my cards out of my purse. At first I couldn't figure out what the deal was. It was just my regular card. My name was correct, as was all the contact information. Crimson over eggshell white. Classy. Then I looked at where "*Books Are Our Passion*" was supposed to be written. Instead, my card read, "*Books Are My Toilet Paper.*"

Every ounce of blood drained out of my face.

I blinked, hoping I had seen wrong. Regrettably, I hadn't.

"Books Are My Toilet Paper."

Not so classy.

My jaw swung open and I looked searchingly into Mary Jo's unforgiving eyes. "I suppose this is your idea of a joke," she said.

"No!"

"Well congratulations!" she exclaimed. "You've given the entire Candlelight delegation a black eye!"

"But I didn't know!" I insisted. "I don't know how this happened."

"Those cards didn't get printed up and hop into your purse on their own, Rebecca."

"I know, but someone—" My mouth snapped shut. Oh, God. *Cassie.* No wonder she had made such a point of waving me off the night before I left. "*I wish I could be there, too,*" she'd said, smirking.

No wonder. She would have loved to see the fruits of her labors resulting in my utter humiliation.

I seethed angrily for a moment. "It was Cassie," I said. "She did it."

"Cassie!" Mary Jo exclaimed skeptically. "Cassie's not even here."

"I know. She was mad about being told she couldn't come. And besides that, she hates me. She's had it in for me from the very beginning. Just ask Andrea."

"That's quite an accusation you're making. What proof do you have?"

Mary Jo seemed to think that I was fingering a suspect in a murder case.

"Ask anybody."

She put her hands on her hips. "Cassie has been a responsible Candlelight employee for four years. Years before you ever got there."

I stuck to my guns. "If this wasn't Cassie, then I'll resign."

Mary Jo's lips pursed. "By the time Mercedes is through with you, you might not need to."

For the rest of the day I was persona non grata at that conference. I apologized to Mercedes, but I was still excused from the "Boardroom to Bedroom" panel. In fact, it was suggested that I might want to look into exchanging my flight back to New York City for an earlier one. It was so humiliating. I'm ashamed to admit that I did not bear up well to the disgrace, either. Instead, I hid in my room emptying out my minibar until I was fairly certain it was the dining out hour and the coast was clear. Then I sneaked down to the hotel bar to partake of some liquor from full-size bottles. Tanqueray had never tasted so good.

I don't know how long I was draped over that bar before someone came for me. In the end, it wasn't Andrea, Rita, or anyone else from Candlelight. My comrades seemed to have forsaken me. No, when someone tapped me on the shoulder and I looked up, it was none other than Dan Weatherby.

"Long time no see," he said.

I could barely see now. The man was definitely blurry, but that smile was so welcome I hardly cared. In fact, I was comfortably past the point of caring about much of anything.

"I heard about your trouble," he said, sliding onto the stool next to mine.

I waved a hand, as if the day's depredations were just so much water off a duck's back. And for the moment, they seemed like it. What mattered more was the fact that Dan Weatherby was here, and he was smiling that sexy smile at me.

"I've been thinking a lot about you lately," he purred.

I wasn't just imagining it, either. There was something definitely come-hitherish about him. I was picking up vibes.

"Why?" I asked.

He shrugged his broad shoulders. "Something I've been reading reminded me of you."

"What?" Right now I felt so pathetic, the only heroine I could possibly empathize with was something out of Judy Blume. *Are You There God, It's Me, Rebecca.*

"It's something new," he said. "But I predict it will be hot."

I snuffled self-consciously and poked his suit jacket with the toothpick from my drink. "Shouldn't you be off schmoozing with clients?"

"My client pooped out on me, so I'm available." He grinned. "For anything."

Good heavens. If he'd kept going on like that, in another half hour I would have ended up in bed with him.

As it was, he kicked it up a notch and it only took fifteen minutes.

What do I remember? Not a lot. With his help I managed to weave up to his room. Then, once we were inside the dark hotel room, it was as if we were in some dark, sensual cocoon. He didn't even bother turning on the lights, which was okay by me. I prefer the dark for these initial encounters, and I was gratified that he seemed to anticipate me on this point. In fact, he seemed to understand a lot about me. In some ways, it was as if we were connecting in a way that I never had with anyone else.

But of course, I was also more looped than I had ever been with anyone else.

When I opened my eyes the next morning to the sound of Dan brushing his teeth, I was still remembering the night before. It was as if no time had passed. At first, I didn't even feel hungover. I felt great. Supercharged, even. I stretched like a cat and sat up, quickly grabbing my camisole top from the night before and slipping it on. I didn't particularly want Dan's first view of my body to be the stretch marks across my middle.

I have to admit, my ecstatic mood wasn't all about ecstasy. I was also feeling a little smug. *Take that, Fleishman*, I wanted to shout. I *had* found someone else—someone, if my soused memory served, who was even much better in bed than Fleishman could ever dream of being.

Of course, the fact that Fleishman had basically been steering me in this direction was a little worrisome. But I didn't dwell on that particular point.

Dan finally came out, so thoroughly flossed and brushed

that his teeth almost gave off a glare. "I hope you don't mind that I ordered breakfast."

He obviously didn't know me. "Not a bit."

"I have a client appointment for brunch this morning at ten o'clock, but I'm starved." He let out a sexy rumble. "Guess we worked up an appetite last night."

Oh God. Was he not adorable? I couldn't believe my good fortune. "It's lucky I ran into you. Otherwise I might have ended up asleep on that barstool."

"Surely someone from Candlelight would have come along and rescued you."

The thought of Mercedes or one of her minions spotting me in that bar made me groan. "I'm glad it was you instead."

"Me too," he said.

By the time the scones and coffee arrived, it occurred to me that this was the happiest I had ever been on one of these morning after occasions. This felt easy. This felt right.

"I was really dreading going back to New York, but now I can't wait."

Dan flashed me one of those million-watt smiles. "Why?"

Wasn't it obvious? Last night I was certain that when I returned to New York, it would be as someone shunned, shamed, and unemployed. But now I could hear the birds twittering and all those other things that are supposed to happen when hope miraculously returns.

When I went back to New York I would probably still be shunned, shamed, and unemployed. But now I had Dan, at least for a while. A fling to get me through the rough patch.

Briefly, I even luxuriated in the vision of us becoming a serious item, inseparables, a publishing power couple. (Once I found another job.) My friends and family would embrace Dan in a way that they had never embraced Fleishman, because . . . well, mostly because Dan wasn't Fleishman. In the estimation of practically everyone I knew, Fleishman was an easy act to follow.

I got so carried away in this fantasy that I allowed myself to gush, "I want to show you off to my friends."

I should have known better. "I want to show you off to my friends" is the man's line. I should have realized—before Dan's face fell like an undercooked soufflé—that I was taking way too much for granted.

Before responding, he spent an agonizing moment considering. A bad sign. Then he cleared his throat. "Maybe I should have said something last night . . ."

In the ensuing awkward silence, I tittered nervously. "You're not married," I joked. "I checked."

He grimaced. "No, but maybe I should have said what we both know, obviously. Which was that this was a mistake."

It was as if someone had given me an ice water injection. "A mistake," I repeated.

"A *wonderful* mistake," he added quickly. As if that amendment would make being dumped easier. His tone was so earnest I suddenly felt nauseated. The scone I had so blithely scarfed down a moment before now felt like a boulder squatting in my stomach.

Apparently, this was not going to be a fling. Or it had already flung itself out.

"Because of—well, because of a lot of things, obviously," he said.

I wracked my brains, but I honestly couldn't think of any of these obvious reasons. Unless he obviously didn't like me. Or he had seen some of my obvious imperfections and changed his mind about me.

"Workwise, this kind of thing isn't kosher," he explained. "There might be complications in the future."

Oh brother. Whatever these complications were—or were going to be—I wasn't much interested in hearing about them. It wasn't as if Andrea hadn't told me about Clea. I knew Dan was a lothario—I just hadn't expected him to be such a jerk, too. It was as if the slightest hint of something lasting longer than six hours made him jump out of his skin.

"I get it. It was just one of those things." I started searching for the garments I had discarded so carelessly, so happily, on his floor the night before.

"What are you doing?"

"Getting out of here," I said.

He let out a huff. "Don't be that way about it."

"What way?"

"Clingy."

I gaped at him. "What are you talking about? I'm *leaving*. Which, in case you don't know, is the exact opposite of cling."

"Yes, but you're upset. I can tell."

What was I supposed to do? Stay, but not stay so long that it made him uncomfortable? Did he expect an alarm to sound at the optimum moment for the one-night stand to end?

The whole situation pissed me off. He arrogantly assumed, just because I hung around long enough to drink a cup of coffee, that I was a psycho-girl who never wanted to give him up. But I wasn't. No bunny boiler, me. Just the opposite! Wasn't I the woman who had watched my ex-boyfriend and roommate squire a string of women around Manhattan? (I might pine, but I didn't cling.) I wasn't unrealistic. I knew once a guy started stammering like Dan was doing, it was game over.

And good riddance, I thought.

"Rebecca . . ."

I tossed my shirt over my head and wriggled into my wrinkled skirt. "Never mind, Dan. No explanations necessary."

He let out a sigh, as if he were the wounded party here. "I should have guessed you'd react this way."

What was he talking about? He barely knew me!

I finally managed to escape that hotel room, but just as I was stepping foot into the hallway, who would I run into? Andrea. She stopped mid-stride on her way to the elevator and looked from me to the door I had just closed. When her gaze alit back on me, she was gaping in something like awe.

"No way!" she yelled.

I put a finger to my lips.

Her hands balled at her sides. "I have been coming to these stupid conferences for years now, and *nothing* ever happens to me. And here you are, two for two!"

"It's not how it looks."

"Well even if it's not, it's better than my night, which consisted of tagging along with a group from Boise for Tex-Mex then coming back at nine, popping heartburn pills, and falling asleep in front of *Batman Begins* on television."

I thought for a moment. "Right now I would do anything to have spent the night watching pay-per-view."

In fact, it was one of those moments when I would have switched places with just about anyone. All things considered, being me wasn't working out so hot.

Chapter 14

By the time I dribbled through my apartment and collapsed in a heap, Wendy and Fleishman were out for the night. Max was my welcome wagon. He struggled his way up on the futon and successfully swiped that stinky little pink tongue across my chin. I was too worn out to do anything more than mop up the puppy saliva with my sleeve.

I was glad to be alone, actually. I rattled around the apartment for an hour or so, dreading going back to work even more than usual. How could I possibly live through the day without murdering Cassie? I'm pretty sure killing a coworker would get me fired. On the other hand, I was probably going to be fired anyway. Mercedes had very coolly accepted my assurances that I'd had nothing to do with the whole business card fiasco. But had she believed me?

No doubt about it, Monday was going to be a very bad day.

Finally I sought some over-the-counter oblivion in a wine cooler and two Benadryl. I was sound asleep after that.

The next morning I tumbled out of bed, fully expecting that this would be the last day there would be a necessity to do so, perhaps for a long time. I put on my favorite dress from Fleishman's mother's wardrobe. I wanted to look my best as I was escorted from the building.

I had to pick my way around the apartment, trying not to

make any noise. Sometime during the night, the prodigal roommates had come home. They were still in full snooze when I left.

On the subway ride to work, I concentrated on Cassie. I still couldn't decide if I should just scream at her or go for the kill. I am not a violent person (I was subjected to the cinematic teachings of Ben Kingsley at a tender age), but these felt like extenuating circumstances, at least to me. The jury of my peers residing in my mind had already acquitted me by the time I reached the elevator.

I stepped on and there he was. Suave Guy, smiling at me. Cassie evaporated from my thoughts. I smiled back and did that awkward face forward.

I wish someone would put something in elevators for people to stare at. Television, for instance. A person stuck in an airport can always find CNN somewhere. Why not people stuck in elevators?

No sooner had that phrase—stuck in an elevator—flitted through my mind than the very floor seemed to dip underneath me and I lurched forward, smacking my forehead against the wall just above the button panel.

Suave Guy reached over to steady me. "Are you all right?" he asked, his hands bracing both my arms.

This gave me two reasons to swoon. One, because I was scared witless, and two, because I had inadvertently landed myself in the arms of the elevator hottie.

"I-I'm fine," I stuttered, though for a moment I wondered if he let go of me, would my knees buckle under me like one of those wooden pedestal toys with elastic for joints.

But he did let me go, and with the help of a wall, I managed to stay upright. The situation was pregnant with sensual possibilities, but the only sense that really took hold of me in that moment was clammy fear. Had the electricity gone out? Why? What was going on out there? *(Terrorist attack!)* Did anyone know we were here?

"What do we do?" The tremor in my voice was unmistakable. In a crisis, I am a pillar of Jell-O.

He pressed the red emergency button. From where we were, it produced absolutely no result. I could only hope that somewhere else in the building a brawny rescuer was hearing an alarm bell. "Unfortunately, that's all I can think of."

"That's more than I had the presence of mind to try," I admitted.

He smiled. And I have to admit, panicked as I was, that smile went a long way in soothing my nerves. He was so calm, so blue-suited. He was like Paxil for the eyes. I stopped hyperventilating, though I feared I was drooling. I couldn't wait to tell Andrea about this. If I lived. Strains of "To Dream the Impossible Dream" thundered through my head with Robert Goulet-like insistence.

My companion tilted his head. "Did you hear something?"

Could he hear it, too? For a moment I worried that I had unconsciously burst into song.

"A knocking," he explained.

"Oh!" I concentrated. "No."

He pushed the red button again. "Probably just wishful thinking on my part."

Now that I wasn't feeling as if I were about to throw up, I tried to be philosophical. "I'm not so sure I want off the elevator, anyway." The man's eyes widened, and I realized at once how that sounded. Like I wanted to stay suspended in this cube with him forever. Which, of course, was true. But it wasn't what I meant.

"I basically came into work this morning to allow them to fire me."

His brows raised in alarm. "But you just started. What happened?"

"You don't really want to know," I said.

He laughed. "As it happens, I have some time to fill." He reached into the little white sack he was carrying and brought out a bagel. "You can explain it to me over breakfast, which I hope you'll share with me."

I hesitated. The last thing I really wanted to do with the elevator hottie was whine about my problems while I shoveled down carbs. Then again, what I really wanted to do with the elevator hottie really wasn't an option, outside of a Hollywood movie or a beer commercial.

"Cinnamon raisin," he said, offering me the top of his bagel, which everyone knows is the best half. What a gentleman.

I accepted the bagel and took what I hoped was a delicate bite.

"Now what's this about being fired?" he asked.

Even the nutshell version of my life at Candlelight thus far still managed to take up several minutes. By the time I was done we had finished breakfast and he had a puzzled look on his face.

"Which one is Cassie?"

"She's blond."

His eyes widened. "The one that looks like Jessica Simpson?"

"No . . ." He meant Madeline. For a moment I wondered if Suave Guy had his own dream elevator girl. At any rate, he seemed fairly certain of his knowledge of the Candlelight staff.

"Jan Brady," he guessed.

I was astonished. "Andrea's right! You are a spy."

He laughed. "Nothing so interesting. Just a humble attorney."

Judging by the cut of those suits, not so humble. "Corporate?"

"Wills and estates. McAlpin and Etting, twelfth floor."

"Are you McAlpin or Etting?"

He conscientiously wiped the last of the butter off his fingers with a paper napkin and held out his hand. "Luke Rayburn, junior partner."

I introduced myself, even though it felt strange doing so to someone who had been an object of so many Candlelight ruminations.

"I've always been curious about your business." He leaned casually against the wall. "It's always seemed odd to be up in my office, toiling away on old ladies' wills, when all that romance was going on down below."

"Now you know. There's no romance going on there at all." Outside of my foolish phone flirtation with Dan and Troy's cover model interviews, this was true. "Just the usual office intrigue."

He looked doubtful. "Nothing in my office matches the Cassie shenanigans you just described."

A juicy idea occurred to me. "You think I could sue her?"

"More likely you'll have to settle for her getting her comeuppance someday."

"That sounds depressingly philosophical. And unlikely to happen."

"I don't see you having much success in pinning this on her in the near term, short of getting a taped confession," he said.

Now why hadn't I thought of that? "What a great idea!"

At that moment, the elevator dipped, and I was pretty sure that I would have no opportunity to put this plan into action. "Oh my God!"

"Don't panic," he said. "I think this is it."

If by "it" he meant our imminent deaths, I was in complete agreement. But there was no way I was not panicking. I was already envisioning the freefall drop, the crash, my parents weeping that their youngest daughter had ended her life as a splatter.

But even as those events were playing through my mind, it began to dawn on me that we weren't in freefall. In fact, the elevator was gliding upwards. It was over.

Luke sent me a reassuring smile, and then the doors opened on my floor. "Made it!" he said, holding the door.

I was a little stunned. Five minutes ago, I had been spilling all my woes out to him. It had seemed not out of the realm of possibility that we might die together. Now it was back to business as usual.

"Thanks for breakfast."

"No problem," he said. "Good luck."

I stumbled out of the elevator and smiled as the doors closed between us.

Then I turned. I had somehow expected to be greeted like little Jessica coming out of the well. You would have thought a crowd would gather for something like this, ready to peer down the elevator shaft at the crushed and mangled car that had dropped to the basement. *Hadn't anyone heard the alarm?*

Instead, the place was deserted. My life-and-death struggle had gone completely unnoticed.

Even Muriel wasn't there. In her place was a stranger with dark teased hair and lots of makeup. She was chewing gum, something Muriel would have disapproved of vociferously.

"What happened?" I asked.

"What happened with what?" the woman asked nonchalantly.

"The elevator!" I practically shrieked. Oddly, now that I was off the thing, I felt more shaky than ever. "We were stuck in there for a quarter hour!"

Eyes thick with mascara blinked in unconcern. "I don't know anything about it. It worked fine when I was on it twenty minutes ago."

"Where's Muriel?" I asked.

"Who?"

"The receptionist."

"I don't know. I'm a temp."

Sensing that I was going to get no more information from Miss Max Factor, I wobbled back to the Pulse Pod, making the compulsory stop at Andrea's office.

"You won't believe what happened!" she exclaimed.

This threw me. Wasn't that my line? "Wait, I've got to tell you. Guess who I was just trapped in the elevator with!"

"I don't know." She seemed oddly uninterested. "George Clooney."

"Close! Suave Guy."

She didn't react.

"We were trapped for fifteen minutes, and I told him all about the office. He gave me his bagel." I realized two things at once: That I was babbling, and that Andrea seemed to have no interest at all in what I was saying. And for her to have no interest in Suave Guy, her Mr. Incredible, something had to be very, very wrong.

"What's the matter?" I asked.

"*Cassie!*" she yelled.

"That's what I was going to tell you," I said, hoping to tell her about Suave Guy's idea. If Andrea couldn't torture a confession out of Cassie, no one could. "Luke—the elevator hottie, that's his name—told me I need audio evidence. A taped confession."

"I don't know what you're talking about, but if you're thinking of getting a confession out of Cassie, forget about it. You're too late."

For a moment I held my breath. Too late for Cassie torture?

"She's gone. She pulled a fast one!"

"Faster than switching my business cards to get me fired?"

"She stole my job!" Andrea exploded.

This was incomprehensible. "*You* got fired?"

Andrea rolled her eyes. "Pay attention, Rebecca. Not *this* job. That little she-skunk was welcome to this job, if it had suited her devious fancy. But no! She got my job at Gazelle! Snatched it right out from under me!"

My jaw dropped. Gazelle? "She's leaving?"

"She's *left.* She cleared out her office on Friday while we were all away and skedaddled off to what should have been *my* job."

I again experienced the sensation I'd had when the elevator dipped, like the floor was being pulled out from under me. I had to sit down. "Unbelievable!"

"Well, believe it." Andrea crossed her arms. "Mercedes is seriously pissed. You don't have to worry about getting fired, at least. She will now believe every evil thing about Cassie you care to tell her."

"Took her long enough," I muttered.

Andrea snorted, which sort of turned into a sob. "It's so unfair! That little rat! Why should she get to escape and not me? I've sent out so many applications."

Poor Andrea. "Maybe there's some reason fate has brought you here," I said.

She surveyed her cluttered desk, the piles of manuscripts, the as-yet-unopened Sunday *Times.* "I'm just doomed to rot here. When I die I'll just be a frustrated old spinster living in a studio in Queens, and I'll have two hundred items on the late list." She slid down lower in her chair. "I mean, look at you! Four months in, and you get trapped in an elevator with *my* dreamboat. Don't talk to me about fate. Life is not fair."

I shut up.

She brooded for a few moments, then angled one of her brows my way. "He gave you his bagel?"

"Half of it."

"Top half or bottom?"

"Top."

She sighed. "A gallant hottie."

"His name is Luke Rayburn. He's an attorney. Wills and estates."

She frowned. "That sounds very dull."

"But lucrative," I pointed out.

She slapped a hand on her desk in frustration. "Yes, damn it! He's good looking, rich, chivalrous, and now he's yours. Even my pathetic little fantasy life at this place has been shattered."

"He's not mine," I assured her.

"Well it's no fun dreaming about some guy someone else has been stuck in an elevator with. Besides, I don't like the name Luke. It reminds me of Luke Skywalker, and that soap opera guy from the eighties with the fuzzy hair." She moaned sadly. "I'm just screwed. I'll be here forever."

"Is it really so bad here?"

Her lips twisted. "Asked the lab bunny in the next cage."

I was wracking my brains for something positive to say, but all at once Andrea's door opened and shut and Troy appeared, grinning ear-to-ear.

"Is everybody happy?" he shouted, complete with jazz hand gestures.

We gaped at him.

"I just heard the news and *had* to rush over!"

"Cassie got the job Andrea wanted," I explained. "At Gazelle."

Troy drew back. "Oh no, girl! No tears over that place. I used to work there."

"And?" Andrea asked.

"It's a madhouse. It's like being on the chain gang. And the models—definitely second rate!"

Andrea laughed. She actually seemed to be perking up. "Really? You like it better here?"

"Oh, yeah! Never mind those people." He lifted a hand. "Besides, I was just interviewing a model who was telling me he had heard that there might be something opening up over at Venus."

She gasped. "Really?"

"I'll look into it."

"And you still haven't opened your Sunday *Times*," I reminded her, pointing to the folded paper in front of her. "There could be all sorts of jobs this week."

Andrea looked transformed. "Maybe so."

"There!" Troy said. "And so in honor of Cassie, let's all join in a chorus of 'Ding, Dong, the Witch Is Dead.' "

We started singing, and after a few words, Lisa came running and joined in. Then Lindsay. By the time were done with three choruses—Troy knew them all—every pod in earshot had joined us. I'm not even sure everyone knew why they were singing, but they seemed ready to celebrate anyway. Or maybe just ready to goof off.

When the merriment was over, I stopped by Cassie's office, which looked pretty much like it always had, except of course her salutatorian picture was gone. (No doubt that was already sitting on her desk at Gazelle.) She had been here—practically lived here—for four years, and if Andrea hadn't told me, I don't think I would have noticed she was gone. Except, of course, I would probably have realized that the person trying to ruin my career was missing.

When I got back to my desk, I was surprised by how edgy I felt. My nemesis was gone. I was safe now. Mercedes wouldn't fire me. (At least not this week.)

So why couldn't I relax?

I was still pondering this question when Lindsay came in and flopped down in the spare chair. She seemed agitated. But of course, she was always in a swivet about something. "Can you believe about Cassie?"

"I'm still trying to absorb it all. And you don't even know what happened over the weekend," I said. "Cassie stole my business cards and—"

She cut me off with a wave of her hand. "Oh, everybody's heard about that!" She made it sound like last month's news. "She really went out with a bang. I wonder if those people at Gazelle are having second thoughts yet about hiring her."

"Give them a week."

She reached around and shut the door. "So, what do you think my chances are?"

I had no idea what she was talking about. "Chances of what?"

She looked at me as if I were being purposefully dense. "Of being promoted."

"Oh!" I had to lean back in my chair so I wouldn't fall out of it. "I didn't know . . ."

She slurped some coffee and nodded. "I know—you don't think of me as ambitious. But I can't be Rita's assistant forever."

"No . . . I can see how that wouldn't be a good situation."

"And anyway, look at all the other people working here. Look at . . ."

Look at me, I thought.

Of course, I wasn't creating mad cock-ups every other day, either. (More like every week.) "I see your point."

She nodded eagerly. "Will you talk to Rita about promoting me?"

"*Me?*" I squeaked.

"Rita likes you."

"Well . . ." I tried not to look too uncomfortable, but the words *no fucking way* were playing through my head in a loop. I didn't want to touch this situation with a vaulting pole. "Wouldn't it be best if you talked to her yourself?"

"But she can't stand me."

That was the problem, all right. "Or what about Andrea? She's more senior than me . . ."

"I talked to her first thing."

"What did she say?"

" 'No fucking way.' "

Now why hadn't I thought of that?

Lindsay leaned forward. "Please? I'll owe you, big time."

"It's really not that great a job," I said. "I mean, it's fine, but don't you like being an assistant? It's less pressure."

"Not the way I do it. I figure as much as I angst over my little screwups, why shouldn't I get promoted and angst over bigger screwups?"

I shook my head and nodded. What she said made sense, in a Lindsay sort of way.

"Besides," she continued, "a promotion means more money. Maybe with more money, I could convince Rowdy we could afford separate places."

Who could argue against more money? "I'll see what I can manage," I finally agreed, figuring they were words I would probably regret. But I didn't know what else to do. I didn't have the forthrightness of Andrea. And I liked Lindsay.

I tried to get to work. There was a manuscript on my desk by a new, unagented author who had written a five-hundred page book about a divorcee who falls in love with her art teacher; the cover letter described the teacher as "the Jackson Pollack of Lawrence, Kansas." I scanned the first page, ready to toss the opus on my "to be rejected pile," when my gaze fell on the opening paragraph.

The only thing wrong about Jared Pickett was that he was completely awful in every way imaginable. For me, of course, it was love at first sight.

I laughed a little at that, and since it had seemed like ages since anything I had read had made me laugh, I kept going right up until the moment when Lindsay again poked her head into my office.

Surely she didn't expect me to have spoken to Rita already! Besides, I still had my own little snarl to wriggle out of. I had been expecting my phone to ring with a summons to speak to either Mercedes or Mary Jo. Or at least Rita.

"Mercedes has called a meeting. All editorial."

The conference room seemed fuller than usual. It would be, would't it? The first time I had to show my face after Dallas, everybody was there. Oddly, however, no one seemed to be the least bit interested in l'affaire de business cards, except that it was common knowledge that Cassie had been at the bottom of that stunt. All the buzz was about Cassie.

Even Mary Jo was polite to me when I slipped into the only free chair available, next to her. "Disgraceful!" she muttered, and so pointed was her reference that I didn't even suspect she was talking about me. "To think I didn't believe you when you said Cassie set you up. And all the while she was back here in New York, defecting!"

"I'm still in shock," I said.

She leaned closer. "Tell me, it was really Cassie who was responsible for my mug falling, wasn't it?"

It was like being handed a gift. "I don't like to point fingers, Mary Jo . . ."

She slapped the table. "I *knew* it!"

I quickly started trying to think of other screw-ups I could blame on Cassie now.

Truly, though, I was a little nonplussed by the outrage her leaving was stirring up among the higher ups. Hadn't people told me that editors left here all the time? But when Mercedes marched in, scarf fluttering behind her, and banged her little gavel so solemnly, I began to understand.

It wasn't that Cassie had left; it was that she had left abruptly, and on her own terms.

"I suppose by now you've all heard the news," she said. "While we were gone, Cassie defected. She went to Gazelle. As you know, she left in a very unclassy way."

"But in a very Cassie way!" Andrea sniped.

Mercedes pursed her lips patiently and waited for the groans and sniggers to die down. "She took her Rolodex with her. Beyond that, we aren't sure what else. We need to touch base with all her authors and make sure they're all still on board." She sighed. "And again, we must redouble our efforts to improve our market share."

"Because of Cassie?" Ann blurted out.

Mercedes zeroed in on her with hawklike intensity. "You can bet word of this incident has spread. We've got to try even harder now to make authors feel like Candlelight is a place they can settle in and grow. Which is why we need to keep looking for innovative new projects. Has anyone found anything along those lines?"

It was an odd question to ask, considering that most of us had been out of our offices for the past few business days.

But to my surprise, I found myself lifting my hand. "I have a slush book. The author meant it for Signature—"

"That's a line for established authors," Mary Jo said quickly.

"I know, I was doubtful. But I read a few chapters anyway, and the author has a really strong voice. It's not your usual story, but I think she'd fit somewhere—MetroGirl, maybe."

"There—perfect," Mercedes said. "That's what I want you all to do. Keep your peepers open. Give that book to me as soon as you're done, Rebecca, *s'il vous plait*. And don't forget to mark it *N*."

She let out a long breath and looked around the table. Her gaze alit on every single face assembled, from the heads of departments to the assistants sitting in the back. "Work is hell, isn't it?"

The question hung there, as if she really expected an answer. Everyone at the table seemed to shift, casting sidewise glances at their coworkers.

"Work eats up our lives," Mercedes said. "We get up, we commute, we sit in cubicles and offices for eight hours, we commute home and then have maybe a couple of hours to ourselves before we have to go to sleep so we can start the process over the next day. *C'est la vie.* We're luckier than workers a few generations back, especially women workers, but that doesn't mean that it doesn't become a grind. It wears you down. I know this. Some of you probably sit in your office dreaming of getting different jobs, or going to grad school."

I trained my eyes on my notepad so I wouldn't look up at Andrea.

"What gerbil doesn't want to jump off the wire wheel eventually?" Mercedes went on. "You get tired of coming in day after day, tired of the same old faces. Mine, probably more than anyone else's."

There were nervous titters around the table. From the tension crackling in the air, you could tell that everyone thought Mercedes had flipped her lid. "You probably feel unappreciated. You hear us say we're a family here, and you sneer. You think we don't mean it, but we do. We are a family here. So please, if you ever feel as if you are going to explode out of your desk like Cassie did, come to me first. I mean it. This may be a big outfit, but we are very serious about trying to keep our family together."

She let that last statement hang in the air while we all sat, silent. Next to me, Mary Jo snuffled. Then Mercedes banged down her gavel. "Senior eds in my office, pronto."

Maybe it was just the day I was having, but Mercedes's words actually hit home in a weird way. More than the usual corporate we're-all-a-big-family nonsense. Maybe it had something to do with my near death experience in the elevator that morning, but I think it was her acknowledgement of the cost of the long hours of work that reached me. And then I thought about all the hours she had clocked there . . . not to mention Mary Jo, and Rita, and even Andrea. They'd all been there longer than I could imagine, toiling away to try to make these books as enjoyable for the readers and as profitable for the authors and company as was feasible. It wasn't glamorous work. But it meant something to a lot of people.

I didn't have to wonder long about what Andrea had thought of the speech. She stuck her head in my office and made a retching gesture. "Can you believe that prissy windbag? And Mary Jo—*crying!*"

Having been on the brink of sniffling myself, I failed to join in her sneering. "She was just trying to make us feel like she understands our day-to-day tribulations."

"Right. She feels our pain. Spare me! If she really felt my pain she'd give me a decent raise."

"So why don't you go ask her for one?"

She blinked at me. "Are you nuts? Do you think she meant what she was saying in there? Boy, you really did fall off the turnip truck!"

I could still hear her laughing as she returned to her office and shook open the classified section of the *New York Times*.

I went back to reading my weird chick lit book. It had definite possibilities, even though the plot seemed to ramble a bit. It rambled in a good way, I thought. I began to feel excited, actually, like editors I had witnessed in meetings describing a book they wanted to go to contract on. They would get this possessive gleam in their eyes, like a farmer who had grown a prize tomato.

It was all luck. This project had landed in my lap. But somehow, now that I had it, I felt a real stake in being the person who was going to midwife it into the world.

Rita sauntered in under an armload of manuscripts.

"What's that?" I asked.

"Your share of Cassie's workload. We're divvying it up."

I frowned as my shelf sagged under the new weight. "Are we going to get a new Cassie?"

"That could take a while. Art has ordered belt tightening."

"Oh." I gulped. Great. More work. Then I remembered. "I guess I just assumed . . ." I shook my head. "But you wouldn't want to do that."

She took the bait. "I wouldn't want to do what?"

"Well . . . why not move Lindsay up?"

Rita actually had to grip the wall to stay upright. "This pod has enough problems as it is."

"But one of our problems is we don't have enough workers." I shrugged. "Well, never mind. I'm sure you wouldn't want to go through all the hassle of finding a new assistant."

That prospect—finding a new assistant—obviously had its appeal. A tiny lightbulb went off over her head. "Do you think she's ready?"

"You could always start grooming her," I said. "Or, if you want, I could work with her, maybe steer her through a few edits."

"You'd really do that?" she asked.

I cast my eye on my recently swollen slush pile. "Sure, if it would help out."

A minute after Rita left, I picked up four unpromising looking manuscripts off my shelf and ferried them over to Lindsay's desk. "You're on your way," I told her.

She gasped. "You talked to her?"

"Yup. Take a look at these and see what you think."

"Wow, thanks!"

Her ecstatic reaction to having more work dumped on her was most gratifying. No wonder people wanted to climb the corporate ladder. Delegating was divine.

"Where've you been?" Fleishman asked as soon as I came home.

I had stayed at work a little longer than usual, finishing the chick lit book about the fifty-year-old art student. Mercedes had already left a note on my desk telling me she wanted to see it ASAP. The next day I planned to run in, type up a memo recommending the book, and hand it over to her. It might just be the quickest turnaround in Candlelight history.

"I thought you'd be back an hour ago, at the most. I've been waiting to take you out to celebrate."

"Celebrate what?" For the life of me, I couldn't think of

what there could be to celebrate. Especially between Fleishman and me.

"Your homecoming, for one thing," he said.

"Right. Finding my way home after work was a great achievement."

He shook his head in exasperation. "Not from work—from Dallas."

I wasn't kidding myself that my homecoming from anywhere was the reason behind his wanting to go out. Something else was afoot here. What could be going on in that feverish brain of his?

Maybe I was making it all too complicated. Could be he was just bored. *Maybe it's just that Renata isn't available tonight*, I thought bitterly.

I was none too eager to go out; I felt like collapsing. Fleishman would want to know all about Dallas, and what was I going to say? That I managed to make a spectacle of myself without his help? That his power of suggestion had sent me into the arms of Dan Weatherby?

The wounds of the weekend were still too fresh to laugh about them with friends. Especially Fleishman.

"I don't know . . ." I said, looking longingly at the couch and the television. If ever there was a night for vegetation, this was it.

"Come on, you look fantastic."

"I do?" This was hard to swallow, given how I felt.

But then of course, I was dressed in his mom's Chanel suit. That's probably all he saw.

Fleishman managed to convince me that I was outing-ready. When we left the apartment, though, I was so tired that I didn't see the fat manila envelope stuffed under his arm. I didn't notice it until we were seated at a Greek restaurant and he shoved it across the blue and white checkered cloth at me.

"There!" The word popped out of him. "You're practically the first person I've shown it to!"

He seemed so excited, but I couldn't help being a little stung by his qualifier. "Practically?" I asked. Before now, I had always been *the* first.

"I wanted it to be perfect before I gave it to you. You're a pro now!"

I opened the envelope and pulled out a manuscript that was three hundred and fifty pages at least. Most plays clock in at a hundred and twenty, tops. "What is this, *Long Day's Journey into the Next Millineum?*"

"That's the big surprise. It's not a play at all!" He paused, then announced, "It's my first novel."

"A romance novel?"

A shadow crossed his face. "Not a traditional romance novel. It's a little hard to categorize . . ."

"You want me to read it as a friend?" I asked.

"Of course. But if you *do* think Candlelight would want to publish it . . ."

The words made me want to weep into my moussaka. It had been hard enough working myself up to reject a book written by a friend of the office receptionist. How was I going to deal with this?

"It's sort of a romance from a male point of view," he said.

"But our readers are women," I pointed out.

"So?"

"So, they tend to like reading about the experiences of women."

"That's absurd."

"No, it's just natural. How many men do you know who rush out to see the latest Reese Witherspoon comedy, or nineteenth century costume flick?"

"I do," he said, sounding offended.

It was true, he did. Then again, he also crashed romance conferences.

Of course, it was pointless to start arguing over a book I knew nothing about. "I haven't read it yet, so . . ."

"No kidding!" he sniped. "You didn't even look at the title yet, and I *agonized* over it."

I looked down at the title page.

CUTTING LOOSE
A novel
by Jack Fleishman

"Jack?"

"It's my pen name," he said. "It's better than my real name, I think. It's more like a normal guy."

Which he so wasn't.

He leaned forward. "But what do you think about *Cutting Loose?* Don't you think that's catchy?" He was convinced enough of its catchiness not to wait for my answer. "I have tons of ideas for the cover. I imagine a woman and a man hanging in space—I don't know, connected by a string of pearls, or a chain with a locket—and then a giant pair of scissors about to lop them apart." He grinned. "Isn't that good?"

"Great." I was surprised he hadn't already manufactured a mock cover.

"Naturally I'm thinking trade paperback, not mass market."

"Naturally," I said. "This *must* be good. I've never seen you so full of prunes about any project."

"Do you think I would give it to you if it weren't good? This could be a big book for you!"

I nodded. "I hope so."

He leaned forward and cocked his head slightly. "You haven't so much as leafed through the first page of that book."

"I was going to read it tomorrow," I said, "when I have time to give it my full attention."

"Don't you want to read just the first page?"

I didn't, but he obviously wanted me to. And if I didn't read it myself, he would probably start reading it to me. We'd be at Mykonos until dawn. Dutifully, I turned the cover page. The next sheet of paper was practically blank, except for one short line written in bold type.

For Rebecca Abbot, who inspired every line.

I felt a catch in my throat. Like the reluctant father who suddenly finds himself weeping when looking through the maternity ward window at the little bundle he'd helped create, I had to blink back tears. Fleishman and I had known each other for so long, but he had never publicly acknowledged that I meant anything special to him.

"What do you think?"

"Thank you," I said. "No one's dedicated anything to me before."

"It's true, you know. You'll see how true it is when you read the book."

I promised I would tomorrow. Now, of course, I was looking forward to it. Just by reading that one line I felt I had developed a personal stake in the success of *Cutting Loose*. Which actually was a pretty good title, I decided.

"Let's have more wine," Fleishman said, lifting his hand to catch a passing waiter. "In fact, let's order a bottle. I feel like celebrating!"

The bottle was ordered and then consumed in short order, as we plotted out how our lives would change when Fleishman was a rich and famous author. Actually, it was his life he was plotting out, but I was piggybacking his prosperity every step of the way, even in his own reckoning. When he mentioned, say, the house in Tuscany he planned to buy when the royalties started streaming in, he would catch my uncertain gaze and add expansively, "You'll love Italy! It's the last place on earth where nobody worries about carbs."

And then I would feel giggly and buoyant for another few minutes until the doubts would start crowding in. What would my role in Tuscany be? Houseguest? Visiting editor? Hanger-on?

Would Renata be there?

Fleishman was in one of those festive, ecstatic moods of his, but it wasn't what I would call a romantic evening. Nevertheless, doubts about my future attachment to Fleishman dwindled in direct proportion to the dwindling amount of wine in that bottle. Forgotten were my bitter feelings of the week before. Suddenly we were back in college again, and Fleish and I were going to take the world by storm, together.

It wasn't until I was weaving home with Fleishman's book under my arm that it occurred to my befogged mind that he hadn't asked me much at all about my weekend, or about Dan.

Which, when all was said and done, was probably just as well.

Your first year in the city is for not doing all those New Yorky things you thought you would do before you lived there, like taking horse carriage rides in Central Park or riding the Staten Island Ferry. Our first New Year's Eve Renata and I didn't *go see the ball drop in Times Square.*

We had planned to. We had even passed on a perfectly good party because Renata was determined to do this crazy thing. She had bought champagne for us to stuff under our coats and little noise makers. "It'll be so cool!"

"It will be so not cool," I told her, when I thought I still had a prayer of wriggling out of this. "There will be thousands of tourists, crazy people, and Dick Clark enthusiasts. And they'll all be drunk."

"I know! How can you resist being a part of all that?"

Very easily. The truth was I didn't want to go. Given my druthers, I would have gone to the party. "Plus, I think the operative word you're looking for is cold,*" I told her. "It's going to be fricking cold."*

"You don't want to go." She started unwinding her muffler and unbuttoning her coat. She pulled a noisemaker out of her pocket and tossed it on the table. She looked crushed.

I felt so guilty. But why? Renata still clung to all these romantic notions about our being here together, but to me New York was like a gigantic playpen with exquisite women in it. I was twenty-three and ready to play.

But I still felt a tug from this woman I'd hauled back with me from college in Iowa. "Of course I want to go," I lied. "I told you I did."

"But you don't want to." She dropped down on the futon couch.

"C'mon," I said, taking her hand.

She shook her head. "That's okay. I don't feel like going."

"Renata . . ."

"It's okay. We can stay here and watch it on television."

Stay home? *I hadn't planned on that. "Don't you want to go to the party?" I asked.*

"No."

I sighed. I hated going places alone. I sank down on the couch next to her. She turned to me with those brown eyes of hers, full of tears. I could never handle it when she cried.

"If you really want to go that much, I'll go," I said.

"You idiot!" she said. "I don't care about Times Square. I wanted to be with you—just us. Together."

Together with all those drunken tourists? "Yeah, but—"

"Don't you ever want that?"

Her hand was holding fast to mine now. She still had a seductive power over me every once in a while. For instance, that night she was wearing a black wool jersey dress that clung to her every curve in ways that I'm not sure she was even aware of. Or maybe she was. She leaned forward. Her lips were crimson and very enticing.

It was *cold outside. And if I went to that party, who knew what would happen? This, at least, was a sure thing.*

Did I sleep with Renata because it was twenty degrees outside and I just didn't want to go to Times Square? Knowing that it was all over between us, did I take advantage of her because of my dislike of going to parties alone? Knowing it would cause all sorts of regrets in the morning, did I surrender to carnal pleasure simply because I was determined never to watch another New Year's Rockin' Eve?

Not entirely. I was no longer in love with Renata, it was true. But I did sometimes feel nostalgic for her. And wasn't that sort of what New Year's Eve was all about?

What the hell, *I thought as I bent down to kiss her.* For Auld Lang Syne . . .

Chapter 15

I was just a wee bit hungover the next morning, so my trip to the office was interrupted with multiple stopovers for cures: A double espresso on the way to the subway. Excedrin at the Duane Reade. Two donuts with sprinkles—a little-known but surefire headache cure—from a cart on Forty-second. A super-tall-grande cappuccino from the coffee shop in our building. I waved to Rita on my way in and scurried quickly to my office. I had a feeling this was going to be a bear of a day to get through, and that was before I had sat down with my coffee, donuts, and Excedrin to peruse the first chapter of Fleishman's book.

I re-read the dedication, savoring it, then began. *For a certain type of man—and I plead guilty to being that type to a T—Renata Abner was like catnip to a lean, hungry Siamese tom.*

That first sentence stopped me cold. There was that name! *Renata.* I had been jealous of Renata ever since . . . but it turned out she wasn't a real person, even.

Yet as I read a few more pages, I came to the scarifying conclusion that she actually was a real person. She was me.

She was so me, in fact, that anyone who knew me even in passing would not fail to miss it, even if they hadn't read the dedication. Inspired every word? I could have dictated the thing. Fleishman hadn't even bothered to change small details. And he had lifted conversations we'd had over the years verbatim. The more I read, the more furious I became. Those donuts didn't last three minutes.

It was as if Fleishman had laid our lives out bare for all the world to see, like one of those guys on Seventh Avenue who sold pilfered goods set out on towels. My life was on the towel. Except he was only telling half the story. I became increasingly frustrated as I read, seeing myself reduced to a whiny former fat girl, a scolding jealous roommate, a clingy ex-girlfriend. The words stung all the more because there was a germ of truth in every paragraph—but it was as if he were staring at my personality through the bottom of a glass. The picture was distorted; I wasn't really that person.

Was I?

I began composing angry rebuttals in my head. Then I would remember—this wasn't a TV talk show; I wouldn't be called upon to present my side of the story. There would be no public shouting match. This was fiction. It would live on, bare and unchallenged, to last as long as the paper this book was printed on.

I finished one chapter and then another, guzzling caffeine as I went. What I really needed was a Xanax. My heart was blub-dubbing so erratically I felt at times that I was going to keel over in my chair. I downed a trio of Excedrin in the vain hope of staving off the migraine I was sure was coming.

And then I came to the descriptions of our periodic and now long-lost sex life.

How could he? Okay, I liked the lights turned off. Was that so wrong? I wouldn't call it a *mania.*

I was so furious I thought I would have to stop reading. Instead, I kept on, possessed to see how much worse it could get. It was like a train wreck unfolding before my eyes; I was ghoulishly rubbernecking for blood spatters.

What made it all the more terrible was that I knew with each passing word that I wasn't just reading a book; I was witnessing the very tag end of Fleishman and me. This wasn't going to be something that we could recover from over a few bottles of Corona at Senor Enchilada's. After years of pushing the boundaries, testing me, Fleishman had finally committed the unforgivable act.

The amazing thing was that in so doing, he made me see each argument, each slight, each snag that had ever occurred between us as unforgivable, too. Only I *had* forgiven him, and now I was being repaid for my foolishness. In spades.

How could he have done this?

And then to have had the chutzpah to *dedicate* it to me?

I spent three solid hours with that manuscript, and during that time it seemed that every single word of that book was branded onto my cerebrum. I read until every last syllable was painfully charred into place. I don't have a photographic memory by any means; if you asked me to close my eyes and tell you what shirt I'm wearing at any moment, half the time I would draw a blank. Yet on that morning my brain seemed to have sprouted extra bandwidth to accommodate perfect recall of this outrage.

It was all there—tales from childhood, losing my virginity, my hang-ups. Did he think those things belonged to him? And there he was, too, poised as the knight in shining Armani, attempting to save me from myself. Helping me to move on. I think that's what made me most sick. For a long time, I had wondered how was it Fleishman couldn't notice that I was still secretly crazy about him. But the truth was, he did know. He'd known all along, and he'd loved it. I *had* been his entourage, as Wendy said. I had fed his ego.

And now I had provided him with a plot.

I was interrupted only once, by Mercedes's assistant, Lisa, who poked her head in my door. "Mercedes has a few hours this afternoon. She wants to know if she could have the book you recommended to her in the ed meeting."

I looked at the art teacher book. It was lying there, forgotten. "Just give me a little time to write up my notes," I said.

She crooned a bar of "We Have All the Time in the World," then closed my door.

I went back to fuming. And reading.

Finally I reached the end—the horrible end when the rascally adorable, rakishly handsome protagonist finally convinces the pathetic, cellulite-ridden ex-girlfriend to get her own life so he can live happily ever after with the gorgeous, glam record producer who had in the meantime fallen in love with him. (*Who was she?* I wondered, drumming my fingers angrily against my desk.) Fatso is finally cut loose, as the title suggests, and as a sop to readers she starts her own business with her chocolate chocolate chip cookie recipe.

Which was just so cliché, wasn't it? Starting a business from a cookie recipe. How many movies had that been in? I mean, *come on.*

And when did I ever bake cookies? I thought defensively. Just once, and that had been at Fleishman's suggestion. It hadn't even been my recipe.

God, I was going nuts. I was debating a piece of fiction.

The most unbearable part of all this—and that was saying a lot, because it all seemed awful—was Fleishman's assumption that I would be *happy* about all this. That I would abet this horrible book's seeing the light of day by actually helping get it published. Did he really think I was that big a masochist?

An angry voice inside me countered, *Have you ever given him reason to doubt it?*

I sat at my desk, basically catatonic except for the war-dance tattoo my pen was beating against my chair's armrest, until what course of action I needed to take finally occurred to me. He wanted me to treat this book like I would any other manuscript? Fine. I would reject it like I would any other manuscript. I took out a large Post-it note, slapped it on the cover page, and tried to think of all the phrases I would use in the rejection letter, which I would savor writing. But all the anger seemed to have clogged my brain. The only phrase that came to mind was *No damn way!* And in fact, I started to scrawl this on the yellow sticky when there was a knock at my door.

It was Lindsay. She didn't even wait for me to say come in, or to ask her to sit down. She just plopped down. Her expression was dazed—and surprisingly sad. "Did you hear?"

I put my pen down. "Hear what?"

"About Muriel," she said. "No one's supposed to know—only of course *everybody* knows."

Everyone except me, evidently. I had forgotten about Muriel. She hadn't been at work since I got back from Dallas. "I assumed she was sick or on vacation or something."

"She's in the hospital. In the *psych ward*."

I frowned. I had always suspected there was a world of strangeness beneath that efficient manner and those Peter Pan collars. "What happened?"

"She tried to kill herself," Lindsay said. "At least, that's what her mother said. She lives with her mother, apparently. Did you know that?"

"No." I really didn't know anything about her.

"Hilary in human resources spoke to Muriel's mom. She said Muriel had been *really depressed* since last week, and then something must have really driven her over the edge, because she OD'd on sleeping pills."

Something must have really driven her over the edge . . . That phrase made my blood freeze.

"I never thought she looked depressed, did you?" Lindsay asked.

Maybe I managed to shake my head, but suddenly I had trouble moving at all. A horrible certainty had taken hold of my brain. That awful book! *The Rancher and the Lady.* Could it have been Muriel's?

Why had I not guessed?

I remembered sitting at my computer, pounding out a rejection letter that was probably the most callous thing I had ever sent to an author, ever. I might as well have scrawled *Loser, get out of my way* on one of my business cards and mailed it off. Every single word of that letter had probably seemed like a poison dart to Muriel.

I slipped down in my chair until I was slumped over in a perfect C-curve. Everything else—all my worries, angers, resentments—fell away from me and left me feeling nothing but pure guilt. I imagined Muriel sitting at that reception desk for nine hours every day, then going home to her parents' house—how dismal was that?—to write *The Rancher and the Lady*. How long had it taken her. Months? Years?

And then she had picked *me*, personally, to read her work. And what had I done? Nothing. I'd just left her hanging. Agonizing. And then finally, brutally, I'd sent her a one-paragraph rejection.

Lindsay squinted at me. "Are you okay? You look pale."

"What hospital is she at?"

She shrugged. "Somewhere in the Bronx, I think. Human resources was going to arrange to send her flowers, so you don't have to worry about that. They'll be sending around a card for everyone to sign this afternoon."

A card. Wouldn't that be great? And wouldn't Muriel just love reading it? Especially when she got to my name—the name of her assassin.

My guilty conscience propelled me out of my chair and out the door.

"Hey, where are you going?" Lindsay yelled after my retreating back.

"The Bronx!"

Getting information was much easier than I had feared it would be. Once I told human resources I wanted to visit Muriel, they assumed that I must be one of her best friends at the office. Why else would I put myself out for a mere coworker?

I played along and got the name of the hospital from them—St. Felicity's—then I headed for the elevator. On the way, Mercedes flagged me down. "Don't forget that book," she said.

I walked backwards a few steps so I wouldn't have to stop. "It's on my desk—I'll get it to you ASAP."

"Excellent!" she chimed.

I had no idea where I was going. The Bronx? It was just the great unknown at the top of the transit map, as mysterious to me as the vast arctic whiteness at the top of a globe. I had never been to a Yankees game, or to the zoo. None of Sylvie's foodstuffs had required me to go farther north than Harlem, so there my travels had stopped. I had to ask a station booth attendant for directions, and then, because I never trust station booth attendants, I made her repeat them to me twice, which caused the line of people hurrying places on their lunch hours behind me to start grumbling in a way that sounded angry and moblike.

New York City is no place for the directionally clueless.

On the train, I hung glumly onto a strap even though there were miles of empty seats around me. Standing made me feel more like a penitent. I had no idea why I was going to see Muriel, or what I would say to her when I got there. I couldn't take back a book rejection. I guess I just wanted to let her know that I wasn't heartless. I wanted to start doing things right for once.

That booth clerk must have known what she was talking about, because St. Felicity's was only a block away from the 210th Street station. I stopped at the gift shop next to the hospital cafeteria and charged the largest bouquet they had that wasn't a funeral spray.

Then I found her room and crept quietly through the door.

Muriel looked up. I don't know what I thought she was going to look like. I knew she wasn't going to be in a padded cell. I guess I expected her to seem more depressed—maybe laid out in bed and hooked up to an IV drip of Valium. Instead, she was sitting in a chair by the window, reading a Candlelight romance. It was *Renegade Lover*, by Missy Martin, one of my authors. That detail made my heart sink even further.

She had on a flannel nightgown decorated with stripes of cabbage roses; over it was draped one of those crocheted bed-jackets that at some point in the history of fashion normal women had actually worn. It was as anachronistic now as a bustle, but it made perfect sense that Muriel would not only have one but actually use it.

Her hair was pulled back neatly, and when she looked up, she even had her customary stripe of blue eye shadow in place. In the middle of a nervous breakdown, the woman refused to be untidy.

Her face lit up when she saw me. "Rebecca! What a surprise!"

I seeped all the way into the room. "Hey, Muriel," I said. "Hope you don't mind a visit."

"Oh, no. I am so pleased to see you here."

She was? Belatedly, it occurred to me that if I were confined to a psych ward in the Bronx, the last thing I would be craving was a visit from a coworker.

"What beautiful flowers!" she exclaimed.

I handed them to her, then sank onto the bed. "Thought they might brighten up your room a little bit." She already had a bouquet of roses on her windowsill.

"They are lovely. Call me a girl of simple tastes, but I have always had a weakness for the humble chrysanthemum."

I smiled. In fact, I felt like my smile was frozen onto my face.

She looked at me, and for a moment a little of her normally brittle façade fell away. "I guess the story of my little incident last weekend has made the rounds at the office."

"Only to a very few people," I lied.

I encircled my hand around the metal side of the bed—the one that could be lifted on both sides to provide a cagelike barrier for the patient. All hospital beds had them, but somehow seeing one on a bed in a psych ward seemed more sinister.

"I think the doctors are going to let me go tomorrow," Muriel continued, "and if all goes well, I hope to return to work the first of next week."

"So soon?"

"I miss it," she said. "And since they can't find anything wrong with my heart, there's no reason to keep me here."

I leaned forward a little. "Your heart?"

"Didn't you hear? That's what was wrong with me—they thought I was having a little heart attack, because I accidentally took a few sleeping pills. But it turns out I am fine. Just one of those things."

Okay. I know Lindsay isn't the most reliable person in the world, but there was no way even Lindsay could have mistaken "little heart attack" for "suicide attempt." And I knew I wasn't in *The Twilight Zone.* I was in the Bronx, in a psych ward. I wasn't mistaken about these facts.

And yet there was Muriel, very calm in her little bed jacket, telling me that it had all just been a big mix-up.

Naturally. She was crazy.

I cleared my throat and for once in my life attempted to choose my words very carefully. "Are you sure you shouldn't take some more time off, just to be sure you're . . . yourself again?"

"I've never felt more myself," she replied.

And now that I considered her words, they seemed true. She looked just like Muriel always looked. Which, now that I gave the matter some thought, could be summed up in one word: Nuts.

It was unnerving. I had come up here wanting to atone for my thoughtlessness, wanting to apologize. But how do you apologize to someone in such complete denial?

"How's your friend?" I asked.

"Which one?" Her eyes narrowed on me with a jarring sharpness. "I have more than one, you know."

I flinched. I hadn't meant to insult her. "The writer."

"Melissa MacIntosh," she reminded me with a hint of scolding in her tongue. "I'm surprised you don't remember. It's only been a week since you rejected her book."

I winced, but this was sort of what I'd come for, so I didn't mind. "I have a bad memory for names."

"You held onto that book for months. After all that time, I would think you'd have memorized the author's name, at least."

"I know. I'm sorry."

"Well!" Muriel said with quiet indignation. "You don't have to apologize to *me.*"

But that was the thing. I did have to apologize to her. It suddenly seemed absolutely essential to my future well-being that I apologize to Muriel-Melissa. Unfortunately, Muriel wasn't giving any quarter, forgiveness wise. She obviously didn't want to admit, even at this late date, that she was Melissa MacIntosh.

How did you apologize to a loopy woman who wouldn't cop to writing the book you rejected?

"Did you read my letter?" I asked her.

"Melissa showed it to me."

Uh-huh. I wondered if she was a clinical split personality, like Sally Field in *Sybil.* I was determined to talk to her about this until she had a breakthrough. (In psychiatric poker terms, I would take her Sally Field and raise her one Judd Hirsch from *Ordinary People.*)

"What did you think of the letter?"

She plucked at the pearl button of her bedjacket for a moment, as if considering carefully how to answer. "It was very blunt," she said finally.

There. Let her criticize me. "I should have taken more care," I agreed.

"The tone was harsh," she added.

"I'm sorry," I said.

"I typed some of Mary Jo's letters once when her assistant had appendicitis, and Mary Jo was never that harsh."

Less kind than Mary Jo. Ouch. I did feel chastised. It felt good, actually. "I'm so sorry."

Her lips twisted. "You don't have to keep apologizing to me, Rebecca. It's Melissa who got the letter."

"Melissa. Right."

"You asked for my opinion on what I thought about the letter, and I am giving it to you."

"I know." I thought for a moment. "It's just that I've considered that letter since I wrote it, and I've felt remorse. Sometimes you wish you could take things back, you know?"

"Well, it is a little too late for that. Melissa read the letter and she was upset."

I shifted, and decided to change tactics. "If I knew Melissa personally, you know what I would do?"

"What?"

"I'd like to sit down with her and, first, say that the letter was written too hastily. It didn't give her any of the encouragement she deserves. Do you know what an accomplishment it is to finish a book?"

Muriel looked skeptical. "Even a lousy one?"

"It wasn't lousy. It was just a little amateurish. The plot felt tired. But with a better hook, a well-developed story, and some interesting characters . . ."

She tilted her head. "You didn't like the characters, even?"

My mouth clamped shut. Damn. I swallowed. "No, I did. They were the best part. But . . . you know . . . if you put Scarlett and Rhett in *The Pokey Little Puppy*, it's still *The Pokey Little Puppy*."

She frowned at me, and I couldn't blame her. Suddenly, I was back at the Portland conference trying to explain how to write a book. I was starting to sweat like I had in Portland, too. "What I mean is, I wish I could sit down with Melissa, have a cup of coffee, and tell her all the things I liked about *The Rancher and the Lady*. I'd like to give her some encouragement, which I probably didn't convey in the letter. I'd hash out some possible ideas for future projects."

She brightened. "Would you really?"

I nodded.

"Well, you know, it *could* be arranged for you to meet with Melissa."

Yeah, I'll bet.

We sat for a little while longer, trying to keep the conversational balloon up in the air by talking about the weather, but after five minutes it was clear that it was time for me to go. I stood up.

"Thank you for visiting, Rebecca." She looked hesitant, then blurted out, "And did you really mean what you said about talking to Melissa?"

"Of course!"

I made what seemed like an overly-pat hospital exit speech. I told her that she would feel better soon.

"I *am* better," she insisted. "I'm perfectly fine."

I was in a gloomy mood when I shuffled toward the exit of

that hospital. How depressing to see the layers of denial and artifice that had been holding Muriel together suddenly peeled away. I wasn't sure that visit had helped her or me.

I was no Judd Hirsch.

Just before I hit the doors to the outside, I heard someone call my name.

I turned, wondering who else I knew in the Bronx. But the person I laid eyes on was the last person on earth I would have expected to see again.

It was Bernadine, Sylvie's old pal. Seeing her in such a weird spot, and feeling so forlorn as I did, I practically fell on her neck as one would a long lost friend.

"What are you doing here?" I asked.

"I have to get my cholesterol tested," she said. "I have cholesterol. And diabetes."

I murmured in sympathy. I was afraid to ask the question foremost in my mind; Sylvie, I was certain, was probably not doing well. If she was doing at all. Her accountant had made it sound like she was on death's door, and that had been months ago.

But, finally, I had to ask, "Do you still see Sylvie?"

Bernadine grunted. "See her! Of course I see her. We play canasta every Tuesday at her place."

"Her place? Did she go home?"

Bernadine waved her hand. "Nah, she's in an assisted living community on Elmhurst Avenue in Queens. A prison, she calls it. An old folks home."

I frowned. "Why doesn't she go back to her apartment?"

"Because of that crook!"

"Mr. Langley?"

Bernadine practically spat. "That's the one." She narrowed her eyes on me. "But of course you wouldn't care about that. Sylvie says you abandoned her."

"I was fired."

Bernadine's mouth was pulled down, as if that was no excuse.

It wasn't, I realized. I had been with Sylvie for two and a half years, and for the past four months, I had barely spared her a thought. I had forgotten her.

"The accountant wouldn't even tell me where she was," I said. "He kept going on about the estate's executors."

"Ha! That's him. Now he has all her money, and Sylvie's living in a cage." She shrugged. "It's actually an okay place, but she calls it a cage. She misses her home."

"Of course." I frowned. So my instincts about R.J. Langley had been correct. "How did she get involved with Langley?"

"He's a relation," Bernadine said. "Poor Sylvie!"

Guilt tugged at me. "I'd like to see her."

"That would be nice. Like she always tells me, inmates appreciate visitors."

I got the address from Bernadine, then I took a circuitous route back to the office, looping through Harlem to get Sylvie some hot pickled okra. I would take it to her this weekend.

By the time I straggled back to my desk, it was almost four. I felt drained. I flopped down in my chair, feeling spent. I couldn't remember now where I'd left off. I tried to think back on what I had been working on when I ran off to the hospital. That seemed ages ago now.

Something about my desk bothered me, but I couldn't quite put my finger on it.

Then I remembered, and I let out a groan. Fleishman! That damn book of his. I had been writing a rejection letter.

I searched the top of my desk, but I didn't see the book. I swiveled toward my bookshelf; it wasn't there, either. I started tearing my office apart, looking for it. When I came up empty, I got up and went to Lindsay's desk.

"Where've you been?" she asked. "Did you go see Muriel?"

I nodded.

She looked eager for news. "How was she?"

For a moment I was torn between the urge to tell someone just how incredibly nuts Muriel was and to protect her. In the end, sympathy won out. I wasn't rock solid, myself. "It was all an accident." I fabricated a story involving a big pill-bottle mix-up, knowing it would circulate around the building in nothing flat.

"Wow!" she said. "That's really awful. And here we've spent the whole day thinking she was crazy!"

It was as good a time as any to change the subject. "Did you take a book from my desk today?"

Her eyes flew open. "I didn't go near your office, I swear!" she said defensively. "Except once to grab a peppermint from the jar on your bookshelf, but that's all I touched, I swear. Oh, and I maybe swiped a few of your Post-it notes from your top drawer. But you had a whole package."

"Never mind," I said.

A niggling oddball idea scratched at the back of my mind, but just to make sure it couldn't be true I went over to Lisa's desk.

"There you are!" she exclaimed. "*Finally!*"

"Is Mercedes here?"

"She went home early."

I frowned. "Did she try to find me?"

Lisa snorted. "Uh, yeah? Like, all afternoon?"

"Oh. I had to leave for a while . . ."

"Well never mind," Lisa said. "She just got it off your desk."

"What?" But of course I knew what. It was just as I feared.

"The book."

My heart sank. "*Cutting Loose?*"

"I don't know what the hell it was called," Lisa said. "All I know is that for about an hour she was locked up in her office with the thing."

"What'd she think?"

"I dunno."

Maybe she hadn't liked it. In fact, there was a really good chance she hadn't. It was a weird book; not right for Candlelight at all.

"But I think she took it home with her," Lisa said, "if that makes you feel any better."

It didn't.

Chapter 16

I practiced my speech to Fleishman on my way home. Not aloud, of course. Not that anyone on the J train would have noticed an office worker babbling to herself, but I still take pride in maintaining the appearance of sanity.

I was not going to be shrill, or a scold. I was going to be so calm, poised, and reasonable, no one would be able to confuse me with that insecure, neurotic nut Renata. Yes, she was just fiction, but in the space of one short day, she had become real to me, like the demented twin I had been trying to avoid all my life who had suddenly found my cell phone number.

One thought sent clammy waves of worry through me: What if Mercedes actually liked *Cutting Loose?* When I had been reading that book, that abomination, it hadn't seemed like a novel so much as an elaborate insider joke. And the joke was on me. Now I had to go over it again in my memory, word by awful word, trying to figure out what the editorial director of Candlelight Books might make of the thing. Where would it even fit in our publishing universe? Signature? Fleishman didn't have a big name. He didn't have any name. MetroGirl? He wasn't a girl. And it certainly didn't belong in any of the more traditional romance lines.

That was one thing that gave me grim satisfaction. Fleishman thought he was such an authority on romance. After four months of reading them and crashing one romance conference, he fancied himself an expert. But look! His first stab at the genre, and it had come out as this insulting, twisted tale of a guy slowly dumping a woman for a rich, sexy blonde.

I was safe.

I was pretty sure I was safe.

God, I prayed I was safe.

I tramped back to the apartment, stunned to find myself crossing my threshold at just a little after five. Wendy seemed as shocked as I was. It was a rarity that we saw each other at this time of day; I was usually just beginning the long march home as she was heading off for another evening aiming Klieg lights on overemoting undergraduates.

"You look like someone just died," she said. "Did something happen at home?"

She meant Ohio, obviously. We were still young enough that home meant where our parents were, not where we spent ninety percent of our time.

"It's nothing like that," I said, being purposefully vague. I looked around for Fleishman. "Where's wonder boy?"

Wendy swooped forward. "I've been home for a few hours and he hasn't been here. Is something going on with you two?"

"Well . . ." My voice I'd been keeping cool, neutral. But now it cracked, and with it I could feel my last shred of composure begin to crumble. Damn. Why wasn't Fleishman here? I was so ready to confront him; I'd screwed up my courage to cast off the friendship we'd been mired in for years. Now all those fine words I had formulated in my head evaporated. The argumentative rug had been pulled out from under me.

I sank onto the futon couch, feeling hollow and trembly. It didn't help that Maxwell jumped into my lap, wimpering. He'd been alone too long with Wendy, obviously, who as far as he was concerned was the wicked stepmother of the house.

I buried my face in his bristly fur. "This has been a hell of a day."

"What happened?" Wendy asked, her voice looping up.

The honest concern in her voice loosened something in me. My entire day came pouring out. Of course I had to give her the lowdown on the book, including a few unsavory details from my past that had now been immortalized in *Cutting Loose*. Also, I had to explain the horribleness of going up to see Muriel in the Bronx, and learning about Sylvie. And then being thrust back into the office and hearing that Mercedes had the Fleishman book in her hot little hands.

When I finally wound down, Wendy was red in the face. "He really wrote about all those things?"

I nodded.

She tilted her head. "Am I in this book?"

I actually hadn't considered this. "No, you aren't."

She rolled her eyes. For some reason, being left out seemed to make her madder than anything. She turned and made a beeline for our communal closet. "That's it!"

"What are you doing?"

"I'm packing his bags for him. Right now." Not one to mull things over, Wendy.

I jumped up. Never mind that I had been mentally packing him up all afternoon. Now that I was seeing someone doing it physically, now that the umbilical cord was being cut, I felt a moment of panic.

"Wait—"

"Wait, my ass. He's outta here. Writing a book about you? This is not okay, okay? I don't care if Fleishman thinks he is the next Jacqueline Susann, this is not acceptable behavior."

"But—"

"This is an intervention, Rebecca. You are not going to give him time to weasel or cajole you into thinking that this is acceptable behavior from a friend. You're my friend, too, and I'm not gonna stand for it. Not this time. No."

If anyone could stage a one-person intervention, it was Wendy.

She yanked the tropical fish shower curtain aside and started pulling down suitcases. All Fleishman's.

The sight of those bags didn't make me feel any calmer. And then Fleishman walked in, his arms weighed down with flowers.

I opened my mouth to speak, but the words that sounded through the room weren't the ones I expected. Wendy had opened her mouth, too, and her lungs had beaten mine to the punch. Forget diplomacy. Forget restraint. That wasn't Wendy's style.

"You sonofabitch!" she yelled, tossing a suitcase at his feet. And when Wendy got around to yelling, the earth shook.

Standing there with his luggage at his feet and the walls rattling around him, Fleishman looked, quite understandably, flabbergasted.

I was, too. I was expecting this scene to take place between Fleishman and me. It hadn't really occurred to me that this would be a momentous occasion for Wendy, too. But she had been with us all these years. And obviously, the apartment, the weirdness between Fleishman and me, and the dog pee had all taken their toll on her psyche. She had snapped.

She zoomed right up to him, making him hold his bouquet of lilies as a protective shield. "How dare you use Rebecca that way!"

He looked mystified. "What are you talking about?"

"Your book! You wrote a piece of hideous garbage about her, and now you expect her to publish it. Well, over her dead body will Candlelight publish that story! Mine, too. Bookstores will sell that book at the same moment they start selling Eskimo Pies in hell."

"Uh, Wendy . . ."

Fleishman's gaze met mine. He looked wounded. "You didn't like it?"

Wendy crossed her arms. "That's putting it mildly."

After a moment of letting the criticism sink in, Fleishman's face looked demonstrably redder. "What was the matter with it?"

I took a breath. "You put in all—"

"You made her sound like a psycho!" Wendy shouted.

His eyes narrowed on me and he quivered impatiently. "But what did you think of the story?"

The story? Was he kidding? He had Wendy bearing down on him in a full-tilt rage and all he was worried about was my editorial opinion?

It was the first moment I ever considered that he might really be an author.

"Do you think it's publishable?" he asked.

I cleared my throat. "I'm not even sure. The only thing I thought while I was reading it was that I hoped it never saw the light of day."

He looked dumbstruck. "Then you aren't going to buy it?"

Wendy nearly howled. "*Hello?* This is what she's been trying to tell you!"

Actually, it was what Wendy had been trying to tell him. But Fleishman wasn't even looking at her. It was as if she didn't exist. In those crazy eyes of his, I was the only one he was focused on, but the attention wasn't at all flattering. It wasn't me he was seeing, but someone who could do something for him.

"I changed the names," he said.

"Barely," I said. "It didn't fool me, and I doubt it would fool anyone we know."

"Well?" he asked. "Do you own everything that's happened to us? It was my life, too. I can write about it if I want."

"That's true."

"You're just being hypersensitive," he said. "Believe me, if you pass on this, you're making a big mistake."

"Fleish—"

Wendy brayed in the background as a flurry of Fleishman's clothes flew out of the closet. "The only mistake we made was letting you stick around for so long. But the ride is over. You are going to have to go, Fleishman."

He recoiled. Then he looked back at me. "Is that what you think, too?"

I swallowed. "Yes."

He put the flowers on the table, then pivoted back to us, crossing his arms. Something in his stance made me very uneasy.

"I'm the one whose name is on the lease," he said. "Remember? I made the down payment."

"So?" I said. "We reimbursed you for that years ago."

"The apartment belongs to all of us," Wendy pointed out, "and we outnumber you."

"Yes, but it's the name on the lease that counts. So if there's anyone who's going to move out of here, it's not going to be me."

"But you can't kick *us* out," Wendy said, feeling the full sting of having the tables turned on her.

"Yes, I can. I have the lease. Legally, I'm the renter."

Wendy and I gaped at him. Then at each other. What could we say to that?

He lifted his hands. "I'll be generous. I'll give you a week."

"*A week*?"

His brows darted up in warning. "That's apparently more than you were prepared to give me."

He picked up a suitcase, crossed to his dresser, and started shoveling things in with his long arms. "I'll go to Connecticut for a few days, and next Wednesday I'll expect you both to be gone."

For some reason, whenever I had imagined the possibility of Fleishman and I—What would you call it? Breaking up?—it had always been in a big theatrical emotional scene. With tears and yelling. Or lots of replaying the events of our shared past. I had never imagined a short squabble over a lease and then ten minutes of strained silence as he threw things into bags. It seemed so cold, antiseptic. We could have been any three roommates having a fight. It didn't seem to be doing us justice.

When the packing was finally done, he picked up his bag, crossed to the front table and grabbed his flowers. "You two can have the television. I'm getting an HD soon." He looked at me sharply. "I've had it on good authority that the book will sell like hotcakes."

Head high, he breezed out the door as gracefully as anyone could carrying two suitcases and an armload of lilies.

When he was gone, Wendy sank down on the couch, looking completely deflated. "Me and my big mouth," she muttered. "My big homeless mouth."

"It's okay," I told her. "No matter what happens, you did exactly right. It was beautiful."

I sat in a chair and put my head down on the dining table like we used to do during naptime in first grade. Maxwell pawed at my leg until I picked him up. "Who do you think he was talking about?" I asked.

"When?"

"When he said someone had told him that the book would sell. Who else do you think he gave the book to read?"

"Who knows? Maybe Natasha. But he was probably just shooting off his mouth."

"Probably, but . . ."

"We've got bigger problems than that book now, Rebecca. How are we going to find a new apartment in a week?"

That was a more immediate conundrum. "Do you have any money?"

"What do you think?"

I sighed. "Neither do I."

"I thought you were drawing in the bucks these days."

"Unfortunately, I've also been spending the bucks. I don't see how you can make more money and suddenly have less, but it's happened."

She got up, crossed over to me, and practically pulled me out of the chair by my armpits. "C'mon, let's go."

"Go where?" I was reluctant for mopey time to come to an end.

But Wendy was good at marshalling the forces, and so we walked to the nearest Korean deli and picked up ramen noodles, a bottle of vinegary Merlot, and the new *Village Voice*. Back at home, I boiled the water for dinner while she poured over the classifieds.

"I'd like something in Manhattan," she said.

I let out a snort. "Upper East Side? A townhouse, perhaps?"

"If we're going to move, we should at least decide what our ideal would be before we have to compromise it," she said.

"Yes, it's always comforting to know what you're not getting."

She ignored my snarkiness. "It would be nice not to have such a long train ride twice a day."

That did sound nice. And while we were dreaming . . . "A slightly bigger kitchen would be nice. With no roaches." I thought for a moment. "A tub!"

"And a real bedroom with a door that shuts."

"God, that would be fantastic!" I said.

We dreamed on in this fashion all through the ramen noodles, so it was a little bit of a disappointment when we crunched the numbers and found out that about all we could afford in Manhattan was a "lge" studio somewhere down in Alphabet City. Actually, we could do better if Wendy would let me chip in more—which I could afford to do—but she wouldn't hear of that. "If it's not an even split, things get hinky."

I started looking at Brooklyn listings, while her brow remained firmly furrowed. "The trouble is you pay a premium for not being able to afford much."

"Huh?"

"A one-bedroom is astronomical in price, but a two-bedroom is only slightly more astronomical."

She was right about that. Not that it did us any good. At the end of the evening, we had circled several possibilities in Brooklyn.

"I guess I'll start calling people tomorrow," she said.

"Or I could."

"No, I will. I work at the coffee shop tomorrow. It will make playing barista more interesting if I'm steaming milk and dealing with real estate agents at the same time."

Wendy always liked a challenge.

I was about to head off to bed when her eyes suddenly bugged. Which was disturbing, since she was staring in my general direction.

"Oh no!" she breathed.

"What's the matter?"

She pointed at my lap, where Maxwell was contentedly dozing. "He didn't take the dog."

I tensed. Did she actually mean she wanted Fleishman to take Maxwell? "Of course not." Maxwell was mine!

"I am not hauling that loose-bladdered furball to another apartment," Wendy declared.

"But—"

"Uh-un."

"But he belongs to me. He's my responsibility. And he hasn't peed on anything for days."

"I thought he belonged to Fleishman."

"Well, he was sort of both of ours, but . . ." Panic made me shameless. "But Fleishman was terrible with him. He spoiled him. Once you pointed out the behavioral problems he's been much better. The crate training was a stroke of genius."

She tilted her head. I don't think she was buying any of it.

"He won't be much trouble," I promised. Max was probably the only vestige of my years with Fleishman worth hanging on to.

"It's hard enough finding an apartment for people," she grumbled. "Finding one that takes dogs? In a week? That's gonna take a miracle."

The next morning I was up and at'em in my usual timely fashion. I was late. I tossed on an old dress and bolted for the door, stopping short when I saw Wendy hunched over the paper, basically where I had left her the night before. "Keep this afternoon open after three," she said. "I'm going to try to set up some apartment viewings."

"Where?"

"There's a huge place on the Upper West Side—way upper. It's only three hundred dollars over our budget."

"Where's the three hundred supposed to come from?"

She tapped her highlighter pen against the classifieds. She

was all business. "I'm not sure. We might have to start selling our ovaries."

I scooted out the door. By the time I was squeezed onto a subway train, my mind had already turned from the apartment hunt back to obsessing over *Cutting Loose.*

The more I thought about it, the more unlikely it seemed that Mercedes would like the book. Yes, it had a few chortles in it. Fleishman was a funny person. Of course, *I* hadn't found it very funny . . . and I doubted anyone else would either. Why would they? To me the thing was about as entertaining as watching someone pick a scab. Mine.

At the office, I dropped my purse in my chair and looked up to find a vaguely familiar man standing in my doorway. He was medium height, with deeply tanned skin and dark hair that was slicked back in a way that made me think of Andy Garcia. When he smiled, his white teeth practically glistened against his Coppertone complexion. "So you're the new one," he observed.

My lips twisted into a wobbly smile. Who the hell was this? "Uh . . . fairly new."

"Mercedes has told me good things about you," he said, waving. "Keep up the good work."

"Thanks!" I chirped toward his back. He was already walking away.

Three seconds later, Andrea poked her head in my door. "My God, what did he say to you?"

I squinted. "Who?"

"Art!"

"*That* was Art Salvatore?"

"Of course! Who did you think it was?" Her face screwed up. "I wonder why he didn't stop by my door."

"Maybe his stopping by mine wasn't such a good thing," I said.

I was already feeling uneasy when I headed for the coffee room. Lindsay fell into step with me as I passed her cubicle. "Are you ready for your closeup?"

Some sort of joke, obviously. It went right over my head.

"Your 'Making Waves' interview for *BM*," she prompted. "Isn't that today?"

Oh shit.

Belatedly, the memory of making the lunch appointment hit me like walking into a wall. I froze in my tracks.

It was one of those moments when, if I hadn't been in a space where I was posing as a professional, I would have just let my knees buckle underneath me and sunk to the ground, beat my fists on the carpet, and wept. This was just too gruesome. I was wearing a dress that was as appealing as an NPR tote bag, no jewelry, and no makeup. Maybe I could have passed for someone making waves back in Khrushchev's Moscow, but now I looked more like something that needed to be sandbagged. I was a disaster.

"I forgot. Completely," I wailed *sotto voce.* "Look at me! I'm in no shape to meet the press!"

Lindsay's face wrinkled in concern for a split second, and then she shrugged. I guess in the annals of Lindsay screw-ups, underdressing for an interview didn't even rate. "You look okay to me . . ."

Those were not comforting words. Andrea told me that Lindsay had shown up for her second day of work in a thrift store tube top.

She gave me a fresh up and down scan. "But now that you mention it . . ."

I groaned.

"Not to worry! You can fix yourself up after the meeting."

Those words stopped my writhing. In fact, they practically stopped my heart. "Meeting?"

"Weren't you headed for the conference room?"

Father in heaven. The weekly ed meeting. I had forgotten about that, too. I was in serious need of a brain transplant.

I galloped toward the coffee room—no way could I face an ed meeting without caffeine—going over my options for the interview. Or my lack of options. I was supposed to meet the woman at noon at some Japanese restaurant. I didn't have time to go home, and it wasn't as if I had a wardrobe closet in my office. I wasn't even sure I had an old lipstick at the bottom of my purse.

Maybe on the way to the restaurant I could swing by Bloomingdale's and partake of free makeup counter samples. It would be tempting to buy a new dress while I was at it, but the night before Wendy had made me take a vow of fiscal responsibility.

All of these thoughts were racing through my mind as I slopped coffee in my cup and poured in a vat of non-dairy creamer. Then I arrowed straight for the conference room, landing in a seat just as Mercedes was bringing us all to order. When she spotted me, she stopped mid-gavel and exclaimed, "Genius has arrived!"

I blushed, assuming this was sarcasm. From the snorts and chuckles that rippled around the table, so did everyone else.

But Mercedes wasn't laughing. "*Genius*," she said again.

I looked down at the pile of paper she had in front of her. To my horror, it was Fleishman's manuscript, and it was littered with little yellow stickies, which meant that she actually had taken it seriously. That she liked it. She'd even brought it to the meeting as a show-and-tell exhibit, something she hardly ever did.

I shrank in my chair.

"Rebecca has given me a book that will open up a whole new direction for us. We haven't done anything like it before. I've already made a copy and given it to Art. He read the first chapter and loved it!"

I slid down in my chair. So *that's* what Art's stopping by had been about.

Mary Jo eyed the book with suspicion. "If it's so different, why do you think it's right for Candlelight?"

"Because it's irresistible," Mercedes gushed. "A combination of Nick Hornby and that Bridget Jones woman, with a little bit of Robert James Waller thrown in."

"Who's Robert James Waller?" Madeline asked.

"*The Bridges of Madison County*," someone explained for her.

Her forehead showed the faintest of wrinkles. "Like that really boring movie? But that was about *old people*."

"I only meant that it's bittersweet and moving. But it's funny. More Nick Hornby than anything else."

Andrea shook her head. "I get it. The new voice in women's fiction is a man. Brilliant."

"This is romance with an edge," Mercedes said. "It's lad lit with a heart. It's got a lovable scamp for a hero who's exasperating and adorable. I could see John Cusack playing him in the movie."

"Oh! I love John Cusack!" Madeline exclaimed. Or maybe the whole table said it. Everybody loved John Cusack.

They were all on board now.

I wanted to bang my head against the table. The phrase *catastrophic success* finally made sense to me.

How could she have liked it? And what was I going to do? My worst fear was coming true. I was going to be immortalized in print as the ex-girlfriend, the neurotic Jenny Craig alumna.

Mercedes tapped her pen against her legal pad. "Which reminds me . . ." She craned to see Lisa, who was in the back of the room. "Lisa, we need to see that this book gets in the hands of production companies, ASAP."

"But it's not under contract," I piped up.

And it never will be. Scenes from the night before flashed through my head. I'm pretty sure Wendy had used phrases along the lines of "over my dead body" and "when hell fills with Eskimo Pies" to characterize Fleishman's chances of having his book published with Candlelight.

This was a bind. I didn't want this book to see the light of day, but if it didn't, I was now screwed. I would be bumped from genius back down to bumbling fool. It was a perfect lose-lose situation.

I tried frantically to look for a bright side. Okay, it looked like the book was a shoo-in to sell. Maybe I had overreacted about the personal stuff. So what if Fleishman had thrown in a little autobiography into the story? It wasn't as if that many people would notice. Maybe a few mutual acquaintances, sure, along with my entire family, but so what?

"There shouldn't be a problem, should it?" Mercedes asked, jolting me back to the question of acquisition. I was slumped in my chair in a panic coma. "I got the feeling this was a first book," she said, "and that you knew the author personally . . ."

The room got very quiet, it seemed to me. I cleared my throat. "That's true, but—"

"From the dedication, I thought you were very intimate with this author, this Jack Fleishman." Mercedes scanned the first page. "*To Rebecca Abbot, who inspired every word . . .*"

Mary Jo shot me a curious glance. "Is one of the characters based on you?"

"Um . . ."

Mercedes nearly slapped her forehead. "You are *so* like the character of Renata, aren't you?"

"Is she the love interest?" one of the editors asked.

"No, she's the one who gets dumped." Mercedes hitched her throat and cut her eyes to me. "Pardon me. She gets *cut loose.*" She leaned toward me. "Did you really lose your virginity in a Chrysler minivan?"

I groaned. "It's fiction."

"Wait a second . . ." Andrea's face was frozen in puzzlement. With a pleading glance I tried to stop her, but she apparently didn't catch my eyeballed SOS in time. "*Fleishman?* Isn't that your roommate? That crazy guy who flew out to Portland when you were at that conference?"

"Yes." My voice downgraded to a mere peep.

She shook her head. "And now he's written a book about dumping you? Cripes! That's humiliating."

It would have felt nice to strangle her at that moment, but maybe it was best to have it all out to begin with rather than coming out in dribs and drabs at other inopportune moments.

Apparently Mercedes didn't mind about my humiliation. "But that's perfect! If the guy lives with you, it should be a snap to get him under contract."

I had to work hard to dislodge the large frog that had taken up residence in my esophagus. "Not exactly. I don't even know if we were the only house he's submitted to . . ."

That last statement created a disgruntled silence shared by all. Multiple submissions—when an author sends the same book to more than one publisher—are frowned upon. For one thing, if more than one publisher want the same book, it creates a thorny problem. The publishers have to start bidding against each other, and they hate that. It takes all the power out of their hands. And Candlelight prized loyalty from its authors. Multiple submissions, even from someone we'd never published before, exhibited a certain disloyalty in advance.

Mercedes bridled uncomfortably. She had obviously thought this would be a slam dunk. "Does he have an agent?"

"No," I said. I was certain of that, at least.

"It'll be a snap," she repeated.

"20K?" Mary Jo asked.

"Tops, I hope."

Twenty thousand? I went all woozy in my chair. I wanted to cry. I was going to have to hand Fleishman twenty thousand dollars for insulting me in print?

As I sat brooding, the late list was distributed around the table.

"Who's the high roller this week?" one of the editors asked.

I looked at it and gulped. I was all over the thing.

Mary Jo let out a laugh and shot me a smile. "Looks like it's the genius."

I did swing by Bloomie's on the way to the interview. And after I had made up my face one counter at a time, I swung by accessories and picked up a scarf. It was on sale—a steal at twenty-three bucks. It looked crisp and professional—like a scarf Mercedes would wear. By the time I left the store, I was at least presentable from the shoulders up.

Alex Keene, the *BM* reporter, had chosen a Japanese restaurant in the basement of a modern building on Fifth. Banquette tables lined the wall. The decoration was stark—lots of black enamel broken by a few decorative pots of bamboo. There was no sound except for the faint burbling of a goldfish pond.

The black pantsuited hostess swayed toward me, but before she could reach me, I was ambushed from behind. "Rebecca?"

I turned and had to crane my neck upwards. In her stocking feet, Alex Keene might have been five-ten, but in five-inch heels she was approaching NBA territory. She didn't teeter on those stilts, either; she had one of those purposeful strides with nothing tentative or wobbly about it. She had been very business-like on the phone, but for some reason I hadn't expected a red-haired giantess in a long black jacket. You would never have guessed she worked for a publishing industry rag. From the looks of her, she belonged in the Condé Nast empire.

"You *are* Rebecca, aren't you?"

I nodded.

She gave me a once-over. "You're not at all what I expected."

Not the *making waves* type, obviously. I smiled. At least I was wearing the newest fall lipstick color from Estee Lauder. It was my only source of confidence at the moment.

The hostess ushered us to our table. I was glad to see we were separated from the next couple of diners by one of those bamboo pots. Nothing like those awkward sidewise glances from diners too close together, pretending that they are not hearing every syllable of your conversation. Thanks to that bamboo, their voices were no more than two masculine murmurs.

Alex and I ordered our bento boxes and sat back, sipping hot weak tea. "Mercedes Coe spoke so highly of you, it really swayed me."

I frowned. "Swayed you?"

"To include someone from Candlelight in the article. We hadn't intended to, initially." She shrugged. "I mean, romances are great. My grandmother buys them by the truckload. They're just not . . ."

"Prestigious."

"Right!"

I smiled as I tried to figure out how to respond to that. Getting up and walking out would have felt good, but Mercedes had really wanted me to do this interview. I couldn't blow it.

"We're always trying to change people's minds about that," I told her. "Maybe I can change yours."

She laughed doubtfully. "Well, Mercedes changed my mind about doing this interview. Mercedes, and the fact that the person I was going to interview from Knopf got fired when I was setting everything up. Mercedes said you were terrific, and you had all these terrific new ideas. Where did you go to college?"

When I told her the name of that little liberal arts haven in Ohio, her eyes glazed over. I was losing her.

I was beginning to feel uneasy . . . and not because Alex Keene so looked like she wished she was eating lunch with some young blade from Random House, say. There was something else disturbing me. And then I figured it out. Those male voices coming from the next table sounded familiar to me. Very familiar.

While Alex bloviated about how worried she'd been that she would be late for our lunch because she was talking to Jonathan Franzen on the telephone, I took the opportunity to peer through the bamboo shoots at our neighbors. I'm not sure if I actually let out a bleat. I certainly heard one in my own head.

Sitting right next to me was Fleishman. But that wasn't even the worst of it.

Sitting across from *him* was Dan Weatherby.

Chapter 17

I stood so abruptly I caused Alex Keene to sploop tea on herself. She emitted a muted shriek and immediately dunked her napkin in her ice water. "What happened?" she asked as she dabbed at herself. "Are you okay?"

It was a ridiculous question, considering the fact that I was so obviously not okay. I stood rigid peering over the bamboo, eyes bulging first at Fleishman, then at Dan, and then at Fleishman again. At first I couldn't make sense of it. What were they doing, comparing notes?

When he spotted me—and how could he not?—Fleishman looked ruffled, too, but he managed not to come unglued. I could tell he was upset by the welts of red just under his cheekbones. His gaze narrowed on me.

Dan composed himself first. Of course. He was half man, half Pat Sajak. One of his eyes fluttered in a wink. "Hiya, Becca."

Hiya? Even under the most casual circumstances, that is not a greeting I care for. I especially don't care for it when the last time I saw the person saying it was just after a mad romp in a hotel room. It had only been three days! *Hiya.* That stung.

At the sound of a familiar voice, Alex's eyes widened and she bobbed her head up, down, to and fro for a moment trying to see around the bamboo. Finally, she just had to hop out of her chair. "Dan?" she squealed. "Dan Weatherby?"

Spotting her, his smile broadened. He stood up, too, and they exchanged an air kiss over the foliage. She rated, apparently. Maybe *she* hadn't slept with him yet.

"Where have you been all my life?" he said.

She rolled her eyes, turning from a no-nonsense businesswoman into a six-foot coquette before my eyes. "Working!"

"I so know how that is."

It was like old home week with those two.

"This has been a brutal couple of months," she said. "Just a terror. Half the magazine's out on maternity leave."

"Must be something in the water cooler." Dan chuckled, then winked at her. "Better watch out, Al."

She hooted. Which was probably just as well, since it covered my groan.

It took the two of them a few more seconds to notice that both myself and Fleishman, who, not to be left out, was now standing, too, were staring at them in stony silence. Dan made the introductions. "Alex Keene, this is my newest client, Jack Fleishman."

I gasped. "Your *client?*"

Dan's brows wafted aloft. "Didn't you know?"

"No, I didn't know," I said hotly. I darted a glare at Fleishman. "No one told me."

Fleishman shrugged. "It's a new development."

"Are you published?" Alex asked him.

He answered modestly, "Not yet." Though I couldn't help noticing that the gaze he aimed at Alex was so intense it was borderline smoldering.

Dan broke in, "That *will not* be the case for long. Isn't that true, Bec?" He was smart enough not to wait for my response. "Jack's going to be the next big thing. The new Nick Hornby."

"Excellent!" Alex exclaimed.

While I gnashed my teeth, I tried to remember that I was supposed to be a business person. I tried to distance myself professionally. Dan was just another agent; Fleishman was just a commodity. Mercedes had ordered me to go forth and buy that book. There was something else at stake here besides my own personal pride. There was my job.

Unfortunately, those stakes involved future public humiliation.

"Mercedes was full of praise for *Cutting Loose.*" I spoke the words so reluctantly, so resentfully, they came out a mere rasp, as if they had been through a meat grinder.

There. I'd done it. I had officially swallowed my pride and brought up the subject. I had inched one step closer to buying that odious book. With his agent, no less.

His agent! That was still confounding me. When had these two joined forces?

But rather than seeming pleased that I was putting professional interest before my personal ones—waaaaaaaaay before—Dan merely smiled blandly.

He and Fleishman exchanged a look.

"That's a good sign, I guess?" Fleishman asked.

He guessed? He knew who Mercedes was. I could feel the wrinkles gathering on my forehead like thunderclouds. "I would say it's a very good sign," I said.

The dastardly duo exchanged another look, and I took more time analyzing it this time around. It contained an off-putting combination of amusement and discomfort.

"Actually, Bec," Dan said, "Jack and I aren't quite sure yet which way we're going to go with the project."

Which I interpreted to mean that the cabal I had just interrupted was a strategy session.

"Naturally he was happy to give the manuscript to you when you asked for it, since you're a close personal friend. . . ." Dan said.

I could only hope they couldn't all hear my teeth gnashing.

Fleishman grinned at me. "The long and short of it is, I've had nibbles."

"How?" I was aware of my voice rising, but I couldn't help it. There was an awful ringing in my ears. "A few nights ago you told me I was one of the first people you had shown the book to, and I haven't had it for two days!"

How could he already be getting responses from other publishers? How could they already be thinking of acquiring it? How could anyone else already be *nibbling?*

Obviously, I had been lied to. The big surprise there was that I was still surprised. I hadn't known that Fleishman had an agent, either. Dan Weatherby!

The waitress came by, carrying two elaborately carved bento boxes. She seemed surprised to see us all standing and chatting across the bamboo. Or rather, to see three people chatting and me yelling.

"Here's our food," Alex sing-songed, looking relieved to have an excuse to put an end to the conversation.

The waitress nodded to the empty seats on the other side of Dan and Fleishman. "You would like to move?"

"*No!*" they all chimed.

We all sank back into our respective seats. *Back to our corners*, I thought.

Alex balanced her chopsticks in her perfectly manicured hands. "Small world." Her voice lowered to adjust for eavesdropping.

Mine did not. I was too mad. "Smaller than you know."

She tilted toward me. "So I take it you know that author well?"

"We live together." I added, "*Lived.*"

Maybe it wasn't kosher to give personal details, but I couldn't help myself. I was in a swivet. I stared at the neatly ordered quadrants of my lunch and tried to sort out the mess that was unraveling. It wasn't making any sense. All I knew was that I was feeling murderous. I grabbed my chopsticks, lamenting the dull edges. *Just when a sharp object might have come in handy . . .*

Alex started talking about her ideas for the magazine article, and somehow in a conversation about up-and-coming editors, she managed to drop the name of half a dozen very famous authors. I half listened. Actually, I half listened for about thirty seconds and then I was off in my own world again.

All the implications started to pile up on me. Dan and Fleishman couldn't be a completely new development. They hadn't just gotten together this week. An agent didn't decide to represent someone overnight. Chances were that even before I had gone to Dallas, Dan had read the book. And that he had known, or at least suspected, that I was the pathetic, needy, easy-to-seduce Renata. I had inspired every word, after all.

And how had I come across in Dallas? Pathetic, needy, and easy to seduce.

In this light, a few of the things Dan had said to me over the weekend began to make sense. Cryptic comments about my wanting the lights out and being clingy. I mean, I had thought at the time that it was weird to call someone clingy five minutes after waking up from a one-night stand. Now it seemed worse than weird. It seemed sinister.

Oh, yeah. This explained a lot.

Like the way Fleishman had practically pimped me out to Dan. I had forgotten about *that.* Those flowers, that whispered comment on the way to the airport. They had been a sort of *You go, girl!* nudge. Had he thought it would improve his chances to have his agent and his editor sleeping together?

Except now he didn't even seem to need me as an editor. Or no, he just wasn't sure. He had *nibbles.*

Nauseating.

Alex leaned across the table and peered worriedly into my face. "Is your lunch okay?"

"Fine!" I gritted out. To demonstrate how fine I was, I gulped down a piece of sushi whole. Then another. I was barely chewing. Just shoveling. Meanwhile, waves of clammy cold and then heat washed over me.

"Maybe you could tell me about what you did before coming to Candlelight. Mercedes said you worked for Sylv—"

Rocket propelled by anger, I exploded out of my chair again. "Did you think it was funny?" I demanded of neither one in particular. It was hard to say whom I was the most angry at anyway.

Dan and Fleishman glanced up, startled.

"The book?" Dan asked. "I thought it was hilarious."

"Not the book," I said, disgusted. "Or, yes, the book. The

book, me, and your pathetically easy Saturday night seduction. You knew just what buttons to push—and no wonder!"

Dan's face went red, and he arched a brow in the general direction of my dining companion. "Bec . . ."

I rolled my eyes. "My name is *Rebecca.* It's not Bec. It's not Becca. And it's sure as hell not Renata."

"Maybe we shouldn't be talking about this here . . ."

"Where, then?"

"In private, maybe?"

"Oh sure," I said with a sarcastic snort. "Sure. I'll just wait for you to call. In fact, I'll bet you were about to call me at any moment, weren't you?"

"Actually, I was," he said.

"To tell you the truth, Dan, I didn't care if you called me or not. Still don't. I haven't given you much thought since Sunday. I've had other things on my mind. But to find out that you slept with me because I was easy game because of something you'd read in Fleishman's crappy book, that makes you an even bigger sleaze than I was already beginning to suspect you were."

Fleishman jumped into the fray. "I *told* you she didn't like the book!"

For some reason, *that* comment almost did me in. Literally.

So far I had been venting mostly on Dan, maybe because what I felt toward Fleishman went so much deeper. I felt betrayed. I was seeing him, really seeing him, for the first time, and it was painful. He had exposed me, betrayed me. Worse, he had made a mockery of six years of friendship.

I sucked in a breath to speak—it was a deep breath, because I had a lot to say—but when I did so, some half-chewed piece of sushi that had been buried behind a molar suddenly jumped into my throat. My diaphragm contracted, then began to spasm, but there was not a whisper of air coming down my windpipe.

I started to make desperate motions with my arms. At first, no one seemed to notice. *Great. Just great.* Death by sushi inhalation would top off my week nicely.

The faces staring at me began to screw up in confusion. "What's the matter?" Alex asked.

I jerked my arms around in a frustrating charade as my companions continued to gape at me. Maybe they thought I was just having an apoplectic fit, but I was sure I was turning blue by this point.

Alex grabbed my arm. "Omigod!" she exclaimed. "She's *choking!* She needs help!"

The words would have made me feel better had I not feared they would be the last I heard on this side of eternity. Which, even though I consider myself mildly spiritual, happens to be the side I tend to prefer.

After registering a moment of surprise, Fleishman jumped up and yanked me away from the table. Then he started pounding on my back. Hard. And just in case you ever need to know, when you can't breathe, it's not so great to have people beating you.

"Wait!" Dan said. "That's not right."

No kidding.

"I remember!" Alex flicked Fleishman aside. "You have to grab her like this."

Like a rag doll, I was grabbed from behind by Alex.

"That's right," Dan said, "you punch her diaphragm."

"With your fists!" Fleishman said. I guess all that first aid knowledge was coming back to him.

Alex followed their instructions and miraculously managed to perform a perfect Heimlich maneuver in one thrust. She was, not surprisingly, strong. I could practically hear a pop as I unclogged and that troublesome piece of sushi went flying across the bamboo, landing with an audible plop in Dan's miso soup.

I've known a lot of embarrassing moments. More than my share, I would say. At the age of twelve I had started my period at camp on trail ride day and spent the rest of my time at Camp Promise hearing snide renditions of that stupid "There was blood on the saddle" song. Actually I pretty much consider my first eighteen years of life one bad moment after another, all strung together.

But choking during my "Making Waves" interview in front

of two ex-lovers definitely rated. Not only were Dan and Fleishman gaping at me (actually, Dan was staring at his soup bowl), the entire restaurant had turned to watch. There was no sound, either, except that burbling fish pond.

It is hard to recover your dignity after an episode of public regurgitation, and my dignity had already been on the verge of collapse.

Only Alex seemed at all animated. "Omigod!" she yelled, delighted. "It worked. I saved your life!"

I mumbled my thanks. I *was* thankful. I just wanted to be out of there.

"I hope I can work this into the article!" she said.

I grabbed my purse. Call me a coward, but I didn't really see much point in continuing on with my publicity lunch. The only waves I was making were the ripples still in Dan's miso soup. "Actually, we might have to continue some other time."

Her brow creased. "Oh, okay . . ." She seemed disappointed. I think she wanted to spend the rest of the meal basking in her heroism.

After that, there didn't seem much left to say.

Except, come to think of it, there *was* one thing I wanted out in the open.

I brushed past Fleishman, then looked Dan Weatherby square in the eye. "Just for the record, Dan. Your new client, the new Nick Hornby? He thinks you're a baloney sandwich."

On the way back to the office, I underwent a complete willpower meltdown. I passed Food Emporium, then doubled back and came out minutes later with an M&M two-pounder. Unashamed, I tore it open on the street with my teeth, sending colored candies flying like confetti. I popped a fistful into my mouth, then barely restrained myself from upending the entire bag into my mouth.

When I got off the elevator, the temporary receptionist gestured to the message wheel. "You've got a bunch."

The messages were all from Wendy. *Left you a voicemail*, one said. Another: *Where the h are you?* Then, *Meet at 3 at the NW corner of 96th and B'Way.*

I groaned and popped another fistful of M&Ms. Apartment hunting. Which meant dealing with supers, or worse, real estate agents. Would this day never end?

"How'd the interview go?" Lindsay chirped at me. She was planted next to the Xerox machine. I murmured abstractly as I whisked by her.

"You look one hundred percent better than when you left!" she called after me.

I shut myself into my office and leaned back in my chair, popping M&Ms by the palmful and letting them melt in my mouth for a moment before starting to chew. God it felt good. I can't tell you. I leaned farther back, then finally just gave in, kicked off my shoes, and propped my bare feet on my desk.

Pure sugar oblivion, that's what I was looking for. And blessed silence.

It's not what I got. As I sank into my M&M reverie, my door opened and closed with a slam. And then, in the blink of an eye, Andrea was on my floor, in a fetal ball, rolling from side to side. And moaning. The most awful sound I'd ever heard was coming out of her—a horrible, otherworldly keening noise. Like a large rodent with stomach cramps. It was as if she were going through some sort of weird reversion therapy.

I brought my feet down and leaned toward her. "Um . . . Andrea?"

She turned slightly. What a sight she was! Her hair was in her face, her skirt was bunched up around her thighs. "I . . . AM . . . SO . . . SCREWED!"

They were the first intelligible words she'd spoken since flinging herself down on my carpet. Maybe this was a positive sign. "What happened?"

The question made her go slack, and she lay facedown on the floor, like a penitent. "I applied for a job . . ."

"So?" She was applying for jobs all the time.

"At *Candlelight!*"

I was mystified. "How could you have done that?"

"I *don't know!*" she howled. "I didn't know what I was doing! They didn't put the name of the company in the ad."

I remembered the ad I'd responded to. I hadn't known I was applying to Candlelight, either. Of course, to me it hadn't made any difference. "Who received your application?"

"Kathy Leo! And instead of coming to me, she bumped my resume right over to Mercedes. The traitor!"

"Shit."

"And Mercedes called a conference with Rita, and Karen . . ."

"Shit."

"And then invited *me*. They ambushed me."

And I thought I was having a bad day.

Andrea heaved a deep, deep sigh. "For a minute there, I thought I was being promoted. Then she brought out my resume and cover letter, and I knew the jig was up. It was over. I was toast."

I shuddered sympathetically. "Oh God."

Her head lifted. "It's worse than *oh God*, Rebecca. I had put in all sorts of cover letter bullshit about how I had been with my present company forever and was now seeking greater challenges. Mercedes read all the awful bits back to me in front of everyone."

"Ouch."

"The worse part is, the ad made the company sound so fantastic! I thought I was applying to this great publishing house that would shower me with money and prestige." In a sign that she was snapping back from adversity, she grumbled, "Kathy Leo ought to try her hand at becoming an author. The drivel she concocted was pure fiction."

"What did Mercedes say to you?"

"Plenty."

"Did she fire you?"

"No—but you know Mercedes. She jawed on forever about what a valued employee I was. And how she was so disappointed that I wasn't happy, but hoped that I wasn't actually planning to leave."

I mulled that over for a moment. "You know, that doesn't sound like you're screwed, Andrea. In fact it sounds like she was trying to be, you know, encouraging."

Andrea rolled her eyes. "When were you hatched? She knows I'm trapped here like a bug on a web. She's got my number now. I'll be watched, tormented, and persecuted. I'll only be sent to conferences in North Dakota. Just when I think I've finally cleared my name, the noose will tighten. *That's* when I'll be booted out."

She seemed to take perverse pleasure in seeing herself as the Jean Valjean of Candlelight editorial. "Maybe Mercedes was telling the truth," I said.

"Oh, no. I'm doomed, I'm sure of it. I'm going to lose my job, my apartment, everything. Not only will I not be able to tread water in Queens, I'll be forced to move back to my parents' house in East Orange. I'll be lucky to get a job as a grocery scanner. I will die a spinster."

"There aren't spinsters anymore." One of Andrea's authors wrote very popular western romances.

"They just don't call them that anymore." She poked at her chest. "Maybe that's where I'll be a trendsetter. I'll single-handedly bring back the pathetic, middle-aged no-hoper."

I tried to imagine Andrea as a modern-day old maid. Zazu Pitts with a potty mouth. "I don't want to disillusion you, but I think you're overreacting. I don't think Mercedes has it in for you."

"*Ha.*"

"Think about it. She had your resume. She could have had it for days. She had plenty of time to sit around deciding what to do with you. But instead of firing you, she called in all your superiors and staged this intervention."

Andrea crossed her arms. "She just wanted to see me squirm."

"Or there's another possibility."

"What?"

"She really doesn't want to lose you."

I was ready to be barked at, belittled, and told I was a

gullible rube. Remarkably, Andrea's head slowly tilted, as if she were actually thinking over what I'd said. "Is that some kind of joke?"

"No, I mean it. Why shouldn't she want to keep you? You're a good editor. I would have been sunk without your help these last few months." Which, I realized, was actually true. In her own curt way, Andrea had been invaluable to me.

"But she knows I want to leave!"

"So?" I shrugged. "A lot of people have their eyes out for better jobs. Didn't you notice Mary Jo looked awfully good a day or so after that ad appeared in *BM* for a senior ed at Avon?"

"Get out of here."

"It's true. And remember what Mercedes said after Cassie left? She said she wanted to prevent that from happening again. Maybe she was actually telling the truth."

We both took a moment to chew over the possibility that corporate groupspeak wasn't entirely BS. That we actually were valued employees. It was an unsettling thought. Briefly I thought I saw tears welling in Andrea's eyes.

Or maybe not. She frowned at the candy bag on my desk. "Jesus Christ. Is that a two-pounder?"

I nodded, ashamed.

"That's disgusting!" she said. "Can I have some?"

I offered the bag, and, sitting cross-legged, she emptied about half the contents into her skirt. "I love these things."

"I needed chocolate therapy."

"Why? What happened to you?"

I hesitated. I didn't want to enter into a game of one-upmanship.

But Andrea egged me on. "C'mon. It couldn't have been worse than what happened to me."

I couldn't resist the challenge. I told her all of it. Andrea's lavish reactions to my tale of woe were very gratifying. Her eyes bugged when I went into the details with Fleishman, she issued profane exclamations when I explained what had happened over the weekend, and she agreed—whole-heartedly—

that my dress was hideous. By the time I told her what went down at the Japanese restaurant—or rather, what came up—she was staring at me, slack jawed.

"That is seriously fucked up," she finally declared.

In the battle of the bad days, I guess it was a draw.

She devoured a few more M&Ms. "What were you doing sleeping with Dan anyway? I thought you were holding out for elevator man."

"Elevator man is the impossible dream. Dan was available."

"I'm beginning to think what's out of reach is safest in the long run."

"You mean abstinence?"

She shuddered. "I *am* becoming a spinster. Maybe I should go out and get a few cats for my apartment."

Apartment! I bolted straight up in my chair and squinted at the clock on my monitor screen. The tiny numbers said twenty till three. "Crap! I'm late."

I jumped up, and so did Andrea. M&Ms went flying. "Where are we going?"

"We?"

"You can't leave me alone here," she said.

There was something almost touching about Andrea in needy mode. "I have to go look at an apartment with my roommate. I've only got twenty minutes to get to the other side of town and up to 96th Street."

Her mouth dropped open. "You're going to live up *there?*"

"We're just looking. We have to find a place . . ."

"Right. The new Nick Hornby has rendered you homeless," she said. "I'm definitely going with you."

Thanks to the unexpected timeliness of all the trains, we were only five minutes late to meet Wendy. She was standing at the corner, arms crossed, looking as if someone had just died.

"I'm not going to install myself in your apartment," Andrea said to her. They had never met. "I just came along for the exercise."

"You're late," Wendy said.

"Just five minutes."

"Well, I was ten minutes early, so I went ahead and looked at the place."

I supposed that's why she looked so grim. "Bad?"

"No, fantastic. It's beautiful. Huge." She sighed. "Expensive."

"So we can't afford it."

"No, we can't." Wendy looked like she was ready to throw herself in front of a downtown bus.

I shrugged. "Oh, well . . ."

"I want to see it!" Andrea said.

"You do?" Wendy asked. She brightened a little. But to me it looked as sinister as the brightness of an addict finding a crack pipe.

"Fantastic, huge, and expensive is just what I love."

"But if it's too expensive," I said.

Resistance was futile. Those two wanted to go in. Masochists.

The super of the apartment was a skinny, scruffy guy named Greg who looked really annoyed to be showing the place twice to the same person. "You again?" he asked Wendy as he handed the key over.

"Sorry to make you knock yourself out," she said.

Greg scurried back into his first floor apartment like a cockroach diving for a crack under the baseboards.

Inside the apartment, Wendy and Andrea were all exclamations.

"This is *so* cool!" Andrea said. "Look at these floors!"

"Parquet," Wendy said. "Lovely!"

"And the ceilings—they have to be nine feet."

"Eight and a half, I think," Wendy said. "But they're coved, so I think they look higher."

The Home and Garden Channel had taken control of Wendy's brain.

It *was* a nice apartment. While those two squealed over glass doorknobs and the river view (I couldn't see it, but I didn't drag an old folding chair out of a closet and stand on it like Wendy did), I took a quick tour. There were two small but real bedrooms and a little room—a bonus. The kitchen was a galley but it was bigger than ours, and the bathroom had a claw-foot tub *and* a shower. It seemed like stupendous luxury.

I made a complete circle in the time it took them to go from the front door to the kitchen.

"Two problems," I said. "It's too expensive, and it's too expensive."

"But look how big the kitchen is," Andrea whined, as if she had a stake in any of this. "It's bigger than mine."

"It's twice as big as ours," Wendy said.

I couldn't believe her. All these years *she* had been the level-headed one about money. She had been the person who counseled frugality, and she had frowned more than me at Fleishman's lack of realism when it came to paying bills. Now—after seeing one nice apartment—her inner spendthrift had come unhinged.

"It doesn't matter if it's kitchen stadium from *Iron Chef*, we can't afford it. Besides, if you wanted to be closer to NYU, this isn't the place. It's geographically farther away than Williamsburg."

"Not exactly," Wendy said. "It's a straight shot down on the subway. And maybe Starbucks would let me transfer to a store closer to home."

"Besides, the layout of this place is all wrong."

Wendy put her hands on her hips. "How much more wrong could it be than the place we've been living? Which, you know, doesn't even have rooms. Or doors on the closets. Little amenities like that."

"I know, but . . ." I looked at the small room, which had obviously been an office. One wall was solid floor-to-ceiling bookcases. For the first time, apartment yearning began to take hold of me, too. It would be the first place I ever lived with enough shelves.

Not that we were going to live there. Why on earth had Wendy chosen this moment to become a head-in-the-clouds dreamer? Last night she had been talking about fiscal responsibility. Now all she cared about was coved ceilings and closet space.

"We can't afford it," I insisted.

"Or maybe you could," Andrea said. I had almost forgotten that she was standing there.

Fifteen minutes later, I had paid Greg the last of my money as a bribe for the dog and we were signing the lease. All three of us.

Chapter 18

Moving out of Williamsburg seemed grim. It wasn't just watching my stuff go into boxes and milk crates that made my misery index rise, it was what wasn't going in: Fleishman's stuff. His books, his tchotchkes, the furniture. I was extra careful not to take anything that could in any way be construed as his. I didn't covet his material possessions; but for so long I had thought of them as *ours.* Our DVD collection. Our rug. The great kitchenware Natasha Fleishman had given *us.*

It had all been an illusion, I realized now. We had never been a real couple. I might as well have been playing house with an imaginary friend. Actually, that would have been better. Now I found myself not only having to deal with being separated from Fleishman, but also from his Viking cookware.

To make things worse, on my way to and from work every day, I had to pass all our places. Our Italian restaurant. Our bakery for weekend mornings. The thrift store where we'd found the Pillsbury Doughboy kitchen clock. Our Korean deli.

I felt wounded in a way I never had before. Part of me wanted to withdraw from everyone, to foreswear friendship and simply do without social interaction altogether. I mean, if someone I had loved and trusted for seven whole years could write a tell-all book that was the literary equivalent of poking my burned body with a stick, if I could have misjudged him so completely, what was the point?

There were moments when I visualized myself living in a cave somewhere, or becoming one of those urban hermits you see around sometimes, the ones who mutter to themselves as they're rooting through garbage cans. I used to wonder about people like that. Now I just wondered how many of them had a Fleishman lurking somewhere in their past.

Fortunately, I realized picking through garbage was not for me. I can't even bring myself to take a sip from someone else's glass.

Another part of what made me not want to renounce society altogether was my friends. Wendy was so great. Even though she was thoroughly obsessed with finding sheers for the windows and picking out paint colors, every afternoon she would rent one of my favorite movies and leave it for me to watch when I came home from work. So instead of brooding alone in the apartment, I would pack while I watched *Ninotchka*, and *Tootsie*, and *Pillow Talk*.

The *When Harry Met Sally* DVD disappeared.

At work, Andrea monitored my mental state, which was increasingly shaky. Every day I had to scrap with Dan Weatherby over the offer we were making for Fleishman's manuscript. Dan decided he wanted a twenty-five thousand dollar advance. Which, for a first book in paperback, was Candlelight's outer limit. Mercedes summoned me to her office several times a day, trying to decide whether Fleishman should be allowed to go where no freshman Candlelight author had gone before.

"You told him we would be doing promotion, didn't you?" she grilled me.

I nodded.

"You told him he'd get full-page ads?"

"Full-page, color."

"And he knows the 20K threshold is sacrosanct?"

I was new at this, so I was doing everything Mercedes told me to, basically. I was her negotiating handmaid.

"He knows," I said, "but Dan Weatherby is not the big believer in the 20K threshold that we are. In fact, I think he just views it like a steeplechase horse views a hurdle."

"*Merde!*" she exclaimed. Then she let out a naughty laugh. "Pardon my French."

I don't think she understood that expression was what you said when you *weren't* speaking French.

After these meetings, Andrea was always there to prop me up. "Don't worry so much about this stupid contract. Or that book," she would tell me as I slumped in despair at my desk. "It's just another book. With any luck, it'll flop."

"Right," I moaned. "It would be great to have a flop on my hands."

"Nobody would blame you. That's the beauty of being an editor. You get all this reflected glory if something hits the bestseller lists—then you're a genius. But if your pet project flops, there's always this great scapegoat: the author."

I wish I could say that the idea of Fleishman being a flop didn't make my heart pitter-pat with delight. But sometimes the vision of *Cutting Loose* on a remainder table was all that was keeping me going.

The night we signed the lease, Andrea, Wendy, and I had been giddy at the prospect of our new digs, so we went for a powwow at a local bar in our new neighborhood. It was an old taverny place—probably the past watering hole of many failed writers of Manhattan—that served generous Rat Pack style drinks heavy on the liquor and the maraschino cherries.

Wendy sucked on a whiskey sour and gave us a soliloquy on color schemes. For Andrea, the excitement was all in the act of moving. She had a brother with a truck, and she was sure she could wheedle him into ferrying her stuff from Queens into Manhattan.

My own jubilation ended sometime midway through my second Tom Collins, when it occurred to me that this would be the first place I lived without Fleishman since my junior year in college.

Wendy noticed me sinking first. "We're losing her," she warned Andrea.

"You want my orange peel?" Andrea asked, stabbing at the bottom of her glass with her swizzle stick.

I shook my head.

"Don't mope," Andrea said. "That's what they want you to do. What you need to do is go out and find yourself a fantastically handsome yet hedonistic sex puppy."

"That's what I told her!" Wendy jumped.

"Sounds great," I grumbled. "But who?"

"What about Elevator Man?"

"Oh, right."

"Well why not?" Wendy said. "Just take the initiative."

What did she mean? Jump him on the elevator? For some reason, the whole thing made me cringe. Taking the initiative had never worked out for me in the past. (Paging Jason Crane . . . or Jake Caddell. Even I was getting my past mixed up, thanks to that damn book.)

"It would never work. He's older. He's rich. He's suaver than shit." I shook my head wistfully. "That kind of guy would never go for me."

"That's what what's-her-name said about Max de Winter in *Rebecca*," Andrea said. "And look who she ended up with. Laurence Olivier!"

I frowned. "Yeah, but she ran around paranoid for months and was gaslighted by a crazy woman."

Wendy frowned. "And then her gorgeous house burned down."

Andrea sighed. "Fine. Leave him roaming on the loose. Someone else will take him—and it might just be me."

Wendy sent me a sympathetic look. "Maybe we should go to Bed Bath and Beyond and pick out a new bedspread for you," she suggested.

She had gone round the bend with this home improvement stuff. "I don't really have money for that."

"Oh! But there's this show called *Design on a Dime* that has all sorts of ideas for fixing up places . . ."

"A dime is about all we have," I reminded her. "I'm not even sure how we're going to afford a man with a van to get us over here next week."

Wendy frowned. "I hadn't thought of that."

"Maybe I could get my brother to swing by your place after he's done with mine," Andrea said.

That didn't seem fair, seeing as how we had nothing to pay him. Also, we had too much stuff.

"Well what if he just picked up the big stuff, like beds and bookcases?"

"And what about the rest?"

"We could just haul it ourselves in dribs and drabs."

"That's a lot of dribs."

"This is when you miss school," Andrea lamented. "Back in the day when for the price of a pizza you could convince your friends to help you move."

"Right," I said.

Wendy's eyes rounded. "Wait a second! I *am* in school. And even the people I know who aren't in school would help us if we gave them free food."

In other words, actors.

"You obviously travel in elite circles."

"Theater people will work for food," Wendy explained. "Hell, they'll actually work for nothing. For food they'll do things none of the rest of us ever would. Otherwise advertisers would never find people to be in Kotex commercials."

Now that we'd pinpointed a group of people we could exploit, Andrea was all enthusiasm. She slapped her hand on the table. "An evacuation party! This could work."

Thirty minutes later we were stumbling into an Internet café to send an all-points bulletin to everyone we knew, telling them to be at our apartment in Brooklyn on Saturday night. They were instructed to wear comfortable shoes and bring their MetroCards. They were promised food, drink, and fun.

I was skeptical about the fun part. I was doubtful anyone would show up.

Then, the next day, Mary Jo stopped by my office. "Should I bring anything?"

I tilted my head, puzzled. "Where?"

"To the party! I make a fantastic spinach dip," she said. "I can't wait to see your place."

I flinched. When we'd invited everybody at work, I'd hoped we could persuade Lindsay to show up. Maybe the mailroom guy. It never occurred to me that Mary Jo would want to come.

Now the reality of having any of my coworkers tromping through my apartment with its shower curtain doors and roach infested closet of a kitchen began to sink in. In horror, I imagined Mary Jo hovering in the doorway in Brooklyn, puffing from the three-flight climb, her nose wrinkling at the faint whiff of doggy odor.

But what could I do? The die was cast. I couldn't uninvite them.

"You don't have to bring anything," I told her.

"But I'd love to! I'm going out to buy a MetroCard at lunch!" she chirped, as if it were part of a treasure hunt party.

Andrea, who had heard the whole thing from her office, came in a few moments after Mary Jo left. She was shaking her head. "It's like when fishermen throw out their nets for tuna and they end up with a hammerhead shark."

"She doesn't have a MetroCard?" I asked, puzzled.

"She lives in Mount Kisco."

"Where is that?"

"Somewhere south of Canada. The subway doesn't reach."

Throughout the course of the day, I discovered that Lisa was also coming, and Troy, who promised to bring good-looking men, and Madeline. Mercedes RSVP'd *non*, thank heavens. Having Candlelight's editorial Big Kahuna there might have done me in.

At the end of the day I button-holed Lindsay at her desk to see if she would be attending.

She tilted her head. "I don't know. I'm getting so many invitations these days." She handed over a card that she'd been studying.

At first glance it looked like a wedding invitation. It was a cream colored card with raised gold lettering.

Marguerite, the Contessa of Longchamps cordially requests your presence at a
showing of her new line of jewelry,
The Contessa Collection

"This just came for Rita, but I think everybody's getting one."

I frowned. The invitation was for two weeks from that day, at two in the afternoon. "It's in the middle of a workday."

"I know, isn't that fabulous? Mercedes is bound to let us all go."

True. She wouldn't want to alienate anyone at the *Romance Journal.*

"And yes, I'll be at your party. Even though it sounds like there will be work involved."

"Don't worry. No one has to carry more than ten pounds."

"Can I bring Rowdy?"

"Of course! Bring any able-bodied person you know." Then I frowned. "Are you still living with that guy?"

"Yeah—he's hard to shake. Sweetest guy, though."

"Well, maybe you'll get lucky at the party. I mean, maybe *he'll* get lucky. There might be some cute Starbucks girls there who work with my roommate."

We had the night all worked out. Books would be ferried in small batches in old grocery and shopping bags. Clothes would be packed in small boxes, as would miscellaneous stuff, like toiletries and random knickknacks. Pictures would just have to be hauled by themselves.

The party began in Brooklyn, with drinks (and Mary Jo's spinach dip, which really was fabulous). Andrea's brother had come by with his truck that afternoon and moved our beds and the television, so the place already looked forlorn, even with Fleishman's stuff still there and boxes and shopping bags stacked everywhere. Within an hour of the appointed time, the apartment was jammed with people, and the noise they made, along with music blaring from Fleishman's Bang and Olufsen stereo, probably would have gotten us evicted if we weren't moving already.

I hadn't expected it to work. Call me an old cynic, but I didn't think an evacuation party would be a big draw. But its interactive nature apparently appealed to some people, who dutifully showed up ready to roll. More than a few brought champagne to christen our new apartment with.

Andrea took several bottles with her when she left with a few of her friends. They were to be the advance team who would be waiting for us at the apartment in Manhattan.

At the appointed time about twenty minutes later, Wendy started whipping our ranks into shape. She was a perfect troop mover, handing each guest just what they were willing to carry. The able-bodied lugged boxes or awkward items like pictures, lamps, or end tables; the rank-and-file hauled two shopping bags apiece; the high-heeled were given comforters and pillows in Hefty bags. My job was to close up the apartment, leave a note to latecomers informing them that the party had moseyed on without them, and to bring up the rear, rescuing any stragglers if need be.

I never thought it would work, but as I stood on the stoop after locking up and looked up and saw two blocks of coworkers, friends, and strangers filing toward the subway station with our stuff, some of my faith in humanity was restored. Which was funny, because they didn't resemble humans so much as a line of ants.

It was Saturday night, and we were not popular on the subway. I barely managed to squeeze on lugging a small chair in one hand, Max in his carrier in my other hand, and all of Max's bowls and other paraphernalia in a duffel looped over my shoulder. My arm got tired and I really wanted to set my chair down, or maybe just sit on it. Then I saw Wendy reprimanding someone for putting down a shopping bag; I decided to tough it out rather than risk the wrath of Wendy.

Even with twenty-five people helping, moving was a pain in the butt.

By the time I dragged myself up to the new apartment, I vowed never to accumulate anything more. If something got lost or worn out, it would have to be replaced with something of lesser weight. For the rest of my life, I would make do with folding chairs and air mattresses. My next dog would be a Chihuahua. Or maybe a hamster.

But those thoughts were driven away as I was sucked into the vortex of the party. The apartment had seemed so big when it was empty, but now it was a mad crush of people, unpacked boxes, and shoppng bags stacked everywhere.

Andrea handed me a glass of champagne. "Circulate," she ordered.

I did as I was told, though I confess that at first my heart wasn't in it. In party situations, I revert to feeling like I'm sixteen again. Maybe everyone does, although sixteen in my case was a disaster.

I swigged down two glasses of champagne in quick succession, which helped put me into a partying frame of mind. Troy had brought dance tunes, which he promptly put into the boom box, turning what little free space there was in the living room into a dance floor. Mary Jo seemed to be enjoying herself, too. She was in the middle of a bunch of Wendy's graduate school people, telling them about the time she had starred in *The Diary of Anne Frank* in high school. Lindsay was everywhere; for the first time, she seemed to fit in somewhere. In the mix of guests, she did not stand out, and she even seemed to blend in with the Wendy crowd.

In the time it took me to circulate around the room once, it felt as if I drank about four glasses of champagne. I felt great until I realized who wasn't there. My friends. Or, more specifically, the few of the mutual friends I shared with Fleishman. I had mulled over the people we had in common and only invited the few who I thought were more mine than his. Apparently I had miscalculated.

"My God, you look like death," Lindsay said, coming up to me.

"Sorry, I didn't mean to be a mopey hostess."

"That's okay—it's your party and you can . . ." She took a swig of champagne. "Well, you know."

"It's like I've been divorced, and all our friends are now his friends."

Lindsay squinted at me. "Then screw 'em." She held up a bottle of champagne. "Here, you obviously need liquid reinforcement."

I let her fill me up.

"Have you met Rowdy yet?"

I shook my head. Poor Lindsay. Still trying to foist that guy off on someone. It struck me as very sad—sad for Rowdy. I took a long swig. The bubbly was really beginning to kick in. Finally.

"I had introduced him to a woman who used to work in production in Candlelight who now is a gopher for Regis Philbin. I'm hoping the celebrity angle will appeal to him." She sighed. "I'm so ready for us to move on."

"Me, too," I slurred decisively. "I'm ready to move on."

"Good for you!" Lindsay's bracing slap on the back nearly toppled me over.

After that, things got fuzzy. I know I made my way to the kitchen to commandeer another bottle of champagne. I felt as if there were a smile pasted onto my face. I was moving on. I was having a good time. Everyone was having a good time.

The last thing I remember clearly was seeing Mary Jo dancing in the middle of Troy's models. Then I have a fuzzy recollection of joining her.

After that, mercifully, I fuzzed out completely.

When I woke up on Sunday, the day was already almost halfway to Monday. All night I'd had awful dreams that I'd forgotten something, or let someone down. That I had come up short, basically. My head felt as if someone had been blasting a trumpet in my ear all night. I was staring at my clock, which, when I forced my eyes to focus, read eleven forty-three. It was strange to see my familiar digital clock radio in a completely new space. Mindful of my head, I rolled over, hoping to go back to sleep until my skull stopped throbbing.

Then I screamed.

The man who happened to be lying in bed next to me shot up to sitting. He wasn't wearing a shirt. His bald chest was pale and freckly; the dusting of hair was just slightly more russet colored than the pumpkin orange thatch on the top of his head.

My first wild thought was of some red-headed obstetrician I'd read about a while back. Maybe this was another horrible dream.

But no. I had a vague recollection of seeing him at the party. Try as I might to dredge my brain for a name, though, I couldn't think of one. I couldn't even remember speaking to him. I certainly didn't remember sleeping with him.

"Oh, hey!" he said, rubbing his eyes. "How's it going?"

Sometime in the past three seconds, I had yanked the comforter from the bottom of the bed up to my chin. Which was a totally superfluous gesture on my part; not just because it was a little late in life to start protecting my virtue, but because I was fully clothed. I was wearing exactly what I'd had on last night—jeans, a tank top, and a fitted snap-front shirt that had come halfway unsnapped. I was even wearing socks.

"Where's your shirt?" I asked. I could only send up a prayer that the rest of him was clothed.

"In the bathroom. I spilled orange juice on it. We made mimosas, remember?"

Oh God. "That would explain the tap dancing rhinos in my skull."

He chuckled. "Yeah, you were really putting it away."

"I do that every once in a while." *And it tended to end badly.* I needed to remember that next time.

I was a little calmer now that I figured out that nothing had happened last night between me and whoever this was. At least I was pretty sure. I'd had many bizarre experiences before, but I had yet to have a man tear off all my clothes only to then put them back on again. That would have been both bizarre and insulting.

Come to think of it, it actually wasn't all that flattering that I could wake up hungover with a guy and still be fully clothed. Not that I was a sexpot or anything, but I like to think I'm a little muss-worthy. Even with a man who had a certain Howdy Doodyishness about him.

Maybe he was one of Troy's models.

No, on second thought, definitely not. He wasn't up to Troy's standard.

"Who *are* you?" I blurted out.

My bed buddy yawned. "Don't you remember? I'm Rowdy."

At that news, I clutched my aching head in both hands. I might have moaned. When I'd first heard about Rowdy Metzger from Lindsay, I had felt so sorry for him. Now I felt like we were one. The unwanted. The dumped. The foistable.

Nice try, Lindsay.

"You want to get breakfast?" he asked.

My stomach churned. "I don't think so."

He sighed. "I'm not really hungry either. But I need time to think how I'm gonna explain all this to my girlfriend. Lindsay—you know her, right?"

"I know her well enough to know that she'll understand."

"Isn't Lindsay great?" Rowdy asked, a twinkle in his blue eyes. The question was purely rhetorical. "I can't imagine life without her."

"I'll bet she can't imagine life without you, either."

I stumbled out of the bedroom into a world I still barely recognized as my own. It was strange, and it was a mess. Empty and half-filled glasses stood on moving boxes. Shopping bags of books had been shoved into corners and under the card table that was at present doing duty in our dining room. Our mish-mash of other furniture seemed pathetic by the light of day. Like pitiful leftovers from a yard sale piled on top of one-hundred-fifty-year-old parquet flooring. In the middle of it all, Greg the super had rolled out Wendy's blue electric blanket on the floor and was sleeping one off. Max was curled up next to him, zonked.

I frowned and felt my way to the kitchen. Andrea was propped on a stool, eating a Pop-Tart. She looked like death. "I'm never moving again," she moaned.

"Who's sleeping in your bed?" I asked.

"No one, unfortunately. Not even me. For some reason, I left my mattress leaning against a wall last night and decided to sleep on the floor."

"Maybe you got the idea from Greg."

She frowned. "I hope this doesn't become a habit with that guy."

"Is Wendy up yet?"

"Up? She hasn't come back."

"Back from where?"

"Who knows. At two AM a bunch of people went clubbing."

"Lindsay's boyfriend is in my room."

Andrea laughed. "Lindsay left with Wendy's group. Gave ol' Carrot Top the slip."

I took a Pop-Tart. "Doesn't it seem reckless just to dispose of a perfectly good boyfriend that way?"

"She's young."

"She's just a year younger than I am."

"You're young, too."

I was just two years younger than Andrea, who was all of twenty-seven. "But I've burned through a quarter century, and what do I have to show for it?"

Maybe that's who I had dreamed I'd let down—me.

Or, no . . . I shook my head. And then I remembered. I *had* forgotten someone. Sylvie. Although that seemed like years ago now, I had told Bernadine I was going to see her this weekend.

Andrea remarked, "Well, pretty soon you'll have a book documenting your early years."

Some comfort that was. Just the reminder of Fleishman

made me sad. And angry. And puzzled. I felt sloughed off; but something else pricked at my conscience. I started poking through boxes that we had stacked in the kitchen.

"What are you looking for?"

"Hot pickled okra," I said.

It took me a while, but I found it. "Could you tell me how to get to Elmhurst Avenue?"

She squinted at me. "Are you kidding? I've spent the past four years trying to get away from there."

"I just need directions."

She looked at me doubtfully, but told me which train to take.

"I'll be back this afternoon," I promised. "Don't clean up without me."

"Don't worry."

Part of me was hoping for forgiveness. And part of me was hoping for wisdom. There was something about waking up from that party that made me crave seeing someone old. That was the trouble with being young, and in Manhattan. It felt like we were all babies toddling around without supervision, creating messes and being no use to each other whatsoever. That morning I felt like seeing Sylvie would ground me.

After some searching, I found her in a large retirement complex in Queens. When she opened the door, I half expected her to spit on me, or toss a few French curses my way for abandoning her. Instead, she smiled. "Rebecca! Come in, come in. You should have called first."

"I'm sorry . . ."

"Well, never mind now. How've you been?"

I frowned. She seemed a little different. Besides being frailer looking; or maybe I had just forgotten how delicate she was—how she was so thin that it seemed like a sneeze could knock her over. Her skin was practically transparent in places, so that an occasional vein would seem dangerously close to being exposed. She wore her old uniform of ironed button-down cotton shirt, elastic waist pants, and Reeboks.

There was something else different about her. I couldn't place it at first.

From what Bernadine had told me, I was expecting Sylvie to be living in the old folks home equivalent of a dorm room. Instead, it was more like an efficiency apartment. There was only one large carpeted room, a bedroom nook, and a bath, but it didn't feel too cramped. There was also a little kitchen area, where she took my gift of pickled okra.

She noticed me looking around the place and rasped, "Isn't it a dump?"

"Not too bad."

"Not too bad, she says."

I frowned. I realized what seemed different. Her voice. She didn't sound like Sylvie. She sounded like Bernadine.

She settled down in her chair, which I recognized from her other apartment. I wondered what had happened to all her belongings. Her apartment in Turtle Bay had been four times this size, and crammed with stuff. "When I got out of the hospital," she explained, "Langley had cleared out my apartment. He'd sold most of my things and arranged for me to live here. I haven't heard from him since."

"That's terrible!" I said. "How could he do that?"

"He thought I was going to die, obviously," she said. "He thought it was all his."

"When he fired me, he kept talking about beneficiaries."

She got a good laugh out of that. "*He's* the beneficiary. He's my nephew."

"Your *nephew?*" I asked, confused. R.J. Langley wasn't French. "By marriage?"

"No, he's my sister's son. She died, so he is about all the family I have left." She shrugged. "He was a lawyer, so when I moved back I decided to let him handle my affairs."

"Moved *back?*"

Sylvie nodded. "Back to New York City," she explained. "Where I was born."

"But—"

She laughed. "I know, I know. I have a confession to make. I should have told you before, but it didn't seem any of your business. I'm not French. I didn't even move there until I was seventeen, after I ran away from home."

I was stunned. Sylvie was not French? It didn't seem possible. It was like hearing that Sean Connery wasn't Scottish, the pope wasn't Catholic, and bears were doing their business in marble bathrooms. It was hard to absorb.

And yet, I now understood the way she had stonewalled the few scholars who used to track her down. She didn't mind giving them a few harmless anecdotes; she just didn't want to talk about herself.

But she had just tossed the news to me so casually, as if people spent decades pretending to be a different nationality all the time. As if living a double life was no big deal.

I leaned forward. "Did Picasso know?"

"Know what?"

"That you were a . . ." *A fake* was the word that leapt to mind. ". . . an American."

She considered for a few seconds. "No, I don't think he did. Or maybe he did and did not care. He was an artist, he understood about creating."

"Is that what you did?" I asked. "You used yourself as a kind of canvas?"

"What else could I do?" she asked. "I did not like my life here. I did not want to spend the rest of my life as Sylvie Arshovsky, stenographer . . . or heaven knows what. I wanted adventure, romance. I wanted to be someone. Don't we all?"

I guessed we did. "Most of us aren't so successful."

"Nonsense! You are doing very well at it yourself."

"I am?"

She crossed her arms. "You showed me a picture once of your family and I did not recognize you. 'Who's the fat one?' I asked. Remember?"

I remembered. I had barely managed to confess that the fat one had been me.

"You did not like that person you were, so you created someone you liked better." She waved her hand. "*Voilà!* Art."

"But you had a whole lot of people fooled." To take the art metaphor to an extreme, Sylvie was a Rembrandt, while I was more like a landscape fashioned from a Bob Ross kit.

"The trick is to believe in this person you want to be. You can't go through life thinking you are an imposter."

I chewed this over for a moment. I could see a certain logic to what she was saying, but on the other hand, there were people like Muriel, who invented themselves right into psychiatric wards.

"Is that why you never wanted to write your autobiography?" I asked. "Or talk to any of the people who came to interview you?"

She gestured dismissively. "No one is interested in me. They just want to hear about Harpo Marx and other famous people. So I tell them a few harmless things, and they go away thinking I'm just an old lady."

That's what I had thought.

"But now," she said, "no one would come here to see me." She looked around her apartment in dismay.

"Why don't you move?"

"I have no money. Langley pays the bills here, but I can't find him."

"He absconded with your money?"

She nodded. "And sold my jewelry!" She seemed almost as upset about that as anything else. "Now I am stuck! I suppose I should be relieved he did not leave me homeless."

"I don't understand how he could have sold all your things."

"I asked a lawyer about that. A man Bernadine brought over. That was before Langley disappeared. He told this lawyer fellow that I had signed over power of attorney when I went into the hospital, and that he had acted in my best interests."

I had known that man was a jackass, but I hadn't thought he was this evil. "There must be something you can do."

"I don't know what," she said. "It's difficult when you're almost ninety-five, Rebecca. It's hard to know where to turn."

I nodded. It put my problems in perspective, a little.

"Who would I talk to?" she asked. "I don't know any lawyer I would trust with something like this."

An idea occurred to me. "I do."

Chapter 19

At nine the next morning I was planted in a leather chair in the reception area of McAlpin and Etting. The waiting room had been all done up to look like someone might think a barrister's office in jolly ole England might look like—it was all wood paneling and subdued lighting and old hunting prints. Or, maybe like the office itself, the prints were only made to look old. Knowing that my own fluorescent-lit office was just three floors down, I got the feeling that I was on a movie set of a lawyer's office.

The receptionist seemed to think I didn't belong there. I suppose, by her reckoning, I didn't. Unlike the two others who had checked in and settled on the faux antique furniture, I had no appointment. I was just there on hope.

The night before, I had consulted with my sister Ellen. She thought Sylvie's story was terrible, but not unheard of. "When someone is old, alone, and has money, there's usually a vulture circling somewhere," she told me. "That woman needs to work with someone who can hunt down this Langley person and put the squeeze on him."

When Luke Rayburn came in, he smiled cordially at me and then breezed right past. A jolt of anxiety bolted through me. He didn't even know me. Would he think this was too weird? Would he think I had trumped up some story just to see him in a non-elevator setting?

A few steps later he stopped, and when he pivoted back to me, his face was puzzled. "*Rebecca?*"

He remembered my name! I fluttered in response as he shook my hand. I would never have remembered the name of a guy I had only met once in an elevator . . . unless of course I had spent months obsessing about him.

"There's a matter I wanted to discuss with you," I said. "I didn't have your card to make an appointment . . ."

He shook his head as if it were offensive that I should think I had to be so formal as to call first. "Never mind that. Come on back."

As we zigzagged through the inner offices, he offered me coffee. I shook my head.

"Sorry I don't have another bagel to offer you," he said.

"That's okay. At least we're not trapped on an elevator."

He laughed. "I almost didn't recognize you just now," he said, showing me into his office. It was also woody and somber. He snapped on lamps and offered me a seat in a buttery leather chair. "You were out of context. I don't believe I've ever seen you on stationary ground."

"You weren't thinking outside the box," I said, before I could stop myself.

He squinted at me, then made a show of laughing at my little joke, which was kind of him but did not stop me from feeling like a doofus. I was feeling out of my element. He was so professional, so together. He even had expensive looking hair—short, shaped, but no visible hair product.

"You said there was a reason you wanted to speak to me," he said. "I hope you're not in any kind of difficulty."

"Actually, I'm sort of here on someone else's behalf."

"A relative?"

"A friend. My previous employer."

Worry lines creased his forehead. "Does she know you're here?"

"I told her that I was going to help her. You see, she's ninety-four years old. Her name is Sylvie Arnaud."

His lips twisted and I could see him casting about to place the name. "That rings a bell. Was she an actress?"

"In a way—if you consider someone's entire life to be a performance."

He asked me to start from the beginning. I gave him the whole of Sylvie's saga, as far as I understood it. It was still difficult for me to believe that she had led this amazing life after having started as a nobody. That she had even faked a different nationality to keep an aura of mystery.

And then, of course, I had to tell him about the creep R.J. Langley, who had installed his aunt in a retirement home and then absconded with her money. While I spoke, Luke sipped at his coffee, nodding at the correct moments but obviously trying to stay neutral. He seemed to think Sylvie's history was interesting, but he didn't seem at all surprised by the behavior of R.J. Langley. Neither had Ellen. It occurred to me that lawyers, like psychiatrists, had probably heard it all.

He didn't even seem to think that Sylvie's story was unusual at all.

"Do you think there's any way to help her get her money back?" I asked. "I think she's resigned to living where she is, but I hate to see her nephew just get away scot-free with bilking someone that way."

"Me, too." Luke thought for a moment. "There are ways we could try to hunt Langley down and get the money out of him, but I'll need to talk to Sylvie herself."

I considered whether Sylvie would want to make the trip. She had been skeptical when I told her I was going to consult a lawyer for her.

"If she can't come here, maybe you could take me to see her," he suggested. "Maybe Wednesday night? After an early dinner?"

I'm not sure if my heart stopped beating, although for a few moments, as I looked into those dreamy brown eyes of his, time did seem to stand still. He was asking me on a date, sort of.

Or maybe he wasn't.

"Why don't I swing down by your office at five and pick you up?"

I nodded. "Thank you." I stood, feeling awkward when it came to business arrangements. "I'm not asking you to work *pro bono*, you know. I want to make sure you're paid for your time."

"Oh, I'll be paid," he said, sending me a sly wink.

He seemed so lascivious, so eager, it was as if he intended to arrange a billable-hour-for-sex trade.

Then he continued, in the voice of a man who really loved what he did, "R.J. Langley will pay, once we've squeezed the money out of him."

"Oh," I said, feeling like a silly hysteric for jumping to the other conclusion.

Then again, in this instance, legal-aid-for-sex had a definite appeal.

Dan Weatherby was driving me out of my mind. Every time I thought we had the *Cutting Loose* contract nailed down, he would call me back asking for a little something extra. A publicity tour. Higher royalties on foreign sales. More money. And then, finally, when I phoned to tell him Mercedes had capitulated to all his demands, he dropped this bombshell.

"Actually, Rebecca, I just talked to Jack. . . ."

It was Jack all the time now.

I bit back a sigh. "Oh? What are his thoughts?"

"We're thinking hardcover."

I squinted into the receiver. I was speechless. *Hardcover?* We had spent an entire week negotiating and the word hardcover had never been mentioned before. I had never even negotiated a hardcover contract before. At Candlelight, hardcover was reserved for the big guns—the women who had clawed their way to the top of the *New York Times* Bestseller List and managed to keep a berth there. I had authors who had written twenty times as many books as Fleishman—that would be twenty—for whom the word *hardcover* was still a distant dream.

"We'd just like to know where you are on this," he said.

"Frankly, we're nowhere on it, Dan. This is an offer for a trade paperback." I added, "And we think it's a pretty generous offer, too."

He chuckled. "Oh, we realize that. But it's not as if Candlelight couldn't do hardcover for a first-time author they really wanted to get behind. . . ."

"I'll have to run this by Mercedes," I said.

"Fantastic!" Dan said. "Oh, and Rebecca . . ."

I bit back a sigh. "Um?"

"Jack told me to tell you that he can't find his iPod. Maybe it just happened to slip into one of your boxes while you were moving?"

He was now asking his agent to accuse me of stealing? "Tell Herbert Dowling the Third that I haven't seen it, but I will go over the apartment with a fine-tooth comb."

Dan chuckled. "Fantastic! And get back to me on the other thing soon, won't you? Jack and I would really like to wrap this up."

When I informed Mercedes of this new hitch in the proceedings, she was livid. "He's yanking our chain. He just wants money."

"He didn't say more money. He said hardcover."

"But he knows that's what it means." She huffed, "This is very unprofessional of Dan Weatherby."

But very cunning.

"Well, we could just say no, couldn't we?" That idea had definite appeal for me.

"Damn straight we can just say no. We could scrap the whole deal." She drummed her fingers, then let out a sigh that deflated her. "Except that Art wants the book. I never should have shown it to him! Now he's taken a personal interest."

I tilted my head. "Why *did* you show it to him?"

She rolled her eyes. "I was in a brown-nosing frame of mind," she confessed. "Every once in a while Art likes to read one of our books, just for show. I thought he'd like that one, because, you know, it was written by a man."

It gave me some satisfaction to know that she had to bow and scrape to a higher corporate power, too. In fact, being responsible for two hundred and seventy titles per year, she was under more pressure than anyone.

She let out a long, weary breath. "Fine. Hardcover."

Maybe Mercedes worried that she would wind up wearing cement shoes in the East River if she didn't get this book deal. In fact, I was beginning to wonder if the mob rumor hadn't been started by Art Salvatore himself. It was a hell of a way to keep employees in line.

She took out a yellow legal pad and started dashing down figures. After five minutes of muttering to herself, she ripped the page off, handed me our offer, and told me to get back to Dan.

"But wait till after lunch to call him," she said.

She wasn't above yanking chains herself.

At one o'clock I called Dan and gave him the terms Mercedes had outlined. It hurt. I was handing over more money than I would see in two years of work for a book that took a few weeks to write (and my lifetime to live). We were offering a five-city book tour, the top royalty rate, and even more author copies than I had heretofore seen offered to any author. All for a book that basically felt like it was peeling the clothes off my body and exposing me, naked, for all the world to see.

And what did Dan say?

"We'll have to get back to you on this." Not even a grunt to acknowledge that I had come through with a generous offer.

"Mercedes is really eager to wrap this up," I said. Which was probably saying too much, but hell, *I* was eager to wrap it up. I really didn't want to spend another week of my life thinking about *Cutting Loose*.

"I'll bet she is," Dan said before hanging up.

As if we were the lucky ones, to have had Fleishman's book offered to us.

When I hung up the phone, I was fuming.

Lindsay came by my office. "Meeting," she reminded me.

I groaned.

"Yeah, I can see why you don't want to go." She handed me an advanced copy of Janice Wunch's production late list. I was all over the thing. I'd barely done anything for the past week that wasn't related to *Cutting Loose.*

When I sat down, Mercedes caught my eye. "Any word yet?"

I shook my head. "They'll get back to us."

After Mercedes gaveled, the main topic of discussion was the big *Romance Journal* party the next week, which was being held in the ballroom at the Helmsley Park Lane. Practically the whole office was going, so it began to take on the aura of a school field trip. "We looked into hiring buses to ferry us over there," Mary Jo said. She had been put in charge of organizing us all. "But it didn't seem cost effective."

"So we just have to walk?" Madeline asked, annoyed.

At this news, there were grumbles heard all around, until Mercedes announced, "But because we know the extra time it will take, we aren't expecting anyone to come back to work after the party."

Forget field trip. It began to feel like Christmas.

One of the books we were set to discuss was the book about the woman who falls in love with her art teacher, which I had given to Rita after Mercedes had been sidetracked with *Cutting Loose.* Rita announced that she had read the book and liked it, but that she worried the heroine was too old.

"How old?" Mercedes asked.

"She's fifty."

"Fifty is the new forty," Madeline said.

"Not when you're having hot flashes, it isn't," Rita grumbled.

Ann, who was the head of MetroGirl—the Mod Pod—

looked cautious but pointed out, "The majority of MetroGirl books now are about marriage and other midlife issues."

Mercedes shook her head. "Marriage is one thing, but Rita's right. Fifty is menopausal. We have to consider demographics."

"I was just thinking about this," Lindsay said. Everybody turned. It really wasn't kosher for editorial assistants to blurt out things at these meetings, though Lindsay tended to blurt out things no matter where she was. "You know that book about the English chick, Bridget Whatsawhosis—"

About twenty shocked people corrected her. "*Jones!*"

"Uh . . . right. Jones. Well, everybody always talks about that book, but it's like, *ancient.* I read it in junior high school, and it was meant for people, you know, in their thirties and stuff. So that means that all the people the book was written for are middle aged anyway," Lindsay said. "So, like, that book Rita's talking about would be perfect for them."

Outside of a funeral, I've never seen so many people get depressed so quickly.

"My God—she's right."

"I read that book in college," Andrea said. "Christ, I'm so old!"

"You're only twenty-seven!" someone yelled at her.

"Almost twenty-eight," she moaned. "I'm pushing thirty."

"That's nothing. I was thirty when I read it," Ann with the pampered dog lamented. "I thought Bridget was me."

"Now Bridget would be a geezer."

"Shit."

Mercedes had to gavel us out of our collective funk.

"And let's not even start on how long it's been since we all read *Hop on Pop,*" Troy added. "We'll have editors jumping out windows."

Mercedes shot him a look. "Actually, Lindsay raises an excellent point. All those early chick lit readers are now smack in the middle of their midlife crises. Like I said, we can't ignore demographics. That's good thinking, Lindsay. We have to keep looking for the next thing."

Rita grunted. "How long before the next thing involves Metamucil and Depends?"

"Wouldn't it be kind of weird to stick a book about a fifty-year-old woman into a line called MetroGirl?" I asked.

"Maybe we could rebrand it," Mary Jo said, tapping her pencil and biting her lip in concentration. "Metro . . ."

"I've got it!" Andrea said. "MetroGrannies!"

"MetroMatrons?"

"MetroGeezers!"

"GeezerGirl!"

The smack of wood on wood cut the brainstorming short. "Meeting adjourned," Mercedes announced.

When I went back to my office, my message light was not flashing. I went to the reception desk to check the wheelie thing, just in case. Muriel was back this week. "Hello, Rebecca," she said. "No messages for you this afternoon. How was your meeting?"

"Fine."

"Good!"

I still felt a pang of guilt whenever I saw her. And I still felt that curiosity to get to know her better. "How are you feeling?"

"Fine," she said. "Just fine."

Those eyes were like a stone wall. I could put my hands on the padded shoulders of her sweater and shake her and she would never confess to having written that book. She would just keep staring at me without those unblinking eyes.

I wasn't back in my office five minutes when the phone finally rang. It was Dan.

"I'm so sorry, Rebecca, but we have to decline your very generous offer."

I was stunned. "The hardcover offer?"

"Yes. Jack has decided to accept an offer from another house."

"Which house?" Maybe I wasn't supposed to ask, but I was so flabbergasted it just popped out. I felt robbed, and a little panicked. At least when *Cutting Loose* was my project, I felt like

I was going to have some control. Now that book would be in the hands of some stranger.

And then it would be in the hands of tens of thousands of strangers . . .

"I don't think I should really say," Dan replied. "But I did think it was the wisest choice, and that is what I advised Jack."

So they had both turned on me.

I hung up the phone and stomped straight over to Andrea's. She was sitting at her desk, reading and listening to headphones. I had to knock loudly enough that she would hear me, which wasn't difficult. The way I was feeling, I could have put my fist though the door.

She looked up. "What's wrong?"

"He went with another house!" I blurted, not even bothering to explain what I was talking about. She knew. "After all that negotiating—he bailed out on us completely."

Her brow knit in sympathy. "What a douchebag!"

I bemoaned having to inform Mercedes of Fleishman's defection, and then I looked down at the little iPod sitting on Andrea's desk. It was one of the minis. "Where did you get that?"

Andrea looked stricken. "Wendy gave it to me. She said she found it in a box and didn't know where it had come from. She thought it might have been left by somebody when we moved. Is it yours?"

I considered for a moment. Maybe this would be the closest I ever came to vengeance. I wouldn't even have to lie.

I shook my head. "No. It's not mine."

When five o'clock rolled around, I still wasn't in a great mood. I almost wished I hadn't told Luke I would go out with him that evening. Almost. I felt like I needed a night of drinking hot cocoa and watching reruns.

But of course, all that changed when I saw him waiting in reception for me. The man was a tonic.

Luke took me to a Thai place near the office, where we were the first diners to arrive. It made me feel a little self-conscious, since we were the only objects of the hovering waitress's attention. Even after a few other tables started to fill up, it occurred to me that she was still hovering. Our water glasses were refilled every three sips.

"I think she likes you," I said after she had made a special trip to check the temperature of the hot water in our teapot.

He grinned. "I'm her best customer. I live just down the street here. I usually come in here in lonely bachelor mode."

I was not sure whether I could believe that. A guy like Luke was probably lonely maybe one or two nights of the year.

"It'll be nice to have a face across the coconut curry," he mused.

"This sad-sack bachelor thing is not an act I'm buying."

He laughed. "To be honest, I had another reason for bringing you here."

Now this interested me. "What?"

"You'll see."

I wondered if it had anything to do with some kind of first-date ritual. Like he had a prejudice against women who didn't use chopsticks, and this was a test. Maybe it was something else. Fried squid, or grilled. The meal began to seem more like a challenge.

Not that I was even sure whether this was an actual date. It felt more like an after-work thing. And he probably considered himself to be on business, because we were going to see Sylvie after.

In the traditional exchange of thumbnail sketch life histories, I went first, but only because he asked. I gave him the bowdlerized version—leaving out weight issues, crushing feelings of insecurity, and anything dealing with my short catalog of disastrous romances. Basically, when I was done the man knew I came from Ohio, I won the citywide spelling bee when I was ten, and I came to New York and worked for Sylvie. (But he knew that last bit already.) I tried as hard as I could to make it sound like a charmed life.

Luke wasn't buying it. "What about Cassie?" he asked when I was done.

I craned my neck forward. I couldn't believe he even remembered her. And I have to say, I wasn't exactly thrilled to have her name brought up on my date. "What about her?"

"You were having a nervous breakdown that day in the elevator, remember?" He would remember that. "What happened to her?"

"Oh . . . she got a job somewhere else."

"I thought she might still be there—you seemed a little stressed out when I picked you up at work."

"Well . . . that was something else. A book deal gone south."

"What happened?"

"I don't think you want to know."

"Sure I do."

"It's a long story."

"I love long stories."

I told him. The unbowdlerized version. I even had to backtrack and tell him about growing up with weight issues, and crushing insecurity, and about how meeting Fleishman made me suddenly feel part of a cool crowd. As if I were giving a rebuttal to *Cutting Loose*, I spilled everything, but from my point of view. Even as the words tumbled off my tongue, I felt I was probably deep-sixing any chance I had with this guy. He looked like he had led a perfect life. But if that were the case, I would rather he knew the worst about me now, rather than getting my hopes up and going out with him only to have him realize later that I was a mess. I thought I was inoculating myself against heartbreak.

Clearly, I had learned nothing.

During the crab fried rice, I finished with a flourish by telling him about Fleishman writing the book, and kicking us out of the apartment, and then selling the book to someone else.

"And that brings you up to today," I said.

He took a moment to sip some tea. "Well, that's a lot more interesting than winning a spelling bee."

I laughed. "It's a big muddle. Maybe I should be asking your advice on whether I could sue him for defamation of character." I shook my head. "Or maybe just exposure of defamed character."

"That's not my line. My only comment would be, success is the best revenge."

"That's what they say. But what reason did I ever give him to take revenge on me? We were friends."

He indulged me with a smile. "What I meant was *your success* could be revenge on him."

"Oh! Right." That thought—having success myself—hadn't really occurred to me lately.

"Don't let him get under your skin. People like your friend Fleishman tend to see a shortcut to success and then fizzle. He'll blow his advance on gadgets and vacations, and then where will he be? I've seen a million of guys like that. Moreover, I've written a million of them out of their parents' wills."

The idea of Fleishman flaming out was so appealing. I still couldn't imagine myself achieving a level of success that would make him envious of me, but maybe I was on the road to recovery.

Belatedly, as we were taking the last sips of tea, I asked Luke for his life story.

He was another Midwesterner, from Chicago. His father was a dermatologist. Private schools the whole way. Hardship occurred when he ran low on cash during a side trip to Greece during his junior year abroad and had to take steerage on a boat to Athens before he could wire home for money. Law school had seemed pretty easy. He got his job with McAlpin and Etting right after passing the bar, which had been no sweat.

No sweat could have been his motto. After the hairy tale I'd laid on him, you'd think for my benefit he could have dredged up something more traumatic than a little discomfort crossing the Mediterranean.

He paid the check. "Shall we go see Sylvie?"

On the street, I turned toward the subway and he grabbed my arm, spinning me back. He was laughing. "Where are you going?"

"The subway's that way," I said, pointing.

He gestured in the other direction. "And my garage is that way."

"Garage?"

His forehead wrinkled adorably. "An enclosure where an automobile is stored."

My lips formed an O. "You're the first person I've met from Manhattan who owns a car."

He took my arm. "It's why I brought you to the Thai place, so we could be near the garage."

It was hard to hold back a sigh of disappointment. Then it had nothing to do with first date rituals. He probably didn't consider me date material at all.

Damn. I could have used my fork.

Chapter 20

You wouldn't think a *Romance Journal* event would be the type of thing Andrea would go for, but at one forty-five sharp she was rounding up people. She was all dolled up in a beige jersey dress with cool five-inch heel boots. I had dressed up, too, but my hair was just normal, while hers was done up as if ready for her style shoot.

She hadn't looked like that when I'd left the apartment this morning. But come to think of it, I hadn't seen her since then. "Where have you been?"

"I splurged for a facial and makeover." Then she added, unnecessarily, "Also, I got my hair done."

"You look fantastic."

"A lot of people in the industry are going to be there."

I shot her a look. "I thought you were staying put."

"I am!" she insisted. "But we're representing Candlelight. We have to look nice, don't we?"

"What a liar!" I said.

Old habits died hard. Some girls dropped off on their pillows dreaming of finding the perfect man; Andrea probably dozed off envisioning the perfect job.

"Let's move 'em on out!" she yelled, as if she were riding herd.

"Okay, okay." I grabbed my purse, laughing. "We don't want to represent Candlelight by being tardy."

Rita hurried over. She was wearing her usual meeting suit, but in a bow to the formality of the occasion she had a smear of lipstick across her lips. "I thought the Pulse Pod could share a cab. *My* treat."

"You're expensing it, right?" Andrea asked.

"Well, yeah . . ."

"Where's Lindsay?"

Rita looked doubtful. "Is she coming?"

"I just saw her a while ago. She was all dressed up."

Of course, in typical Lindsay fashion she was all dressed up in a silvery satin top decorated with aquamarine sequin dolphins. It didn't exactly go with her blue skirt, but it was hard to see what exactly that shirt would have matched. Clearly, however, she had made an effort.

Andrea tugged us all along. I think she didn't want to be caught in visual proximity to that dolphin shirt. "Your protégé will catch up."

Ever since I began my effort to get Lindsay promoted, Andrea had taken to calling her my protégé. For fun she liked to spin *All About Eve* fantasies in which Lindsay played Eve to my Margo Channing.

"*All About Eve*, the slapstick version," I'd say. "There's not even a hunky guy for Lindsay to steal."

"What about Luke?" Andrea said.

Luke was a frustrating subject. He was working on hunting down R.J. Langley for Sylvie. He liked to take me out for dinner or for drinks and keep me updated on the case. But he hadn't made any moves toward more.

When I pointed out this fact, Andrea was incredulous. "It's only been what? One week?" And then, later, "Relax. It's only been what? Two weeks?"

At Sunday brunch just days before, he'd spent most of our time together telling me about all the ways people could abscond with money and hide it offshore. Of course I had to come home and spill my frustrations to my housemates.

"Two weeks and he hasn't become any more intimate than holding my hand as he hauls me out of a cab's backseat."

"Well?" Wendy asked. "He's a gent."

"Too much of a gent," I lamented.

"But he keeps asking you out," Andrea observed.

"Only because of Sylvie. He's acts like we're on a case together. It's like we're Holmes and Watson."

"Hm. Maybe *I* could be your Eve and steal him away from you."

"You probably could," I said, dispirited.

Andrea thought for a moment. "It might make our living arrangements a tad uncomfortable . . ."

"We're used to that," Wendy deadpanned.

The hotel was on Central Park South. In the lobby there were signs pointing to the *Romance Journal* party on the second floor . . . but you could have just followed the trail of gussied up women. Some meeting area called the Boardroom was having a reception sponsored by a new sports channel. Anything male was filing in that direction. It was tempting to peel off from the crowd and go with them.

In the ballroom, an impressive scene greeted us, along with the soothing sound of a flute and harp duo playing Debussy's greatest hits. The room was huge and elaborately decorated in a way Liberace might have appreciated. The whole place seemed dripping with cream and gold, except for a strip of crimson carpeting that split the room in half and led up to a dais at the front of the room. There were round tables set up with white cloths with a centerpiece of creamy roses arranged in a ring. Rising from the middle of each ring was a plaster bust spray-painted gold; each was wearing an elaborate costume jewelry piece.

"What's the purpose of the red carpet?" I asked.

"Looks like we're going to have a fashion show," Andrea said. She had to speak loudly to be heard above the crowd, which was approaching a roar. The place was so thick with editors and authors and other industry folk that it was hard to see how we would all fit at the tables.

I recoiled a little as I scanned the room. I had known there would be people there I recognized—a lot of people from the conferences I'd attended. But I hadn't really been thinking that, given my history as the Calamity Jane of industry functions, these might be people I wouldn't want to see again. Everywhere I looked now I spotted people I'd inadvertently insulted with business cards, had stage fright in front of, and vomited on.

"Okay," Andrea announced, "I've got to mingle before the Contessa makes us sit down."

She disappeared. I stayed with Rita. "I don't see Lindsay," she said, visually sifting through the throng of people.

"It would be hard to find her in this crowd."

Rita looked at me as if I were out of my mind. "In that dolphin shirt of hers? It would be impossible to miss her."

She was right, although Lindsay would not have been the only besequined person there, by any means. The Contessa herself was sparkling around the room in a dress with a gold sequined bolero-style overjacket. I had never seen her before, so this was exciting for me; I only recognized her from her pictures in *Romance Journal*.

"Maybe Lindsay's gone to the wrong Helmsley," Rita conjectured. "There's one in Midtown."

I had told Lindsay she needed to keep being assertive; now I felt compelled to assert for her. "I'm sure she'll find the place. She's really been knocking herself out lately. Haven't you noticed?"

"It's true, she's not quite the fuckup she used to be," Rita admitted, albeit reluctantly. Then, as she stared over my shoulder, she exclaimed, "Well! Look who's here!"

I turned, expecting for some reason to see Lindsay. I couldn't have been more wrong. Standing so close that I nearly stepped on her foot was Muriel and a friend.

Rita greeted her like a long lost friend, even though Muriel had been behind the receptionist desk when we left. We had last seen her about a half hour before.

Though I might have glanced at her answering phones, I really hadn't looked at her. Because, I have to say, Muriel really had her geek on that day. She was dressed up in an empire waist blouse with ruffled sleeves over a long shapeless blue velvet skirt. Little black ballet shoes complemented the ensemble. If that skirt had gone the extra three inches to her ankles, the outfit might have been suitable for prom night, 1976. It was couture to listen to *The Best of Bread* by.

"It's good to see you here, Muriel," Rita said.

"Thank you, Rita. Kathy Leo was kind enough to offer me her invitation, since she couldn't make it. I brought my friend, Melissa."

We all said hello to Melissa, who I have to say looked more normal than Muriel, but a lot more nervous. "All these people!" she said. "And I recognize a lot of them from their book jacket photos. Look—there's Valerie Martin, the romantic suspense author!"

Valerie Martin was talking to the Contessa.

"Are you a romance fiction reader?" Rita asked Melissa.

The woman nodded. "I read a lot."

"This is Melissa MacIntosh," Muriel said, looking straight at me.

Which was weird, since the woman had already been introduced. We nodded politely.

Rita nudged me with her elbow. "I'm going to sneak out on the terrace for a little bit."

"Okay," I said.

Muriel was smiling at me. "Melissa has been dying to meet you, Rebecca."

"Really?" That was a first. I wasn't exactly one of the celebrities in the crowd.

"Or, actually, I should say that she has been dying to meet you in person."

I felt my smile freeze. Something weird was going on here. I trained my gaze on Melissa, who still had that anxious glaze in her eyes that I had seen somewhere before. It took me a moment to place it . . . and then I remembered. It was the expression I had seen on the faces of some unpublished authors during editor-author appointments at conferences. Was she an author?

I couldn't quite recall . . .

Oh God. I swallowed back a gasp of sudden recognition. *Melissa MacIntosh!*

My heart sank, even as my brain whirred in confusion. This *couldn't* be Melissa MacIntosh. Muriel was Melissa MacIntosh.

Or maybe she wasn't.

"You rejected my book," Melissa said, unnecessarily by now. "*The Rancher and the Lady?*"

"Oh!" I attempted a bright tone. "Right!"

"Melissa was so excited when I told her that you would like to sit her down in person," Muriel said.

I had said that?

Maybe I had. In the hospital. But that had been when I assumed Muriel was Melissa MacIntosh. I hadn't known I would *really* have to talk to her.

"She said you had all sorts of ideas," Melissa said.

She looked so hopeful. And I couldn't even remember the book.

Well. It wasn't even a question of remembering. I had never read all of *The Rancher and the Lady.*

Instinctively, I cast my gaze about, longing for rescue. Hoping Andrea would be coming back toward me, or Rita. Anyone who would know how to defuse this situation. I had never been confronted with one of my rejectees before.

That's when I saw her. I was already feeling frantic, and then I caught sight of my old nemesis.

Cassie.

I don't know why I hadn't expected to see her here, but I hadn't. Frankly, in the past weeks, I had almost forgotten about her. But there she was, barely recognizable because she was so happy looking and radiant, and yet essentially so Cassie that there was no disguising her. She had cut her hair; her page boy had been lopped off and layered. She was wearing makeup and dangly earrings off her chunky little lobes. And—most amazing of all—her figure was encased in Natasha Fleishman's purple and turquoise Mainbocher dress.

My dress, I thought, outraged. Except of course I had never worn it.

And it was never exactly mine.

But what was Cassie doing with it?

My gaze shifted a few degrees, and there he was. Herbert Dowling Fleishman the Third and Cassie Saunders. A team.

I stood there with my mouth agape. It was as if the floor were going wobbly.

Was I a fool? In the week since Dan Weatherby told me that someone else had bought *Cutting Loose*, the identity of the rival editor had never crossed my mind. I had been so focused on the idea of my losing that I hadn't stopped to consider who had won. If anything, I had wondered more about the publishing house than the individual editor. That's what had consumed Mercedes's curiosity about the whole affair.

But this was worse, much worse, than anything we had imagined.

All those months I had spent nights at home moaning about Cassie trying to undermine me. Cassie making my work life a hell. And who had Fleishman let his book go to?

Cassie.

Maybe he had even *told* Dan he wanted Cassie to look at it. He probably thought Cassie would move heaven and earth to wrestle the book from me.

He was right.

As I gaped and gasped, basically feeling like a tugboat that had just been torpedoed, Dan Weatherby sailed into view, joining them. That completed my own private axis of evil.

I must have been radiating distress, because at that moment, Dan's head rotated and he caught sight of me. He lifted his hand in a wave—he had been hailing people all across the room with more than his usual amount of smarm. His smile to me wasn't even the least bit tentative, either. We might have been old buddies.

Fleishman's eyes followed the wave to me. *He* at least had the decency to look just the slightest bit discomfited by the situation. Though it nearly killed me, I stretched my lips into a grin. I even unfisted my hand and forced my fingers to trill in greeting. I probably looked manic.

But it fooled Fleishman, who, with relief, smiled and nudged Cassie. When she caught sight of me, her smile was more of a smirk. And who could blame her?

I felt sick then, and had to turn away. But the view right next to me wasn't much better. Melissa MacIntosh was still aiming her anxious little smile at me. I had forgotten about her, frankly. The last three seconds seemed to have crawled by like a decade.

One of the circulating waiters came within my reach just then, and I grabbed a glass of some kind of red wine off his tray. I gulped half of it down. I desperately needed some artificial fortification.

"Muriel told me you had some really interesting insights," Melissa said.

"About what?" I was still in a daze.

"About my book—well, and writing in general."

What the hell is Cassie doing in that dress?

I had to flick a gaze back and stare at it again, just to make sure I had seen correctly. Yes, there it was. The more I thought about it, the more bizarre it seemed. I mean, come on. She was his editor, and they had only known each other two weeks! How had they reached a point where he was giving her his mother's clothes?

Unless . . .

My eyes lasered down to that hand at her elbow. That possessive hand. I gulped down more wine and pivoted away.

Fleishman and Cassie. Cassie and Fleishman. It was too horrible to contemplate.

Melissa piped up, "I have all sorts of ideas for revisions!"

"Really?" I was standing there like a normal person, but in my mind I was clutching my head and shrieking like that figure in the Edvard Munch painting.

She nodded. "One of the things you said about *The Rancher and the Lady* was that it wasn't original enough. At first that confused me, since I thought Candlelight wanted books like what they were already publishing. But since then, I've come up with all sorts of ideas to make my book seem more original. For instance, instead of being a cattle rancher, Raif could be an ostrich rancher."

"Um."

Could they actually be sleeping together?

"Would you like to hear more?"

I told myself not to turn back. "More what?" I mumbled.

"More of my ideas."

I lost the battle. I turned back.

He was whispering in her ear, and I could swear he was looking at me out of the corner of his eyes. She tossed her head back and laughed gaily.

"Oh God," I said, shuddering. I leaned against the table for support.

"What?" Melissa said.

"Are you all right?" Muriel asked.

Do not lose your composure. That was just what they wanted.

"Sure, fine!" I turned to Melissa. "Tell me everything."

"Everything about what?" a voice asked.

I jumped. Cassie was looming so large in my mind, that I turned, girded to see her right next to me. But it wasn't her; this time it really was Lindsay. Thank heavens. I could have hugged her, even though she did look like a kook. Somewhere, she had acquired a Yankees baseball cap, which she was now wearing as if it were a formal fashion accessory.

"Where have you been?" I asked.

She rolled her eyes. "I must have missed you guys, but I came with the God Pod. But then, after we got out of the cab I got so confused! I ended up down in some other place with a bunch of sports guys. It was so fun. I mean, *kick ass!* It took me a while to realize that, like, there wasn't anybody from our office there. So I asked this guy I'd been talking to was this the *Romance Journal* thing, and he laughed at me. But I got a free hat, see?"

"We were worried," I said.

Lindsay, who was holding a plate of finger food, stuffed a tiny mayonnaisy looking sandwich in her mouth. "No way!

You think I'd miss this?" She held the plate out to all of us. "Sandwich? Petit four?"

Muriel and Melissa shook their heads.

"I mean, this is amazing. Did you see Valerie Martin over there?"

I introduced Lindsay to Melissa. "Melissa wrote a manuscript called *The Rancher and the Lady.*"

"Oh! I loved that book!"

If Melissa looked stupefied, she had nothing on me. Lindsay had never laid eyes on that manuscript. "You know," I cued Lindsay, "that book we turned down?"

"Oh! And now you're going to fix it?" Lindsay asked. "That's great."

No, it wasn't great, but Lindsay had no way of knowing. I had told her once she needed to learn how to schmooze, but this was going a bit too far.

"I didn't know anyone else had read it," Melissa said.

"Oh, I read tons around the office," Lindsay said. "*Tons.* I've been working with Rebecca a lot. I could help you with revisions."

"That would be so great!" Muriel exclaimed.

How could I disagree? I could barely focus on what they were saying at all. I kept cutting my gaze back to the triumvirate of terror—and then the Contessa swooped up to the microphone. The flute and harp stopped. "May I have your attention, *madames* and *messieurs*? Please take your seats! The show is about to begin."

The lights dimmed, except for a spot at the top of the red carpet and a pinlight on the Contessa, who nudged a pair of bejeweled reading glasses up her nose and read from a script as models—always in man-woman pairs—made their way down the red carpet. I don't know why there needed to be men involved, except as eye candy. The women were wearing all the jewelry, which you couldn't really see too well from afar. In any event, it was the same stuff that was on the busts on all of the tables. Everybody clapped a lot anyway, and made appreciative noises. Flashbulbs started going off as if this were fashion week.

I took advantage of the relative darkness to watch Fleishman and Cassie interacting. He was constantly leaning in to her and whispering little comments in that conspiratorial way that would make her chuckle or give a little eye roll. It was the same behavior I remembered from college lectures when we would have a class together.

Every once in a while I would have the fortitude to look away, but I couldn't keep my focus off of them for long.

Once I looked back and saw Fleishman staring not at me, but at everyone else at my table. From Muriel to Melissa to Lindsay in her Yankees cap. I darted my eyes toward the red carpet before that critical eye could land on me. My cheeks burned, both because I knew what he was thinking—I was at the freak table—and because I was embarrassed for being self-conscious. I was just like Andrea not wanting to be seen next to the aquamarine dolphin shirt.

Worse, actually. It was as if I were back in high school, embarrassed to be sitting at the loser table in the high school cafeteria. But these people were only losers to Fleishman, because he didn't know them, and because he was a twit.

Defensiveness welled in my chest. Maybe she was crazy as a bedbug, but Muriel was a more original personality than the underappreciated wit and genius that Fleishman pretended to be. His book wasn't any more original than Melissa MacIntosh's; she might have been a pale copy of other romances, but he had simply plagiarized my life.

I was steamed, and naturally, some of the heat found its way to Cassie. How pathetic was she, sitting there with that smug little smile on her face, as if she'd been made valedictorian at last. Hadn't she bothered to read the book she'd spent so much money to get under contract? She was a perfect overlooked gal for Fleishman to attach himself to.

The show ended, the lights came up. I gulped down the rest of my glass of wine and looked around desperately for another waiter. Everybody was standing up in preparation for more socializing.

Fleishman and Cassie got up. They were coming my way.

To gloat.

I set my jaw. They would not get the best of me. I would not act jealous. What had Luke told me? *Success was the best revenge.*

On second thought, that advice wouldn't serve me well . . . I hadn't succeeded at anything yet. Maybe in this instance not caring was the best revenge.

Damn. Where is a waiter?

Fleishman stopped and I stood up. "Well hello, stranger."

"Hi."

Cassie smiled at me. The thought of smashing my fist into her upturned little nose flashed through my mind.

I smiled back. "Hi, Cassie. Or is it Nibbles?"

She pouted at me in confusion.

"Congratulations on your new job," I said.

"My new job, or my new find?" She clutched Fleishman's elbow.

Oh yeah. A real discovery.

"Both!" I chirped.

Fleishman was gazing beyond my shoulder and I could tell that my table was gathering behind me. Which meant that I would either have to make introductions or look like a rude bitch. "Fleish, this is Lindsay and Muriel, who work with me, and this is Melissa MacIntosh . . ."

I wasn't going to tell him who Melissa was. Let him think she was a coworker of mine. But I should have known I wouldn't have to tell him. He always remembered names.

His jaw dropped. "Not the the author of *The Rancher and the Lady?*"

A waiter was coming. Oh thank God.

Fleishman's voice carried such astoundment, Melissa could be excused for thinking that he considered her opus to be the second coming of *The Flame and the Flower.* Maybe only I saw the mischievous gleam in those eyes of his. I hoped so.

"I read that book!" he exclaimed.

Melissa turned to me in confusion. Everyone, it turned out, had read her manuscript. No doubt she was wondering how a book I had circulated so widely could have received such a harsh rejection.

"Fleishman's a fellow author," I informed her.

Melissa stammered, "Oh, I'm not published yet."

"But you will be!" Lindsay exclaimed.

I wanted to kick her. Or kick something. Mostly, I just wanted to grab a drink off that tray that was inching ever so slowly our way . . .

Fleishman turned to me, and his expression was one of sheer astonished dismay mixed with a hint of glee. *Surely you haven't sunk that low*, that gaze said.

I felt a thunderbolt of anger, both at him and myself. What had I seen in this person? He was all preening ego, and for so long I had indulged him in his ambitions. I had been an accessory, just like these foolish paste creations on the busts in the centerpieces.

I lifted my head. "We think *The Rancher and the Lady* shows great promise. After revisions, it could be a bestseller . . ."

As the words came spilling out, I knew I would regret them. Moreover, I was using some poor author's career as a way to bicker with my erstwhile boyfriend and ex-roommmate. It was shameful.

But not as shameful as what I did next. That waiter finally made it to me, and I reached out my hand for another glass. But as I reached—just by accident, mind you—I jutted my elbow so that the wine tray tipped over. The waiter tried valiantly to make a save, but he was not successful.

And wouldn't you know that the tray would have to spill all its contents on poor Cassie?

Glasses broke as they hit the floor and each other, and gasps went up all around us.

I lifted my hands. "Oh, I'm *so* sorry!"

Cassie hunched in shock and flapped her arms, which sprayed burgundy on everyone. People who cared about their dry cleaning bills hopped out of her range, clearing a circle all around us. Making us even more of a spectacle, you might say.

I was beyond caring.

I quickly turned and grabbed a napkin off the table and began mopping up Cassie. "What a shame!" I exclaimed. "And it's such a great dress. Mainbocher, isn't it?"

She glared up at Fleishman, seeming to will him to do something terrible to me to retaliate. But he just looked on in amazement as I continued to pat her down. I wasn't really worried about his reaction anyway. There was nothing more he could do to me.

"Of course it's a Mainbocher," I cooed. "I know that. It used to be in my closet."

She swatted my hand away. "Leave me alone!"

I stood back and looked from her to Fleishman and then back again. Then I pressed my sodden napkin into her hand. "Honey, you're alone already. You just don't know it yet."

After leaving the Contessa's shindig, I fled into the park and flopped myself onto the first bench I came across that didn't have bird poop or a person sleeping on it.

I was still shaky from having to apologize to the Contessa, and Cassie again, and then to Mercedes. Not that Mercedes seemed to care too much. ("*It was an accident!*" she had assured me as she looked on in satisfaction as Cassie was led away to the ladies' room.) As Andrea said, I might have represented Candlelight badly, but I had scored one for the home team.

I sank down on the bench, wishing I felt some kind of satisfaction. A wine waterfall cascading down on your rival only took you so far, I discovered to my dismay. This was the third public spectacle I had made of myself in the three industry events I had attended. Before I started working for Candlelight, I had never created a scene. I had always been a quiet person by nature. Now I felt as if I were regressing into a tantrum-tossing, sippy-cup-throwing toddler.

I needed to stop.

I needed something in my life besides this crazy job. By

some miracle I might have reinvented myself as an editor, but though others were buying my performance, I hadn't convinced myself. But was that really so surprising? I had been a size ten, give or take a size, for six years, but when I looked in the mirror I still saw a size sixteen.

That was the difference between Fleishman and me. Some people have delusions of grandeur; I had delusions of failure. I was my own underminer.

I wondered if there was a self-help tome for people like me. Or maybe they were *all* for people like me. But I'd never seen my double on *Oprah*. Whenever she focused on people who had lost weight, they were always jubilant about their transformations. They were ready to go out and conquer the world in their new jeans. Or they were men who became women and went out to conquer the world in lipstick and new brassieres.

But what about the people who didn't buy the personal transformations?

I got up to go home, but instead of walking west, I went the other way. Toward the subway, and to Queens.

Thirty minutes later I was knocking on Sylvie's apartment door. They knew me in her building now. Ever since I had donated four boxes of Candlelight books to the community library, I was welcomed with open arms.

When Sylvie opened the door, she seemed surprised to see me. Or maybe she was just surprised to see me alone. "Where's Luke?" she asked, poking her head around to see if he wasn't behind me somewhere.

She liked Luke. Who didn't?

"He's at work, I guess. I came over spur-of-the-moment."

"Yes, that's obvious." She shrugged. "Come in. Would you like a cookie?"

She was still eating those chocolate orange cookies. Old habits died hard. "No thanks," I said.

"What have you been doing?" she said.

Did she really want to know? Moreover, did I really want to tell her?

"Actually, I've been thinking, Sylvie. You should write a book."

She laughed. "Ah, a romance you mean?"

"No, you should write your life story."

"But I already told you why I do not want to write that," she grumbled as she puttered around what there was of a kitchen in that place. "I confessed my deepest, darkest secret to you."

"But why keep it a secret from anyone? It's a great story. It's got everything. Rags to riches. Personal transformation, with a twist. Celebrity. And yeah, romance." I knit my brows. I was assuming it had romance. The money she was living on—and the stuff that had been stolen—had to have come from somewhere. "It does have romance, right?"

She tilted an impish smile at me. "Oh, I don't think I would disappoint you in that area, Rebecca."

"See? You've got me hooked." I took a step closer. "Plus, I just want to know how you did it."

"Did what?"

"Transformed yourself. I could use some help in that area myself."

She leveled a very Sylvie look at me. "You just want to know about Cary Grant."

"That, too."

She clucked her tongue. "No, I do not think I could write a story. Definitely no."

I hadn't given up hope. We drank tea and talked about everything and nothing. About R.J. Langley, about Luke, about my new apartment, about how she missed her old place. As the time ticked by, my clownish antics at the Helmsley seemed blessedly remote.

Several times, I again slipped in the possibility of her writing a book.

"No, no. How could I write a book? I can't even type."

"I can."

"You have better things to do."

I laughed. "I'm beginning to think I need a keeper, actually."

"And what if I should die? What then?"

"You're not going to die. Not while there's a jar of hot pickled okra left in the city, you're not."

She grumbled. "I think it's not such a good idea."

A little later I got up to leave. Sylvie put up a good front, but visits took it out of her. I took a shopping list with me and promised to come back on Saturday. At the door, she asked, "I would need one of those computers, wouldn't I?"

"Not necessarily."

"They're expensive. Where would I get my hands on one?"

"You'd be surprised. Desperate people sell them on eBay all the time."

At the mention of eBay—or anything that had anything to do with the Internet—she shut down. She began shaking her head, as if I had just told her that writing a book would involve snake handling. "No, definitely not. This is not a good idea."

I nodded. "Well, it's up to you. I'd still love to be involved."

"You should do what they say on TV. *Get a life.*"

"That's what I'm trying to do."

"Your own life."

"Okay, Sylvie. See you Saturday."

"Maybe I'll talk it over with Bernadine."

"What?"

"Our book," she explained, as if I were dense.

"You mean the one we're definitely not writing?" I asked.

"Exactly."

Chapter 21

Nine months went by.

(Sorry, Rita.)

Of course, nine months is a loaded number. Nine months in a Candlelight book means only one thing: pregnancy. But in publishing, nine months is the amount of time that generally lapses between when a manuscript is turned in and when a bound book hits the stores. For a book that's generating buzz, or to cash in on a trend, a publishing house can speed up the process. A president's memoirs can appear on bookshelves a couple of months after he turns it in. A *National Inquirer* flash-in-the-pan can go from headlines to book deal to remainder table in less time than it took my grandmother to prepare a fruitcake.

Gazelle did a really fast job on Fleishman's book. I was humiliated in time for Christmas.

The nine months I was referring to, though, were the nine months that it took for Sylvie and me to finish her memoirs. From September to May we toiled every weekend and sometimes a few nights a week. While I was working at Candlelight, Sylvie would get her thoughts together and scrawl notes on legal pads Luke provided. Then when I saw her next, we would type up a few pages and read through them.

Other things happened in those nine months. Luke tracked

down R.J. Langley and Langley coughed up most of Sylvie's money, in the apparent hope that she would decide she was too old to make it worth her while to try to get her hands on everything.

Then Luke filed suit against him for the rest.

While I was working on Sylvie's book, I became less spastic about my job, and about Fleishman. I was even too busy to worry about Luke, who was gentlemanly to the point of insult. Occasionally we would go out for drinks, or for lunch. At my invitation, we went out to see a movie once. Afterwards, we went out for drinks and talked about Sylvie's case. Then he offered to pay for my cab and sent me back uptown.

I seemed to have a knack for latching on to guys who blow hot and cold. There's a self-help section in Barnes and Noble for that, too. Believe me. I've been there.

For the first time in my life, I let all that relationship business go and concentrated on something I felt was more important than myself—namely, getting the book done. I can now testify that a good way to save your own life is to concentrate on someone else's.

It helped that Sylvie's life was amazing. I had expected a pastiche of parties, travel, and name dropping. But it turned out that was the least of it. Her French mother and Polish father had emigrated to the United States at the beginning of the last century, but they had died in the flu epidemic of 1918, leaving young Sylvie and her older sister in the care of distant cousins (who just happened to have a baby named Bernadine). Sylvie ran away when she was old enough to pass for eighteen, and went to France, which of course her mother had told her all about. In Paris she found work as a model and became known as a party girl until she attached herself first to a famous writer and then a painter. This was her *Where's Waldo* period, in which all the photos were taken.

But it was what came after that stunned me.

While she was still with the painter, a wealthy young man fell in love with her. His parents would have none of her; she might have seemed glamorous to us, but to the old aristocracy she was basically a Jewish tramp. When the war came, she and her young man got married in secret before he left, but he was killed in the early days, and she was left on her own to walk to Switzerland. His family wouldn't help her.

Believe me, when I heard Sylvie telling me about fleeing the Nazis on foot, my little work kerfuffles and Fleishman friction seemed like nothing. Nothing.

What was it about these old people? How could they have gone through all this stuff and kept quiet about it so long? Even when we were working on the book, I was having to pry details out of Sylvie, especially if she thought something was too grim or unpleasant. But if these things had happened to anyone from the baby boomers on down, there wouldn't be a Barnes and Noble big enough to hold all the tell-all memoirs. My generation couldn't keep its collective yap shut about anything.

I became so absorbed in Sylvie's life that at night I would sometimes dream I was her, spending the night in a wheat field, not knowing what had happened to my husband, forgotten by my famous friends in the glitterati; or, after the war, fighting to get a small portion of my late husband's wealth. When I woke up, for the first time I knew what it was like to be glad to be me with my non-problems.

During this time, Andrea became less spastic, too. I could tell by the way that she would occasionally show up in her best interview suit that she was still trying to get out. But then something amazing happened. An office shakeup. An earthquake, really. Art Salvatore promoted Mercedes to Vice President in Charge of Editorial, and Mary Jo became Editorial Director. Mercedes, in her first decision as Queen of the Universe, promoted Andrea to editor and put her in charge of Mary Jo's God Pod. Andrea was the youngest editor in charge of a line.

In this same spirit of creative personnel maneuvers, Rita finally promoted Lindsay. (Also, she was desperate for support staff.) Truly, this move was not as crazy as it would have seemed even six months before. In helping me clear out some slush, Lindsay found some real gems, including a vampire anesthesiologist manuscript I had completely forgotten about. Retitled

Got You in My Blood, the book was right up Lindsay's alley, and she developed a real enthusiasm for what she was doing that seemed to ground her, a little.

After the *Romance Journal* party, Lindsay did some homework and called up Melissa MacIntosh with some ideas for *The Rancher and the Lady*, turning the ranch into a sperm bank and the lady into a cop with a history of infertility who stumbles into mysterious deaths at an in vitro fertilization clinic. It wasn't a quick fix, and I think Melissa was reluctant at first to take the story in such a different direction, but by the time they were finished with it, Melissa and Lindsay turned *Seed of Doubt* into the Pulse line's bestseller for its month. After that, Lindsay developed a reputation for being a miracle worker, and her screw-ups, verbal faux pas, and funky wardrobe started to be viewed more as odd little quirks than career killers.

And in March, she got married. Rowdy finally convinced her that twenty-four was not too young to find the guy you want to grow old and dull with. (He also got her pregnant.)

In Lindsay's place, Rita hired a recent Swarthmore grad named Brea who is shockingly efficient. Even so, Rita was never able to get herself away on vacation, though Andrea, Lindsay, and I did convince her to work from home one week rather than forfeit some of her paid leave.

There were other changes, too. Madeline left Candlelight to become a fiction editor for a fashion magazine. Mary Jo bought a new house five blocks from her old house in Mount Kisco. Ann adopted a dachshund. Troy went to Cancun—not with the Calvin Klein underwear guy, but with someone he said was just as juicy.

Muriel was promoted to Janice Wunch's assistant and hasn't had any obvious depressive episodes since. She seems to derive quite a bit of personal satisfaction from generating the late list for her boss.

Compared with everyone else, my life seemed reasonably static. The article came out in *BM* saying that I was making waves, but I didn't. The piece turned out to be very complimentary toward me and Candlelight; after the incident at the

Japanese restaurant I sent Alex some flowers as a small thank you for saving my life. We did another phone interview that went much more smoothly.

I stayed in my same job, my same office. I went to one conference in Wichita Falls and another in Boston and at both I managed not to make an idiot of myself. At home, everything was working out. We were near enough to the park that I could walk Max over every morning and night, which I loved. When I first moved to New York, I was wary of Central Park, just because of the stories I'd heard growing up of famous crimes that had been committed there. But it's like having the country right in the middle of the city, except it's a good kind of country. The kind where you can walk five minutes and catch a cab to escape it.

Wendy finally graduated and landed an incredible job as an assistant lighting engineer for a firm that puts together large rock concerts. Good-bye, Starbucks.

Soon after her graduation in May, Wendy, Andrea, and I woke up one Saturday morning, made waffles, and proceeded to sit down to breakfast at our card table, which we had dressed up with a tablecloth my mom had sent.

The card table wobbled when Andrea put her plate down. She let out an exasperated breath. "I've about had it with this table."

"What's the matter with it?" Wendy asked.

"It's flimsy."

"So?" It was serviceable, that was the thing.

"So here's an idea for what we can do with our Saturday," Andrea suggested. "Let's go shopping for a table. A real table. You know, made of wood."

Wendy and I stared at each other uncomfortably. I think we had both been waiting for Andrea to crack up someday.

"Maybe we could really go insane," Andrea continued, stabbing at her waffle, "and buy matching chairs."

"That would be expensive, wouldn't it?" I felt bad complaining, since not long ago I had purchased a new laptop to use working on Sylvie's memoirs.

With agonizing calm, Andrea put down her fork. She looked from Wendy to me. "Have you checked your bank account lately, Rebecca?"

I shrugged. "I have some money saved up . . ."

"*And* you paid off your Discover card."

She was right. I had.

She turned to Wendy. "And you're making . . . what? About *ten times* what you were making serving coffee part time?"

Wendy frowned. "Yeah."

"And I'm raking in more than either of you schmucks. We have to face facts here, girls. We're successful. We made it. We're in our mid-twenties and we've got good jobs and decent salaries. I don't know how it happened. I'm not sure how long it will last. But I do know one thing. We can afford to go out and buy a cotton-pickin' breakfast table!"

My God, she was right. For a few moments, Wendy and I were like those guys in old war movies when the battle was over and they had to let the fact that they were still alive sink in. We had survived the battle of the crowded Brooklyn railroad flat. The struggle for financial aid. The ex-boyfriend blitz. When we looked at each other, it was with happiness and relief and even a little tearful nostalgia for what we'd been through.

"When it comes right down to it," Andrea said, slowing down a little, "we could probably afford to move to a bigger place . . ."

"Or even our own smaller places," Wendy said, frowning.

I froze. Neither of those options appealed to me. I liked where we were. Wendy and Andrea were like my family. And hadn't Andrea hated life in her little efficiency? True, she could probably afford an efficiency in Manhattan . . .

Couldn't we wait to uproot ourselves again until we absolutely had to?

"I've got an idea," I said. "Why don't we just buy a new table?"

Wendy and Andrea studied each other for a moment before laughing in relief.

"New table," Wendy agreed.

"Right."

"I'm glad you thought of that," Andrea told me.

We submitted Sylvie's memoir, *Inventing Myself*, to a small but well-known press and kept our fingers crossed. Now it was my turn to be the nervous author. I worried Sylvie would fret about it all as much as I did. But she was cool as a cucumber.

"Nobody's going to buy a story about an old lady," she said.

"Your story's not about an old lady," I said.

But she was convinced that what we had just done was an exercise in vanity. Or maybe she was just better at hiding her nerves than I was. Besides, early in the summer Sylvie was busy moving from Queens to a place that had come open in Bernadine's building in the Bronx, back in the neighborhood she had fled nearly eighty years before. I was worried that the move would be too much for Sylvie, but instead it seemed to affect her like a tonic. I helped find her movers and insisted she pay for someone to pack for her, too.

"You've got money again," I reminded her. "You should use it."

She laughed at me. "That's Andrea talking to me now, isn't it?" I had finally taken Andrea and Wendy to meet Sylvie, and they thought she was a trip. Andrea and Sylvie really seemed to hit it off. "She told me that I needed to get a new television. I told her that I was so old that I might not even live much longer. And then she said, 'So you're not only planning to take it with you, but you expect to get it repaired when you get there?' " She cackled with glee over that.

Andrea was telling everybody to spend their money these days, apparently. She convinced me that for the big RAG convention, which was being held in New York City this year, I needed to get a new dress. Something really great.

That wasn't for vanity so much as self-preservation. Fleishman was going to be there. *Cutting Loose* had been nominated for a Raggie in the category of Best Romantic Comedy (comedy to *whom?*) and I worried that, since he was one of the few male writers ever nominated for anything by the romance writers, he would come out the big winner. If I was going to have egg all over my face, at least the rest of me should look good.

Whether he actually would win was a raging debate both at our office and elsewhere. At first he seemed the odds-on favorite, since the initial review of *Cutting Loose* had been favorable. Gazelle had managed to get his mug all over the *Romance Journal.* In the month of December he was in a full-page color ad, a feature article entitled, "Good-bye Chick Lit, Hello Laddies!" and he received a four-and-a-half kissy review. Other publications were not quite so fawning. *BM* said, "*Yet another entry into the world of lad lit, with an emotional twist. Jack Fleishman might be the male answer to Jennifer Weiner, but one may ask oneself, was a response really necessary?*"

Ouch.

When I finished reading that review, I leaned back in my chair, luxuriating in the thought of Fleishman reading it, too. Schadenfreude never felt so good.

In spring, just after the nominations were announced, controversy started to rage in earnest in the pages of RAG's monthly magazine, *The Romance Voice.* "Back to the Double Standard" was a rabble-rousing article about how it seemed to some that books written by men automatically were given more respect than those written by women. Women's voices were dismissed as "chick lit" while Nick Hornby—and others—were written up in the *New York Times Book Review.* Publishers who treated their bread-and-butter, paperback romance novels like so many widgets to be cranked out in a month suddenly were taking out full-page ads for first-time male authors writing books that were essentially no different from what their female counterparts were writing.

The author of the piece even got a quote from Fleishman. "*I'm a huge fan of romance. Huge. But I wanted to write something that would appeal to everybody—that wouldn't, you know, be branded as just a woman's book.*"

It was like tossing a crippled wildebeest in front of a pack of hyenas. From our office, you could almost hear the collective howl go up across America—the howl of royally pissed off women writers.

Andrea came into my office with the article, gleeful. "Give a blowhard enough rope . . ."

The famous authors in the article who responded to Fleishman's quote pointed out that they also tried to appeal to everyone, though they were rarely marketed in such a way that this would come through to anyone casually browsing through a bookstore.

"It's blowback," Andrea said. "It's wonderful. Savor the moment!"

The moment dragged on. The next month, letters poured in to *The Romance Voice* either supporting the idea that the romance industry was primed for a hostile male takeover, or that the writer of the original article was fostering gender conflict among the very people who write books *celebrating* equality and respect. Then a second wave of angrier letters poured in, with one side calling the other Susan Faludi-wannabe-flame-throwers, and the other side claiming its critics were passive-throwback-mealy-mouths who wouldn't see the error of their beliefs until the market for women's fiction had dried up and left them self-published and royalty-free.

By May, some authors were pleading "Why can't we all just get along?" but by then no one was listening. They were especially not listening to Fleishman, who wrote a letter of apology emphasizing his respect for the RAG, all of its members, and the romance industry as a whole. One of the proudest days of his life, he wrote, was when he was nominated for a Raggie. He said his quote had been taken out of context.

I had a few authors up for awards whom I would be sitting with at the ceremony. One, Riva Nash, was up against Fleishman for her middle-aged art student book. I tried not to let it build up in my head as a big me-against-him battle, because essentially, it had nothing to do with me. It was about them. I mean, about their books.

Besides, if Fleishman lost that would be so fantastic. And I wasn't that much of an optimist.

For the big event, Wendy and Andrea helped me find a knockoff Missoni dress that was somewhere in the realm of affordability. It was simple, but the colors were bright and it had flow. It was also a size twelve, which depressed me. I was sliding. Too many nasty chocolate apricot cookies, which I was actually beginning to like. When I looked in the mirror, I saw a blob.

"Would you shut up about the size?" Andrea said after listening to me moan. We were all squeezed into a Bloomie's dressing room. "So it runs small. You look fantastic."

"Look," Wendy said, poking at me with a forefinger. "That bone sticking out is your collarbone. And there's your waist. It's smaller than mine."

"Mine, too," Andrea complained, though I don't think that was true.

Wendy looked into my eyes and spoke very carefully. "You're the same size you've been since I've known you, Rebecca. You can relax. This is you now."

I stared into the mirror.

I looked . . . well, okay. Better than okay. If someone had told me when I was sixteen that I would look like this in ten years, I might not have been ecstatic, but I would have been pretty damn happy. I glanced into the faces of the two other people hovering in the mirror—especially Wendy beaming proudly—and I felt a load of anxiety slipping away from my shoulders. And believe me, that was the best weight I ever lost.

"Thanks," I said, biting my lip so I wouldn't make a scene. "I don't know what I would have done without you guys."

Wendy put her arm around me, and Andrea folded her arms so that she looked like she was hugging herself. "No sweat," Wendy said.

"Right. I'm sure you would have managed to find a dress on your own," Andrea grumbled.

"No, I didn't mean just to—"

"We *know* what you meant," she said. "So shut up already and buy the dress."

* * *

And the winner was . . .

Riva Nash, author of *Life Is an Art.* Publisher: Candlelight. Editor: *Moi!*

The banquet room of the Marriott Marquis was so packed with women in formal wear that it was a little overwhelming to a newbie. I had skipped the awards banquet the year before, in Dallas, so I was unprepared for the momentous feel of it. I mean, there was music, and strobes, and presenters. It was like the Oscars minus men. Actually, there were a few tuxedos—agents, mostly, and the handful of male authors and coauthors who braved the scene. I had spotted Fleishman and shamelessly picked a seat where I could watch him. If he won, I wanted to be able to report back the awfulness of the moment to Wendy.

He was sitting at a large round table halfway across the room with Dan Weatherby and Cassie and some other people I recognized as being part of the Gazelle crew. Cassie looked kind of frumpy to me, even though she was wearing a dress that went over only one shoulder. I think it was supposed to be sexy, but on her it just looked lopsided or something. Her hair kept getting shorter, too, but that wasn't turning out so well, either.

"Look at that," Andrea hissed in my ear, "it's like an albino afro."

I laughed, and at that moment, Cassie turned and glared my way.

I looked away. Andrea's eyes bugged. "Do you think she bugged our table?"

"What does she look so pouty for?" I wondered aloud.

Andrea smirked. "Maybe because Fleishman hasn't spoken more than two words with her since they sat down."

Fleishman was yucking it up with Dan. Both of them looked great. Of course. They always did.

With one exception. The moment the emcee called Riva's name, Fleishman did not look so hot. The proactive smile he had frozen on his face for protection—or anticipation—momentarily fell away. His head jerked toward my table. To me. I, of course, was beaming.

Riva grabbed my arm. "Come with me!" she yelled over the applause as she lifted me halfway out of my chair.

I shook my head.

"Go!" Andrea gave me an unceremonious shove that propelled me to my feet.

It was so great to see Riva win. Not just because of who lost, either. She was so giddy, so shocked, her happiness infected the entire room. She spent about thirty seconds exclaiming how she never expected to win. "Never!" she drawled. "I mean, I'm a middle-aged real estate inspector from Nebraska!"

Then she gathered herself and found her way back to the traditional script, somewhat—she thanked her agent, me, Candlelight Books, her children, her parents, her grammar school teachers, Louisa May Alcott, Rona Jaffe, Susan Isaacs, Jennifer Crusie, and her divorce lawyer.

She brought down the house, but by the time she wobbled off the podium clutching her statuette, she was a mess. "I wish you'd gotten me off before I made a damn fool of myself!"

"You were great," I told her.

From there on in, our table was in such a party mood that I barely spared Fleishman a glance for the rest of the ceremony. After it was all over, though, I did run into him. His half-empty table was on the path to the doors. Cassie was gone, and it was just Fleishman sitting alone. Dan was turned away, talking to another author.

I stopped. I had to. This was too sweet to pass up. "Hey, stranger."

He looked up at me with a wary smile. "Hey yourself."

"How did you like your first awards banquet?"

He smiled almost sheepishly. Almost humbly. "Better luck next time, right?"

"Oh—have you written another book already?"

He shrugged. "I've been working on a proposal . . ."

"Let me guess," I said. "It's about a woman who always

thought she was being passed over—you know, at school, for promotions, in her love life. Maybe she was salutatorian of her high school class?"

He shook his head. "It's *fiction.*"

Dan Weatherby suddenly cut in on us. "Hello, Rebecca. Gorgeous dress!"

"Thanks, Dan."

"I hope J.F. here isn't spilling too much about his new story." He lowered his voice. "It's supposed to be Gazelle's option book, but you never know . . ."

I scrunched my nose. Something told me Cassie hadn't liked the proposal. "Editors can be so fussy sometimes."

Dan laughed. "You always make me laugh, Becca!"

Fleishman wasn't laughing. "But we're sure it will be picked up somewhere. After the reviews of the first book . . ." He was in full spin mode now. "I've got other projects on the burner, too."

"Yeah, well, you know the formula. Creativity plus dedication plus time."

"Plus I'm still working on that play," he said.

That play. For heaven's sake. He seemed so pathetic to me suddenly that I almost felt sorry for him. Almost. "That's great. I wouldn't want to think you were a Fleish in the pan."

He blinked at me. I patted him on the arm and walked away.

Dan, laughing, hollered after me. "I'll be calling you soon, Bec!"

As I left to go barhopping with the gang plus several writers, I thought briefly about Luke. He was right. Success really was the best revenge.

Epilogue

Later that summer, I had cause to wear my Missoni knockoff dress again. *Inventing My Life* was sold, and to celebrate, Luke treated Sylvie, Bernadine, and me to a big dinner.

It was great. Sylvie ordered wine and got a little looped, but hey, she was entitled. It was the first time I had ever seen her out on the town, or out anywhere. She looked even frailer in the surroundings of the French bistro Luke had chosen than she did in her own place, and I wondered if this might be her last hurrah. I wondered if she wondered that, too.

I got a little loopy myself, drinking to Sylvie's frequent toasts. She was grateful to me, and Luke, and Bernadine. It was sweet of her to be so demonstrative, but I felt a little uncomfortable accepting thanks from someone I owed so much to myself, and I told her so.

"This book saved my life," I said.

"Nonsense!" Sylvie said. Then she asked, "How?"

"I was spinning in circles. Working on this—working through your life—made me realize how upset I was becoming over trivialities."

Sylvie drew back. "And you think I wasn't concerned with trivialities, too, when I was young? That I didn't go out and make a big dope of myself?" She laughed. "You see, you don't know me so well after all!"

"You'll have to write a sequel," Luke joked.

Bernadine leaned back and laughed. "She's right, Rebecca. You should have seen her the night we got our hands on Papa's peppermint schnapps!"

Sylvie shot her a look, then glanced back at me gravely. "Believe me, when you write the story of your life when you're ninety-four, you won't be talking about these little episodes—you'll be focused on the friends you lost, your family, the people you loved. The other stuff is just what you survive to get to the things that matter. It's the same if you're living through a war, or . . ."

I smiled. "A new job?"

It just didn't have the same drama, but I could sort of see what she was getting at.

After dinner, Luke put Bernadine and Sylvie in a cab. We started walking—the subway I could catch to my apartment was a few blocks away. Luke took my arm.

I hadn't been expecting that.

"You know . . ."

I tilted a glance at him. "What?"

"I'm pretty much done working for Sylvie. I think Langley will finally be forced to cough up the rest of the money."

"I know—Sylvie told me. That's so great."

"For so long I've felt this conflict . . ."

I narrowed my eyes at him. "Conflict?"

"That is . . ."

He stopped. This was so weird. In all the months I'd known him, Luke had never been tongue-tied. He'd never been inarticulate. He'd never had those brown eyes fastened on me with such dopey intensity.

I felt my stomach begin to flutter, but I tried to stop it. I was getting better at that.

"The thing is," he blurted out, "is that you came to me sort of as a representative of Sylvie, and Sylvie became my client, and you were part of that, and . . ."

I tilted my head. "Luke, are you telling me that you didn't

want to become involved with me because you thought it might be some kind of conflict of interest?"

He nodded, looking relieved.

I confess I was relieved, too. And impressed. His ideas of tact and propriety were a little over the top, but then, given the meatheads I'd gotten involved with in the past year, that wasn't entirely a bad thing.

I swallowed, not quite trusting the little stream of joy beginning to course through my veins. "So now . . . ?"

"Now I'm declaring an end to the conflict," he said.

He bent down and touched his lips to mine, tentatively. But there was nothing tentative after that first kiss. He put his arms around me and we performed a full body smooch right there on the bustle of the east twenties.

When we came up for air, it was as if the sidewalks had suddenly morphed to puffy cumulus clouds. My step had a bounce—not easy in four-inch heels. I leaned into Luke as he held his arm tightly around me. I'd never felt so happy, so wonderfully alive, and yet at ease. The world was perfect. Everything was just as I wanted it. It was a not-too-hot August evening, with plenty of Saturday night stretching ahead and a Sunday after that. Just for Luke and me.

It felt like a Candlelight romance, only it was real.

If, in that moment, you'd asked me about what I'd been doing for the last year and a half of my life, I might have even drawn a blank. It was just like Sylvie had said. People were what mattered. Love was what mattered. All that other stuff fell away.

I couldn't imagine foolish trivialities and petty little conflicts getting to me ever again. I'd grown up. I'd matured. I'd moved on.

And Fleishman? That part of my life was over and done with. Thank God.

I'd forgotten where we were going. Luke steered us onto an Avenue—First, or Second—where there was an off-off-Broadway theater. The marquee was dark, but I stopped abruptly to stare at it. I couldn't help myself, even though doing so nearly made Luke spin in a circle.

"What's the matter?" he asked.

I gawked up at the small marquee and pointed at the large black letters over our heads. My voice wasn't functioning.

OPENING SEPT. 3
A NEW PLAY BY JACK FLEISHMAN
YULE BE SORRY